Broken Records
Belle Chapin

Copyright © 2021 by Bree Bennett, republished 2023 by Belle Chapin and Danvers Writing and Publishing, LLC

All rights reserved. No part of this publication may be reproduced, stored or transmitted in any form or by any means, electronic, mechanical, photocopying, recording, scanning, or otherwise without written permission from the publisher. It is illegal to copy this book, post it to a website, or distribute it by any other means without permission.

Designations used by companies to distinguish their products are often claimed as trademarks. All brand names and product names used in this book and on its cover are trade names, service marks, trademarks and registered trademarks of their respective owners. The publishers and the book are not associated with any product or vendor mentioned in this book. None of the companies referenced within the book have endorsed the book.

This book is a work of fiction. Names, characters, places, and incidents are products of the author's imagination or are used fictitiously. References to real people, events, organizations, establishments, or locations are intended to provide a sense of authenticity and are used fictitiously. Any resemblance to actual events, locations, organizations, or persons living or dead is entirely coincidental. All products, songs, and song titles are used for reference and a sense of authenticity and are the property of the respective songwriters and copyright holders.

For Papa, who taught me how to feel music.
For Mama, who let me be unapologetically weird.
And for Mia and Gio, who showed that a house full of family was magical.

Second Edition

This book was originally published as *Broken Records* under the pen name Bree Bennett. No new material has been added to this second version.

Content Warning

While *Broken Records* has many light-hearted moments, it does touch on some heavy topics. This book references past domestic abuse, gaslighting, alcoholism, and drug use.

Contents

1. Chapter 1 — 1
2. Chapter 2 — 10
3. Chapter 3 — 19
4. Chapter 4 — 33
5. Chapter 5 — 45
6. Chapter 6 — 54
7. Chapter 7 — 67
8. Chapter 8 — 78
9. Chapter 9 — 88
10. Chapter 10 — 99
11. Chapter 11 — 110
12. Chapter 12 — 118
13. Chapter 13 — 129
14. Chapter 14 — 143
15. Chapter 15 — 158
16. Chapter 16 — 169
17. Chapter 17 — 178
18. Chapter 18 — 188

19.	Chapter 19	198
20.	Chapter 20	207
21.	Chapter 21	214
22.	Chapter 22	222
23.	Chapter 23	230
24.	Chapter 24	240
25.	Chapter 25	249
26.	Chapter 26	256
27.	Chapter 27	269
28.	Chapter 28	277
29.	Chapter 29	284
30.	Chapter 30	293
	Epilogue	301
	Acknowledgments	306
	About the Author	308

Chapter 1

Forty dollars and an hour of peace at last.

Lucy stood outside a hole-in-the-wall record store with two crumpled twenty-dollar bills clutched in her fist. The building was nondescript, a white two-story with chipped paint and a hand-lettered sign that read *Raymond's Music Store*. Sandwiched between a deli and a Cuban takeout place, anyone could have wandered right by it and not realized it was there.

But not Lucy.

That morning, she had searched for record stores in the area and found this one just a two-mile walk from her temporary Airbnb apartment. It was completely worth the battle against the roar of traffic and brusque pedestrians to find a place where she could relax for the first time since coming to that godawful city.

The window front was crooked and grimy, but wide enough to get a sense of the place. A slim man operated a wooden sales counter while an older woman browsed a shelf of vinyl records. It wasn't crowded at all. She could handle this.

She entered with a bracing breath, the bell's *ting-a-ling* announcing her like a musical butler. The man at the counter lifted his chin in greeting and offered help if she needed it.

She didn't.

She was surrounded by her friends.

The atmosphere was infused with the scent of plastic and patchouli, topped with the musty, worn smell of pre-owned things. Pre-*loved* things.

Lucy had no set purpose there, so she chose a shelf at random, leafing through the vinyl albums. Some of the records for sale were brand new, the cellophane unbroken and clean. Others were used, vintage copies that held forgotten memories like an explorer's journal. She picked up the soundtrack to Elvis's live NBC television special, a favorite of hers, but her copy was back at home in Indiana with the rest of her things. She outlined the familiar cover with her hand—the nebulous red lights, the solitary figure crooning into a microphone. It was like clutching a security blanket, and her mind stopped racing at last.

A figure stepped into her peripheral vision, but she didn't acknowledge them. She believed that music stores should be treated like a church—holy and reverently. Silent except for the sermons of singers past and present.

A rough, calloused hand with long fingers flipped through the albums next to her. It selected Elton John's *Greatest Hits*, and her hand jerked. She pressed her lips together and gritted her teeth. The urge to speak bubbled like molten lava inside her, a reflex she had fought her whole life to control.

The hand turned over the album to the tracklist on the back. Lucy's toes curled inside her shoes, and she tightened her lips until they ached. Her hands were balled fists, her nails biting at the palms.

"You don't want that one," she blurted out.

The hand stilled. With reluctance, Lucy hauled her gaze from the album to discover a lean torso in a rust-colored leather jacket, a rugged jaw, and a face shadowed by a washed-out ball cap.

"I don't?" His voice was low and rough, like molasses poured over broken glass.

"No." She ducked her head, studying the carpet and toeing the frayed seams. "That one is from 1974. The songs are definitely classics, but his best albums are from the years before. You're cheating yourself if you just get the *Greatest Hits* album."

A pause. "But these are the songs I like."

Her eyes darted to the tarnished zipper pull on his jacket before she plucked an album from the display. "*Goodbye Yellow Brick Road* was his seventh studio album. It's widely considered his best. It's from the year before the *Greatest Hits* album and has some of his best songs, like 'Saturday Night's Alright for Fighting' and 'Bennie and the Jets' and 'Candle in the Wind.'" She clenched her hands to prevent her fingers from flickering and dancing. "I think it's gone platinum eight times at this point."

She gave him the record and chewed on the inside of her cheek so she wouldn't say anything further. He turned over the album and skimmed through the credits, verifying all the facts she had just spewed at him.

He didn't need to do that. Lucy knew it was all correct.

"Huh." He returned the *Greatest Hits* album to the rack and tucked *Goodbye Yellow Brick Road* under his arm instead. "Thanks."

She bobbed her head, a curt military-like nod. He lingered next to her for a few seconds more, his gaze burning into her, but she kept her eyes focused on the floor. The carpet pattern was mud brown with flecks of green and blue threaded through, and she followed it with her eyes, tracing it until her shoulders relaxed. *Green green blue. Green green blue.* When she eventually looked up, the man was gone.

She browsed through the rest of the Elton John records, examining a vintage copy of *Madman Across the Water*. When someone tapped on her shoulder, her muscles seized. Icy fear dripped down her spine, and she wrenched her shoulder forward to break contact. The hand fell back, and she whirled around.

"I scared you." There was a pause long enough for an apology, but the man in the ball cap didn't offer one. "I have some questions about the Beatles albums over here."

Of course—he thought she was an employee. It wasn't the first time it had happened to her in a music shop. Complying was less stressful than explaining, so Lucy trailed behind him as he led her to the expansive section dedicated to the Fab Four.

A stolen glimpse toward his eyes barely revealed long lashes amongst purple shadows. Lucy detected the woodsy scent of whiskey, but it didn't bother her. This was a record store. Alcohol was probably the least of the vices found here.

"What do you know about this one?" He held up a used copy of *Rubber Soul*. She tilted her head, scrutinizing the foppish gentlemen on the cover.

"Probably the best place to start if you want to dig into their evolution from teenage idols to experimental artists. It's their sixth album, so they're slowly breaking away from the manufactured 'boy band' style. It dips into both the folk and soul genres. Plus, they were on a lot of drugs by that point, so the lyrics get a little wild."

He made an amused noise deep in his throat and added the record to the Elton John one sandwiched in his elbow before beckoning for her to accompany him to another shelf.

"What about this one?" He held up Prince's *Purple Rain*. Lucy nearly purred with approval.

"One of my favorites. That's his sixth album and the soundtrack to the movie of the same name. Did you know that it's the reason Tipper Gore got the Parental Advisory sticker put on albums? She did it because of the song 'Darling Nikki.'" She rapped her knuckles on the song's tracklisting.

"Oh yeah? Why's that?"

"Well, because Nikki is a stripper, and they mention masturbation and grinding, and such."

He choked, breaking into a coughing fit. Her cheeks and neck burned hot.

Filter yourself, Lucy.

"Sorry, that was inappropriate," she said. "I shouldn't have said that."

"No, you're good," he wheezed. "You know a lot about music, don't you?"

"Yes." She stroked her fingers against her palm over and over. He gaped at her again, then leaned over, pulling another album from the shelf behind her and laying it in her hand.

"Tell me about that one."

"Jack Hunter?" She glanced at both sides of the record sleeve. "He's decent. This is his debut album, *Slow Down*. There's a lot of blues influence on this one. If I remember correctly, it went double platinum, and he won two Grammys for it."

He rubbed his thumb against his stubbled jaw before selecting another album from the same shelf.

"What about this one?"

"That's his second album. *Wayward*."

"What do you think of it?"

She hissed an exhale through tensed teeth. "It's okay." She kicked at the faded carpet again.

"No, really." He tapped Lucy's shoulder insistently with the corner of the album, and she twisted away from him. "What do you really think of it?"

She sighed. "It's not his best. All originality shown in his first album seems to be lacking here. It didn't do well with critics or in sales."

Several awkward moments passed, and Lucy got the feeling that she had answered incorrectly. He reached for another album. "What about this one?"

She squinted up at his shadowed face. "Are you a Jack Hunter fan?"

His scowl intensified. "Indulge me. What did you think?"

"That's his third album. It...it's not good. Unless you like it, of course. That's okay too."

Again, he stayed silent. Lucy had messed up something, but she wasn't sure what exactly. She often misread social cues. Panic ratcheted her lungs, and she worried a few loose strands of the carpet with the edge of her sneaker until he spoke again.

"Thanks for your help." His tone was glacial, with a note of defeat, further cementing her suspicion that she had said something wrong.

Filter, Lucy. Girls like you shouldn't speak their minds.

She jerked her head down in acknowledgment, and when she dared to look up again, he was gone from the store.

When Lucy left the store later, she passed by the rickety wooden counter only to see, abandoned and scattered across the counter, a stack of albums with *Goodbye Yellow Brick Road* on top.

Lucy ended up back at Raymond's Music Store at the same time, on the same day, the following week. Structure and schedule were as necessary to her as oxygen, and having something special to look forward to every Thursday at six o'clock sharp eased her scattershot mind.

She should have been looking for a more permanent apartment, as she only had two more weeks in her temporary rental. Moving to New York City had been a necessary evil, but the unfortunate paradox was that to find an apartment, Lucy needed to leave the apartment. Outside, the city was a tornado of noise and lights and confusion, whereas the old brownstone apartment building in Brooklyn had thick walls to block out the cacophony outside.

She wasn't really looking to buy another record at Raymond's. Her budget was significantly tighter, even though the apartment had been a steal, easily affordable for a few months while she got her bearings. Besides, buying another record without her record player—left behind in Indianapolis—was like buying tires without a car. She could admire them, but they weren't going to take her anywhere.

Inside, the same slender clerk stood behind the old wooden counter. He flashed Lucy a smile, and, although she didn't return it, she paused long enough to regard him. His hair was jet black, with streaks of green running through it in a pattern that mollified her senses. *Green black green black green*. Simple and clear.

"You're back," he said. Her eyes flicked to his nametag: *Sully*. "Can I help you with anything?"

Don't say it, Lucy. Don't say it.

She gritted her teeth together, but it was too late. "You only have two rings in your left eyebrow as opposed to three in your right."

He blinked, and her lip trembled. Sully's eyes shot to her mouth, and his perplexed look dissolved. "You're right. I lost the third ring on my left this morning. The ball must have come loose."

Her throat clenched, and she scurried off to peruse a display as far away from Sully as possible in the cramped store. Her embarrassment faded when she picked up a used copy of Aerosmith's *Pump*. It had a yellowed price sticker from its previous life, too stuck to remove without damaging the sleeve, but otherwise, it was in excellent condition. Her fingers dawdled down the tracklisting, and she murmured the songs aloud like a rock n' roll Hail Mary.

"'Love in an Elevator.' 'Monkey on My Back.' 'Janie's Got a Gun.'"

She thumbed through the rest of the Aerosmith collection, oblivious to the rest of the store, and didn't catch the scent of whiskey and leather until it was too late.

The heavy curve of a male hand grasped her shoulder. Instinctive fear, deep-rooted and conditioned, blasted through her body, along with a surge of adrenaline and a dash of fight or flight.

Janie's got a gun, but Lucy had a mean right hook.

She pivoted in place, shrugging the man's hand away. Her right fist slammed into his face. Panicked, she didn't aim correctly, and instead of landing the blow on his jaw, it caught him squarely in the nose. His head snapped back, and his navy blue ball cap flopped onto the floor.

Lucy blinked at it. She knew that cap.

"What the absolute fuck?!"

Even muffled by hands that cradled a bloody nose, she knew that voice.

Her ribcage was a vise of humiliation and horror as she elevated her gaze to the enraged eyes of the man she had met in the store last week. Her throat constricted as if she had gulped down a glass of pure lemon juice. Her lips were numb and cold, and she drew in a rushed gasp. He took a halting step toward Lucy. His broad palm pressed against his swelling nose, and blood dribbled through the cracks of his fingers.

"What the hell was that?" he said.

She stumbled, desperate to get away from him, but her back slammed into the shelf, knocking a cardboard sleeve of albums to the floor. Her heels skittered for purchase, but she toppled backward into the mess, accompanied by the screech of cellophane and the crack of splintered records.

Too loud too loud too loud too loud

She squeezed her eyes shut and covered her ears, trying to ground herself and let logic replace the panic.

Look what you did, Lucy. You messed up again.

An ominous silhouette fell over her, obstructing the cold fluorescent light. Against the plea of every brain cell she had, she glanced up at him.

He glared down at her, his brows knitted in confusion and anger. Slowly, he dropped his bloodied hands from his injured nose, and her stomach sank.

Lucy knew that face. Not personally, and not usually covered in blood, but she knew it.

That face was trouble.

The right thing for her to do would have been to apologize, to help him clean his face, to pick up the display, and offer compensation for damages.

She didn't do the right thing.

She made a noise like an agitated badger, sprang to her feet, and ran out of the store as fast as her legs could carry her.

She dashed through the streets, dodging pedestrians and earning the occasional middle finger. When the stitch in her side became too pinched to ignore, she slowed to a hesitant walk, but whipped her head around every few moments in case she was being followed.

It wasn't until she was panting in front of her apartment door that she let herself relax. She locked the door behind her and dropped her head back against it, sliding to the floor and hugging her knees to her chest.

Oh God, she thought. *I punched a rock star.*

Chapter 2

Jack was confused and bleeding. It wasn't the first time in his life he had experienced that combo.

He gawked at the door where the girl had vanished, ignoring the blood that dripped from his nose onto his ruined shirt.

Sully jogged toward him with a crushed box of tissues. "What the hell was that?" he asked. "You okay?" He shoved the box into Jack's hand. Tiny red drops fell onto the exposed tissue, spreading like watercolor paint.

"Son of a bitch." He blinked rapidly, his eyes watering and stinging. "That hurt."

Sully scanned him up and down. "What did you do to her?"

"What do you mean, what did I do to her?" he snapped, but Sully simply raised an eyebrow.

The question wasn't that out of the ordinary. He was, after all, Jack Hunter—*Mad Jack*, as the media liked to call him, due to his temper and what he called his *worldly adventures*.

Or, as everyone else called them, his *drunken shenanigans*.

Some of his well-known antics included punching his drummer mid-concert, setting a hotel bed on fire, storming off *The Late Show with Jerry Manning* mid-interview, and dozens of other sordid stories guaranteed to find a spot on the latest gossip blog. If you looked Jack Hunter up online, the first story you'd discover involved the Pope, a capuchin monkey, and a graham cracker. They weren't always true, but too many of them were.

This time, though, he swore it wasn't his fault. At least he didn't *think* it was.

When the raven-haired girl with the head full of rock trivia had returned to the store, Jack ventured out from the storeroom to talk to her. She had amused him during her previous visit, and that was a difficult thing to do. Her frankness was refreshing, even if her critiques of his albums had been depressing—but accurate.

He must have frightened her when he touched her, but he had only wanted to get her attention. Her response wasn't normal—it was self-defense, plain and simple. Maybe her running act was self-defense too. She had taken off like a jackrabbit pursued by a coyote.

"I didn't do anything," Jack assured Sully.

"If she comes back—which I doubt—I'll let you know," he said. "You can press charges if you want."

"Nah." Jack fondled his nose, prodding the swollen tissue. It was tender but not broken. He would know—it had been broken twice before. "But tell me if she does come back. I want to talk to her."

"She was so shy when I talked to her earlier. Didn't seem like the fighting type." Sully smiled. "She was more concerned about my eyebrows."

"Your eyebrows?"

"Two rings here," he pointed. "Three rings here. I think it bothered her."

Jack squinted at him. "Now it's bothering me too." He flicked at Sully's temple just above the incomplete jewelry. "Fix it." With that, Jack waved him off and headed back upstairs to his rooms above the store, not bothering to wipe the blood from his face as he drained another glass of whiskey and shot daggers at his dusty guitar. Unable to play, unable to write, he waited for inspiration to invade his worthless mind.

The word *impromptu* was a terrible word. It sounded like something a crabby woman would yell while criticizing your manners. Also, it ended with "u," which just pissed Jack off.

Impromptu meetings with his manager were even worse.

Impromptu meetings with his manager and his lawyer while he was hungover and bruised were the worst of all.

When he blundered into the main conference room at Derelict Records, his vision was blurry and his head was pounding. Kim, his manager, had scheduled the meeting at the Manhattan-based label for the ungodly hour of nine in the morning, a fact that he would complain about as soon as the itty-bitty jackhammers in his head went away.

"What the hell, Jack?" Kim's voice echoed inside his head like a screech owl in an empty barn. "Your face!"

Trent, his lawyer, just shook his head and returned to typing away on his laptop.

"What happened?" Kim asked.

Jack shrugged at her. "You wouldn't believe me if I told you." He barely believed it himself.

"I usually don't, but somehow, your stories always end up true anyway." She blew out an exasperated breath. "Which, to be honest, is why we're here."

The musician slumped into an office chair and glanced over at Trent, hoping for some sort of hint, but the lawyer's face remained grave and impassive. Next to him, an unfamiliar man with shaggy dark hair tapped away at his smartphone.

"To get to the point," Kim continued, "Derelict Records isn't happy with you."

"That's not news," Jack said, picking at one of his calluses. "They never are."

"True. But after the Prince Harry incident—"

He groaned and leaned back as far as his chair would go, pinching the bridge of his nose and wincing at the garish fluorescent lights above him. "It's all blown out of proportion. He's fine. I'm fine. The moose is fine."

"Jack." Trent's deep rumble commanded attention without the need for extra volume. "There's a moral turpitude clause in your contract."

"What? Like paint thinner?"

Kim moaned. "No, Jack. That's *turpentine*. The moral *turpitude* clause holds someone to a certain behavioral standard. You, on the other hand, have no standards."

"Frank wanted to cut you completely," Trent said, "but we talked him into a probationary period."

Jack shot up straight in the chair. "What?" Frank Taylor was the founder of Derelict Records and more indulgent of his antics than the rest of management. Losing Frank's support would be the quickest way to kill his already-struggling career.

"They don't want you anymore, even with one more album left on your contract. You're too much trouble." The lawyer's eyes met Jack's with a touch of pity. "Too much trouble with no return on their investment."

"That's ridiculous."

"No, bozo," the unknown man piped up, looking up from his phone for the first time. "It's a fact."

"Bozo?" Jack stared at him. "Who are you?"

"This is Martin Tan," Kim said. "He's in public relations. From an outside firm."

"Where's Rashida?" He peered around the room as if expecting his usual PR representative to magically appear.

"She's been assigned to other clients. Martin's specialty is..." She touched her tongue to her teeth. "People like you."

"People like me?"

"Problem children." Martin smirked. "Look. You're still a big name, but it's not because of your 'music.'"

Jack wanted to slap his air quotes out of the air.

"You haven't had a hit in years. When people think of you, they think of the Vitamix incident. Or the Thai lingerie shop. Or the bar fight with that guy from *Baywatch*. They don't think *rock star*." The PR expert tented his fingers solemnly like he was delivering a terminal illness diagnosis. "You've already turned the corner onto Has-Been Street, Jack, headed toward Whatever-Happened-to-That-Guy Lane. Possibly with a pit stop at Obscure-*Jeopardy*-Answer Avenue."

Jack fumed, and it took all his willpower not to lunge across the table, grab Martin's phone, and smack him with it upside the head.

"You're wrong," the rock star said.

"No, he's not," Kim said. "I don't think you understand how serious this is. Derelict didn't even want an album you're obligated to give to them. They aren't going to want to re-sign a contract."

"So I'll sign with someone else."

"*Who*, Jack?" Her voice had that same pitying note that Trent's had. "Who is going to want to deal with Jack Hunter?"

"I asked Frank if anything would change his mind," Trent said. "Basically, if this album is a success, and you're a perfect gentleman from this day forward, they'll consider renewing your contract."

"Well, how the hell is that supposed to happen?" Jack snapped. "I'm *me*."

"That's where I come in." Martin proffered that damn smirk again, and Jack wanted to wipe it from his face and possibly the planet. "It's too late to do damage control. At this point, we've got to reinvent you completely.

A whole new strategy. Some sort of life event that shows you're ready to do a 180, to go on the straight and narrow."

"Like what? Save someone from a burning building?"

"Nah." Martin waved dismissively. "Too hard to plan." He leaned forward. "You could adopt a kid."

Was he serious? Jack looked to Trent and Kim for assistance, but there was nothing but concern in their expressions.

"I'm not Daddy Warbucks. And I don't like kids."

"Volunteer for a charity? We could get you a dog, and you could do an animal rights campaign. Sad commercials with Sarah McLachlan crying in the background, that sort of thing."

"I don't have time for a dog." It was a flat-out lie. All Jack did was lay around and try to write songs that refused to be written. A dog would probably be a step up in productivity—at least he would get some exercise.

"What about something with your mother?" asked Martin. "A baking show, or a *60 Minutes* special?"

"No," Trent and Jack replied in unison. Neither had a favorable opinion of Jack's mother. Both had been in the middle of enough legal tangles with her to last a lifetime.

"If only you were in a relationship," mused Kim. "The true love angle always works. And if we could get a wedding out of it..." She tapped her fingers to her lips in a chef's kiss gesture.

"That's a possibility." Martin rubbed his hands together like a cartoon villain. If he had possessed a mustache, he would have been twirling it. "Ruby Li did that after her DUI, and now she and her husband are America's favorite couple."

Jack snorted. "She married the CEO of that toothbrush company. A toothbrush company! So boring. He's her exact opposite."

"But that's why it works!" Kim scrolled through her phone and showed him a picture from Instagram. "And he's a decent guy. Or at least he seems to be, which is all that matters. And look at the squishy face on that baby! I just want to eat her up." Her eyes twinkled, and she added another "like" to the thousands already there. She shoved the phone into Jack's face and scrolled through more pictures of Ruby Li and her husband performing boring domestic activities—painting a nursery, sitting in front of a fireplace, making cookies and dabbing dough on each other's noses. Between the sickly sweet images and the remains of his hangover, Jack wanted to hurl.

But from a PR standpoint, none of these posts brought to mind the three-year-old video of Ruby Li screeching expletives like a banshee while being arrested half-naked on the shoulder of I-5.

"Are you seeing anyone?" Martin swiped through his phone. "There aren't any women on your Instagram account."

"I don't date." Jack shuddered at the notion of any commitment longer than twenty-four hours. Although, a few months previously, he had had a fantastic weekend with a Swiss heiress that had lasted two whole days, so maybe he was getting better at this whole commitment thing.

If only he remembered her name.

"A fake relationship, then." Martin chewed on his lip, lost in thought. "At that point, might as well go all the way. Fake marriage. Plenty of celebrities do it."

"Sure they do." The musician's smile was anything but pleasant. "I'm pretty sure my mom's second marriage was one. Maybe her fourth too."

"So you're familiar with how they work, then," said Martin. Jack was pretty sure he was going to slug him before this meeting was over.

"You have to admit, it's got merit," said Kim. She showed a photo of Ruby Li, her husband, and their baby, all in matching flannel pajamas.

Jack laid his aching head on the table and banged his forehead on the polished wood. "Even if I went the fake marriage route—and I'm not saying

I would ever do such a stupid thing—who would we even get to play my w- my wi—" He couldn't even say the damn word.

"We could find an actress or a model," said Kim. "Set up a marriage contract, NDAs out the wazoo."

He lifted his head enough to waggle a suggestive eyebrow at her. "Or you could do it."

Kim looked as if she'd swallowed her tongue. "Um, no. We'd kill each other in two hours. How we haven't already is a miracle."

"Come on, babe." He winked. "I'd treat you right."

"Well, you're not known for your celibacy," interrupted Martin. "Was there anyone you could handle more than a night or two?"

Jack's feet involuntarily started scrambling under the table. "No. A hundred times no. A thousand times no."

"What about that blonde you took to the People's Choice Awards last year?" asked Kim.

"No. She stole my soap dispensers afterward."

"Oh yeah." Her face fell. "Those were really nice soap dispensers."

"The model from New Year's?" suggested Trent. "The one with the—" He swallowed. "Unusual laugh."

Jack imagined his townhouse, chilly and gloomy except for the constant echo of that godawful guffaw, every day for years to come, like a Stephen King novel come to life. He gulped and shook his head.

"Is there anyone out there that would benefit from hooking up with Jack?" Trent asked with plaintive despair.

No one spoke. Jack resumed thumping his head against the table.

"What about that lady from the toilet paper commercial?" asked Kim feebly. "The one that got caught shoplifting."

"Stop." Jack shoved his chair back from the table and stood. "I'm not adopting anyone—human *or* animal—and I'm not marrying minor criminals just to make some jerks in suits happy. It should be all about the music. All about the album."

"And how's that album coming, Jack?"

Kim might as well have thrown a javelin through his chest for as much as it hurt. She was the only one who knew he hadn't written anything in months.

"Just fine," he said with mock cheer. "I should be able to lay down some tracks soon."

"Uh-huh." She clicked her pen as if she were cocking a pistol. "One week, Jack. Have a plan to fix your reputation in one week, or we're doing it for you." She smiled a little too sweetly. "I'm still rooting for the Daddy Warbucks angle."

Chapter 3

Two days later, Lucy was back outside Raymond's. It was not a Thursday. It was not six p.m. And she was not there to buy a record.

The store bell dinged as usual, but this time, it felt like it was heralding her execution, not her approach. She clutched a linen bag to her side and trudged to the counter. Sully watched her with a smug smile.

"Hi," she said, trying to quell her shaking hands. She focused on the hideous carpet, tracing the pattern as if the activity would ward away any discomfort. "I, um, assaulted a man here two days ago." She didn't want to reveal his identity outright if Sully didn't know who he was. "You were here."

"I was." There was a hint of amusement in his voice. "By the way, there are three rings in each eyebrow now."

She glanced up to validate and offered him the smallest of smiles. "Yes, there are." She set the tote bag on the counter. "Does he shop here often? I've seen him twice now. I have some things for him, and I thought maybe I could drop them off, and you could give them to him the next time he's here."

Because once she left that godforsaken store, she was never, ever coming back.

"For Jack?" He peeked in the bag. "Just a sec." He tapped out a quick text on his cell phone. After a response arrived with an electronic buzz, he shot her an ominous smirk. "He'll be right down."

"Wait, what?" Lucy said just as a door in the back of the store swung open with the scream of hinges and slammed shut behind a hulking, sulking figure.

She would have felt better if Jack Hunter had stomped over to her, shouting and screaming, threatening to tear her from limb to limb, cursing her mother's name. It would have been awful but over quickly.

Instead, he sauntered toward her like a hangman with no hurry to get to the gallows on time. Thinly-carpeted floorboards creaked under his deliberate, torturous footsteps. His nose was still swollen with streaks of yellow and green bruising on the bridge, but it didn't have the twisted look of being broken. He halted his leisurely ramble just inches away, glaring down at Lucy with bitter brown eyes, his lips set in a condescending sneer.

She swallowed against her instinctive response, but it was too late—she went full speed ahead like the Titanic into the iceberg. "Hi I'm Lucy Meyer and I'm sorry I hit your nose and made you bleed but I thought you were trying to attack me," she said in a single, expedient exhale.

He blinked. The fury on his face softened to something like confusion.

"I brought you some things," she continued when he didn't reply. "I made chocolate chip cookies." She tossed him the plastic container as if it were the target in a game of hot potato. "But then I thought that would be bad if you were gluten intolerant or allergic. So I got you some root beer too. It's locally made." She stacked a four-pack of glass bottles on top of the container of cookies. He opened his mouth as if to say something, then snapped it shut again. He looked bewildered, but most people had that look when talking to Lucy.

"I also got you a reusable ice pack, but you have to put it in the freezer first." She added it to the pyramid of presents. "And a card. I wasn't sure what type of card to get, and all the 'I'm Sorry' ones didn't seem to apply to our situation, so I made you an 'I'm Sorry I Hit You in the Nose' card."

Again, no response, so she tucked the card between the root beer bottles and the ice pack.

She handed both Jack and Sully a neatly printed index card. "This is my contact info. I can pay for your deductible if you needed medical care." She gestured at the shelving as she spoke to Sully. "And let me know what I owe you for the display I ruined. Or I can help out in the store to make up for it. I'm still looking for a place to live in the area, but I'll be available. And I'm good with music. I have a—" she glanced at Jack, who raised his dark slash of an eyebrow, "—a thing."

Sully wrinkled his forehead. "Huh?"

"Sully," Jack murmured, speaking for the first time. "Name a song." His voice was harsh and growly, but not unpleasant. Lucy balled her fists and forced herself to raise her head and truly meet his gaze.

When she locked onto his velveteen brown eyes, a shot of bizarre awareness smacked her in the chest. Despite the black and blue coloring around his lids and nose, his eyes were handsome, but also weary and unhappy. She had the oddest impulse to comfort him.

"Okay..." Sully's voice dripped with skepticism. "Um, 'Livin' la Vida Loca'?" Jack and Lucy broke eye contact and rotated their heads in unison to Sully. His cheekbones flushed. "I was under pressure; it was the first one that came to mind."

Her hand twitched, her fingers flying mid-air like an impassioned conductor. It was a tic; a tell that she was concentrating, one of the few habits she had been unable to learn to hide. She blinked at Sully and took a breath. "'Livin' la Vida Loca' is the first single from Ricky Martin's self-titled album released in 1999. Although the album has gone platinum seven times in the United States and was considered the reason for the Latin Pop craze in the late nineties, it didn't win any Grammys."

Sully's eyebrows raised. "'I Wanna Be Sedated.'"

She scoffed at him. "Track seven on *Road to Ruin* by the Ramones. 1978. Probably their best-known song."

His back straightened. "'Three Little Birds.'"

She mimicked his posture. "Bob Marley and the Wailers. 1977. From the album *Exodus*."

"'Monkey Wrench.'"

"Foo Fighters. *The Colour and the Shape.* 1997."

"'Applejohn Blues.'" Sully's smile unfolded like a panther stretching after a nap.

Well-played, she thought. Her jaw tightened. "Jack Hunter. *Slow Down.* 1998."

"I'm impressed," Sully said. "I'll contact you if I ever need some help in the store."

Lucy's nod was sharp and blunt. "I'm really sorry," she said, cringing at the uncertainty in her voice.

Jack's mouth twisted into an uneasy grimace, and he shared a glance with Sully. "Thank you," he finally said, but his voice raised at the end as if it were a question.

"Please don't arrest me."

His lips twitched, with no indication if he were about to shout or laugh. He stroked his chin, his eyes sweeping over her, and she became hyper-conscious of her appearance. She was built more like a street waif than the buxom beauties he probably entertained, and she gazed up at him like an orphan asking for more gruel from a Dickensian villain.

"I'll let it go this time," he said.

Lucy bobbed her head solemnly, but this nightmare situation needed to end. Her brain was frazzled and overburdened. Before anyone could say anything further, she turned and bolted out the door.

She attempted a slow pace down the sidewalk, but she felt crushed by everything loud and bright shrieking around her, like being trapped inside a speeding comet. She collapsed on a nearby bench, gulping in fresh air by the gallon.

The world was fuzzy and clamorous, and if she didn't get herself under control, she'd be lost to the heady spiral of sensations. The traffic hummed and droned, like furious wasps instead of vehicles, punctuated by the incessant flashing of traffic lights changing. She was drunk and drowning in a pattern that she couldn't control.

Cars lights noise cars lights noise crowds people lights noise crowds people lights cars—

Jack shrugged at Sully and set the girl's myriad of offerings on the counter, working two cookies out of the Tupperware box.

"And that's the end of that," he said, tossing Sully one of the cookies and biting into his own. It was still warm and gooey, as a good cookie should be.

Jack was a sucker for a good cookie.

"Dude." Sully gawked at the front door. "She's like Wikipedia. I should call her and see if she wants to host a trivia night here at the store or something like that."

"Doubtful. She doesn't seem like she'd want to be around people. Too quiet."

"Nice of her to bring you presents, though. Nice of her to consider that some people are gluten intolerant too." He threw Jack a meaningful look before returning the cookie and cracking open one of the root beers.

"Sorry, I forgot." *Again.*

"You're just annoyed she didn't say anything about you being you."

Jack paused and stared at him. "You're right. She didn't." Besides acknowledging that "Slow Down" was a song on an album by someone named Jack Hunter, she hadn't said a damn thing about him. He had expected at least an autograph request from someone so fascinated by rock music. It was a little ego-bruising but also...intriguing.

"Nope." Sully took a long sip as Jack fixated back on the front door. An impossible idea—no, a *shenanigan*—began to form.

"Didn't she say she was looking for a place to live?" The musician attempted a nonchalant look, but Sully's eyes narrowed over the neck of his bottle.

"You have your scheming face on. Didn't you learn anything from the Prince Harry incident?"

"Not one thing." Jack shoved the rest of the cookie in his mouth and dashed out through the front door.

Nearly choking on cookie crumbs, he whipped his head around, hoping to spot Lucy before she got any further. Luck was with him—she was sitting on a bench at the end of the block. He sprinted toward her and skidded to a stop. She flinched and clutched her purse closer as if he were going to mug her.

"You," he panted, making a mental note to hit the treadmill more often. "Lunch. Now."

She looked around as if he were talking to someone else. "What?"

Jack swallowed. "Have lunch with me."

"Why?"

"Because I'm hungry."

Her face was moonlight pale. Jack held out a hand to her, just as a courtesy to help her stand. Her head tilted, and she stared at it as if he were offering her a dead fish.

"You have a scar on your index finger," she said.

"Um...yes?" He wiggled his fingers in an impatient gesture.

"Why?"

"Not paying attention while cleaning up a broken glass." He flicked his fingers more insistently. *Take my damn hand.*

Her hand trembled as she slipped it into his, and he felt her fingers flutter against his palm in succession as if she were keeping rhythm to her own silent song.

Pinky, ring, middle, index. Repeat.

He pulled her to her feet, and for a moment, they simply stood there, hand in hand. He felt a strange sense of tranquility in her presence, and from her surprised look, she felt it too.

But when Jack pulled her to her feet, she dropped his hand like a hot pan. She stayed silent during the short walk to the Batter Up diner just around the corner. The baseball-themed restaurant was a staple of the area, and the Petrakis family—the owners—had known Jack since he was a teenager.

"Jackie!" crowed Adrian Petrakis when they arrived, straightening his Yankees jersey. He and his wife, Marina, were the only people still alive who were allowed to call him that. "It's been months!" He shook Jack's hand, the fierce motion rippling from his fingers to his shoulder like a soundwave.

"It's only been two weeks, and that's because I'm still full from last time."

"Your usual table then?" He didn't wait for an answer, leading Lucy and Jack to a little table hidden from view at the back of the restaurant. He handed them two menus, slapped Jack on the back with enthusiastic affection, and left to greet a new customer.

"They like you," said Lucy, looking at a crooked framed photo of Adrian, Marina, and the musician hanging above their table.

"Yes. There are a few people who do." Her eyes snapped back to him, and he pointed at the menu. "I recommend the Rookie's Reuben."

She scowled at him. He scowled at her. They were off to a great start.

"I'm really, really sorry I hit you," she said, laying the menu on the Formica table, aligning it perfectly perpendicular with the edge. "But why am I here?"

Jack waved away her apology attempt and leaned forward. "Do you know who I am?"

Her dark eyebrows rose. Under that shy rabbit persona, Jack suspected a little spitfire was buried deep down.

"Yes. You're Jack Hunter."

"Hmm." He clucked his tongue. "You didn't say anything in the store, so I thought maybe you didn't know."

Her nostrils flared, and she held up her hand defiantly, ticking off facts on her fingers. "You're Jack Hunter. Genre: Rock. Instruments: guitar—both acoustic and electric—and piano. First album: *Slow Down*, 1998. Also, the name of your first single. Four Grammy nominations, two wins. Second album: *Wayward*, 2002. Two Grammy nominations, one win. Third album: self-titled, 2006. No nominations. Fourth—"

"That's enough. I don't need a dissertation on my dwindling success." His retort came out harsher than intended. "You didn't say anything. You didn't freak out."

She studied him, and her voice softened. "Do you need me to freak out? I mean, I can, if you need it as like, some celebrity mojo thing."

"No." He stared at her, blindsided. "My celebrity mojo is fine. It was just...unexpected."

He sent a precursory glance to her left hand. No ring. "Tell me about yourself, Lucy. What do you do besides stalk record stores and punch celebrities?"

"I'm a freelance technical writer," she answered in a clipped tone.

"What does that mean?"

"I write technical things."

He mouthed a curse at the ceiling. "But what does that mean?"

"Companies contract me to write things like training and instructional manuals. I'm finishing up a first aid document for a manufacturer right now. I handle the distribution of the materials too."

"That sounds awful."

She shrugged. "I know. But it's easy for me; it keeps me busy, and I get to work from home."

"Did you grow up around here?"

"No." She scrunched up her nose, apparently having judged NYC and found it lacking.

"But you're looking for a place to live here?"

"Yes."

He restrained a frustrated growl. It would be easier to get more information from a KGB spy. Luckily, Adrian rounded the corner, ready to take their orders before Jack lost his temper. Jack spouted out his usual order and jutted his chin towards Lucy.

"I will have the Grand Slam Grilled Cheese," Lucy said, abandoning her gruffness. "And the side fruit cup—does it come directly out of the refrigerator?"

If her odd question threw him, the older man didn't miss a beat. "Yes, ma'am, it doesn't sit out at all."

"I'll just have a side salad then." She smiled at him as he returned to the kitchen, and it completely changed her face. Her polite numbness cracked just a little, like a porcelain veneer, revealing something wholesome and genuine.

"Can I ask—?" Jack stopped when her smile vanished like a tendril of smoke. She reached for the bundle of silverware wrapped in a napkin and unrolled it, aligning each utensil in soldier-straight lines.

"I don't like cold fruit." A flush crept across her cheekbones.

"That's cool. I'm like that with apples. I don't like biting into apples whole. I need them cut up."

She jerked up her head, and her gaze met his. Like in the record store, Jack got the feeling that this was a rare thing for her to do, but holy hell, he wished she would do it more often. Her eyes were pools of melted milk chocolate, deep and velvety, with a fringe of long, lush lashes.

"Look." Jack cleared his throat, taking advantage of her wayward attention. "When I saw you this morning, I had an idea." His collar was suddenly too hot, and he scratched at the scruff of his neck. "As you know, I have a unique reputation. And my manager and PR team had a 'Come to Jesus' meeting with me. I'm on probation, essentially. I'm lucky the label hasn't terminated my contract completely. I've got to make the next album solid."

"Okay." She shrugged.

"Okay?"

"So do it. Get a good producer, put the time in, and you'll make a good product."

Jack shook his head. "It's not that simple. I've got nothing. Literally nothing. I haven't written anything good in months. Maybe longer. Unless this next album is a hit, the label doesn't want to re-sign my contract."

"Really? But you're very talented."

He threw his hands into the air. "You literally told me how terrible my last two albums were!"

"They were terrible. But your first one wasn't."

"That was a million years ago." He wished he could jump into a time machine and warn his eighteen-year-old self not to squander all his inspiration in one album. "In addition to all that, I've got to fix my reputation. No more of this Mad Jack nonsense."

She made a noise that could almost be called a laugh. "That's a stupid nickname. It makes you sound like a pirate. Might as well start singing sea shanties."

"They'd probably do better than anything I've written lately," he grumbled.

"But I don't understand their concern—isn't all press good press?"

"Then they want a little less 'good press.'" He rapped his knuckles on the table. "I've laid low since the Prince Harry incident—"

"That's true then?" Her face remained impassive as if he was describing the weather and not an international incident.

"Depends on the version you hear. About sixty percent of what you read is true. But unless I manage a hit album without any more bad press—true or otherwise—they won't even consider renewing my contract."

Her lips twisted in thought. "But do you want to sign with them again?" She said it with the same ease as choosing between two pairs of socks. "There are other labels. Other ways to keep making records. If that's what you really want."

"Of course, it's what I want. I'm a musician. Music is my life." It was a canned, rehearsed phrase recycled from years-old interviews. "And no other label is going to want me. I haven't been a good investment for Derelict Records in a long time."

"It's difficult to be yourself when an investment dictates who you ought to be," she said, her lashes lowered. A cold fist squeezed his heart as her words rang true.

"Basically, I gotta reboot who I am, present a whole new Jack Hunter to the world." He conjured up his best sheepish grin. "That's where you come in."

She stayed expressionless as Adrian brought their meals before she blasted him with another brilliant smile. What exactly did Jack have to do to get one of those on his own?

"Explain," she said when the manager left.

"It seems you and I have a connection. That connection being, well, your fist, but other than that, I thought maybe we could enter a mutually beneficial agreement." Jack paused, Reuben inches from his mouth as she cut her grilled cheese into perfect squares. "You're eating your sandwich with a fork?"

Her inhale was brusque. "This agreement?"

He peeked around the cafe as if initiating a drug deal. "I need a wife."

"A wife."

"My PR team thinks a new, wholesome romance would do wonders for my image."

She stroked her bottom lip. "It might."

"Do you still need a place to live?"

He held his breath as she put two and two together. Her face fell, her nostrils flared, and she raised her eyes to the heavens in a "why me, Lord?" expression.

"New York real estate is expensive," he added. "Much more than—where is it you're from again?"

"Indiana," she answered through clenched teeth.

He pulled up a real estate site on his phone. "Looks like the cost of an apartment in Indianapolis is—"

"I've lived in Indianapolis. I know the prices."

"And I've lived in New York. I know the prices." Jack swirled a French fry in ketchup. "How much does a technical writer make again?"

She gazed off in the distance, but her eyes flickered back and forth like she was solving a complex calculus equation. She pursed her lips and drummed her thin fingers on the table. "You want to marry me to change the public's perception of you from insane drunken buffoon to romantic musician with a heart of gold. And you'll give me a place to live in return."

"Yes!" He clapped and pointed finger guns at her. "You've nailed it."

"No." She speared another piece of grilled cheese and put it in her mouth.

"Great! Wait—what?"

"No." She took a napkin and wiped her hands with light, meticulous movements.

"Come on, hear me out."

She raised her eyebrows like a parent who was about to ground their kid, but was at least listening to their excuse first.

"You need a place to live. I have a place to live. You like music. I make music." She shook her head, and Jack began blurting out words faster. "You didn't fawn all over me because of who I am."

"You barely know me."

"I already know you more than any of the actresses my manager is going to line up to play my wife. It'd be business only. We can negotiate a contract. It'd be essentially an acting gig with room and board." She stayed silent, and he continued. "I obviously have money. You'd be set for life. And if this really works, and the next album is decent, I'll get a tour agreement out of it too. We'd never have to see each other."

She reached for a fresh napkin and wiped her hands again. "No."

"But why not?" Jack knew he was whining, but he was used to getting his way. Sure, it was an unorthodox request, but no one had ever turned him down. He was *Jack Hunter*. Former teen idol, smoldering heartthrob, and worldwide rock star. *Jack motherfucking Hunter.*

"Oh." She looked surprised at his question. "Because I don't want to. What else do you have?"

"To offer you?" An exasperated noise escaped him as he shoved his plate away.

"No," she waved her hand dismissively. "What other options for your reputation? Surely your PR team has some ideas."

He kicked his chair back from the table, glowering at her. "This is our best one. Other than that, not much. Bringing peace to the Middle East. Joining a monastery. Saving the rainforest." He leaned forward. "Come on. You're perfect. We're nothing alike. I'm cocky and flashy, and you're—" He gestured at her old AC/DC T-shirt and loose pigtail braids. "Um...charmingly rural? The press would eat it up. Opposites attract and all that."

Her jaw ticked, and she swiped at her hands with another napkin, adding it to a growing pile. Jack stared at the stack, his wounded ego entirely to blame when he growled, "How many times are you going to wipe your damn hands?"

Her back stiffened, and the framework of her defensive walls snapped back into place one by one as her eyes dulled.

"And that's why I won't do it," she said. She pushed her chair away from the table, wincing as it squeaked against the linoleum. She stood, her eyes darting toward the unused napkins.

"Thanks for lunch, Jack," she said with a neutral smile that just made him angrier. He had finally gotten her to smile, but it was in no way genuine. "And good luck with your...venture."

And with that, his rabbit ran off once again.

Jack glared at the remainder of her diced sandwich, the untouched salad, and the pile of used napkins before raking his fingers through his hair in disbelief.

What the hell just happened?

Chapter 4

Lucy paced the sidewalk, her fists clenched as she attempted to psych herself into walking into a New York City bar for the first time in her life.

She had passed the Blue Monster bar on each of her trips to Raymond's Music Store. The bar was covered in garish blue paint the color of a postal box, but it was well-lit and decently clean on the outside. Her ex had taken her to bars before, but they were the posh, sterile environments that most lawyers took their high-end clients to, lacking the vibrancy of something lower-class. For her first authentic bar experience, the Blue Monster seemed to be just perfect.

Two women walked out of the poster-plastered door, giddy with laughter as they snuggled each other. Lucy peeked through the swinging door behind them. The bar was packed, as it should have been at that time of night. Her heart raced, but she needed to try this, needed to know that she could do this.

No one acknowledged her as she slunk inside. People laughed and talked, the two noises fighting for dominance like springtime stags. The air was thick and heavy as if she were stuck under a cotton sheet, trying to breathe through the fabric weave. She tapped her fingers to her palm and headed to the bar.

The bartender grinned at her as she approached, and she returned a shy smile.

"Can I get you something?" he asked, tossing a damp towel back and forth between his hands with the ease of a circus juggler.

"Can I have a Shirley Temple?" she asked, lowering her voice. "But, you know, make it look like I ordered something more adult." She didn't like drinking, primarily because of the loss of control. Every part of her very being was held together with constant concentration. Losing that would be catastrophic.

He winked at Lucy and poured some grenadine into a glass. "You're a tourist, then?"

"Not exactly," she said. "Why?"

"Trust me; I can tell who is local and who isn't." He flashed another glittering smile. "Where are you from?"

"Indiana."

"Oh, yeah? I've got family in South Bend."

"I'm—no, I *was* from Indianapolis. South Bend is nice, though. There's a bakery there that makes the best olive bread." She bit her lip. *Was olive bread considered an appropriate topic in this situation?*

"Was?" he asked, sliding the pink drink to her.

She caught it, letting the cold glass chill her sweaty palm. "I moved here a few weeks ago. I'm still looking for an apartment."

"New job?"

"New...start." She smiled weakly, her gaze dropping to the bar. She traced the condensation her drink had left on the bar, swirling the water into figure eights.

"Well, I hope you like it here." He stuck out a hand. "I'm Tyler."

"Lucy." She grimaced at his hand for a beat before placing her fingers in his for a hurried handshake.

"I gotta keep working," he said. "But I hope you stop by again. We're nothing fancy, but we're fun, and we've got our regulars." On that last word, his eyes darted behind Lucy before he shook his head with a disapproving frown. He gave her a final smile and turned to a rambunctious party that had sidled up to the bar.

Lucy squinted through the crowd, people-watching like a pro. She saw a man and a woman stiffly sitting together, both on their respective cell phones. Two men canoodled in a corner, their eyes starry with mutual affection. And behind them, she spotted a figure wearing a familiar ball cap and an even more familiar scowl.

Jack Hunter was here, he was alone, and he didn't look well.

She wormed her way through the crowd, wincing at every invasive touch and bump until she reached Jack's table. She waited for him to notice her presence, and when he didn't, she tapped him on his shoulder.

"What is it?" he drawled, his head lolling up at her like a broken bobblehead. He blinked rapidly, and his brows furrowed. "Cottontail?"

"No...I'm Lucy. Remember?"

Jack tipped his taut, ashy face toward her. Puffy, violet circles outlined his weary eyes, blending down into the yellow and green splotchy remainders of his bruise.

"You're here." He whipped his head around as if expecting some sort of magical portal that had transported her there. "Alone?"

"Yes."

"Ah." He drained his drink, and his foggy eyes traveled over her red knit dress. "Well, have fun." He flicked his hand at her in cold dismissal.

Lucy slid into the seat across from Jack. He sipped at his empty drink, his shaking hands drumming against the glass.

"You're drunk," she said, neither lauding nor accusatory.

"I am."

"Why?"

"Because I drank alcohol." He shot finger guns at her, whispering "Pew, pew!" under his breath before breaking into a hoarse cough.

A sandy-haired waitress stopped by the booth. "Anything else for you?"

"Yes," Jack said, using his finger gun to stir the melting ice in his cup until it clinked and swirled against the glass like a frozen tornado. "Another one of these."

Lucy met the waitress's eyes and dismissed the order with a subtle head shake. The woman nodded and hurried off to the register.

Jack leaned forward, his dark hair falling into his eyes. The timbre of his voice matched the hum of the bar. "Wanna get married?"

"No." She rubbed her temples, trying to wrest away the misplaced sense of responsibility she had when it came to this ridiculous, broken man. "What happened tonight?"

"Nothing." He tapped his forehead. "Nothing here." A pat to his chest, just above his heart. "Nothing here." He broke into a wheezing spell, and her curiosity turned to worry.

"Are you—are you dying?" she asked.

He snorted and tipped the glass until the remains of an ice cube dropped into his mouth, clinking off his back teeth like a missed golf putt.

"God, I wish." He slid across the booth's cracked leather seat. "I'm going to use the facilities," he said with unnecessary solemnity. "Don't hop away."

Lucy laid her head in her hands and gripped at her hair. There was a television on the wall showing the Jets game, and even at a low volume, the announcer's booming voice and the crowd's cheers wriggled their way into her subconscious. She should leave now, while he was in the bathroom. She could go back to the apartment, put on her pajamas, and relax with a movie. And yet, she stayed, resigned to playing therapist to a drunken guitarist.

The waitress brought her the check and a cheap ballpoint. Lucy pilfered through the pockets of Jack's coat for his wallet and handed a random credit card to the waitress.

"He's always here," the waitress said in a low voice. "No one has ever come for him before. Women leave with him, but no one comes for him."

Jack walked, or rather, moseyed back to the booth, his limbs not quite in sync. He snatched up the check, moving it back and forth in front of his face like a trombone slide.

"There are only three drinks on here. I shouldn't be this drunk after three drinks." He crumpled the receipt and threw it on the floor before turning to her. "And you're here too—my twitchy little musical rabbit. Everything's off tonight. Maybe I'm in Wonderland." He waggled his eyebrows at Lucy.

She thought he was trying to be coy, but it just looked like two cobras doing a mating dance. An unsuccessful attempt at a wink followed.

"Can you get your jacket on?" she asked. "I'm going to take you home. Either put your jacket on or carry it." He looked at his jacket and lifted a sleeve as if questioning its existence.

She took Jack's hand in hers, threading their fingers together. His hand was as warm as a leather car seat on a July afternoon.

Jack pressed their entwined hands to his face. "So good," he murmured, nuzzling her knuckles. "So nice and cold."

She snatched her hands back in alarm. "My hands aren't cold—you're burning up." A timid pat to his cheek confirmed her suspicions: not only was he drunk, but he was running a fever. Add to that the bruises on his face, and he was a wholly miserable mess of a man.

"I'm going to take you home," she repeated, arranging his arm so that he appeared to be embracing her, not leaning on her for support. If there were any sneaky cameras in the bar, they looked like two smitten lovers on their way home instead of a lonely, drunken, former teen idol and his…whatever she was. At the moment, she felt like his parole officer.

She tugged at him to start walking, but he didn't move. He gazed down at her with such surprise and amazement that a heated blush rose on her cheeks.

"Gotta be Wonderland," he murmured, caressing the line of her jaw with his shaking index finger. It was sweet and simple, and yet her skin sizzled with electricity.

"And you're mad as a March Hare," she said, yanking him through the crowd and out into the bitter autumn evening, where he promptly vomited onto the sidewalk.

Jack had no idea where he was.

The air was crisp and chilly, yet sweat dripped down his temple. Someone was tugging at his hand. Jack batted at them, swatting as if at a pesky mosquito, but the motion was weak and kitten-like.

"Keep walking, Jack," a clear voice said.

He flinched, wobbling his head around to find the source. "It's her," he whispered to some unknown audience. "It's my killer porcelain rabbit."

Lucy posed his arms around her like an articulated action figure, his full weight sinking into her shoulder as she led him down the sidewalk.

"I need your address," she said. Jack looped his fingers through her messy braid, twisting and playing as he hummed a wordless, off-key tune.

"Jack, where do you live?" she repeated.

"In my house."

She took his haggard face in her slender hands, squishing his cheeks until his lips pouted forward like a fish. "Tell me your address so I can take you home."

He bit out the address in mumbled fragments. Lucy propped him up between her hip and a street sign while she ordered a ride. He rolled his forehead up and down the metal pole, sighing as his hot skin rubbed against the cool steel. When the car arrived, he whimpered when she dragged him from his snugglefest with the sign.

"You're still here." He squinted at her. "Are we getting married after all?"

"No." She blew a strand of hair from her sweaty face. "Get in the car." She half-lifted, half-shoved him into the gray sedan. The driver was thankfully quiet, though his eyes narrowed with obvious recognition of the musician. Jack slumped against the seat like a season-end scarecrow and fell into a twitching sleep for the remainder of the ride until he lurched awake when the car stopped outside his townhouse.

"You're still here, Cottontail?" he panted, clutching at his chest.

"Still haven't gone anywhere," she assured, grunting as she hoisted him into a standing position. "Why do you keep calling me that?"

"You're jumpy. Like a rabbit. Like Peter Cottontail." His muffled chuckle transformed into an off-the-hinge cackle as he booped the end of her nose. "Hippity, hoppity..." She ducked from his touch and rummaged in his back jeans pocket for his house keys. "Whoa, buy a guy a drink before you do that."

"You don't need another one," she said.

Jack wanted to tell her she was wrong, that he would always need one more drink, but his tongue was impersonating a moldy peach.

She braced him in front of his alarm system until he punched in the security code, then tested a few keys in the door before finding the correct one. She yanked him into the entryway with the gentleness of a mule and couldn't hold back her gasp when she saw the trashed travesty of his townhouse.

"If the Plaza and the Bates Motel had a baby..." she whispered, tripping over a crumpled Amazon box. Structurally, the townhouse was beautiful, but months of slovenly living gave it a haunted, dingy look.

She led him to the nearest room, his home music studio, and shoved him down on the sofa. He couldn't figure out where to focus, so his heavy head bobbled back and forth. He felt like he was on a runaway carousel, and the horses were plotting against him.

"Do you have someone you can call to stay with you? An assistant maybe?" She snapped her fingers in front of his face to keep his attention. He went slightly cross-eyed, trying to follow her hand.

"I don't have a PA anymore. She got pregnant."

"You got your PA pregnant?"

His head snapped up with indignance. "No. Her husband did. She resigned to stay home with the baby. I'm not always a walking tabloid article."

A strawberry-colored flush tinged her skin. "Well, what about friends? Or family?"

He stared at the hardwood floor, ignoring her until she tapped her foot insistently. His curls tumbled forward as he shook his head. Humiliation sank deep in his stomach, adding to his nausea.

"Well, then. Do you have a thermometer?" Lucy asked.

His reddened eyes widened, and he shook his head again. She placed her inner wrist on his forehead, and every one of his senses reeled. He let out a pitiful whimper and leaned into her arm. She smelled like cocoa and lavender, two scents he had never imagined together, and in the future, would never imagine one without the other.

"You have a fever," she said. "You need to rest."

Equal parts dread and panic niggled at the back of his brain. *I can't go to bed yet,* he thought. *I'm supposed to be doing something.*

"A song!" he gasped. "I have to write a song." He stumbled to the piano, sliding onto the bench and hitting a few keys with errant fingers. Swaying on the seat, he began playing a few improvised chords.

"Jack. What are you doing? You need to go to bed."

Through the whiskey fog, he remembered an argument with Kim from this afternoon—another fight about bad reputations and contracts and an aging catalog of songs. About finally setting a date to go into the studio and record songs that hadn't even been written. He wanted to explain this to Lucy, but his thoughts and sanity were flying around his brain like shingles in a tornado. Instead, he sneered at her and played a raucous, bluesy rendition of "Peter Cottontail."

"Stop it. You look like you're going to pass out." Her fearful, drawn expression was replaced by an annoyed glare, and he was secretly pleased. His rabbit had claws after all.

"Would you like something more your style?" He transitioned into a pounding "Goodbye Yellow Brick Road," his entire body trembling with the effort. After a few measures, he moved into a bone-rattling "Great Balls of Fire." Sweat dripped down his temple and splashed the ivory keys. He hit one wrong note, then two, the missteps squawking like angry crows surrounded by songbirds. After several more mistakes, he howled and slammed his hands onto as many keys as he could, unleashing a cacophonous roll of musical thunder.

"Finished with your tantrum?" Lucy folded her arms and frowned at the feverish, piratical lunatic. Jack snarled, his sweat-dampened curls falling over into his eyes. He clawed at his hair before returning to the keyboard to play "Chopsticks" in a mocking, singsong rhythm. His head bobbed closer and closer to the keyboard until it fell onto the keys with a dissonant crash.

"Key of C-sharp major," he said, pointing to his forehead before collapsing to the floor, unconscious.

Lucy left Jack sprawled on the floor next to the piano bench. It had been enough of a struggle to support his weight earlier; dead-lifting his unconscious body was simply not going to happen. She placed a dusty couch cushion under his head as her stomach twisted with worry. He was extremely drunk, with a fever on top of that, so dehydration was her first concern. She checked his breathing once more—steady but raspy—and went to find some water.

His kitchen was both a dream and a nightmare, with marble countertops, an inset cutting board, and a wide island perfect for laying out an expansive meal. The walls were farmhouse white, with an accent wall the color of a sea storm.

That kitchen was beautiful. That kitchen wanted to be loved.

It clearly was not.

The island had a blanket of dust, uninterrupted except for the warped imprints of glasses and bottles. The cutting board had a burgundy stain that Lucy really hoped was just wine. There were no pots, pans, or utensils on the counters. Even a potholder would add warmth to the stark room, but there was nothing but a crumpled roll of paper towels.

When she opened the refrigerator, she found a gallon of expired milk and a Styrofoam box of moldy mashed potatoes. She threw out the food and searched through his cupboards, but found nothing there. The man apparently lived solely on takeout and booze.

She pulled out her phone and ordered some basic groceries, adding some basic adult necessities—like a thermometer—and arranging for it to be delivered.

Jack was stirring when she returned to the studio with a cup of water. His face had a verdigris pallor, and when she touched his shoulder, he jerked away.

"How come you can touch me, but I can't touch you?" he demanded.

She blinked, surprised at his perceptiveness and unable to think of a proper response. The complicated answer was so much more than his simple question.

"I don't like being surprised," she said at last. "I don't like being startled. But you can touch me."

She offered a quivering hand. He stared at it for a moment before poking her palm like a wasp's nest.

"Can you sit up?" she asked. "I want to take you to the bedroom."

"That's what they all say." He squished his face into the cushion, unabashedly nuzzling the upholstery.

"I think you'd be more comfortable there. And I can't carry you."

Eyes closed, he swiveled his body, and she placed a firm hand on his shoulder blade. She yanked him to his feet with an "Alley-oop!", ignoring his protesting groan. Taking the brunt of his weight, she shuffled him down the hall and upstairs in a cumbersome two-step. He gave her a self-satisfied grin when they entered his giant loft bedroom.

"Aww, you're carrying me across the threshold. It's a real marriage!" He chucked her under the chin, and she resisted the urge to drop him like a bag of rocks.

Like the rest of his townhouse, his bedroom was stark and cluttered. The sheets on his king-sized bed seemed clean, despite being balled at the foot of his bed. Lucy guided him to the mattress, uncrumpled the sheets, and pulled them over his shivering shoulders. Finding a spare blanket on the floor, she rolled it into a firm tube, placing it against his back and bracing it with extra pillows.

"What are you doing?" he mumbled.

"Putting a blanket behind you, so you don't roll over onto your back. I don't want you to throw up and choke."

"Why not? It's a family tradition," he said with feeble mockery, and she froze at her thoughtless words. Most people were familiar with the story of rising star actor Connor Vincent, who had overdone it on pills and liquor and died in that same way. His legacy, other than a handful of cult movies, was leaving behind his pop star girlfriend and their unborn son, Jack Vincent—better known by his stage name, Jack Hunter.

"I'm sorry," she said, but his fluttering lashes were the only indication he had heard her at all. She bit her lip, glancing between his sleeping body and his bedroom door. Propriety would have her wait downstairs until he woke up, but as he shifted and moaned a little in his sleep, she couldn't leave him alone. With a sigh, she removed her shoes and crawled onto the bed, laying as far from him as possible, and began her vigilant watch.

Chapter 5

Jack woke up two hours later with a spluttering cough. Lucy rolled the new thermometer across his brow, frowning when it trilled cheerfully.

"No birds in the house," he said, swatting it away with a sweaty palm.

"It's just a thermometer. Let's try and sit up."

He shook his head like a petulant toddler and buried himself under his comforter. She slid her hands under his lean arms and tugged upwards at his shoulders.

"I'm not ticklish." He shoved her hands away.

"I'm not trying to—I'm trying to lift you. Sit up."

Like an engineer trying to redesign a ramshackle building, she surveyed him for the best angle before using her shoulder to push him into a forward position. Her socks slipped on the hardwood floor, and she fell to her knees, face planting into the blankets.

"Please. Sit. Up."

He groaned, coaxing his body to incline against the pillow. Lucy placed a thermos of microwaved chicken broth into his hands.

"Drink it."

"I don't want it."

"Drink it."

Intense irritation spread like a thundercloud across his face.

She stifled a shudder and tapped her fingers against her palms.

"Why are you so jumpy? Like a fucking jackrabbit."

"You're stuck on this rabbit thing, aren't you?" Her nostrils twitched, and he pointed to it as damning evidence. "Please, drink the broth."

His gaze slid to her vintage-style shirt. "Elvis sucks." His jaw locked in arrogant defiance, challenging her, baiting her.

"Drink the damn broth."

His lips quirked, and he looked quite pleased with himself before he took a hesitant sip, swallowing with a pained grimace. "Is Elvis your favorite singer?" He gestured at the shirt with a surly expression.

"I don't really have a favorite. But he holds a special place in my heart." For Lucy, listening to the King was like wrapping herself in the plushest of blankets, or drinking the sweetest of cocoas. It was music that transcended cruel laughter and busted lips and the darkest nights.

Jack grunted in disapproval, so she pushed the mug toward his lips again. "Sip it."

"No." He closed his eyes, shaking his mop of damp, tangled hair. "Tired."

She chewed on her lip, fretting. Jack needed to drink more fluids before she would be comfortable enough to go back to her own apartment. Her father had had his own unique trick when any of her brothers and sisters were suffering from the inherent stubbornness of illness. Perhaps it would work on Jack. "Drink it, or I'll start telling jokes."

He lifted his lids just enough to peer at her through his long, thick lashes. "No."

"What do you get when you cross an elephant and a rhino?" She paused. "Elefino."

He groaned at the auditory pun and took another sip, wincing again.

"Good boy. One more."

"No."

"Why did the scarecrow win an award?"

"Fucking hell."

"He was outstanding in his field."

He took a hurried sip and glared at her, shoving the thermos into her hands. "No more. Jokes or broth."

"You did well." She left the thermos within his reach on the nightstand. "Sleep some more, okay?"

He grumbled something incoherent and hid his face under a pillow.

After he drifted back to sleep, she explored his townhouse. It was unkempt, and not in a lived-in, comfortable way. Minimal decor adorned the walls, except for in his studio, which had his platinum records on the wall, glittering relics from another age.

It felt like the house itself had given up on life—a little like its occupant.

A shelf held a framed picture of Jack and B.B. King. Physically, he looked the same—a little leaner, perhaps, and his mop of chin-length waves didn't have that dusting of silver at the temples. But his smile was giddy and unabashed. He was a young man on top of the world, unaware of the drunken mess he would become.

On the second floor, there was a guest room with a television in it. The bed was neatly made, though the dusty nightstand proved no one had been in there in a while. Lucy laid down on the bed like a sleepy Goldilocks. Was this what it would be like to be Jack's wife, or rather, glorified roommate? If that night had been any indication, it would probably be more trouble than the free room was worth. Still, walking around this lonely house, there was a tiny bit of her that wanted to take him up on his offer. They were both living alone in the dark. Maybe they could look for a little bit of light together?

Lucy awoke from her unplanned nap to two sounds rarely heard together: the gentle plink of piano keys, followed by the guttural heaving of someone vomiting. She bolted downstairs to the music studio.

Jack sat on the piano bench, bent in half over a trash can. He wiped his mouth with the back of his hand and gulped in gasping breaths. His other hand laid on the keys, curved in the shape of a chord.

"What are you doing?"

"I thought you left," he bit out, his face green and roughshod. The alcoholic bliss had worn off and left a feverish animal in its stead, wounded and ready to strike.

"I was in the guest room, that's all."

He waved her off and turned back to the piano, plunking at the keys with frenetic chaos and swiping at his sweaty forehead.

"Stop this. Are you trying to recreate the death scene of *Amadeus*?"

"I'm working on a song." He stopped and clutched his stomach, closing his eyes as if in prayer.

"It can wait."

"No, it can't." He swung back to the piano, running his fingers over the same keys, over and over like a hesitant spider, before roaring and slamming his hands down in a loud chorus of chords. Then he bent over again and retched into the trash.

"You're going to throw up on your piano," Lucy said. He flipped her his middle finger between heaves. She ignored it and waited for his body to finish casting up whatever was left in his belly. When he straightened with a pained gasp, his expression was a mixture of humiliation and pure misery.

She took a tentative step toward him as if he were a stray dog—possibly sweet, but also possibly rabid. He glared at her outstretched hand as if it were responsible for his misery.

"Do you want help going upstairs?"

"I don't need your help!" he snapped. "Not from you, not from anybody. I can write music and save my career on my own, so just fuck off already!"

She yanked her hand back as if bitten. "Fine."

"I don't need help," he repeated with a vicious snarl. His white knuckles clenched around the lip of the piano bench. "Not from some rock groupie."

Oh, hell no. Not the g-word.

"I am not a groupie," Lucy spat out. "I am the farthest from a groupie you'll ever find. And even if I were, I'd hardly be a groupie to *you* of all people."

Jack's eyes darted between her and the trash can, possibly regarding them as equal worth.

"Good luck, then, with this." She gestured at the whole mess—the trash can, the piano, the musician—before rushing to the front door. He retched again, but she didn't turn back. As he had so vehemently stated, he didn't need help.

Throwing the front door open, she pulled up the rideshare app to order a car and plopped down on the bare stoop to wait. Wind leaked into the neck of her jacket as she tugged it tighter around her. She could have waited inside the house, but she didn't want to be anywhere near Jack Hunter—no, *Mad Jack*, because the press was right. The man was insane.

Once the car arrived and she was safely inside, her phone buzzed with a text alert from an unknown number. There was no message preview, so she ignored it. *Stupid spam texts.* She didn't need a new car, a credit check, or a penis enlargement.

The text alerts didn't stop once she was sheltered and cozy inside her apartment, her cell vibrating in her pocket like an angry bumblebee. Annoyed, she unlocked her phone to find that they weren't regular texts, but recorded audio messages. She tapped the first one and listened with apprehension.

"I'm too sick to text. The alphabet keeps spinning." Jack's voice was slurred and distant, as if the phone was barely near his mouth. With a frustrated groan, she remembered she had given him her number in case of any medical costs from his Lucy-inflicted injury. She opened the next few in succession.

"Oh God, you were right. I got sick on the piano," he moaned. "Cottontaaaaail."

"Not my name," Lucy mumbled, but curiosity had her listening to the next messages.

"I can't get the water bottle open." Next.

"There's water all over my fucking shirt!" Next.

"Luuuuucy," he said on the next one, before several clunks like a runaway bowling ball when the phone was obviously dropped.

"I'm using the wet shirt to clean the pia— Awww, fu—"

"I spilled water all over the piano."

The next clip was just Jack gagging and sputtering. If Lucy had no conscience, she could have sold these to a radio comedy show, but the ridiculousness of it all gave her a warm feeling deep in her chest, like a fresh sip of sun tea.

It wasn't until she was in bed at last that the final message, a real text message, came through on the screen.

JACK: I'm sorry.

She sighed heavily. The whole mess with Jack Hunter had been a—well, if not exactly fun, an *interesting* detour from her plans, but it was time to get back to business. She had to find a place to live, and a new life to carve out in the city.

LUCY: Don't worry about it. Feel better soon.

The next day, Lucy redoubled her efforts to find an apartment. She spent the morning hunched over her laptop, alternating between browsing real estate websites and formatting a hazardous materials manual for a client. She found a handful of places in Brooklyn that fit her simple requirements—a place to cook, a place to sleep, a place to work.

A place to be alone at last. To be safe.

While she threw together a simple salad that afternoon, her phone shook with an incoming text. She lifted it, expecting her daily check-in message from her mother.

JACK: You left your wallet here. Send me your address and I'll send a driver with it.

She frowned and checked her purse for confirmation. She must have left it on the counter when she ordered his groceries. She tapped out her information, went back to her computer, and checked out a listing for a minuscule studio apartment in Cobble Hill.

A harsh knock on the door an hour later interrupted her concentration. She peeked through the eyehole and let out a groan. A bleary-eyed rock star glowered back at her through the fisheye glass, looking like the victim of a zombie bite.

Lucy opened the door. "You're not your driver." Jack stumbled in, dressed in a ratty tartan bathrobe and green moccasins like an illustration from Eddie Vedder's Christmas cards. He tossed her wallet at her.

"I'm sick," he said. "Marry me."

"No." Her chest twinged as he clutched the back of a chair for support. "You look awful. I would've come and gotten the wallet if you needed me to."

He waved her off. "Don't make me talk. Just come back."

"Come back?" she repeated. "Why?"

"I didn't mean what I said. I was sick." He scrubbed at his face with shaking hands, his eyes wide and wild. "I don't like being sick."

"Ah yes, as opposed to the many people who love it." She reached for the front doorknob and twisted it open, sweeping her arm as a gesture for him to leave.

"I shouldn't have yelled. Kim and I got into a fight before you found me. I have to write. She booked studio musicians and a recording date. I mean—fuck. Just come back." He swayed like a cattail in the breeze. "Please."

"Why?"

"Because."

"That's not an answer."

"I'm sick as hell," he said.

"Yes, you've said that." His ashen face tugged at her heartstrings, but she wasn't in the mood to return to his house just to get snapped at or proposed to again.

"Come stay with me. Until I feel better." He met her eyes, and though she tried to look away, his hangdog expression drew her in. "I don't have anyone else."

Silence yawned between them. "What about Sully?" she asked.

He frowned. "He's my tenant. I can't ask him."

"What?"

"The building," he said. "With the record store. It's mine."

She blinked at him in surprise. Dilapidated commercial buildings weren't exactly something that usually attracted someone in his tax bracket.

Jack tried to straighten his posture, but a racking cough overwhelmed him. "Are you coming now?"

"No."

"Please." His hand darted out, circling her wrist, his calloused fingers brushing against the sensitive skin. "I'll let you tell one joke."

She snorted. "Why me?"

His mouth tipped up in a shadow of a smile. "You treat me like I'm normal."

Perhaps she and Jack had more in common than she thought.

"I really shouldn't," she said, swallowing back any pity and half-heartedly pointing at the door again.

"Oh." He had a stunned look of betrayal, like someone who had just taken a dodgeball to the face in gym class. His shoulders fell, and he broke into another coughing spell.

"Can I just stay here?" he asked with a half-hopeful look.

Lucy sighed. "For a few minutes." She went to make a cup of herbal tea for him, partially because it would probably do him good, and partially because she didn't want to be expected to make any additional conversation. Despite everything, she was starting to become a little attached to Jack. He was like a licorice twist—sharp, bitter, and liable to give you a tummy ache.

Lucy was rather fond of licorice.

When she returned, Jack's head was on the table, cushioned by his folded arms. Lucy patted his shoulder, and he snored. With a sigh of exasperation, Lucy sat down across from him and sipped at the tea, suddenly feeling a tummy ache coming on.

Chapter 6

There was an elephant on Jack's chest and a snake in his bed.

Jack hated snakes.

Elephants were hit or miss.

His eyes flew open, and he choked out a gasp of terror, scrabbling halfway up his pillow. Quickened footsteps intermingled with the ominous hissing.

She was there. His Cottontail. His elation at the sight of her battled with panic over his imminent demise.

"Snake!" he warned as her figure slipped through the doorway. Instead of shock, her doe eyes filled with sympathy, and that was the moment Jack knew he was going to die, either poisoned by snake venom or crushed by pachyderm pressure.

She advanced toward him like an angel of death, her wrist dipping to his forehead. He couldn't die, not when he'd just learned about the wonder that was that wrist. He moaned and pressed against her cool skin shamelessly.

"You're warmer than this afternoon," she said. "I'm going to retake your temperature, okay?"

"No, Lucy." His tongue was thick and clumsy. She tried to work her hand away, but he pinned it in place with sweaty fingers. "The snake will get you."

"Snake?"

"Yes, snake." He hissed hoarsely and stuck his tongue out.

"Jack, that's the humidifier." She lifted her wrist. "You're hallucinating."

"The elephant then. On my chest. Make Dumbo go 'way."

Her eyes narrowed. "Your chest feels tight?" He ducked his chin. "Come on, let's get you sitting up." She laid a gentle hand between his shoulder blades and coaxed him upward. He felt the scratchy, corded upholstery underneath him, and he remembered he wasn't in his bed. He was in Lucy's tiny rental apartment with a thin comforter pulled over his body.

"Snakes, huh?" she asked, handing him a glass of water.

"I hate them."

"They're not so bad. I think they're kinda cute."

He halted, the glass halfway to his lips. "You ever see a snake blink?"

"No."

"Exactly."

She clicked her tongue and left, returning with a pair of white pills and a glass of water. Jack took them without argument and turned to thank her, but she had already disappeared again.

Jumpy as a jackrabbit.

When she reappeared several minutes later, holding a mixing bowl, her eyes were red-rimmed and weepy. Jack was sure he was really sick because, for some reason, the sight made his chest hurt even more.

"What's wrong?" He jerked up in the chair. "What happened?"

She wrinkled her nose, still sniffling. "Nothing, I'm fine." She held up the mixing bowl. "I made you an onion poultice to help your chest."

"Like a chicken dish? I don't know if I can eat right now."

"No, that's *poultry*. This is a *poultice*. The onions go on your chest and the vapors help you breathe."

She retrieved a lumpy, folded dishtowel from the bowl. Even with his congested nose, Jack could smell the pungent onions.

"Don't you dare." His paltry threat came out as a raspy croak, dismissed with a single shake of her head. When she came closer, he reached for the cool skin of her wrist again, but she shrugged him away. She eased his T-shirt upward, tucking the hem at his neck like a bib. Her fingers caressed his stomach, and with that single motion, he forgot all about her wrist. He shut his eyes and reveled in her touch, and for the tiniest millisecond, the universe and life itself were amazing and wondrous.

Then she shoved a slimy dish towel onto his sternum and yanked his shirt over it. His nostrils splayed, and he sputtered and coughed, assaulted by onion odor.

"I changed my mind," Jack yelped. "I don't need you or your witchcraft." She raised an eyebrow and tucked the comforter around his arms, jailing him inside the world's smelliest cocoon.

Lucy backed away from him and sat cross-legged on the sofa on the other side of the room. Her mouth was a slim white line of tension.

"What's wrong with you?" he sputtered. An onion jostled free inside his shirt like a slippery eel wriggling against his skin. He almost wished he were back to his stand-off with the hallucinatory snake.

She swallowed. "The smell. It's, um, very strong."

He stared at her, unable to determine if he was mad that she'd pushed her strong smell struggle off on him or touched that she was fighting her own senses for his health.

"You don't need to stay in here with me," he grumbled.

"If you can handle it, so can I."

"How long do I need to wear this?"

"About twenty minutes."

He threw his hand around for his phone, and finding it in the folds of the comforter, set a timer for twenty minutes. He refused to wear the poultice for a minute longer.

Lucy's face twisted up in thought, her hand tapping itself in a nervous staccato. Jack had started to identify it as some sort of motion to soothe anxiety, which frustrated him. He could handle the dumbstruck reactions of fans, but Lucy was reacting to him as a person. The only time she emerged from her emotional fortress was when he challenged her, so he went for it.

"Stop opening and closing your mouth. You look like a goldfish."

Her eyes blazed, and her pattering fingers froze mid-tap. "I am not."

"You are. I'm waiting for air bubbles to float from your mouth at any moment." He poked a little more to test his theory. "If this is some delayed starstruck reaction, then I don't want you here."

The blaze in her eyes turned into a bonfire. "I don't get starstruck."

"Then say something. Or ask me for my autograph. Just get on with it."

"Autographs are creepy."

He squinted at her and bit his lip to keep from laughing. "Well. That's a statement we're going to have to unpack at some point."

The hand tapping began again, and she gritted her teeth as if he were forcing her to speak at gunpoint. Her focus was trained on the floor, and her words were stilted when she finally spoke. "Sometimes, I just—I need to make sure I'm saying and doing—the right things. I can't always tell. I don't want to make mistakes."

"You always consider what you're going to say before you say it?"

"Almost always." Her eyes flicked to his for a millisecond. "For some godawful reason, I have trouble with it around you." Her words were charged with bleak, drained frustration.

Jack grunted. "I've had people sucking up to me my entire life. It would be really refreshing to hear the goddamn truth sometimes."

Her lips twisted and pursed. "No."

"No?"

"No."

Jack sighed. She was back to the one-word answers. He rested his head back on the sofa arm. "You've punched me, and I've vomited in front of you. We're beyond filters."

Her shoulders slumped. "I'm sorry I hit you," she said. "I really didn't mean to. You just startled me."

"I'm sorry too. I won't sneak up on you again."

She peered at him with a mixture of grief and awe, and the peculiar pinch in his heart ratcheted tighter.

"I think we'll be okay," she said. "You're not the quietest person around."

Jack snorted. The medicine was kicking in, and his eyelids were as heavy as ship anchors. He didn't want to fall asleep, though, because he smelled like a roadside diner. "By the way, my manager, Kim, will probably stop by with an NDA sometime soon about all this."

"So I can't publish your sickbed confessions then?" She slipped him a slight grin. The smile lit up her elfin features, transforming her from a shuddering shadow into something wild and wonderful. He had finally drawn a smile out of her, and it was glorious. Between the coughing, the onion torture, and that fucking smile, he wasn't sure if he would survive the night.

"There's nothing to write about. I'm a perfect angel."

"Too bad. I'm sure the *National Enquirer* would love an article about Jack Hunter's snake phobia."

His lips curled in disapproval. His stage name didn't sound right coming from her. "Vincent. My real last name is Vincent."

Her smile faltered. "I know."

"Of course you do. You know everything." He burrowed into the blankets, trying to recall better scents than the onion burrito he had become. Roses. Fresh-baked cookies. Cocoa and lavender. "What's with the rock and roll history thing, anyway?"

The twenty-minute alarm shrilled through the room, and Lucy sprang from the sofa without answering. He plucked the poultice from his shirt, shivering at the sliminess.

"What are you thinking right now?" he asked, dropping the poultice into the mixing bowl with a moist plop. "No filter."

"Honestly?" She blinked at him, and the corners of her mouth slanted up. "You need a shower."

As soon as Jack stood, Lucy regretted her shower suggestion. He shook like a leaf in a rainstorm, although his skin was a tad cooler and his breathing a little less labored. Regrettably, he also smelled like a fryer, but a hot shower would go far in clearing his lungs.

"You sure you can do this?" she asked once they were in the apartment's bathroom. He set his jaw and nodded, tugging at his shirt to pull it over his head. During his feeble struggle, a few loose onion slices dropped to the floor with a squelch.

"Lucy," he said, his head half-buried inside his shirt. "Help."

"Sit." He hunkered on the side of the tub, his arms haphazardly tangled in his sleeves. Lucy stood in front of his outstretched legs, arranged his arms, and removed his shirt.

"There you are," she said when he was rescued. His forlorn, dark eyes gazed up at her. There was an exhausted rawness sick people had, where all their pretenses were torn away by weakness, and their true self shone through. Jack exhibited that look then, and she could barely breathe. It wasn't his sharp jawline or messy curls, or slightly crooked nose that captivated her. It was the exposed, unabashed emotion reflected in those umber brown eyes—loathing and weariness and utter sadness.

"There you are," she repeated, and her hand took on a life of its own, reaching out to cup the length of his stubbled jaw. At her touch, he closed his eyes, and his abrupt inhale cracked through her haze.

"You don't have any tattoos," she blurted, surveying his lean chest as she dropped her hand. He furrowed his forehead, and she crimsoned. "Sorry, that's a musician stereotype."

He mumbled something incoherent.

"What was that?"

"The first rule of ass tattoos," he said. "Don't talk about ass tattoos."

"Oh." Her fingers twitched, and she slid her gaze to the floor. "I have a tattoo too. But it's on my back, not my ass."

"Let me see," he said, a hint of his devilish spark back.

"No."

"I'll show you mine if you show me yours." He attempted a half-grin but could barely manage it. Even his lips were trembling from the effort.

"I don't want to see it," she said. "I'm going to stay in the bathroom while you shower. My eyes will be closed. If you feel like you are going to faint again, I'll try and catch you."

"How are you going to catch me with your eyes closed?"

Lucy ignored him, starting the shower. He goggled at the water as if it were Mount Everest and he had lost his Sherpa.

She shut her eyes. "I'm ready. You can drop your pants."

She heard the swoosh of fabric falling to the floor. Jack took a breath, hesitating. "This is, without a doubt, the sexiest moment of my life."

She raised her eyebrows but kept her eyes pinched shut. "Really?"

A scoff. "No." The glass shower door glided open with a metallic whine. "Pretty sure you're the first woman ever to close her eyes while I'm standing naked in front of her. I'm going to develop a complex."

She remained vigilant to the sounds of the shower, listening for a tell-tale stumble or anything else that would indicate a fainting spell. After a few minutes, the rustle of his movements ceased.

"Jack?"

"Yeah, Cottontail?" His voice quavered.

"Are you done?"

"Yeah." The shower water continued to spray with no other sound indicating movement.

"Jack?"

"Yeah?"

"Do you need me to turn off the shower?"

A long, grateful sigh. "Please."

She felt her way against the humid tiled wall until she found the shower door. She cracked it open, and after a few tries—and a soaked shirt sleeve—she shut off the water. His hand clamped onto her wrist, warm and wet. She was so startled by the fact that she *didn't* startle that she let out a squeaked "Oh!" He released her immediately.

"No," she said, flapping her arm in his general direction as if aiming for a piñata. "It's alright. Use me for balance if you need to." After a moment, he rested his hand on her arm again, and a frisson of awareness shot through her. She fumbled for a towel and thrust it at him.

"Covered?"

"Uh-huh."

She finally opened her eyes. Fatigue rolled off Jack in waves as he clung to her arm with damp fingers. He zombie-walked to the bedroom, slipping back into his rumpled clothes while Lucy looked away.

"I'm dressed," he said finally, his shoulders slumped in exhaustion.

"See, that wasn't so bad. Go on, lay on the bed. You don't need to go back to the couch."

He gave her a sleepy-eyed glare. "The couch is fine. I'm feeling better anyway."

"Oh?" she pushed on his arm, and he fell back onto the bed, dazed. "That's what I thought." He grumbled as she tucked the covers around him.

"I'm going to go in the living room," she said. "I'll check on you soon." She headed toward the doorway until his hoarse voice called out.

"Lucy. Stay with me."

"Why?"

The side of his mouth curved up. "The snake might come back."

It was a terrible idea, and yet she joined him, slipping under the blankets and making sure that a reasonable amount of distance was between them. His breathing steadied, and Lucy followed him into sleep as the rhythm of early evening rain provided their naptime soundtrack.

When Lucy woke, it was well past nightfall, and she was drenched in sweat. She tried to kick off the cumbersome blankets, but they weren't blankets at all.

Jack was snuggling her. His arm was flung over her side, cinched tight against her belly, and his knees curled up behind her in a perfect spooning position.

Any other day, she would have frozen in place, her brain racing from zero to sixty with panic. But all she could think was *he's too hot*, and not as a measure of his attractiveness.

She tossed back the covers and lay her wrist on his forehead. His face had a ghastly pallor, splashed with flushed red. His shivers were gone, replaced by damp sweat and dry heat. He didn't even wave away the thermometer when she rolled it over his temple.

"Alright, Jack," she said. "Let's get some of these blankets off." She paused for one of his snarky responses, but he was silent. She peeled back all the blankets except the sheet. Heat radiated from his body like an antique oil heater. Grabbing a wet washcloth from the en suite, she smoothed it over his forehead. He stirred, opening his eyes weakly.

"You've got quite a fever there, Mr. Vincent," Lucy said with false cheer. He blinked, shifting his head and studying her. His hand extended and traced her jaw with one finger. She covered his hand with hers, wishing she could transfer a little of her health into him through touch alone.

The compress slipped from Jack's forehead. She adjusted it back on his temple and sat next to him on the bed. To her surprise, he slid his hot hand in hers, looping their fingers together.

"You don't need any more body heat," she said, but he shook his head.

"I'm sick. You have to do what I say."

"I'm pretty sure that's not how it works." She yielded and let him cling to her hand. "Do you want to go to urgent care?"

"No. I don't need a doctor. I have you and your hillbilly witchcraft." He rubbed his chest where the onion poultice had been.

"I'm not a hillbilly. I'm just from Indiana." He lifted a judgmental eyebrow. "Well, I did grow up on a farm. A non-working one."

He groaned as he rocked into his pillow. She lifted his head and flipped it to the elusive "cool side," and he nodded his gratitude.

"Tell me about the farm," he said with all the ardor of a Steinbeck character. He patted at the mattress next to him, and she sat, overlooking the way her heart stuttered at his proximity.

"The farm's outside of a town called Sparrow Hill. My great-grandparents used it as an actual farm, so there are still some old buildings left." She scrolled through her phone, showing him a picture of her parents she had taken during a fleeting visit last summer. "This is the backyard, but you can see the granary and the barn in the background."

"Are those your parents?"

"Yes," she said with proud affection. "My dad's a general contractor. My mom is a stay-at-home mom. I'm one of eight kids."

"Holy shit. Which one are you?"

"Number four." She held up fingers to count off. "It goes Nico, Violetta, Matteo, me, Ariana, Dante, and then Elena and Sophia are the twins. And Gianna is the only grandchild so far. She's Violetta's—Lettie's. Ma is second-generation Italian and insisted we all have good Italian names if you can't tell."

"Lucy is Italian?"

"My full name is Luciana," She drew out the pronunciation as *loo-chee-ah-nah*. "Everyone uses Lucy with the soft 'c' though. It's easier than correcting them and having to explain how it really is said."

"Hmmm." His heavy-lidded eyes skimmed over her face. "I like Luciana, though." Her lips tugged to the side, and she tentatively smoothed an errant curl away from his forehead. "Is there anyone else?"

"No." She hesitated. "Well, except for Lincoln and Larry."

"Who are they?"

"Lincoln is the cat. Larry is the pig."

"You have a pig."

"He's just a little guy. He won't hurt anyone."

"I'm not scared of the pig, Luciana." Her belly fluttered as he said her full name.

"That's good. He'll probably cuddle you at some point, and it startles people." She frowned at the awkward statement. Larry wouldn't ever cuddle Jack because he wouldn't ever meet Jack.

Jack's eyes drifted to her mouth, but the movement was sluggish and labored. "The pig is in the house?"

"I said he was little. And litter-trained. Such a good boy."

She flipped through different photos from the past few years, narrating through each one. Jack's stillness was only broken by coughing fits and hoarse rasping. After a particularly racking cough, he laid his head on her shoulder. She froze, her heart trip-trapping like a billy goat over a troll's bridge. She couldn't remember the last time her heart raced for any reason other than fear, and yet it was happening, simply because a man who was probably infecting her with influenza at that very moment was snuggling her shoulder.

She shook her head to clear it before pulling up more photos: Lettie, beaming in front of her farm, her greatest source of pride other than her infant daughter. Nico, Matteo, and Dante fixing up the old barn. Elena and Sophia moving into their first college apartment together. Ariana and her mother hugging, most likely taken before another argument about Ari's bright purple pixie haircut. And finally, a picture of Lucy and Gianna, the first day she came home from the hospital.

The day everything had changed.

"Hold up." He stabbed a finger at the picture. "How come she gets such a big smile from you?"

"Because she's a baby!"

"Psshhh. I've gotten one smile like that, and I can walk and talk."

A delicate warmth blossomed inside her chest. "You're keeping track?"

"You never smile," he said. "Except for babies and men who run diners."

The blossom of warmth wilted. "I don't smile a lot. It doesn't mean that I'm not happy. I just don't always think to do it."

He responded with a neutral humming noise. Lucy switched to a picture of Larry sprawled and napping in front of a brick fireplace. "There you go," she said. "Proof of the pig."

"You really have a pig." He shook his head but didn't lift it from her shoulder. It almost felt like an affectionate nuzzle. "Your family is weird."

"I know."

"You're weird."

"I know." It was only the millionth time she'd been told that, but there was no malice in his words.

His eyes fluttered shut, and he shifted, rubbing at his chest with a grimace. His body crooked closer and a surge of protectiveness crashed over Lucy, unexplained and unyielding.

"Hey, Lucy?" he whispered after a moment. "Weird is okay."

Chapter 7

The late afternoon sun glowed through the cracks of the curtains when Jack woke up next. His chest was tight and his joints sagged with fatigue, but he was in his right mind at last.

And Lucy's apartment smelled fantastic.

Like a toucan mascot, he followed his nose to the kitchen. A pot simmered on the stove, filling the air with the delicious aroma of chicken soup. Lucy bent over the counter, chopping carrots and swaying to a Queen song. The entire scene was so comfortably domestic that it made Jack's heart ache.

"I'm alive," he said, and she jerked her head up. She put down the chopping knife and settled her wrist against his forehead.

"Your fever broke. Probably why you've been asleep so long. Do you want to try some soup?"

She dished out a tiny serving for him to try. Not only was it good, but after days of barely keeping anything down, his body's natural urge was to devour it like a starved panther.

"This is delicious, Lucy. Marry me."

She shook her head, not even responding to his proposals anymore. "I'm glad you like it. I'm making vegetable soup as well. I'll pack them up for you when you leave."

But Jack didn't want to leave. He liked this moment out of time, where the real world didn't matter—an oasis in a desert of boredom and irrelevance. He drank the soup as she dumped the carrots into the soup pot with a splash of steam, washing her hands afterward.

"How many band shirts do actually you have?" He gestured at her Led Zeppelin shirt. It clung just perfectly to her figure. He may have been half-dead from the flu, but he could still appreciate the way her waist dipped in and the slight curve of her breasts.

She reached for a zucchini, slicing it into thin discs. "Forty-two. And a half."

Of course she knew the exact number. "A half?"

"My Aerosmith one has a hole in it." Her bottom lip curved downward.

"Any Jack Hunter ones?"

Her responding 'hmph' answered that.

"Well, that needs to be fixed." He made a mental note to have Kim send a few over.

She shook her head again with a faraway smile and rewashed her hands before moving on to another zucchini. Her hand flew over the cutting board, dicing and slicing like a pro. When she finished that zucchini, she cleaned her hands again, and realization struck Jack.

Grilled cheese eaten with a fork. A pile of napkins on a Formica table. Constant hand washing while cooking.

Lucy didn't like her hands to be dirty.

He sprang up and went to the table, grabbing all the napkins from the holder and thumping them down next to the sink.

"Marry me," he said, motioning to his offering. "I'll buy you napkins."

Her chopping stalled, and she frowned at the napkins first, then him.

"That's a new one," she said. "Finish your soup."

"Come on. We get along well."

"We barely know each other."

"Look, I'm not stupid. I know how crazy this sounds." He tugged at his hair in frustration. "Isn't there anything in the world you want?"

He should just give up and stop pushing her. Kim could send a courier with a dozen dossiers of potential fake spouses within the hour, and he could have his pick. But for some insane reason, his stubborn heart was set on Lucy.

"I want to say yes." Her hand shook when she finally spoke. "I like helping people. I like being helpful." She nipped at her lip, clearly distressed.

"Luciana," he said, drawing out her full name like a rollercoaster car on his tongue, wild and thrilling. "No editing your words here. Just talk. Or don't. But don't practice everything in that big brain of yours ahead of time. Not for me."

She drummed her hand along the underside edge of the counter. "Honestly, this marriage of convenience thing could be nice."

"Nice?" Jack had never heard any relationship with himself described as *nice*, and he wasn't sure how to take it.

"But I can't do it."

"Lucy." He swallowed. "I don't want to just be remembered as a drunken one-hit wonder."

Her expression softened. "That won't happen."

Jack cast an askance glance at her. "Go through that big music catalog in your head. I'm sure you can name a hundred musicians whose behavior overshadowed any talent they ever had." Her guilty silence confirmed it.

"It's not really fair, is it?" she said after a moment. "Yes, you've done some idiotic things. I mean, that thing with the kayak in Norway—"

"Lucy—"

"—or the raccoons on Yom Kippur—"

"*Luciana*. You're not helping."

"Oh." She blinked. "What I'm trying to say is, it's not really fair that you have to work really hard on an album and also prove that you're not a hot mess. You should just be allowed to be a hot mess and leave it like that."

Even though his head still throbbed a little, he threw back his head and barked out a laugh. "From anyone else, that would not be a positive statement, but from you..."

She nodded, her face lighting up. "Exactly. You understand."

"And I wouldn't ask you to marry me if I weren't so desperate," he said.

She joined him in laughing, a peal of bell-like giggles that elevated the atmosphere of the entire room. The sound thrilled Jack even more than her smile.

"So romantic," she said, her eyes twinkling.

His heart flipped like a pancake at her sunny grin. It had been hidden the entire time they'd known each other, and now that it was out, he never wanted her to hide it again.

"I am serious, though," he said. "Who am I if I'm not Jack Hunter?"

Her smile fell so quickly that he winced at its loss. "Marrying somebody isn't going to help with that." She tossed the last of the zucchini into the pot, added a dash of seasoning, and covered it before stifling a yawn. "This needs to simmer. I'm going to watch television."

Jack gave her some time alone before peeking inside the room. Lucy had burrowed herself in an oversized comforter on the sofa like a sleepy hedgehog, watching an old sitcom on the television. He gestured at the opposite end of the sofa, and she gathered up the folds of the blanket, allowing him a cushion's worth of room.

He shifted his attention to the television screen. "Are you watching *Full House*?" he asked in dismay.

"It's my favorite show. There's a marathon."

He groaned at the dated studio audience's laughter. "I take back all my proposals. This is a dealbreaker."

The edge of her mouth tipped up, but she didn't take her eyes off the screen. They watched in comfortable silence for a few minutes before Jack couldn't take it anymore.

"There's no way these men are happy," he said, pointing to the three leads. "Look at them. If this was real life, they'd all be at each other's throats."

"They love each other. Like brothers. So they make it work."

"No. They secretly want to kill each other. I bet the dad is plotting Uncle Joey's murder every time they talk. And the catchphrases! Jesus."

To punctuate Jack's point, Uncle Jesse strutted across the stage with a growly *Have mercy!* which was answered by catcalls from the studio audience. "So corny. There's no way he's working that into everyday conv—" He halted, catching sight of Lucy's face. Her cheekbones were tinged pink, and she was biting her plump lower lip.

"Luciana?"

"Yes?" Her voice rose an octave.

"Do you have a thing for Uncle Jesse?"

Her cheeks flushed further from pink to ruddy red, and she twirled a tendril of hair that had escaped from her messy bun. "Everyone has a thing for Uncle Jesse."

"I don't have a thing for Uncle Jesse." He raised an eyebrow.

Lucy turned to him with the most solemn of gazes. "You should. Now just watch the show." She nestled further into her blanket burrow, but he could still see her blushing face above the comforter. It was the most adorable thing he'd ever seen.

Until Uncle Jesse strode onstage with a guitar, and she made a noise like a chipmunk on acid, clapping her hands together. Jack glared at her, and her eyes rounded before she hid her hands.

"So how is it," he began, "That I, the greatest musician ever to walk the earth—"

"That's debatable," she interrupted, but he held up a single finger for silence.

"As I was saying, the *greatest musician ever to walk the earth* can propose to you a dozen times and you don't blink an eye, but a fictional guy from the nineties picks up a guitar and you sit there and squeak at him?"

"He just—" Her eyes glazed over as the character broke into song, barely paying attention to Jack as she continued. "He induces squeaks."

"I'll induce some squeaks from you," he growled, but she didn't even acknowledge him. He glowered at the screen, reduced to jealousy over a made-up character. He rubbed his hand over his face and accepted the truth.

He couldn't go through this crazy scheme with anyone else but her. She was the weirdest, most fascinating creature he had ever met. Blowing out a sigh of resignation, he started browsing through charities on his phone, trying to find one that might take on a drunken has-been as their new representative.

She watched the screen with her hand pressed over her heart, her face enraptured. When the show was over, though, she glanced over at Jack with a rueful smile.

"You're feeling better now, aren't you?" she asked, but it wasn't a question. "I'll pack up the soup and you can head home."

"No, wait, I might get a fever again," he protested, trying to maintain their little pit stop away from reality for a little longer.

"You'll be okay." She stood, folding up her blanket into a neat square. Her dismissal was obvious in the curt way her hands wrapped the blanket into itself and laid it across the back of the couch, as if she were resetting the entire room.

"Thanks for doing all of this," he mumbled. "Not a lot of people would do that."

She looked at him with a grave expression. "But they should."

"Is there something I can do to repay you?" She lifted her eyes to the ceiling, and he clarified, "Not marriage-related. Just as a thank you."

Her fingers twitched and danced at her side, and Jack wished he could peek inside her mind. She reminded him of a computer, constantly processing and calculating.

"There's one thing," she said as if it pained her to vocalize. "Will you go look at apartments with me?"

Jack blinked. "You want me to help you find apartments when I've offered you a free place at my house?"

She flushed. "You're right. It's silly." She ducked her head and went toward the kitchen area.

"Lucy." He raked his hands through his hair. "Yes, I will help you look at apartments."

"Really?" She brightened. "I'll meet you at your place tomorrow then. I'll text you a time when I've got an appointment set up."

"See you then," he said, ignoring the tight feeling in his chest. Lucy put together the soup canisters within five minutes, and then she was pushing him out the door, and the real world came back to roost at last.

Hands down, searching for apartments with Lucy was one of the worst experiences of Jack's life, and that was coming from someone who had once been sequestered in a broken elevator at the Grammys with rival opera singers.

The next day, Lucy showed up with a neatly printed list of Brooklyn-area apartments in hand. When she gave Jack's driver the list, he grimaced and flashed Jack a suspicious look. He shrugged, unable to combat Lucy's palpable good mood. The driver shook his head and drove them to a whole new world—a world that didn't adhere to building codes.

The first apartment they visited was tiny, plain, but possibly livable.

"My record player could fit there," Lucy plotted. "And my desk over here. I could get a pull-out couch. What do you think?"

"It's small," Jack said with an attempt at diplomacy. "But the neighborhood seems quiet." Her eyes brightened at the observation.

"Let's go look at the bathroom," she said, walking an uncomfortably short distance to the room. The door stuck, and when Jack finally forced it open, they found an inch of tepid standing water.

"Oh, look, it comes with a pool." He poked in a finger and found it much more viscous than water should be.

Lucy's face fell. "This is only the first one. The next one will be better."

At the next apartment, the landlord recognized Jack. He gave him an autograph, winking at Lucy as she frowned at the paper in consternation. While she examined the room, the landlord elbowed him in the ribs.

"Nice," he said, openly ogling her ass. His jocular expression dropped when Jack fixated him with a murderous glare.

"Lucy," he called out without breaking his death stare. "We need to leave. I found a cockroach."

"Oh," she said, disappointment coloring her tone. "Well, don't hurt it. Maybe we can catch it and put it outside."

Jack rubbed the heels of his hands into his eyes. He wasn't sure if Lucy wasn't ready for New York, or New York wasn't ready for Lucy.

At the third apartment, a scruffy man opened the door. "Lucy?" he asked in a voice decimated by cigarettes.

"Yes," she said with a clearly artificial smile. "Are you the landlord?"

"Landlord," he said, flopping down on the couch and indicating to an armchair for her use. "And roommate."

"Oh," she said, her lips thinning as she pressed them together. She nudged herself a little closer to Jack, who placed a protective hand on the small of her back, tamping down a zing of triumph when she didn't pull away from his touch.

"I didn't want a roommate," she whispered out of the corner of her mouth.

"We can move on," he whispered back. The landlord/roommate jerked his chin up as some sort of mute acknowledgment, then pulled out a pocket knife, picking at his toenails while staring intensely into Jack's eyes. Lucy gulped, and they backed out of the door one by one.

By the time they got to the last place on the agenda, both were in foul moods. Jack had snapped at the driver twice, and Lucy looked as if someone had stolen her puppy. The landlord met them outside a ramshackle piece of architecture that could have been called a building at one time in its existence. He led them up three flights of stairs—no elevator—and had to jiggle the key in the lock for two whole minutes before the door finally opened.

"Just your basic studio apartment," the guy said, chewing on a worn toothpick.

There might have been just enough room for a twin bed and a dresser in the living area. The kitchenette contained a banged-up mini-fridge straight out of a fraternity house bedroom, a rusty sink, and a microwave yellowed with age and who knew what else. Exposed piping lined the room, disappearing into a bathroom the size of a telephone box. The air was somehow both chilly and humid. Lucy shivered, looking around the room with a heartbroken expression.

Jack stalked the perimeter of the apartment, surveying the pipes, examining the electrical outlets, and running a finger over a water stain on the floor.

"No." He crossed his arms and glared at the landlord.

"Hold on a minute," Lucy said. "Stop shooting down each place. You're not the one living here."

Jack stared at her. The landlord peered between them and rolled his eyes. "I'll let you two talk." He tapped a cigarette out of its carton and headed through the creaky front door.

"I could make this work." Her jaw jutted out in defiance.

"Not gonna happen."

"Really. I don't have much stuff I'd bring here, and I could save up for a bigger place later."

Jack inhaled several times, scratching the bridge of his nose. "There's exposed plumbing everywhere."

"It gives it a modern feel. Like a hipster brewery."

"There's loose wiring in the 'kitchen.'"

"I can tape it up."

"That outlet," he indicated, "isn't even real. It's just a faceplate screwed into the drywall. And there's more mildew visible than actual grout."

"Then I'll get some bleach." She tried to smile, but her lips trembled.

"You are not living here." He enunciated each word in a low voice. "Let's go."

"No." She lifted her chin. "This is what I can afford. It's not as bad as you're making it."

"Lucy!" Jack exploded, her name reverberating across the vacant room. "This place is a firetrap waiting to happen! Which, hey, at least you'd be warm because the thermostat doesn't work! There's black mold everywhere, the lock barely works, and if you'd been paying attention, you'd have seen the fucking junkie laying in the hallway four doors down! There's no way in absolute hell you're living here, so let's get the fuck out and go back home!"

They stared at each other in the ensuing silence. Jack's breathing was choppy, roughened with aggravation that surprised him.

"I'm—" her voice warbled. "I'm going to check out the bathroom." Before Jack could apologize, she dashed to the bathroom, slamming the door. The false outlet cover fell to the floor with a metallic clang.

Chapter 8

The bathroom door opened outward into the apartment, a miracle of forethought in the otherwise badly constructed dump. If Lucy twisted her body just right, she could stand between the yellowed toilet and the door and still have a little room to breathe. She dropped her head back against the wall, coughing when a few plaster shavings shook loose into her hair.

She inhaled deeply—once, twice, three times—trying to will away the tears. She hadn't had a full-on cry in months, and she would be damned if she cried over a stupid apartment, stupid Jack Vincent, and stupid, stupid New York City. She pressed her lips together until they hurt, balling her fists as her nails drove into her palm.

She turned her head at a scuttling noise from the shower. Blinking back at her was a sleek gray rat the size of a kitten.

The first tear fell.

Her back slid against the wall until she slumped on the floor, squished against the toilet bowl.

And she cried.

She cried because, at last, she was truly on her own, and she was failing miserably. She cried because she missed her home, her real home, not some cookie cutter luxury home in Indianapolis. She cried because she had no idea who or what she was anymore, or even what she was fighting to become. And she cried because she just wanted to push the easy button and go back to Jack's house.

The rat tilted his head, blinking his shadowed eyes. "Don't worry," Lucy hiccupped between stifled sobs. "I'm not going to hurt you. Let's be miserable together." His tail flicked in response, and his tiny paws rustled his whiskers.

There was a soft rap at the door. Both the rat and Lucy tensed.

"Lucy?" Jack's voice was muffled through the particle-board door. When she didn't answer, Jack peeked his head in, frowning. A crease appeared between his eyebrows as he examined her pretzel-like position. "What are you doing?"

"Looking at the bathroom." She waved at the near-prison. "It's state of the art, don't you think?" She emphatically patted the toilet like a used car salesman. When she drew back her fingers, they were covered in unidentifiable moisture, and she gagged a little.

His brows furrowed further as he leaned against the doorway. "Look, I'm sorry I yelled. I was only try—Jesus Christ!" His voice changed into a horrified yelp. He snatched up his shoe and hoisted it above his head, aiming it like a discus at the animal in the shower.

"No!" she threw herself in front of the rat, skinning her elbow against the chipped tile. Jack stumbled and jerked back his arm mid-throw. His eyes rounded, and he swept her with a terrified look.

"That's a fucking sewer rat, Lucy."

"You don't know that," she sniffled. "Maybe he's just visiting from the country or something."

He tipped his head at her very, very slowly. "It's a sewer rat," he repeated, quieter this time. "This isn't a Disney movie."

She hummed, unable to speak for the lump in her throat.

"It probably has rabies," he continued, still in that heavy, cautious voice.

"Maybe not. Maybe you're just a rat-ist. Maybe he's got a family back where he came from. Maybe he's just up here exploring and living some beautiful ratty dream, and tonight he's going to go home and snuggle up with his family in his giant rat's nest and dream about the adventure he had today."

Jack's cheek twitched. The rat's nose twitched.

"This isn't about the rat, is it?"

"I don't know!" A sob escaped her throat, and she lost her last thread of composure. Jack's baleful expression melted as he slipped back into his shoe. He took a step toward her, and because every wall, every defense she had was cracked and lost to her tears, she flinched. Her arms shot up, clasped together as a shield for her face. He froze, his eyes widening. His cheeks paled, and his lips pressed together into a firm, white line.

"Luciana," he said, too softly, too calmly. "May I sit next to you?"

Control yourself, Lucy. Now you've made him uncomfortable.

He dropped to a crouch, rocking on his heels. "Can I sit there?" She lifted a limp shoulder, and he wormed his way into the bathroom, squeezing himself between the door, the toilet, and her. He hugged his knees to his chest to fit his long legs, and more plaster tumbled from the wall, falling into his curls like dirty snow. Ever so slightly, he tugged on her sleeve until she leaned into his shoulder. It was tender and strong and safe, something she hadn't felt in many years. She allowed her head to drop and her tears to flow.

She didn't know how long they sat there—the rat, the rock star, and Lucy. At one point, Jack entwined his fingers with hers, massaging her knuckles in a soothing rhythm. He removed a handful of single-ply tissue, rough as cardboard, from the toilet roll and offered it to her.

"Alright," he said. "Out with it."

"This isn't how this was supposed to go. This was my chance to make it on my own, to prove I could do things by myself. I can't even find a place to live without screwing it up. And I couldn't even do that—I had to bring you."

He stroked his jaw with his thumb. "Doing things on your own, it's not dependent on whether you do things right or wrong. It's about having choices. You could screw up every decision from here on out, but at least you're the one making the decision. As much of a hissy fit as I had out there, if you really want this apartment, it's your choice." He sighed with more than a little dramatic flair. "But, if you live here, providing you with 24/7 security will really do a number on my expenses."

She huffed out a laugh. "You're not getting me a bodyguard. You barely know me."

He gazed down at her with an odd expression that made her feel shaky and fizzy, as if a million soda bubbles were traveling in her bloodstream. "I know you, Luciana Meyer."

"I guess so." She leaned her head back against the wall. "Thanks. For this. And for today."

His hand tightened around hers. "That's what friends do."

"We're friends?" She blinked back another onset of tears. She hadn't had a friend of her very own in a long time.

His lips curled in a half-smile. "You and I are friends, Cottontail," he said. He turned his attention to the rat. "But you and I, we're not."

Someone pounded on the door. Her rat friend squeaked, and Jack's nostrils flared.

"The hell is going on in there?" snapped the landlord.

"Just a minute, we're looking at the shower." Jack shot a cautionary glance at the rat, who preened himself near the drain.

"Time for one of your on-your-own decisions," Jack said, nearly toppling over as he climbed back to his feet. He pulled her to a standing position, which squished their bodies together, chest to chest. "Is this the apartment you want?"

She let her head fall, a slightly jerky motion, until it lay against his collarbone. It felt a little like surrender. "No. I don't want it."

"Then I agree and support your decision. Now," he leaned in closer, whispering against her temple. "The rat looks hungry. Can we go?"

Jack had the driver drop them off at a gourmet pretzel shop near her rental. His wolfish, surly scowl was out of place in the cutesy store, adorably named "Oliver's Twists." It smelled of salt and warm bread and comfort.

"I haven't been here in years," he said, gazing around before he sauntered to the counter and ordered two regular pretzels.

"Aren't you Jack Hunter?" asked the cashier as she packaged up the steaming pretzels in parchment paper.

"On occasion, yes," said Jack, flashing his standard-issue half-smile.

"You were so awesome," she said. "My sister had the biggest crush on you. Can I get your autograph?"

He smiled as he signed a napkin, but it didn't reach his eyes. When the cashier disappeared to grab a bag, his smile drooped.

"Were," he repeated with a sardonic gaze. "You *were* so awesome. I'm reduced to *were* instead of *are*. *Had* instead of *has*. *Was* instead of *is*."

"Maybe you just have to work your way back to *is*," Lucy said.

He gave her a sullen look, but the tension in his shoulders dissipated.

The cashier returned and handed the bag to Lucy, but Jack intercepted it.

"Not yet," he said. He went to the shelf of condiments and pulled out one of the pretzels, folding several napkins around the bottom before handing it to Lucy without so much as a glance.

"Oh," she breathed out as he doctored his own pretzel with an absurd amount of mustard.

He had wrapped her pretzel to keep her hands clean.

They walked the few blocks left to her apartment. It was dusk, and for once, the city didn't seem so loud to her sensitive ears. Perhaps it was because of the delicious pretzel giving her something to focus on, or maybe it was the grouchy rock star at her side, making her feel more grounded.

"Time for another favor," he said, sucking a glob of mustard off his thumb. "I'm looking for a roommate."

"Sure you are," she said, pressing her tongue against her cheek. "And what does Jack Vincent look for in a roommate?"

"Someone about yea high—" he held his hand to her hairline, "—with dark hair and brown eyes."

"Uh-huh."

"I'm not done." He took another bite and continued, half-muffled. "Someone about yea high, dark hair, brown eyes, and who likes my music more than Elvis."

"He's *Elvis*."

Jack rolled his eyes. "Fine. I can be flexible with the last part. For now."

"Fine." Her resolve was disappearing like early morning fog. "What would being your roommate entail?"

Besides bathrooms that don't flood or have rats or roommates with suspect hygiene routines.

"Just roommates. You could have the guest room. No strings attached." He tapped his left-hand ring finger. "I promise."

She thought about his earlier words. It was an opportunity, and even if she wasn't living entirely on her own, it didn't mean that she wasn't in control of her decisions.

She expelled a long sigh. "Fine. I want to pay rent."

"Fine." He shrugged, stuffing more pretzel into his mouth, but his eyes had an excited glint.

"And utilities. And I'll contribute to groceries."

"Fine," he repeated, not bothering to hide his smirk.

"Fine. We'll put a lease together."

He paused, searching her expression. "Is this an on-your-own decision?"

"I promise," she said. "You're very persuasive and often annoying, but yes, this is an on-my-own decision."

"Good," he said, and a ghost of a smile tripped across his lips.

"What about your future wife, though?" Lucy asked. "We could make the lease month to month if that helps."

His smile dissolved. "Nah, I've decided against that."

"Really? One girl turns you down and you give up?"

"What can I say?" he said, pressing a flippant hand to his heart. "I'm sensitive when it comes to my fake romances. I've been looking into different charities instead. Making a list of causes to support."

"Did you land on anything?"

"No." His laugh was humorless. "Other than the fact that there are no causes out there that I'm passionate about. I don't have a 'thing.'"

"Nothing at all? Saving the whales or childhood literacy or plastic straw bans?"

"I mean, those are all good things, and I support them, but there's no life-changing passion driving me. I guess I don't have room to be picky, though. Whoever will let me tie their name to them will have to do." He threw her a sidelong glance. "Got anything you want me to support?"

"How do you feel about homeless pigs?" She scrolled through her phone and brought up a picture of Larry on his first day home from a pig rescue organization.

"I dunno. It depends on how homeless pigs feel about me." He sighed, a sound drenched in disappointment and self-pity.

"I really am sorry your fake marriage idea didn't work out," she said with all honesty, taking in his slumped shoulders and harrowed face. "But it wouldn't have been a good idea with us. I like you."

His toe caught a crack in the sidewalk, and he stumbled mid-step. "You like me?"

"Yes. You said we were friends." She paused, suddenly nervous that it had been just comforting words to stop her tears. "In the creepy bathroom."

"It *was* a creepy bathroom." His tone was cautious as he started walking again. "We are friends."

"Why would I want to lose a friend, then? Marriage leads to all sorts of uncomfortable situations, and next thing you know, poof! Friendship gone."

"You don't want to marry me," he repeated, "because we're friends?"

"Exactly." Surely, it wasn't that hard of a concept to understand.

He halted at the sidewalk corner, and she tumbled into his back, dropping the last bits of her pretzel and nearly pushing him into the street. A lazy pigeon snatched the ruined pretzel in his beak. Jack whirled and caught her by the waist with the span of his hands. It wasn't a casual embrace between friends. It was a claiming, a plea spoken through touch that seared her skin despite the layers of clothing.

"You made me drop my pretzel," she whispered, because what else could she say? All her previous thoughts were lost in an abyss bordered by gripping hands and dangerous looks.

"You do understand that—" He let go with an annoyed growl, scraping his hands through his hair. "Lucy, I have a *lot* of money. If you marry me, I will give *you* a lot of money."

"To...buy another pretzel?" She examined the way his mouth was set, the way his brows were knitted together. There was some sort of social cue she was missing, and her throat tightened because she *just didn't understand*.

Jack made a strangled noise and stepped away, his hands clasped around the back of his head as he mumbled a few curses. She winced at the metallic echo when he kicked a nearby lamppost, and again when he returned with a pronounced limp.

"Luciana." Jack's voice sounded strange, far away. "Please marry me. Be my fake wife. This is the last time I'll ask, I swear. It's an on-your-own decision." His usual bravado was nowhere to be found.

"And we'll stay friends?"

"Pinky promise." His apprehension disappeared, replaced with his arrogant grin once more. He searched her face and pumped his fist. "You're going to say yes, aren't you?"

Another deep breath, and then Lucy made an on-her-own decision based on nothing more than napkins wrapped around a pretzel, the slide of a hand in her own, and a whispered *Weird is okay.* "I think so."

Jack squeezed both of her hands, and then they just stood there in silence, surrounded by the deafening non-silence of the city around them.

"This feels anti-climactic." He rubbed his whiskered jaw. "Let me do it better. You deserve a real Jack Hunter proposal."

He looked both ways, stalked across the crosswalk, and stopped, mid-street. Brakes screamed, and a cab halted inches from his body. The honking and squealing tires were immediate, from cars trying to maneuver around the crazy man in the middle of traffic.

"The hell, Jack?" she yelled, covering her ears. The cab driver leaned out of their window and spouted fiery, colorful language, backed by a dozen car horns. Jack raised a lackadaisical middle finger, his eyes solely on her.

"Lucy!" he shouted above the horns. "Marry me!"

This was the circus she was joining, and the ringmaster was right there, prancing in the middle of Brooklyn traffic.

"You idiot! You're going to get yourself killed!"

The traffic jam thickened around him, a bustling, angry Red Sea around a very cocky Moses. The taxi nudged forward until their front plate tapped the back of Jack's knees.

Lucy bolted across the street, yanking him to the other side. A chorus of horns and shouts assaulted them as traffic reverted to normal.

"You bastard," she panted, smacking him on the chest.

"Sorry. Grand gesture and all that," he said with a triumphant smirk.

"You scared me half to death." She cupped her ears again and fought the urge to rock in place.

He leaned closer, peering at her. His smile froze, then fell like shattered ice. "I did scare you. I'm sorry."

She finger-combed her wind-blown hair. "Your shenanigans have consequences. You could've gotten hurt."

His eyes widened, and he swallowed. "But I didn't."

"This time." Their eyes met, and though instinct begged her to look away, she stood firm.

He took a tentative step closer and caressed her jaw, stroking the side with his thumb. "Marry me?" he asked.

"Yeah, fine," Lucy said. "Somebody's got to keep you alive."

His phone rang. He glanced at the screen, then placed the call on speaker.

"Jack." Kim's robust voice was eerily serene. "Why are there pictures of you standing in the middle of traffic on Twitter?"

"I got lost," he said with bored calmness.

"Uh-huh."

"By the way," he said, his wolf-like grin growing, "set up a meeting tomorrow with Martin. I've got a solution to our PR issues. Trent needs to be there too."

"What?"

"I'll explain tomorrow." Jack disconnected the call. "Come on, Cottontail. We've got a marriage to plan."

Chapter 9

Lucy arrived at the Derelict Records office in Manhattan ten minutes earlier than the scheduled meeting time, armed with two notebooks and a slew of pens and sticky notes. A perky intern at the front desk directed her to a chair in the foyer, where Lucy waited.

And waited.

Ten minutes after the scheduled meeting time, the door to the building flew open with a metallic bang, and Jack sauntered in, strolling right past her. Each footstep was imbued with celebrity cockiness until he stopped and retraced his steps to where she sat, her purse clutched to her chest.

"Cottontail?" he asked, sliding off his sunglasses like a crime show hero. "Why aren't you in the meeting?"

She frowned. "Because I don't know where to go. Or who to see. Or what to say."

He scrutinized her, and his lip quirked. "Those are good reasons." He held out a hand, and she took it, letting him lead her to a posh conference room where three other people waited.

"This is Kim," Jack said, gesturing to a taller woman in her forties. The woman gave Lucy a cordial but confused smile and held out her hand. Lucy stared at her hand for three interminable seconds.

You'll be fine, Lucy. Just for God's sake, don't be you.

"Nice to meet you," she said, clasping the woman's hand in hers. Kim's gaze was calculating and assessing, and her eyes narrowed as they darted back and forth from Jack to Lucy.

Jack pointed across the table to where two men sat, both typing at their respective laptops. The first man exuded tension as he shifted back and forth between his computer and his smartphone.

"That's Martin," Jack said. "He sucks." Martin held up his middle finger, his busy eyes never abandoning either screen.

"And that's Trent. He's my lawyer. He also sucks."

The second man stood when she approached him, holding his hand out. Lucy had to keep her jaw from dropping. He was one of the most handsome men she had ever seen, with jet black hair, caramel brown eyes, and a robust and sensual jaw. In fact, he almost reminded her of—

"Have mercy," she breathed out.

Jack's eyes shot from her to Trent, and then he rolled his eyes. "Well, fuck. Can't unsee that."

"Nice to meet you," she quavered, making eye contact with Trent for a few precisely calculated seconds.

"It's lovely to meet you, Lucy." His eyes crinkled when he smiled, and she tensed her fists to keep from fanning herself.

"Come on, Lucy." Jack grabbed a paper cup of coffee and an obscene amount of sugar packets and led her to a set of chairs. She didn't sit, though her knees were nearly knocking with nerves.

"Lucy, if you want to wait for Jack while we meet, there's a little kitchenette just down the hall," offered Kim.

Lucy glanced at Jack and started inching her way toward the door as the others took their places around the table.

Without looking up from his coffee, he snapped his arm out and circled her wrist with his fingers. "No running this time, Cottontail."

She sighed in surrender and lowered herself into the chair next to him, immediately preoccupying herself with the uneven groove on the side of the table.

"Jack?" Kim asked with a warning note.

"Lucy stays."

Kim and Trent's gazes stayed glued to Jack as he prepared his coffee with dramatic precision. By the time he slowly—*very* slowly—took his first sip, Kim released her frustrated groan.

"All right, Jack," Trent said, gracious but serious. "What's going on?"

Jack took another delayed sip. "I decided on a plan to fix my reputation."

Martin's brows perked. "We're gonna go with the fake marriage angle. Picture it now." He raised his hands as if pitching a newspaper headline. "Insane Musician Tamed by True Love." He pouted his lips and made a squeaking, smooching sound.

Lucy rubbed the middle of her forehead to ward against an impending headache. Miracle of miracles, Martin raised his head from his phone. Lucy took it as a hopeful sign.

"You're getting married," scoffed Kim.

"I'm getting married."

"To who?" His manager crossed her arms expectantly.

"I believe it's 'to whom,'" Jack corrected. Lucy couldn't hold back her facepalm.

"To whom, then." Kim accentuated every syllable through gritted teeth.

"To Lucy. Say hello, honey."

"Hello, honey," she said, raising her head and smiling nervously at Kim. Kim's jaw dropped, and Trent looked dumbfounded. But Martin...Martin was *intrigued*.

"Yeah, this is good. I can work with this." Martin bobbed his head as if ideas were flying at him from all angles, and he had to duck from his own brilliance. "Okay, we gotta build a narrative first. Start from the beginning. How'd you two meet?"

"Mutual friend," said Jack.

"I punched him in the face," Lucy said at the same time.

"You did that?" Kim considered Jack's fading bruises with renewed interest.

"It was an accident," Lucy said. "I swear."

"Um, yeah, so *no*," Martin dismissed them with an Oscar-worthy eye roll. "The point is to *not* show Jack involved in anything less than savory. Got anything else?"

"She stayed with me while I had the flu," Jack offered.

"Yeah, that's what I'm talking about! Little Miss Nobody nurses you back to health, and you fall madly in love. People eat that shit up." Martin's fingers flew over his keyboard. "Is it even worth asking how you proposed?"

"Which time?" Jack asked, sliding a laconic glance toward Lucy.

"He was very annoying about it," Lucy added.

"I had a fever for most of them. That nullifies the annoyance factor." He peered over at his lawyer with an impatient scowl. "The hell you smiling about, Trent?"

"Absolutely nothing," said Trent, leaning back in his chair with a wicked grin, his gaze bouncing between the two of them.

"Once again, not going to work," huffed Martin. "It's autumn in New York. We'll stage something and get some good pictures. And pictures are going to be key with this campaign. This isn't just a few appearances with the paparazzi. We're recrafting Jack's whole life. We start with slow hints on social media, introducing the idea that Jack is new and reformed. Add some thoughtful, stupid quotes about how life is fleeting and changes all the time and bullshit like that, and hint that he has fallen in love. Then BAM!" Lucy jumped as he pointed at her with enthusiasm. "We introduce you. His love nurse."

"My love nurse." Jack's skepticism was unmistakable.

"We'll work on the name." Martin waved him off. "Once we get her introduced, we really take off. Photos of the two of you, romantic walks, laughing at each other's stupid faces, blah blah blah. Pictures doing domestic, fluffy shit that people will go nuts for. We'll get you your own Instagram and Twitter accounts, Lisa—"

"Lucy," corrected Jack, his eye twitching.

"Yeah, yeah. We'll have you get married as soon as possible. Girlfriends only stay exciting for so long, so the sooner you're married, the better. You're not the Duchess of Cambridge; we don't need to draw out the wedding anticipation. The focus is the necessity of this relationship, the power that you have to pull Jack from the dark, tragic hole he lives in now."

Lucy had to admit, Martin had an enticing plan. If she were watching this unfold on social media, she'd want to find out what happened next. Jack, however, was shifting in his chair like a toddler at the dentist, his eyes round with panic.

"Holy shit, we're really doing this," he wheezed. Lucy tentatively reached out her hand, starting at the contact of his skin against hers. She squeezed his hand, a single pulse of comfort. His head tilted as he stared at her fingers, and she hoped he understood what she was trying to say with her simple caress.

I'm touching you, and it doesn't bother me. I trust you. And you can trust me.

Without facing her, he flipped his hand palm up, and their fingers laced together naturally as if they had been holding hands for years. It was a subtle reply, but she read it loud and clear.

We're partners. We're equals. We've got this.

"Actually, Jack, I wanted to talk to you about a possible way to kick this off," Kim said. "Laser Wolves was supposed to play the Big Apple Harvest Festival this Saturday. Patrick Hodelle broke his leg in a jet ski accident.

If you took his place, it'd give you some karma points in the eyes of the public."

"Patrick's an idiot," mumbled Jack, his opinion of the Laser Wolves's lead singer apparent. Kim curled her lips around her teeth, most likely holding back stories of Jack's own jet ski antics. "But I'll do it."

"Good," Kim said. "Lucy, you're welcome to come, of course. Maybe someone will get a picture." Lucy gave a noncommittal shrug, but her stomach contracted with nerves. A chaotic concert was not the best place for her.

"It's a good start," said Martin. "Helping out a fellow musician, and it's a charity. It'll tide us over as we prep the whole relationship and marriage narrative."

"Do they actually have to get married?" asked Trent. "Legally, I mean. If it's all just for illusion, they could fake it."

"Twenty years ago, yes," sighed Martin. "Now you're in the age of instant information. TMZ checks marriage license records for every celebrity marriage. Showmances used to be so much easier."

"Got it," nodded Trent, turning his attention to Jack and Lucy. "This isn't my first marriage of convenience contract, so it should be easy to draw up. As long as you're both American citizens and not doing anything nefarious or illegal, it should be pretty standard." He flashed that swoon-worthy smile, and she tried not to flutter her eyelashes like a cartoon character. "Are there specific terms you've discussed?"

Lucy tensed. They hadn't discussed anything significant yesterday, other than her acceptance of the proposal and her living situation.

"Lucy stays with me at my townhouse," started Jack. "With a monthly allowance in a separate account to use at her discretion. A set lump sum should we divorce." He glanced at her. "Anything else you want?"

She blinked, her mind momentarily emptied not because of the amount of money, but that he had said *should* we divorce instead of *when* we divorce. A simple slip of the tongue, but it still set a few butterflies skittering around her belly.

"And in return, Lucy agrees to enter into a marriage with you for..." Trent waited for Jack to fill in the blank.

"Two years?" he asked, raising his eyebrows at Lucy in question. "That would cover recording an album, promotional time, and a subsequent tour. Even if the album sucks—" he held up a finger to stop Kim's impending protest, "—which it won't—it should still get a lift in sales from the publicity. Then we break up, and I get to make a kick-ass broken heart album." He punctuated his point with a righteous air guitar riff.

"Two years is okay," Lucy repeated, her head wobbling in an over-enthusiastic nod. Two years she could handle. Two years was nothing compared to the hell of the last fourteen.

"Lucy, what's your background?" Trent asked. "Are there any skeletons that might come up? We already know all of Jack's."

She peered around the room as she tried to recall anything troublesome she had done in her past. "I got detention my junior year because I helped the class cheat in Spanish."

There was a moment of stunned silence, and she felt her skin flush.

"You devil," said Jack proudly, smacking the table. "How did you help the whole class cheat?"

"When the teacher left the room, I translated the answers in my head and then read them all to the class."

Another quiet moment passed. Jack continued to grin like a jackal until Trent cleared his throat.

"Well, Lucy, I'm sure you're very remorseful about that," he said. "But, um, we were thinking of illegal activities. Petty theft, that sort of thing."

She shook her head, and Trent continued. "What about past relationships? Are you divorced?"

Lucy's muscles tensed, and her mouth went dry. "I, um, was engaged until recently."

Jack froze beside her, and his fingers tightened around the cup until it crinkled like Christmas-morning wrapping paper. "You were? You never told me that."

She bit her lower lip. "You didn't ask."

"Are they someone we should worry about? Would they make trouble in the press?" Trent asked in a gentle tone.

She cocked her head, frowning. "I don't think so. Brock was very much about appearances, and this wouldn't look good. It's bad enough his fiancée left him, but if it gets out that I left him for, uh—" she waved her hand to indicate Jack's entire body, "It wouldn't look good for him at all."

"How long were you together?" Jack asked, his forehead creased in disapproval.

"Fourteen years."

Jack choked on his over-sugared coffee. "You—what? What?!"

"Do you two need a moment?" offered Kim, studying the shock on Jack's face. "We could take a quick break."

"No," said Lucy, just as Jack answered, "Jesus, yes." He sprang to his feet and headed out of the room. She stared at the door for a moment before reluctantly following him down the hall.

Jack hauled Lucy into one of the label's studio spaces. Inside, she immediately released his fingers, her eyes wide with wonder as she looked at the recording booth. If Jack hadn't been there, pacing and cursing, she probably would have snuck in to visually feast on the rows of buttons and screens and instruments. As it was, he had to flap his hand in front of her face to reclaim her attention.

"Did you know that the Beatles had to record *Sgt. Pepper's Lonely Hearts Club Band* using a pair of four-track tape recorders because eight-track tape recorders weren't available yet?" she spouted, trivia flying from her like ticker tape. Her fingers swirled mid-air as she recited, dancing on a stage all their own.

"What?" spluttered Jack. "No, no, no. Stay with me, Cottontail. Focus."

With reluctance, she dragged her gaze from the booth to Jack.

"You were with your ex for fourteen years?" Jack hissed, shock spurring his heart into a breakneck speed. It was a miracle if he stayed with a woman for fourteen hours, let alone fourteen years.

Lucy wandered away from him, trailing her hands over a music stand. "Yes."

Jack exhaled a languid breath. Lucy's mood had switched from reticent to—well, more reticent, and getting any information from her in this state was impossible. He took a moment to reform his questions.

"Dating since high school then?" he asked, before huffing out a laugh. "I mean, I assume so. Jesus, I don't even know how old you are."

"I'm thirty," she said. "So yeah, high school. We were sixteen when we started."

"I'm forty." And he certainly felt it today. "You know, the media will probably point out the age gap. Although ten years is nothing in this industry."

She shrugged and eased herself into a metal folding chair. Jack took one next to her, attempting to appear nonchalant.

"So, I'm not your first fiancé, then?"

Again, a simple head shake, and for reasons he couldn't explain, intractable jealousy rammed itself through Jack's senses like a runaway train. "How long were you engaged?"

"For about a year. It ended when I came here." Her face clouded, but her fidgeting had slowed.

"Why did you break up?"

Her fingers sped up again, drumming against her knee, and she looked back at the recording booth.

Jack cursed and covered his mouth with a broad palm, dragging it across his face. This conversation was like a game of snakes and ladders, with too many snakes for his comfort.

"Would you come home with me?" she asked, her eyes snapping to his with cut-glass focus. "To tell my family before we announce all this."

Jack gawked at her, his head spinning from the sudden topic switch. "Why? Do I have to ask for your hand in marriage or something?"

For the first time since they'd entered the room, Lucy's eyes glittered with amusement. "I would pay money to see that." Her expression relaxed. "Brock—my ex—he's from Sparrow Hill, too, and he had—" She paused and shook her head as if resetting herself. Her lips worked through a few silent words before she said, "I only saw my family when we went home for holidays with his family, and only for a few hours at a time."

"I don't understand." He peered at her. "He didn't want you to spend time with your family?"

Her smile was as sweet and sad as spring rain at a picnic. "He was strict." She swiveled her head away, scanning the room, looking everywhere except at Jack before murmuring, "I just want to start this engagement off right. I want it to be good." Her breath hitched on the last word, and a niggling suspicion rose in Jack's mind. He tamped down a flare of rage, but it was something he couldn't address. Not yet.

"Do you miss him?" he asked instead, his throat constricting. "Would you ever go back?"

Her brow furrowed. "I miss who he could sometimes be. He was capable of being very nice, I think."

"Capable," Jack repeated, his fingers pinching a permanent crease in his jeans. The ordinarily positive word left a sour taste on his tongue. "You think."

There was a weighty pause, then she shook her head, words spilling out of her in a frantic flow. "I don't want to talk about this anymore. I'm tired. I want to go back to my apartment." She wrung her hands over and over until Jack worried she would hurt herself with her own nails.

"Alright, Lucy, alright." Jack sighed. "And we can go see your family next week, okay?" He had once performed karaoke with the Osmond family; meeting his future in-laws would surely be a piece of cake in comparison.

She brightened. "Really?"

"Really. And hey," he offered a hand, and she took it without hesitation, "you can visit your family as much as you want, as long as you want, as long as nothing is going on with our little plan here. If I get a tour, you can stay there the whole time if you want."

Chapter 10

An early morning knock on the door jolted Lucy awake with a gasp.

He's here he's here run run run

Her hand flung across the bed, but the other side was vacant, the blankets smooth and immaculate. Her heart hammered, and her breathing was shallow as she sat up. Her eyes adjusted from sluggish fog to objective alertness, and she remembered where she was.

Brock isn't here, she recited, each word a careworn bead on a mental rosary. *He can't find you. You're safe.*

She made her way to the front door and peered through the peephole. At the sight of her visitor, she groaned and thumped her forehead on the wood.

"Why are you here?" she asked, unlocking the door for Jack. "You're not supposed to be here."

"Good morning to you too," he said, gliding inside and taking a seat at the kitchen table, his legs sprawling on either side of the chair.

"I don't like surprises. You're not supposed to be here."

He gave a noncommittal shrug, tossing a bent manila folder onto the table. "I'm here to help you pack."

"Why? I have until the end of the week on this place."

"Because I'm tired of going back and forth. I'll have a key made for you to make it official." He hesitated. "Speaking of..." He opened the manila folder, rotating the marriage contract toward Lucy with a dramatic hand flourish. "Trent will be by later to get this."

The contract was simple, stark, white and black typography with legal jargon and their names sporadically sprinkled throughout, yet it contained the threads of their entire future, broken down into unemotional chunks of Times New Roman. She perused it, making sure all the essential bits were in the right places before searching through her purse for a pen.

"Ready?" she said.

He scoffed at the Elvis-themed pen, but plucked it from her hand. "I guess so." He scratched out his jagged signature on the appropriate dotted lines. Lucy took a breath and signed next to his name, her swirling, lacy cursive contrasting with his angular letters, different as two signatures could be.

"Okay, Mr. Vincent?" she asked.

"Okay, Mrs. Vincent," he replied, his expression tight.

Even though she had spent time at Jack's house before, the final ride from her rental to his was one of the most nerve-racking events of her life. Jack stared at his shoes the entire ride, and she gripped her purse like a life jacket. The closer they got to his place, the more Lucy's stomach twisted into a sailor's knot of anxiety.

"Stop that," Jack threw his head back with an exasperated groan. "You sound like the big, bad wolf over there. You're huffing and puffing, and I'm about to lose my damn mind."

"Sorry," she said, her voice a tinny squeak. "Nerves."

"Chill, Cottontail," he said, though his own leg was bouncing like a basketball. "I never thought I'd get married, but if I did, I would want it to be to someone who didn't go into cardiac arrest at the thought of me."

The car stopped in front of their home, and they gaped at the townhouse like frightened teenagers outside a graveyard.

"Well?" she whispered.

"I'm getting out of the car," he said, but he didn't move, his throat working.

"Count of three?" she asked. He nodded, and she counted off on her fingers. "One...two...three."

Neither one stirred. The driver cleared his throat.

"I just remembered," said Jack with robotic enthusiasm. "I need to work in my studio. The other one. The one that is not here."

"Fantastic idea," Lucy agreed, and with a word from Jack, the driver delivered them to Raymond's.

Jack gripped Lucy's elbow awkwardly as the familiar bell announced their entrance. Sully glanced up from the register and his eyes nearly popped out from his skull.

"Uh...hello," he stammered, his eyes flying from Lucy to Jack and back again.

"Hi, Sull," said Jack. "Got a second?"

Sully made a choked noise but followed them to the back room. Jack tapped Lucy's shoulder several times when she got distracted by the memorabilia around her. They went through a storeroom filled with cardboard boxes and up a creaky wooden staircase to a scuffed green door.

Inside was a sparse but homey studio apartment. The kitchenette could have been lifted straight from a 1950s sitcom, but the living room was cluttered with recording equipment, electric guitars, and amplifiers.

Jack and Lucy sat down on the sofa, misshapen with age, but Sully remained standing, gawking at them. Jack folded a tentative arm around her, and she stiffly reclined back. They looked like two middle school kids on their first date at the movie theater.

"Huh," said Sully, his eyebrows soaring to his hairline.

"Short version," Jack said. "Lucy and I are getting married."

"Huh."

"Yes, love at first sight or something like that." Jack sounded anything but convincing.

"Huh." Sully snorted. "Congratulations?"

"Yeah, thanks." Jack waved him off. "I thought maybe you could show Lucy around the store."

Sully's expression went from perplexed to thoughtful. "Really?"

Lucy gave him a bashful smile. "I would love a tour."

His eyes flicked to Jack, and confusion clouded his eyes once more. "You coming, Jack?"

"Go ahead," Jack said, choosing an acoustic guitar and plopping into a patched armchair. "I'm going to play around up here."

"You're really getting married?" Sully shook his head over and over, still baffled, as he led Lucy downstairs.

"Yes."

"To Jack?" He pointed to the ceiling, where the vibrations of guitar chords drifted down.

"Yes."

"Huh. You must have hit him harder than I thought." Sully scratched his beard. "It's about time to open. Come on, I'll show you around the front. Maybe even let you touch the register."

The store didn't get its first customer for a half hour. Lucy sat back, ready to observe Sully's customer service skills, but he indicated that she approach the middle-aged woman wandering the aisle with uncertain movements.

"Can I help you?" Lucy asked, her stiff arms pressed tightly to her sides.

"I'm trying to find an album, an old one," the woman said. "There was a song called 'I'm Sorry,' and I think one called 'Dynamite' or 'Dynamo' or something like that."

The peculiar gears in Lucy's head began whirring and clicking. "I know that album! Brenda Lee's self-titled album, 1960. Let's go look for it."

She took her over to the "L" albums and flipped through to find the one she needed. The customer's gasp of surprise filled Lucy with shy pride.

"My mom passed away last month. We used to listen to this all the time," the woman said, holding the record with shaking hands. "Thank you for finding it." Lucy gingerly patted her shoulder.

Sully rang the woman up and grinned at Lucy. "Wanna try another?" he asked, with the mischievous smirk of a preteen prankster.

The next customer arrived just a few minutes later. This time Lucy was ready.

"My daughter's birthday is next week," he said with that mix of irritation and love possessed by all parents of teenagers. "She wants that album about juice from that Bouncy lady."

After a moment of puzzlement, she steered him to Beyoncé's *Lemonade*. He thanked her, but she didn't want his gratitude. She was on a high she had never felt before.

She had found her kingdom, and she was the queen.

Over the next few hours, she connected customers with Johnny Cash, loaded up a lady with Lizzo, and recommended the Rolling Stones to a young teen just beginning his journey into classic rock. Jack emerged from his musical man cave and ran out for bagged lunches at Batter Up, which he left in the backroom until she was ready.

It was nearly four when Lucy heard an annoyed cough behind her. She turned to offer assistance, only to find Jack frowning at her with a paper bag in his hand.

"Lucy." He held up the grease-stained sack. "You didn't eat."

"Oh." She dropped her gaze to the floor. "I forgot." Her traitorous stomach took that moment to growl.

"You forgot." His tone was anything but amused. "Did you eat breakfast?"

She gnawed her lip and shifted her attention to a shelf of vinyls. His fingers brushed her chin, and he pivoted her face back to his.

"You didn't."

"I forgot." She flicked her eyes away from his scrutiny. "It happens sometimes."

"I find it hard that someone who can recite the discography of the Temptations—no, that's not a request—can forget something as easy as eating." When she didn't respond, he shook the bag of food. "Let's go upstairs; we can heat it up." He tipped his chin up at Sully, and they headed to the apartment.

Lucy tried to take the bag from Jack, but he motioned her to the couch. "I know where everything is; you don't."

"Did you write anything?" she asked. His responding growl reverberated through his chest. "Okay, then...how'd you end up with a music store?" she tried again as he plated her food and put it in the microwave.

His shoulders stiffened. "I'm sure you can guess that things at home could be...intense sometimes."

Lucy shuffled through her memory, ascertaining what she knew about his mother. *Rita Rae. Genre: pop. Instrument: vocals only. First album: 1979. Second album: 1982. One Grammy. Last album,* A Rita Rae Christmas, *two years ago.*

"I don't know much other than her career," she confessed. "My trick—if you want to call it that—it's like baseball cards. For the most part, I know stats. I don't usually know people. She's a bit of a diva, right?"

He brooded over that for a second. "My mom is a very hedonistic person. Sex, drugs, gambling—she's done it all. She's gone bankrupt several times."

"But she's so successful. Doesn't she host that singing contest show?"

"It doesn't matter how much you make if you spend it all as soon as you have it." He rifled around in a drawer, pulling out a table knife. "You should see her apartment. It's all tacky glitz and gold shit that no one should ever need or want. It makes Trump Tower look like a hovel. It wasn't a fun place to grow up."

"I'm sorry."

"There were drunks and junkies and celebrities all over the place. One time I went to brush my teeth, and there was a TV star doing a line of coke at my sink. Not that I was deterred from that sort of thing either. Once I got older, I used to look for other places around the city to go instead of sticking around there. I found this place and ended up striking up a friendship with Raymond, the owner. He had this apartment up for rent, and once it became available, I paid him to keep it open for me so I'd have a place to escape. I kept a guitar up there and would stay for days at a time, lost in my own world. I loved it. I couldn't let the building go to anyone else when he died. It was my sanctuary, you know?"

He handed her the plate, and her gasp caught in her throat. He had cut her grilled cheese into precise squares. She met his eyes, unable to vocalize her gratitude.

He slid her a bittersweet half-smile. "Eat your cheese squares, Cottontail, so we can finally move in together."

Jack had never had a roommate, but he was pretty sure that you were supposed to see them at some point. Passing awkwardly in the hall before bedtime, maybe colliding into each other while getting the mail, that sort of thing. But from the moment he showed Lucy to her room, she had simply disappeared.

He gave her the rest of that night to get herself sorted, retiring to his bedroom with half a bottle of Kentucky bourbon and his neglected guitar. He even allowed her to have the next morning, though he paced the kitchen as he drank his coffee. Having Lucy in his house but not near him unsettled him, and then the fact that he was unsettled tended to unsettle him more, until he was cross-eyed from the paradox of unsettled unsettledness. Jack knew she was alive because every time he wandered by her room—on the way to his own room, of course, and not because he was checking on her—he heard David Bowie's nasal crooning through the door.

By the eighth time he strolled by her room—because he was doing laundry and not for any other reason—he realized that "Space Oddity" had been playing on repeat for nearly an hour. He set the hamper down and rapped at her door.

"Lucy?" No answer. He turned the brass doorknob and froze.

It was locked. Despite their growing friendship, Lucy still feared him enough to lock the door against him in his own home. In *her* own home.

"The door's open," she called. "Come on in." He frowned in confusion, attempting the door again with no luck. After a muffled rattling from the other side, commingled with a few inventive curses, the door stuttered open on stubborn hinges.

"The door sticks," Lucy said with an apologetic grimace. His tense shoulders slackened with relief. She hadn't meant to keep him out after all.

"I wasn't sure if you'd fallen asleep in here with your music on repeat." He gazed around at her room. She had cleaned it, but it looked nearly the same as before—severe and isolated, without any decor. "Are you picking up the rest of your stuff when we see your family?"

"No." He waited for her to elaborate, but instead, she swept her hand toward her open closet door. "Thanks for the housewarming gift, by the way."

His face split into a grin at the sight of three brand new Jack Hunter T-shirts hanging crisply from plastic hangers. "Well, they do say to dress for the job you want."

She rolled her eyes and picked up her phone, restarting the song once more.

"Lucy," he said gravely. "No matter how many times you listen to it, Major Tom is not coming back from outer space."

She cackled and flopped back onto the bed, stretching long legs out across the quilt. "Oh, that. Don't you ever just listen to a song and dissect it?" Tiny flecks of gold in her eyes glittered at him with eager sincerity.

"I mean, I guess that's what you kinda do in a recording studio. Break it apart and see what needs redone."

"No, I mean, *really* listen." Her lips thinned with indecision, and then she reached a hand around his bicep and dragged him down onto the bed until he was flat on his back.

"Lu—"

"Listen." She covered his mouth with gentle fingers, and he grumbled a protest against her skin. "Right there. Hear that buzzing electronic piano sound? That's a Stylophone. It was a weird miniature metal keyboard that was popular in the late 60s."

He squinted an eye, trying to parse out the sound of the dated instrument, but the only sensation he noticed was the delicate brush of her arm against his as she breathed, as carefree as he had ever seen her.

"Now, I'm going to restart it," she said, jarring Jack from thoughts of warm skin and silken caresses. "There—that weird hybrid piano flute noise? That's a Mellotron. Between the two instruments, it just sounds 'spacey' unless you know what they are."

"Groovy." He gulped against a lump in his throat as a tendril of her hair tickled his ear. Inexplicably, he wanted to rake his fingers through it. "I don't think anyone's gone through one of my songs like that."

"Nonsense." She made a disbelieving face. "If a song is out there, someone has overthought it. Instruments, chords, lyrics, it doesn't matter. Besides, you've got tons of fans. I bet that right now, someone somewhere is laying in a bed just like us, wondering things about 'Slow Down.'"

"Sure they are." He rolled onto his side to face her, close enough that he could count the scant sprinkle of freckles on her nose.

She parted her lips, and he could almost see her thoughts wind up like a yo-yo, about to slingshot into the universe. "Well—why did you choose to use a violin for the bass line on 'Applejohn Blues'? Why did you write 'Midnight in New Orleans' in 5/4 time? Why did you use the name Natalie instead of something more alliterative, like Lady or Lula or Lacey, in 'Lullaby for Natalie'? Why is there a banana peel on the right-hand side of the cover of your third album?"

Jack blinked at her, and his jaw went slack. Rosy banners of color soared high on her cheekbones.

"You sure you're not a Jack Hunter fan?" he asked, his index finger tracing the satiny skin beneath her blush.

"He's okay, I guess," she murmured, and Jack's laughter dissolved whatever magic spell had entranced him earlier.

"Those are much better questions than I usually get," he admitted, tapping his lower lip in thought. "I used a violin because I wanted to make it sound busy under the melody, like a bumblebee. Natalie was the name of my favorite nanny. The 5/4 time was because my manager—the one before Kim—bet me a thousand bucks that I couldn't do it."

"And the banana peel?"

"The photographer was a prick during the cover shoot. After I had a banana for a snack, I left it on the ground out of spite. They thought it was some artistic metaphor." He stretched his foot out and hit a folded piece of paper lying on the edge of the bed. "What's this?"

"Nothing!" She sat up and tried to snatch it away, but he gripped it between his toes in a surprisingly acrobatic movement. He glanced over the words before raising his eyebrows at Lucy.

"It's a list," she said, her shoulders slumped. "Just little things I want to do, now that I'm out here. New York-y things."

He skimmed the list, stopping at the first item. "Go to a bar? Is that what you were doing that night?" She shrugged. "Shit, did I mess up your goal?"

Lucy gave him a baffled look. "I wanted to go to a bar, so I went to a bar. Whether I found an inebriated rock star there is inconsequential to the completion of the list."

He lifted a hand in surrender to her logic and read further down her list, pointing to item eight. "I can help you with this one." She leaned over his shoulder to read, the curve of her chin nestling into the notch by his neck.

"Really?" she asked, straightening. "You would go with me?"

"We can go right now," he said, offering his hand. Lucy settled her hand in his, her fingers wiggling against his palm in their familiar dance.

Pinky, ring, middle, index. Repeat.

"First, though," she asked. "Can we go to a florist?"

Chapter 11

The wind snapped at their ears as they crossed Central Park West. The tissue paper in Lucy's hand rippled with every gust, but the chill didn't deter her enthusiasm. She bounced on the balls of her feet, excitement escaping in an ecstatic gasp as they arrived at their destination. She covered her mouth and staggered forward before kneeling in front of the black and white mosaic in the middle of Strawberry Fields, the tribute to John Lennon in Central Park.

Jack felt like he was witnessing something holy. Her hands trailed over the tiled word *Imagine*, brushing the letters in feather-like strokes. Others who had made the same pilgrimage that day left bouquets, candles, and notes. Lucy bent over the memorial and laid down a rose, perfectly aligned with the black line in the mosaic peace sign. Next to that, she placed a golden sunflower, bountiful petals smiling up at the gray sky. The breeze battered silky strands of hair loose from Lucy's hat, and she shut her eyes, rocking back on heeled boots. Jack knelt down beside her, looping his arm through hers when she started shivering.

"I like the pattern," she said after her vigil. "It's soothing."

Struggling to maintain their balance as they crouched on wobbly ankles, Jack craned his neck at the artwork. "I suppose it is."

"It makes my brain quiet." She sent a heavy gaze toward him. "It's never quiet."

"Take your time," he said, wishing he could crawl inside her mind and investigate what exactly was so loud. Her eyes were unfocused as she immersed herself in the pattern. When she finally sat back, content with the tiles, her face was illuminated with serenity.

"Doesn't it feel odd to mourn them?" he asked, helping Lucy to her feet. "You don't even know them."

She scrunched up her mouth. "So, there's this theory I have. I call it the Bubble Theory."

"The Bubble Theory," he repeated with a wry smile. "Please explain."

"So, songs—and paintings, and books, and any other kind of art, are like bubbles. And the artist is the person holding the bubble wand. Once that bubble is created, it floats off into the world, no longer tethered to that artist. It belongs to the world."

She formed a circle with her hands, waving them around in the air. "And everyone sees the bubble differently. Some focus on its size, or the direction it's blowing, or the colors they see inside. No matter what they are focused on, though, the bubble doesn't belong to them or to the bubble blower."

"What if the bubble blower—" he grimaced at the clumsy phrasing, "—doesn't interpret the song the same as the listener?"

"Does it matter? Go back to 'Space Oddity.' Do you think Bowie really cared what people thought the song meant? Probably not. The magic is in experiencing it on your own like we did. Are you really worried about what John Doe from Nowheresville thinks 'Applejohn Blues' means?"

"I guess not." Jack thought of other musicians, legends past and present who had abused their fame.

He thought of his mother.

"But sometimes the bubble blowers are really shitty people."

"Sure. But that doesn't make the bubble, the song, affect people even less. The bubble is now separate from them." She gestured to The Dakota across the street, the building where John Lennon had lived and been murdered. "It applies to that too. I can be sad that a man was killed, but I have no claim to the grief or love or anger of his family and friends, nor to the struggles and rights and wrongs of the man himself. But I can mourn the experiences I have had myself concerning his art."

"How so?"

She hesitated before continuing on in her linear, documentative fashion. "Well, as you know, my family is huge; private time with a parent didn't happen often. But one night, my dad asked me to watch a show with him. Just me. He made nachos, and I was allowed to have a Coke at night, which is a big deal to a kid. We sat on the couch, just the two of us, and he put on Elvis's NBC TV special, his big live comeback concert. I'd never seen anything like it. I was glued to that screen, every song, every sound, every word he spoke, like it was real-life magic. The next morning, Dad showed me where to find the concert soundtrack in his album collection and gave me a few others to try, and that was it for me. I went through every album he had—all the greats, even the not-so-greats—and then we'd go off to consignment stores or record shops to find more. I'd sit in our den, wearing these clunky headphones that were too big for me, listening to record after record, reading every book I could find on rock and roll. It was all fascinating, but more importantly, music was magic, and it was comforting and familiar. Like an old friend."

Her bronze-brown eyes met Jack's. "When someone like that dies, I don't mourn the person. I think about a special time with my dad, or rediscovering those albums for the first time." She tipped up her mouth in a smile. "And now when I hear 'Space Oddity,' I'm going to think of you and your inability to open my bedroom door."

Jack scowled at her, but Lucy cleared her throat. "Speaking of how bubbles affect different people," she said, jerking her head toward two figures barreling toward them, "you've been spotted."

"The plight of the bubble blower," he whispered just as two women stopped and squealed at him.

Handling fans was always tricky for Jack. There was a tenuous line between catering to the people responsible for your fame and losing yourself in the process. Many people marched right over that line as if it were a rough sketch drawn in sand.

Jack plastered on a synthetic smile as the first woman curled a strand of blonde hair around her index finger like ivy around a sapling. "Can we get your autograph?"

"Of course," he said. "Always great to meet fans."

"I've been a fan since I was sixteen," squealed the second, a redhead wrapped in a stylish woolen peacoat. "I had all your posters. You were my first concert ever." She rummaged around her tote and retrieved a pen and scrap piece of paper. She ripped it in half, giving one side to the blonde for her own. After he signed the two slips, Jack glanced at the other side, which read *milk, eggs, deodorant*.

I'm signing grocery lists in the middle of Central Park, he thought. *This is what my life has become.*

He looked over at Lucy, who had stepped back behind a tree, observing the exchange. The women thanked him for the autographs, but the blonde followed it by spider-walking her fingers up his jacket. "We're on our way to a party at our friend's place. You should totally come."

"I appreciate the invite," Jack said. Three months ago, he would have taken her up on the offer in a heartbeat. "But—"

"Come on," said the blonde, though her redheaded friend was yanking her away, flashing Jack an apologetic look. "It'll be a blast. We could really have some fun." She shimmied a little closer and whispered a few details that curdled his ears—words that were arousing under the influence of booze and drugs, but felt oily and manufactured under the sober gray sky. Words that made him a product, not a person.

A choked gasp interrupted them. Jack turned his head and met Lucy's wide, alarmed eyes. She clutched at her chest, releasing a keening sound before her eyes rolled back, and she fell forward, first to her knees and then into a crumpled heap on the sidewalk.

Shards of icy fear speared through his veins, his heart thundering with panic. He shoved past the women and sprinted to Lucy, sliding to his knees to bend over her limp form.

"Lucy?" he shook her arm. Her face was starlight pale and her eyes tightly shut, but her mouth opened and closed in a *blink-and-you'll-miss-it* motion. He lowered his ear to her lips, her breath tickling his cheek.

"I'm giving you an out," she whispered from the corner of her mouth. "Milk it."

He stared at her, unable to decide whether to hug her or scold her.

Foolish, clever girl.

"Okay, honey, up you go," he said, cupping a hand under her elbow and supporting her to a sitting position. His fans watched him with a mix of horror and amusement on their faces. "My friend is having one of her spells," he called out. "She has a bad...spleen."

Lucy let out a noise like a baby elephant choking.

"She looks fine to me," said the blonde, but her friend shushed her.

"Gotta take a raincheck on that party." Jack pulled Lucy to her feet. She moaned and clutched at her forehead in proper damsel-in-distress style. "You know what the doctor says, dear."

"At least one walk per day keeps the spleen feeling okay," Lucy recited. He tipped his chin at the two confused women and led Lucy further into the park, his lips pressed together.

"My spleen?" she hissed once out of earshot.

"I wasn't prepared!"

She glanced behind them with a shudder. "They were scary. And touchy-feely. Are fans always like that?"

"No, thank God. For every fan like that, there are a dozen good ones."

"Still..." She looked at him warily.

"I'm not gonna lie; you might get some attention," he said. "But it's me they want. For my bubble wand." He gave her a lascivious wink. "It's part of the whole fame package. And the way they were with me, they may not be with anyone else. I'm not Jack Vincent to them. I'm Jack Hunter—just a product. I'm Coca-Cola. I'm an Oreo."

"I guess so." She kicked at the sidewalk, her nose wrinkled in irritation. She muttered something under her breath.

"What was that?"

"You're not an Oreo," she said.

Jack was strangely touched by those four simple words, so naturally, he fumbled out an inappropriate response. "I could be. You could crack me open and sample the creamy goodness inside."

Lucy's nose flared as wide as humanly possible, and she slowly turned her head to gawk at him. Her disgusted grimace deepened as she glanced over him, and she wiped her hands on her jacket.

"Sorry," he ducked his head, "That metaphor died as it lived—a bit crumby and in need of a tall glass of milk." He reached into his coat pocket for his phone to call for a ride, and found the box that a courier service had delivered to his house earlier that day.

"Oh yeah," he said. "Lucy, c'mere." He led her under a nearby maple tree, bare and skeletal, its colorless leaves scattered around the trunk like week-old confetti.

Lucy shivered, her hands thrust in her pockets, and peered at the box.

"This was dropped off today," he said. "You should probably start wearing it." He flipped it open to reveal a yellow sapphire flower surrounded by diamond petals. He scratched at the scruff on his jaw and glanced down at the cold, muddy patches of grass. "Do I have to get on one knee?"

"Oh, please don't," she said, spellbound by the glittering ring. "Anytime someone gets on one knee, spectators come popping up out of nowhere like groundhogs. And then Martin will lose his perfect engagement photo."

"Well, we don't want to make Martin mad," he said, nudging her shoulder. She scanned the area to make sure no one was watching and held out a slender finger. Jack pulled the ring from the box—and his frigid fingers promptly dropped it into the mass of leaves below.

"Shit!" he said, dropping to his knees, a slurry of damp, cold mud from last night's rain seeping into his jeans as his splayed hands searched through crunching leaves. "Just hold on a sec, I'll find it."

Out of the corner of his eye, he saw Lucy kneel as well, and he let out a choked noise. "No, you'll get all muddy!"

She gave him an odd look. "It's fine, let me help."

"But you don't like to get dirty," he protested, reaching to help her stand but instead forcing his knees further into the dirt. "Stand up, quick, before it soaks into your pants."

Her eyes widened for a moment, and she looked away, a slight tremor around her lower lip. When she turned back to him, her eyes were glistening, but she was smiling. "That's only my hands that really bothers me."

"Oh, well, good to know for future mud-wrestling events," he said, plunging his hand into a particularly soggy leaf pile. "Aha!" He hoisted the ring into the air with Gollum-like glee—and then frowned, shaking it as muddy water sluiced off the sides. "Your hands, you said?"

She took a jagged breath. "I'll be fine. Put it on before someone sees."

Instead, he unzipped his jacket and wiped the ring as cleanly as possible on his no-longer white shirt, leaving behind a muddy Rorschach pattern on the fabric. Still teetering on their knees, he took her hand and slipped the ring on her shivering finger. "So, is it a yes? Because if not, Luciana, I'm sending you the dry cleaning bill."

She shot him an insouciant glare, and then, without warning, she hugged him, knocking the breath from his lungs as her arms wrapped around his waist. It was a cumbersome tangle of crisscrossed legs and soggy knees and bits of crunched leaves sticking everywhere. Still, as the autumn wind tore through their hair and battered their ears, and the damp chill of the sidewalk seeped into his jeans, Jack felt as if he had just been granted something absolutely extraordinary.

Chapter 12

The idea of having a social media presence had never bothered Lucy. Some people dreaded comments and negative viral attention, but to her, they were simply words, written by unseen faces masked behind blue-lit screens.

Jack, however, was a veritable mess.

On the day they were to begin their foray into the jungle of social media, he snapped at Lucy for everything from how her eggs were cooked ("How can you eat them when they are that runny?") to the state of his own blue jeans ("What the hell is the point of this little pocket?"). She ignored his nervous bumbling and focused on her own plans for the day.

She was pouring two tall glasses of water, one for her and one for her guest, when she heard Jack amble down the hallway outside of the kitchen. His footsteps stopped abruptly, the volume increasing as he returned.

"Lucy." He stood in the doorway, arms folded over his chest. Soggy spots covered his shirt where his freshly-showered hair had dripped. "There's a man in our living room."

"There is." She gathered up the glasses, wondering if she should add lemon to the water or if that was too pretentious.

"Who is he?"

"That's Parker."

He leaned his head to one side, more water trickling from his dusky waves. "And who, by chance, is Parker?"

"Your—our—new assistant."

Jack's head tilted further. His hair flopped directly onto his shoulder, and Lucy made a mental note to grab him a dry shirt before their meeting. He really should have dried his hair with a towel.

"Kim?" he asked, and she nodded. "I didn't want a new assistant. They're annoying and bossy."

"They're the annoying and bossy ones, and yet you're the one who's had five assistants quit on him." She arched a challenging brow.

He lifted his fist to his mouth, running his teeth along his knuckle. "He's rather young. And good-looking." He spoke the last word with the same derision as a leprosy diagnosis.

"That's really sweet, Jack. I'm sure he'll appreciate the compliment." Jack sighed in exasperation. "He looks young because he is young. He just graduated from NYU this past summer with a degree in Music Technology. He could use some exposure in the industry."

"And getting our groceries is going to help."

"You're cranky today," she pointed out. "Come meet him." She seized Jack's hand and escorted him down the hall. After a moment, he gripped her hand back, threading their fingers together.

"Parker, this is Jack." Parker stood at attention, and Lucy couldn't help but agree with Jack's assessment. Parker *was* good-looking, with a charismatic disarming grin, brownish hair, and eyes to match. He stood several inches over Jack's six feet, a long-legged bundle of youthful enthusiasm, like a frolicking newborn giraffe.

Parker held out his hand to Jack. "It's great to meet you, Mr. Vincent," he said with a tremor of starstruck excitement.

Jack frowned at the assistant's outstretched hand. Lucy pinched his fingers until he let out a yowl and returned the handshake. "Call me Jack," he muttered. "I like my coffee with two cream, five sugars. Don't get pregnant." With that, he turned on his heel and went back to his studio, slamming the door.

"That's not even coffee, that's syrup," Parker said, his mouth half-open in disbelief. He flicked a hand at the empty doorway. "Is he always like that?"

"Cantankerous? Usually. Will you be treated like Bob Cratchit? Often. Still want the job?"

He mirrored Lucy's knowing grin. "Absolutely."

They sat down at the table to plan out his duties. By the end of it, he had assignments to set up a housekeeping service, help Kim and Martin with any last-minute wedding items, and assist Jack at the recording studio once work on the new album began.

Five minutes before their scheduled video meeting, Jack stalked back to join them. Parker had set up their webcam and laptop to meet with Martin and Kim. Jack thanked him with a tolerating grumble.

"First off, nice work yesterday with the fainting stuff," said Martin, not bothering with a greeting. "You were trending for a few hours."

"Fainting stuff?" Jack asked.

"Yeah, whatever Lucy did," Martin said. "There's an out-of-focus photo of you helping her up off the ground. The responses were generally positive, portraying you as some kind of hero. Although some people think you pushed her over, but that's the Internet for you."

"Fantastic." Jack folded his hands over his eyes and groaned. "People expect the same behavior from me that they do from an angry goose."

"Now, you guys ready?" asked Martin through the video feed, dramatically swirling his finger in the air above the keyboard.

"Ready," Jack and Lucy said, locking apprehensive gazes.

Martin clicked on his laptop just once, and the first Instagram post of their absurd scheme went live. It was a simplistic picture of Jack, taken in front of the baby grand piano at the record label's office. His face was turned away from the camera, his long fingers splayed on the keys. In calming, classic black and white, the photo was accompanied by inspirational words about change and the future.

As soon as the post went live, the comments flowed in like water from a broken pipe. As expected, a few were nasty and ruthless, with blatant jabs at Jack's previous escapades and lackluster albums. Lucy dismissed them, but Jack's forearm flexed and tensed, pressed against her own. Parker tracked the feedback from his own phone, jotting down ideas on a notepad.

"Look." Lucy tapped on the laptop screen above one of the comments, which was just a screaming emoji accompanied by the words "NEW ALBUM?!?!" and then *#jackhunter4ever*. Whoever had the username *@jh-penguin* was going to be thrilled with the campaign. They'd get that new album and a hell of a lot more.

Jack's jaw went as rigid as a steel rail as more and more comments filtered in regarding the new album. "Are we done here?"

Martin didn't seem fazed by Jack's hostile tone. "We're good. I'll keep an eye on the comments and reactions. In two days, we'll post something hinting again at the new album, and then we'll come in from left field with the engagement photos." He grinned like he was planning a worldwide takeover, not an engagement announcement, and hung up without a goodbye, leaving only Kim still connected.

"Parker, great to have you on board," she said. Jack emitted a very audible, very displeased grunt but said nothing. "I'll email over all the details for the concert on Saturday." Parker scribbled copious notes while still maintaining animated eye contact with Kim.

"And Jack," she continued, switching from warmth to wariness. "Next week, the studio is assigned to you to start laying down tracks. You can get in a couple days before you leave for Thanksgiving." Jack's lips curled into the slightest sneer. "Good," she said, her tone anything but good as she began disconnecting. "See you soon."

"Parker?" asked Jack. "You've got your tasks then?"

"Of course," said Parker, his eyes bright. "Plenty to prepare for—"

"Good," Lucy's oh-so-cheerful fiancé interrupted. "Go home and do it."

Parker looked at Lucy, who granted him an assured smile. "Text me with your questions and updates any time. I know we'll work great together."

Once Parker was out of the house, she whirled on Jack. "What's wrong with you?"

His dark brows drew together in consternation, and he flexed his fingers like raptor talons before blurting out, "You know I don't have any songs."

Lucy searched his somber expression. Beneath that sullen attitude was a layer of pure panic, teetering on a foundation of years of self-doubt.

He doesn't need coddling, she thought. *He needs courage. Or a swift kick in the rear.*

She grasped his shoulders firmly and spun him in the direction of his studio. "Then go write."

Jack stomped off to the studio and slumped into his chair, snatching up his guitar. He tuned his guitar angrily—yes, it was possible to angrily tune a guitar—until a string snapped and stung his fingers. He hurled the string into the trash with no less than a dozen curses.

"Do you need me to do anything?" Lucy asked, appearing in the doorway. "I can talk, not talk, play music, whatever you need."

Jack gave her a glare infused with every ounce of sarcasm he could muster. "Whale songs."

"Really?" Her luminous brown eyes sparked, and she retrieved her phone from her pocket. Before he could stop her, the crooning wail of a whale echoed through the room.

"I was kidding." He scratched at the back of his neck as the sounds of a colossal sea mammal bellowed in the background. "Maybe if you come in, work on your laptop, it'll put some imagined pressure on me."

She vanished through the door and reappeared with her computer, flopping down in the armchair and losing herself in concentration.

Jack plucked a few chords to warm up, and then worked through a few of his older songs, looking to the past to grant him some hint of future inspiration. Every once in a while, he glanced over at Lucy for a reaction, but she was oblivious. Even when he threw a Bruce Springsteen song into the mix, she had the focus of a Buckingham Palace guard.

Too jittery to work on a melody, Jack laid his guitar down and reached for his notebook.

"Play 'Freebird.'" Lucy flicked her eyes up from her screen, and the edge of her mouth lifted.

"Really?"

"Nah. I just always wanted to be the one to say that." She mimicked an invisible lighter in her hand, waving it in the air in tribute to concertgoers from decades past. "Although, I'm not likely to see Lynyrd Skynyrd in concert any time soon, so you'll have to do."

Jack twiddled his ballpoint in his hand like a drumstick. "What concerts have you been to?"

Her gaze slid back to her screen. "None."

"None?" He scoffed. "Are you serious? You, of all people? I thought you'd have a pallet full of ticket stubs back at home."

Her lips compressed. "Not a lot of tours go through Sparrow Hill."

"Oh, come on. You're not far from Indianapolis or even Chicago. All the good tours hit those. I've played them both at least ten times."

She tapped at a key with unnecessary force and didn't answer.

"Well, at least you'll be at the Harvest Festival," he added.

"You don't need me there. There won't be time for pictures."

"No, I don't need you there," he said, although, now that the idea was there, the thought of seeing her out in the audience as he performed sent a glow of contentment through his body. What would it be like to play for a crowd, knowing that someone was out there in the audience not because they were a fan, but because they were there for you and you alone? That they were, God forbid, proud of you? "Seriously, you would have fun. Come to the concert. Please."

She bit the side of her thumb. "Fine. I'll go."

"It's not a death sentence. I'll even let you come backstage. You can get my autograph."

She rolled her eyes. "Autographs are creepy."

"You keep saying that."

She thrust a slender index finger upward, like a lawyer on a mission. "Someone admires you, so they give you a piece of paper. You write your name on it and give them back the paper. Not a letter, not instructions, just your signature. And then they treasure it forever and ever for some reason." She dropped her voice to a gruff rasp. "Hi, my name is Jack. See? I can write my name. Take it and show your great-grandchildren."

"I don't sound like that at all," he corrected before elevating his voice an octave, adding a nasal Midwestern twang to his vowels. "Howdy, I'm Lucy. I secretly want Jack to sign everything I own because he's my favorite singer ever."

Her eyes spoke of intended murder, but her lips struggled to hold back her amusement. "It's weird."

"It's a time-honored tradition. I think."

She side-eyed Jack. "It's a creepy-ass tradition. Just give them a sample vial of blood while you're at it."

"I really am going to sign everything I give you from now on," he said, waggling the pen threateningly in her direction. Lucy sniffed and motioned to his dog-eared notebook.

"You start with the lyrics first, then?"

"Sometimes. Elton John style. Except, in this case, I'm both Bernie Taupin *and* Elton, but neither side is feeling inspired." He glanced at her. "Do you have a favorite song of mine? Maybe I can try and mimic the style a bit."

"'Applejohn Blues,'" she said immediately. "Your bluesy songs are always stronger than your standard ones."

"Really?"

She nodded. "The structure is solid, the tempo is upbeat without being obnoxious, and you use bent notes to accentuate the lyrics rather than overpower them. And your voice. Mmm." She clapped a distressed hand over her mouth, her eyes as round as dinner plates.

"Lucy." He lifted a roguish eyebrow.

"Yes?"

"Cottontail."

"Not my name."

"Did you just make a..." He paused for dramatic effect, flourishing his hand out like a Shakespearean actor. "A yummy noise about my voice?"

Her face was the color of a raspberry. "You sing very effectively."

"Effectively?"

"Effectively."

"Lucy." He diminished his voice to a near-purr. "What does *effectively* mean?"

"Well, you have a growly, howling sort of quality that is..." she gulped, "pleasant."

When she met his gaze head-on, he gave her a smile as sweet and feral as honey dripping from a bear's claws.

"Effectively, indeed," He threw her a first-rate smoldering look and returned to his notebook.

She cleared her throat. "Do you want me to look at what you've written so far?"

"There's nothing here." He held up a page with a few lines of schlock and a sketched stick figure of a guitarist with a speech bubble that read "KILL ME."

She tapped her lips, her eyes shooting back and forth like she was reading a line of invisible code. "Hand me the notebook." She whipped her palm out.

"No."

She shut her laptop with a snap and came closer, her hand out. "The notebook?"

"Make another yummy noise."

Her eyes blazed. "No." She snatched the notebook and sat down on the couch next to him. "I learned this trick in a creative writing class in college." She scrawled on the top of the page. "You need to stop trying to write a Jack Hunter song and just write. Even if it's dumb."

She held the notebook up to his face so he could read her prim handwriting.

It was a dark and stormy night

"You're kidding." He pushed the notebook away.

"Nope." She shoved the notebook back at him. "There's the first line to a song. You're just trying to get your creativity flowing in another direction."

"No."

She wrote another line.

And your hair looked such a fright

"This is ridiculous."

She stole his hand and attempted to pry his fingers open. He stiffened them just to be contrary. Once she lifted the last finger, her tongue jutting out of the side of her mouth with the effort, she forced the pen into his grip and fastened his hand around it. She covered his hands as if he held something priceless instead of a cheap ballpoint, and a zap of electricity tripped over his skin. Her breath snagged, and she jerked her hands away, narrowing her eyes as if the tangible heat between them was all Jack's doing.

"Fine. Are we going with four-line rhymes or just couplets?"

She shrugged. "I'm not the writer here."

"No, apparently just my tormenter." *In more ways than this ridiculous exercise.* He jotted something down and flipped the pen at her. She caught it, read the notebook, and began chortling.

My socks are too damn tight

"You're not even wearing socks." She laughed and checked her shoulder into his.

"You didn't say it had to be factual."

"True. You never wear socks."

"Neither do you!" he scoffed, snagging her bare foot. Her toes had been supplanted by ice cubes. He took her other foot and cupped his hands around her digits, rubbing them back to room temperature.

A brief moment of realization passed, and their mutual gazes fastened on his long fingers.

"Huh," he said, because nowhere in their contract did it say they were responsible for warming each other's toes. Yet, there he was, massaging Lucy's feet to the tune of dramatic whales warbling wordlessly about something like krill or kelp or talking wooden puppets. He patted her feet once and lifted his hands away as if to say, *all done!* Her copper-colored eyes traversed up his body before settling on his mouth. He nearly made a yummy noise of his own.

"You've got the basic idea," she said, sliding off the couch. "I'll leave you to it." She was gone from the room—jackrabbit fast as always—before he could even conjure up a reply.

Jack recovered the pen and tried to list all the words he knew that rhymed with night, but without Lucy in the room, the exercise once again felt pointless and, well, *difficult*. Too difficult for his washed-up brain.

He closed the notebook with a level of indifference several decades in the making, crossing the room to his bar. Overfilling a shot glass with whiskey, he toasted the unknown whale still pouring her marine soul out, and focused on getting very, very drunk.

Chapter 13

Jack didn't believe in magic. Sure, he was a closet Harry Potter fan, and he was still convinced that one girl in Croatia had done some sort of voodoo on his junk, but other than that, logic clearly proved that magic didn't exist.

Until Lucy emerged from her room clad in some sort of fashion sorcery that transmogrified his hands into magnets. He actually had to trap his hands—the magnetic knots of lust that they were—deep in his pockets so he wouldn't maul her like a bear returning from hibernation.

Instead of her usual braids or messy buns, her hair swirled and cascaded down her back like a waterfall. Her band shirts had been usurped by an emerald green dress that caressed every curve, topped off with a plunging neckline that left little to the imagination. His brain short-circuited, and all focus he had built up for that night's event disappeared in a poof of desire.

And what an event it would be. After being roped into replacing Patrick Hodelle for the Laser Wolves set at the Harvest Festival tomorrow, Jack was expected to be at the celebratory dinner, an event designed for self-promotion under the pretense of charity. It would be a good practice event for Lucy. Most of the attendees were rich but not famous, and there wouldn't be any significant media presence other than a stray camera here or there. It was a chance to dip her in hot water before throwing her into the pot completely.

She checked her hair one last time in the hall mirror. Jack knew he should say something suave and gentlemanly like, "You look wonderful tonight," but all that fell out of his clumsy mouth was a barked, "Aren't you ready yet?"

She beamed at him, her full lips colored cranberry red. "You're the one whose bowtie isn't tied yet."

He fumbled with the limp fabric at his neck before she plucked his fingers away. She sidled up to him, so close that he could just seize her hips and yank her against the swell in his pants, and they could forego the bowtie and the rest of their clothes altogether.

"How do you know how to tie a bow tie?" Jack asked, steering his gaze skyward, because if he looked down at her bare, elegant neck, he might go full vampire on her.

"Three brothers, two proms each." She tugged the ends and leaned closer, outlining the fabric to verify every angle was absolutely straight. "Plus, Nico's wedding, so that's another four bowties counting my dad."

"I don't even know what I'm wearing to our wedding, but if it's a bow tie, I'll call in your expertise." She inclined his chin with her finger for better access. He restrained from nipping the end with his teeth. "Any of your other siblings married?"

"None of them are. Nico and Jenny divorced years ago. Someone else better get married in the next two years, or the Meyer record is going to be oh-for-two."

"I think my mom is oh-in-four or oh-in-five. There was a remarriage there somewhere."

"Well, then. We're just following in our family's footsteps." Her smile wavered.

"We still need to come up with a good story on how we met," Jack said, shifting the subject away from their impending divorce, especially when the impending marriage hadn't happened yet.

"I was held in a warehouse by kidnappers. You saved me, and we drove off into the sunset just as the warehouse exploded."

"Whoa there, Michael Bay," he said. "We don't want to be boring, but we need something believable."

She huffed. "Fine. We met at a record store."

"We did."

"It was love at first sight." She flapped her eyelashes like a soap star.

"Classic, but it works."

"You took me out to dinner."

"Where?"

"McDonald's."

"I am a classy guy." He folded his arms. "Where, really?"

"I dunno. Some Italian place. I was too enamored to look at the name." She sighed, and beneath the false drama rang a wistful note. "And then you wooed me passionately."

"I wooed you."

"You wooed me."

"We aren't using the word 'woo.' I don't *woo*."

"You wooed me. Then you took me to Central Park. We looked at the leaves changing. You realized I had been properly wooed, and you proposed under a tree."

"What kind of a tree?"

"A maple." She flashed a rare, mischievous smile. "It was simply *woo*-ti-ful."

He groaned. "*Woo*-nderful."

"We know it's a short engagement, but we couldn't help ourselves; we're so in love. You even wrote me a poem. Roses are red, violets are *woo*—"

"Jesus." He hauled her closer under the guise of assisting her with her coat. "I should send you back to Indiana."

"Oh, and you were going to sing a song for me when you proposed. Ask me why you didn't."

"Oh darling, lovable, not-funny-at-all fiancée of mine, why didn't I sing for you at our proposal?"

"Because all you could think of were *Woo*-Tang Clan songs." She shifted to catch his expression and burst into giggles, her eyes watering with mirth.

Jack touched his forehead to hers. The vibration of her laughter tickled his skin. "Cottontail, I swear..."

Her snickers faded into quickened breaths. Her scent was perfect cocoa and lavender, and inhaling it gave Jack enough courage to be incredibly stupid.

"Luciana," he said, his lips against the fragile sweep of her temple.

"Yeah?"

"We're going to have to act in love at this event too."

"Oh." Her breath caught. "I suppose I can act really happy to see you."

"Mmm-hmmm." He skimmed his mouth over her brow. "Cottontail?"

"Not my name."

Jack tipped her head, and her lips parted by instinct.

"I'm going to kiss you."

She wrinkled her nose. "Why would you do that?"

"Practice. We don't want to be awkward in public together."

"Right," she said with a witchy half-smile. Her eyes dropped to his lips, the black velvet edge of her lashes an elegant contrast to her flushed skin. "Because we're never awkward together."

"Oh, hush." He quelled her sarcasm by grazing his lips over hers, intending to be quick and chaste. She squeaked, and for a moment, their lips compressed together, hard and unyielding as competing bumper cars. Then with a surrendering sigh, she slackened against him, and *quick* and *chaste* became the most difficult words in the English language. Her lips were so delicate and supple that it took every ounce of Jack's focus to keep it simple. After one more kiss, he drew back. Her eyes drifted open, lazy and demure.

"How did we do?" he asked.

She frowned. "Needs work." She grasped the lapels of his tuxedo and yanked him to her. He crushed his lips against hers, and *quick* and *chaste* changed status from merely difficult words to "words Jack wanted outlawed from the dictionary." With a coarse, hungry noise, he tangled his hands in her thick hair, bowing her head to a new angle so he could devour her without grace or mercy. His other hand clawed around her hip, and he jerked her flush to him. Her breasts pressed against his chest in a gasping rhythm, and she moaned against his mouth. He backed her into the wall, and her coat crumpled to the rug, forgotten. She twined her leg around his, hooking him closer, and he shifted a shaking knee between her legs. His hips carelessly rolled against her, a barely perceptible movement that was rewarded when she quivered against him. Then she shoved his chest, and he pitched backward, interrupting the kiss.

"We're good!" she said. "No more practice needed." Her lips were delectably swollen, her lipstick as smudged as an impressionist painting.

"Yes, I think we've got it down," Jack said. He turned from her to regain control, but his brain only remembered two instincts: breathing and tossing her over his shoulder like a Neanderthal.

For both their sakes, he focused on breathing.

She grabbed her coat from the floor and stalked to the front door on spindly heels. Jack followed, still reeling from the lust cyclone inside his head.

When they arrived inside the Manhattan event hall, Jack turned to Lucy for a last-minute pep talk. To his astonishment, she was utterly calm and poised, like a porcelain doll on a collector's shelf.

He didn't like it.

"You're going to be alright with this?" he asked.

She proffered a wholly disconnected smile. "Of course, Jack." She tucked her arm into the bend of his elbow. The engagement ring winked in the panes of light drifting down from the overpriced chandeliers. Jack liked how it looked on her hand—tangible proof that she was *necessary*. Maybe even that she was meant to be there and had always been. That somehow, they were just naturally each other's people.

Once inside the ornate ballroom, Jack escorted her to a nook between tables where they could speak without being overheard.

"Look over there." He indicated a cluster of guests across the room, huddled together like penguins on the ice. "That older man, that's Frank Taylor. He founded Derelict Records. He's the one who will have the final say on whether I get a new contract."

"Got it."

"The blond man next to him, that's his son Keith. Frank is pretty much grooming him to be his successor. Keith has a hand in all decisions for the label, officially or not."

"Keith Taylor," Lucy recited it several times under her breath.

"All right, Cottontail. Like it or not, it's showtime." He steered her toward the Taylors and their gaggle of acquaintances.

"Jack!" Frank Taylor's voice boomed. He was in his early sixties, but time had been benevolent to his appearance. His dark hair had faultlessly spaced streaks of gray, and his mannerisms and attire were more like that of a boisterous sea captain than a businessman nearing retirement. "I'm glad you could make it! I can't remember the last time I saw you out at an event like this." His smile was sincere, but a reluctant tautness around his eyes made Jack wary. "And this is the fiancée." Frank grasped Lucy's hand, patting the back of it in a fatherly manner. She tensed at his touch but didn't push him away. "I'll tell you what, I could hardly believe it when Kim told me. Jack Hunter! Engaged!"

"I can hardly believe it myself." Jack smiled at Lucy in a way that said, *look how much I adore my fiancée!* It wasn't too difficult to manage. "This is Luciana Meyer."

"Call me Lucy. It's so lovely to meet you." Her voice was silky and lithe, and it stunned Jack how comfortable she appeared, as if she had been trained for society events her entire life. His own smile slipped away.

This wasn't his Lucy. This was someone else entirely.

"Lucy, you must be a saint." Frank released her hand and slapped Jack's shoulder so hard he felt it reverberate in his ribcage. "How did you tame this jackass?"

"I didn't have to tame anyone," she said, her rosy mouth crooking upward, eyes sparkling with pride, unconditional and pure. "Jack is absolutely wonderful the way he is."

Jack had fallen once while running onto a stage, years ago. A loose wire had hooked around his shoe, and he had tumbled forward, crashing into the planked stage floor and slamming the air from his lungs. He had laid there, gasping for air, ribs bruised and aching, all the while aware of the hundreds of people staring at him as he was stripped to the core by unadulterated shock. And yet when he had staggered to his feet, he had realized that the whole episode had taken place just inside the curtain's edge. The audience had been completely unaware of the way he had just fallen completely apart.

He felt the same way as he did sprawled on that long-ago stage, the breath knocked from his chest, shock scorching its way through his veins, and yet the world spun on around him, oblivious to the effect of Lucy's whole and absolute trust.

He brushed his lips against her temple, lingering against the delicate pulse point. *Thank God it was you that walked into that record store.*

Frank coughed. "Lucy, this is my son, Keith." She stretched her hand out to the younger man, and Jack recalled all too late how much of a charmer Keith Taylor actually was.

"Pleasure to meet you," says Keith, flashing a set of pearly white teeth and flicking oceanic blue eyes toward him. "Jack, she's absolutely stunning. Well done."

"Don't tell me, tell her," he grumbled. "She's my fiancée, not some fish I caught."

"My apologies." He grinned at her, and Jack saw he had dimples. *Dimples, dammit*! He clenched his jaw as Keith lowered his voice. "Lucy, you're absolutely stunning." Lucy blushed like a debutante and beamed at him, patting him on the shoulder with a sugary laugh.

"And don't forget me, now." A heavier-set man with a smug leer bustled forward, his hand out to Lucy. Jack groaned internally upon recognition.

"This is James Thurston," Frank said. "He owns Cruise Records." The middle-aged mogul grabbed Lucy's hand and pumped it. He was saturated with the essence of New England old money, but with an extra sheen of music industry political smarminess.

"Nice to meet you, Lucy." He dropped her hand and reached for Jack's with a wink. "Jack, if you ever want to talk when these two knuckleheads aren't around..." He dipped his chin toward Keith and Frank.

"Thanks, James," Jack said, dragging his hand away. "I'll keep that in mind." He wouldn't.

A godsend of a waiter appeared with a tray full of champagne flutes, and Jack snagged one each for Lucy and himself. She declined hers with a smile, but it wasn't the prized, genuine smile he craved. It was false and rehearsed, yet everyone was lapping it up like kittens with saucers of cream.

"So when's the wedding?" asked Frank.

"Soon," said Lucy. "We're finalizing the details now." She delivered a convincingly contrite pout. "I'm so sorry we won't be able to have anyone there, but we wanted to keep it just the two of us. Especially with some of the bad press Jack has been getting lately."

Frank admired her with calculated appreciation. "That's exactly right. Right now, the best thing for Jack is staying low-key." He shot Jack a heavy glance. "The best thing for the label too."

Jack swallowed, grasping the executive's meaning. *All work and no play make Jack a lucrative asset to Derelict Records.*

James launched into one of his blustering stories about his sordid past, an activity that usually commanded most of the social gatherings he attended. That night's long-winded saga was from his younger days as a trust-fund bachelor, something about a Clinton election night party, Freddie Mercury, and a few has-been 90s movie stars. Jack shifted from foot to foot, looking enviously over at a round table and chairs. If they had to listen to James's self-absorbed stories, they should at least be allowed to sit while doing it.

He glanced at Lucy, expecting to find that "Grace Kelly at the Oscars" high society composure. Instead, she glowered as if James were declaring to a room full of children that Santa wasn't real.

Jack draped a hand around her waist and pulled her close enough to murmur in her ear, "Everything okay?"

Her hand flexed and thrashed, like a wolf pawing the ground before pouncing. "No, you didn't," she blurted out, bringing James's story to a screeching halt. James blinked at her with eyelids puffy from a life of unencumbered inebriation. Lucy's cheekbones were dusted with pink indignation, and her sculpted persona vanished.

There you are. There's my real Lucy.

Jack sipped his champagne nonchalantly and stepped back to watch the show.

"I'm sorry, what was that, dear?" James accentuated the "dear" like a patronizing uncle.

Her eye twitched, and Jack almost felt sorry for James. Almost.

"Why would Freddie Mercury be there?"

"Why wouldn't he be?" He glanced around at the rest of them with a *can you believe this girl?* look.

"He wasn't known for mixing in American politics," she said.

"That doesn't matter. It was a hell of a party, and he was invited."

"Sure. It's just that Bill Clinton was elected in 1992."

"So?"

"Well, it would be hard for Freddie Mercury to attend, considering he passed away in 1991."

The group was stricken speechless. Jack drained the rest of his champagne flute while satisfaction rippled through his chest.

Well done, Cottontail.

Keith erupted into laughter, clapping the astonished man on the back. "She's got you there, Jim."

"Must have been some other British singer, then." He mumbled something excusatory, waving at another party guest and weaving their way to bore them instead.

"We've all wanted to call him out," Keith said, wiping his eyes. "But you actually did it. Please come with Jack to all events from now on. Hell, come without Jack if you want. You're a treasure."

Jack grinned at Lucy, but her expression was blank as a slate.

"Excuse me," she said. "I'm going to find the restroom." Keith jumped at the chance to steer her in the right direction. She thanked him with that icy smile and walked away.

Keith stood next to Jack, rocking on the balls of his feet as he watched Lucy disappear down a hallway.

"How did you, of all people, manage to win *that*?" he asked. His tone held subtle notes of both admiration and degradation that turned Jack's blood volcanic.

"I wooed her," he said and dashed after his fiancée.

Lucy did not go toward the restroom, opting instead for a hallway clouded with savory kitchen odors and tempered by a chilly blast of air from the back entrance. The door yawned open into a cramped alley stuffed with greasy cardboard boxes, used metal drums, and a rusty dumpster.

You messed up, Lucy.

Brock's velvet and cashmere voice droned in her head, over and over like a wobbly record. Ten minutes into the event, and she had ruined everything. She *knew* she could be polite and quiet and charming. Brock had made her rehearse enough before any social event. She *knew* the right way to smile, to stand, to touch another person, or shake that person's hand.

She didn't like it, but she *knew* how to do it.

The back door swung open with a squeal of rusty hinges, and Jack stepped outside, scowling at the sunlight like a grouchy fruit bat.

"Lucy? You out here?"

"I'm here," she said, resignation coloring her voice.

"They're starting to serve the food."

She didn't answer, preferring to examine a discarded glass bottle with half of the label missing. If she positioned the ball of her foot on it just right, she could roll it back and forth in a peaceful rhythm without toppling over on her heels.

"Hey." He softened his tone. "What's wrong?"

"I messed up." She shrugged, but the cadence of her breathing was abrupt and jagged.

"What did you do?" He started to pat her down like an injured child, his hands running up and down her arms until she twisted away.

"I didn't fall; I said I messed up."

"How?" He tossed his head from side to side as if the proof of her mistake was something tactile lounging out in the alley with her.

She rolled at the glass bottle again until Jack stepped on it, blocking it with his dress shoe.

"No editing, Luciana. What's going on in there?" He tapped her furrowed forehead.

"I'm working on it," she bit out, because she honestly didn't know what to say, what the right words would be, and most importantly, what not to give away.

"Okay, then. When you're ready." He released the bottle from his foot and stepped back.

She took a knife-sharp breath. "I let *me* out."

"You?"

"I couldn't let him be wrong," she bit out. "He was saying the *wrong things*. And now I've ruined everything."

Look what you did, Lucy. You fucked up.

Jack rubbed at his mouth, but his shoulders were twitching with stifled laughs.

"It isn't funny," she said, suppressing an indignant foot stamp. "I messed up. I should have kept my mouth shut and stood there and smiled and—"

"Oh, Lucy," he said with a headshake. "You're doing just fine. They loved you in there. What do you want me to do? Punish you for being charming?"

Like that of a chained dog, a terrified, inhuman whine escaped her throat, and Jack's mirthful look plummeted. He reached for her, but she shied away, stumbling backward. The bottle under her foot betrayed her, switching reassurance for imbalance. His hand shot out to steady her, but when his fingers coiled around her wrist, she released another unearthly wail.

"Lucy. Look at me."

She jerked her head, her eyes screwed up tight, waiting for the hot surge of pain and salty ooze of blood. His hand grazed her jaw, and she clamped her teeth together.

Just take it, Lucy. I'm just trying to help you. You just need to learn.

"Luciana. Honey, look at me."

The *Honey* snapped her from the flashback, leading her through the murky fog of memory like a lighthouse on the rocks. She blinked several times and forced her eyes to travel to Jack's face. His expression was desolate, and his fists hung rigid at his side.

"What did you think I was going to do?" he asked.

"I messed up."

"No, you didn't," he ground out, a definitive pause between each word. "What did you think I was going to do?"

She whipped her head back and forth, looking at everything in the alley except Jack. The man just wanted his life to stay the same, and there she was, mucking it up with her inability to hide anything true about herself.

"I thought you were going to punish me," she finally whispered, and his neutral countenance melted into a torrent of distress and anger.

"I would never—" His throat bobbed, but she shook her head, waves of dark hair swishing back and forth against stiffened shoulders.

"I don't want to have this conversation," she said, enunciating the words as if each syllable were a protective shield.

"We will," he said. "And soon. But not tonight." He tucked a wayward tendril of hair behind her ear. "Lucy, just be you. For the love of God. I don't want anyone else. If I wanted the stereotypical perfect woman, I would've picked one of the actresses that Kim wanted. Someone we could mold into what we needed."

"I can be perfect. I can try harder."

A slight tremor in his thumb syncopated his touch as he stroked the cuff of her ear, the hollow of flesh behind the lobe, the ridge of her jawline. "This whole PR stunt is a shitshow. Let's at least have a little fun. Besides, you're a success already. You calling out James has gained you instant adoration from Frank and Keith."

She flushed. "I just want this to go well for you."

His hand drifted down to hers. "You know, I've done ten tours in twenty-some years, and those each lasted nearly two years. There's no time to be lonely. There's no time to be anything. It's go-go-go, twenty-four hours a day, every day. And...sometimes I hate it."

"What?! Then why are we doing this?" She flapped her hand between their chests.

"I don't know how to do anything else. So here we are." He hesitated for a beat. "Look. I'm an asshole, and you're a weirdo, and we get along just fine. I'm not pretending to be anything I'm not, and you don't need to either. If they don't understand either of us, they can screw right off. Let's just have fun for the next two years and raise a little hell along the way." He extended his hand for a mock handshake.

"Thanks, asshole," she said with a skeptical chuckle, her palm meeting his.

"You're welcome, weirdo." His gaze dropped to her mouth, and for a brief moment, she thought she might kiss him again.

"Come on," he said instead with an auspicious wink. "Let's go raise some hell."

Chapter 14

The following morning, Jack picked up a complimentary Marriott Hotels pen, leftover from one of his tours, and began to write.

Inebriated indifference had been a lousy muse for the past few years, but after the previous night's events, he suddenly possessed an entire palette of emotions, raw and ready to be used.

He wrote anger.

He wrote fear.

He wrote frustration and uncertainty and shame, and he wrote a brand new emotion altogether, one that captured the scent of cocoa and lavender.

The incident in the alley solidified his suspicions that Lucy had been hit, and often. But now that he knew, he had no idea what he was supposed to do next. In the movies, the hero always hunted down the abuser and subjected them to some radical torture scene that brought in gazillions of box office dollars and the promise of multiple sequels.

But that wasn't how it worked in real life.

When Lucy had flinched from him, his pulse had begun galloping like a spooked racehorse. Instinct didn't spur him to fight. It made him want to take Lucy home where they could lock the door and hide away, and no one would ever, *ever* cause that look on Lucy's face again.

Lucy came into the music room with a sheepish smile. Jack snapped his notebook shut as if the crinkled lined paper would betray his thoughts. "You look suspicious," he said, securing his guitar in its case.

"I, uh, thought I should wear this today." She tugged on her shirt hem, displaying a silhouetted guitarist and stylized logo. Jack's face split into a self-satisfied grin.

"Why, Miss Meyer," he drawled. "Is that a Jack Hunter shirt?"

"I didn't have a Laser Wolves shirt, so I had to go with this old thing."

He rolled his eyes and hurled a pillow at her. She caught it and set it back on the couch at a perfectly measured angle.

"Come here." He rifled through his desk drawer and pulled out a marker, hiding it behind his back. "Close your eyes."

She grimaced but shut her eyes as he moved behind her. He said, "I'm going to touch your hair," because he didn't want to startle her and get whacked in the nose again. He swept her long braid back, exposing the delicate skin of her neck. He autographed the shirt with huge, swooping letters—yet another signature binding his life to hers.

She stiffened. "Did you really just sign my shirt?"

"Maybe."

"That's creepy."

"I'm well aware of your feelings on autographs." He capped the pen, and she whirled around. "Most people love my autographs. And I've signed a lot of things." He waggled his eyebrows.

"Like?"

"Photos. Guitars. Cars. Breasts."

She peered downward at her own chest, then back to Jack with a frown. "But then how do they remove it?"

"I'm...sorry?"

"They'd probably have to use something caustic, I'm sure. Rubbing alcohol, maybe. Coconut oil might work, too." Her nose wrinkled, and she rubbed at her skin.

"Maybe they want it to stay on. We could experiment if you're really wondering." He uncapped the pen and winked at her, wielding it like a sword. She hopped out of the marker's radius and tipped her head toward the notebook.

"What were you working on?"

"The usual," Jack said, flopping back down on the sofa. "Trying to unstick my stuck brain."

"Well, maybe you need to talk it out." She sat down next to him. "What do your songs feel like?"

"Feel like?" he simpered. *They feel like failure.*

"Yeah, you know." She rotated her hand in the air, grasping for a description. "The emotional response they evoke. Or physical." She tapped her nails to her teeth before snapping her fingers. "Like 'Juke Box Hero.'"

"The Foreigner song?"

"Yes." She nodded, as if affirming an internal argument. "First, you've got that intro beat. *BR-ahw, buh-boom buh-boom, buh-boom.*"

"*Br-ahw?* That's a word?"

"In this case, yes. That single beat makes you feel like you're all alone, but in a good way. You feel like you're in the rain like the narrator in the beginning. You feel the excitement and anticipation. And then *Hwah-CHA!*" She waved her arm like a manic conductor. "You get zapped by lightning, just like the singer, all based on the way it feels. It feels like newness. It feels like possibility."

"Got it," Jack nudged her playfully. "'Juke Box Hero' feels like *Br-ahw.* Or *Hwah-cha.* And whatever other words you have in your sound effect language there."

Her nostrils flared, and she retrieved her phone, scrolling until her eyes lit up. She lifted the phone to show Jack the album art.

"Neil Diamond?" Jack blinked. The soft rock artist wasn't exactly Jack's style.

"Yes."

"Neil," he clarified.

"Yes."

"Of the Diamond family."

"Yes." She sighed like an exasperated school teacher. "'Forever in Blue Jeans' is a perfect example of 'feeling' a song. First, you've got a simple picked melody and a rhythmic bass drum beat. It's clean, fresh; it sounds like summer. He starts with the chorus to get you hooked. The lyrics aren't deep, and they don't need to be. He uses easy rhymes like 'money' and 'honey,' and 'walk' and 'talk,' but hooks you in with that bass beat, and you just want more. Like engaging in musical foreplay."

Jack's spine went rigid, and his belly fluttered. "Neil Diamond is foreplay?"

"No. Yes. Sort of. Hush." She shook her head and raced onward. "So you're hooked by this simple chorus, simple beat, and it just feels so promising and exciting. And then he does those quick synth chords like he's leading up to something so good—*bum bum bum bum bum bum bum.*" She tapped it out on the side of her thigh. "And you're just vibrating with the need to hear that chorus again, and do you know what he does?"

"No, Lucy," he said in a deadpan tone. "Tell me what Neil Diamond does next."

"It's all a tease!" She flapped her hands in a tempestuous flourish. "He goes off into this bridge about a fireplace! But that beat keeps going underneath, and it finally emerges into those damned piano and guitar chords again and finally, *finally*, we get our chorus again, even louder than before, and it's just this release that makes you feel powerful and fulfilled. Do you get what I'm saying?"

Jack paused. "You're saying that Neil Diamond is really good at sex."

"Lord, give me strength." She inhaled, her eyes raised skyward. "Here. Just listen."

She started the song on her phone. A guitar intro saturated the room, low and simple. She shut her eyes, and her fingers plucked along near the slight curve of her belly. She reached for Jack's hand, pausing as if asking for permission.

"Isn't this the song from that Gap commercial?" Jack asked. Lucy groaned and snatched up his hand, pulling him to a standing position along with her. She set her palm over his before restarting her invisible guitar concert, with his hand along for the ride.

The rational part of Jack's brain was screaming *danger!* but since he generally didn't listen to that part, he shoved the thoughts away. He wrapped his other arm around Lucy as she swayed with the light drum beat, but she went rigid as she backed into his chest. With a flare of disappointment, he began to tug his arm from her, but her beloved synth chords—*bum bum bum bum bum bum*—echoed through the small room, and her body relaxed. Instead of fleeing, she tiptoed backward to nestle in the hollow of his arms. His chest tightened as if open to the frigid November winds outside, and he found himself coming to terms with the fact that he was half-aroused because of *Neil fucking Diamond*.

Starving nerve endings tamped down any further logical thoughts, and Jack rested his hands at her ribcage, his thumb sweeping in figure eights to the crescent curve of her waist.

She inhaled sharply, but the tremor in her voice proved she wasn't immune to his touch. "Focus, Jack. Close your eyes if you need to."

The chorus returned, rich and pure. Lucy murmured the words to herself, and her face cracked into a mischievous grin. She guided his hands in a strange sort of movement, like playing air guitar and acting as the bandleader all at once. It wasn't true dancing. It was a messy mix of shoulder shimmies and impish hip sways and air guitar struts, all while punctuating notes with hand waves and gesticulations.

The music tunneled and reverberated from Jack's fingers to his toes. It surged and encompassed them in the zero-gravity eye of a tornado of magic and solace, if only for the span of a song. It rose in volume and intensity, and Lucy's face flushed with almost holy devotion, and Jack was pretty sure he would die if he didn't kiss her soon.

And then it ended. Neil was silent, having said his piece and left Jack torn and very confused. He dropped his hand from Lucy's waist but laid his head on her shoulder, attempting to recover his breath and a bit of his sanity.

"You okay?" she whispered.

"Yeah, sure." *Not remotely.*

"I get it," she said. "Neil Diamond."

"Sure." Jack nodded against her neck. "Neil fucking Diamond." He stepped away to pack his supplies, wondering how three minutes of seventies folk-rock had flipped him entirely inside out.

"Are you ready for today?" she asked, her words level and cautious.

"I think so. It's only a half-hour set. Two of my songs, three of theirs."

"Are you sure—" she stopped, worrying her lip. "Are you sure you don't want me to stay backstage and wait for you?"

"Definitely not," Jack said. "This is your first real concert experience. Go out and enjoy it."

There was a lengthy pause. "All right. Just for your set, though."

"Fine with me. Gets me out of there faster. I'll see you there." Jack shouldered his guitar and hurried out of the house, ready to lose himself onstage and forget everything he had just finally realized.

He was falling hard for his fiancée.

The arena was too loud.

In the lobby, free of wailing guitars and screaming fans, the concertgoers hummed and buzzed like a wasp's nest. Big Apple Harvest Festival banners hung everywhere, garish orange and brown monstrosities covered in painted leaves and vomiting cornucopias. The Big Apple Harvest food bank had donation stands set up throughout the lobby, ready to reel in donors between sets. Lucy found a covert corner behind a booth and hugged her back to the wall, boxes of canned goods at her feet. There, she could at least breathe without being jostled by another person.

She should have told Jack the truth, but she hadn't wanted to pile anything else on him after the previous night. But there she was, cowering behind a charity booth and trying not to panic.

The arena doors swung open, and a handful of attendees swarmed out, using the intermissions between sets to snag merchandise, gorge on overpriced snacks, and stand in mile-long bathroom lines. Lucy waited until a doorway cleared enough to enter without bumping shoulders with too many people. She showed her pass to an usher, who guided her to her seat, for which Lucy was extremely grateful.

On stage, stagehands in dusty black clothes switched out instruments and adjusted microphones for Jack and the Laser Wolves. Her seat was close enough that she could glance into the wings if she stretched forward, but Jack wasn't in sight. Would he be able to see her once he was on stage, or would the bright lighting make it too difficult?

A low rumble of applause turned into a freight train of screams and cheers. Lucy's skin ached, nearly feverish, but she stood with the rest of the audience as Jack and the band stormed the stage. He pumped his fists high in the air, and the crowd whooped and hollered. She clapped for him with shaking hands, but her throat was too tight to call out.

He raised his hand to shade his eyes, scanning the audience. His eyes lit up, and his mouth widened into an unbridled grin as he pointed at Lucy, wriggling his fingers in the shape of rabbit ears. It was a surreptitious motion, unnoticed by anyone else, but the gesture warmed her, numbing her for the briefest moment against the tidal wave of sensations barreling at her.

She was his friend.

She was his fiancée.

She was his Cottontail.

She could do this.

He slid the embroidered guitar strap over his neck, beckoning for the crowd to quiet down. He glanced around to the rest of the Laser Wolves, nodding to each before addressing the crowd.

"Hello, New York!" he yelled, milking the audience's reaction. "I know you were expecting Patrick, but you'll have to put up with me instead."

There were a few errant cheers, but one man heckled, "Go set a hotel bed on fire!" as if it were the cleverest thing he could come up with.

Jack's consequent expression oozed arrogant charm. "Let's get two things straight," he said, his face crinkling in a lewd grin. "I was drunk. And there were bedbugs. Now," he punctuated with a riff on the guitar, "who's ready to slow things down?"

Laser Wolves's guitarist struck an opening chord, and the arena was flooded with the raucous tones of Jack's first hit, "Slow Down."

Lucy closed her eyes and grasped at the familiar notes for comfort, but panic coiled itself around her ribcage, squeezing like a boa constrictor. She took deep breaths through her nose but couldn't exhale without gasping. The harder she tried, the shallower her breathing became.

Her teeth rattled from the sound system's vibrations, and her knuckles strained and cracked against her tight fists. The lights swirled and stirred like an overflowed cauldron. All around her, people touched and crowded and squeezed her in their nightmare dance.

Lights music loud crowd noise lights music pushing squeezing loud crowd lights screeching screaming stop stop stop

Bang.

A stage light popped, the bulb shattering with a sound like an errant firework. The overall lighting effect is unchanged, and Jack even worked the incident into his performance, laughing and gesturing while he strummed out the refrain.

But there in the audience, Lucy tipped over into an abyss.

Tremors shook her from head to toe. Her chest rose and fell like bellows in a fireplace, but she couldn't catch enough air.

She was present, and she was not present.

She was inside of her head and outside of her body.

She had to get out. She had to leave.

The song ended with a surge of applause like the roar of a stormy ocean. Jack peered out into the crowd, and their eyes locked. He froze, still as a statue in front of an audience of hundreds.

Lucy shook her head adamantly, mouthing, "I'm fine." His head tilted, but his body was still suspended in place.

The drummer began a count-off to the next song. Jack shook his head as if dazed and spun to face him, making a stretching gesture. He jogged to the wings, disappearing off stage. Lucy bit down on her fist to stop a low whine, unable to impart to Jack that she would be fine, that this night wasn't about her.

Jack strutted back on stage with a lazy smile and picked up his guitar, hitting the first chord with a crush of electric notes. He didn't look back at Lucy.

Coppery blood hit her tongue as her teeth cut into her finger. A warm, gentle hand pressed between her shoulder blades.

"Come on, Lucy," Parker said, his voice soft as he leaned into her ear. "Let's go."

Parker escorted her out of the arena and down a back hallway to Jack's dressing room. He led her to a well-worn couch and then shut off the sound monitor to the stage.

"I'll be fine," she said, teeth chattering. "You can go back to Jack."

"I can stay with you; it's not a problem." His eyes were filled with concern, but it wasn't pitying or pretentious. It was the austere countenance of one person wanting to comfort another, and Lucy hated that she couldn't accept that comfort in the way that everyone else could.

"It's just a panic attack," she said, wiping at her tearless face over and over. "A meltdown. It'll stop if I'm alone. I'm sorry. It's not you, I swear."

Parker gave her a heavy, assessing gaze, then nodded. "The set is almost over. We'll be back soon."

As soon as he was gone, Lucy laid down on the couch, squishing herself tight against the back and arms, like a baby opossum against its mother. The pilled upholstery, the tension of her body against the cushions, and the dressing room's beautiful silence brought her back down to earth.

The tremors became shivers.

The shivers became nothing.

Footsteps echoed in the hall, and Lucy flipped the sound monitor back on. She heard the sounds of an audience shuffling around. Jack's set was done.

She peered into the hallway, where Parker was making his way back.

"You okay now?" he asked, blocking her from the roadies lumbering down the hall, arms full of electrical equipment.

"Yes." She found a fishhook-shaped nick on the wall and traced the curve of it with her fingers.

Parker's eyes narrowed, and he led her back to the sofa. "Want some tea?"

"You don't have to do that."

"I'm your assistant. Let me assist." He filled a mug with an herbal tea bag and steaming water from a thermos. Stealing a water bottle for himself, he pulled up a folding chair next to her on the sofa.

"Jack will be along soon. He had to do a soundbite backstage for the charity." Parker wrinkled his forehead. "Really, are you okay?"

She wanted to lie, to tell him that everything was terrific, that it was a one-time fluke and she couldn't wait to see the next concert.

But she was so very, very tired, so all she said was, "I don't like crowds."

He took a swig of water, wiping his mouth. Instead of offering mundane advice or the usual platitudes, he said, "Does Jack know?"

She shook her head. "Not fully. I'm sure we'll hash that out tonight."

"Don't worry. The guy is crazy about you."

She managed a chuckle but didn't respond, too exhausted to analyze the tangled web of her relationship—fake or otherwise—with Jack.

The door swung open, slamming into the wall, the brass doorknob thudding like a broken cymbal. Jack glowered in the doorway, his eyes erratic and wild.

Parker rose from his folding chair, nearly knocking it over in his haste. "Hey, Jack." He glanced at Jack's animalistic expression, then back at Lucy with an *I told you so* look. "Aaaaaaaand I'll see you two later."

He tiptoed out of the room, and Jack smacked the door shut behind him with the flat of his hand. He stared at Lucy, his chest heaving and his forehead slicked with sweat like a prize marathon runner. His hands were balled at his sides, the knuckles white and taut.

She managed a strangled squeak, but no words came.

Jack said nothing, his eyes as stormy as a hurricane.

She swallowed. "Jack. I'm sorry."

A distressed growl rumbled in his chest. He stepped forward, stiff as a rusty tin soldier. "Don't apologize."

"I know, but—"

"I said, don't apologize." His voice quivered. Another halting step forward, then he knelt on the floor in front of her, as if in prayer. He didn't touch her.

"Did someone hurt you?" he asked, rocking back on his heels. "Did someone touch you?"

Her mouth fell open. "Oh, no, not that. Nothing like that." She tucked an escaped curl behind his ear.

He pushed her away gently, his brows slanted in angry slashes. "Tell me who it was. They might still be out there. I'll find them. There are cameras everywhere. Just tell me."

"Jack, please calm down." She lifted a hand when he pulled back, affronted. "Nobody touched me. I had a panic attack, nothing more."

Jack's expression was a stunned slurry of wrath and confusion, and he rose to his feet again. "You what?"

"I, uh, have sensory issues. Crowds. Loud noises. Lights. Dirty hands, as you already know. It causes panic attacks. Meltdowns."

"And I made you go to a concert." He flopped down on the couch next to her, his head thrown back against the cushions. "Fuck."

"You didn't make me do anything."

He gave her a frustrated look. "You okay now?"

"I'm okay now. See?" She feigned the cheesiest grin she could, but he just muttered under his breath, digging the heels of his hands into his eye sockets.

"What else?" he asked, rubbing his hand over his face, causing his eyebrow hair to stick up a little.

"I don't understand."

"What else do I need to know to keep this from happening again?"

"You don't need to keep anything from happening," Lucy said, slightly alarmed. "I can handle it myself."

"Lucy." He sent her an exhausted look. "I know you can handle things by yourself. I've known that since you tried to move in with a rat rather than live with me."

"He was a cute rat," she whispered.

"We'll discuss your rodent bias at another time," Jack said. "Now tell me. How can I help?"

"Well—" She stopped. The words were there, but to admit them was a struggle. She'd been punished so many times for these traits, she wasn't sure how to vocalize them anymore.

"I don't like crowds." *Four words to start.* She could do this.

"All crowds?"

She tipped her head. "Actually, no. Just chaotic crowds. Where I'll get touched. But something organized like the park, or a movie theater, that's okay."

"So no concerts." He held up a finger, counting. "What else?"

"Lots of lights and sounds. It's too much."

"Got it. No raves in the back of a police car." He raised a second finger. "What else?"

"I talk too much."

Jack dropped his hand and looked at her, astounded. "I can barely get you to talk half the time."

"Well, like with music, I have to be careful because I'll go on and on, like a broken record. I can't always tell when I'm talking too much or at the wrong time."

His hand slid next to hers, just enough that their pinkies touched. He brushed his back and forth, a rhythmic, soothing cadence. "What else?"

She looked down at their fingers. "I usually don't like being touched."

He froze, and she skimmed her own pinky against his. "I said 'usually.' I—I don't mind so much when it's you. I don't know why."

She did know why. She suspected it had something to do with the new skittering rhythm of her heartbeat.

There was a long, empty silence, with only the tinny speaker of the stage monitor for noise. Then, his hand lifted from hers and skimmed across her back, pausing to caress between her shoulder blades. Every movement was part of a meticulously plotted course that ended with his arm around her.

She sighed, a bare whisper of a noise, and her head sunk into the niche between his neck and shoulder.

"What else?" He rested his cheek on the top of her head with perfect, calming pressure.

"Well, I'm good at hiding it for the most part. I've practiced—a lot. But sometimes I slip. With you, even more so."

"So that's why you edit yourself, making sure you say the right or expected thing."

"Exactly."

He pulled back, tipping her head with calloused fingers until they met each other's gazes. "But not with me, right? Never with me, promise?"

She studied his brown irises, mahogany bleeding into rusty velveteen up against a black fringe of eyelashes. There was a moment of calming *brown black brown black brown*, and then clarity swept in. Lucy pried his fingers from her chin. "If you need to change the terms of our arrangement, I'll step down; I won't fight it."

"What are you talking about?" His nose crinkled.

"It doesn't look good if you have a wife who can't even attend your concerts."

"Oh, come on, Lucy."

She shrugged his arm off. "Your life is loud and bright and crowded. It's not for me. I should've told you from the beginning."

"Luciana." His voice lowered. "I don't need someone else."

"Don't be silly. I have all sorts of anxiety issues."

"And I'm double-jointed in my right elbow." He lifted his shoulders.

She blinked. "What?"

"Oh, sorry. I thought we were just saying random facts about ourselves."

She summoned her most serious of glares. "I have meltdowns in crowds."

He glared right back. "I'm really useful when the remote falls down behind the couch."

"I talk too much, or not at all. I say the wrong things. I'm awkward as fuck."

"And this isn't?" He folded his elbow back on itself like a disfigured paper clip, readjusting his arm back to normal when she choked in horror. "Look, I really don't care. It's part of what makes you Lucy, and that makes it good."

Her legs grew shaky, and she felt a little drunk.

That makes it good.

He continued. "I don't need anyone else. We work well together. We're partners."

"Partners." She nodded. "And still friends, right?"

An odd, pained look flickered across his tired face. "Yeah. Still friends."

Chapter 15

Jack sauntered through the door of Kim's favorite restaurant, ready to eat his weight in scrambled eggs and toast. He had barely eaten dinner the previous night, spending the time in his studio writing like a frantic college student with an overdue thesis paper. The result was a quarter of a composition notebook filled with ideas—some good, some bad, but at least they *existed*.

Kim sat at a secluded table in the back, sipping her standard black coffee, no cream, no sugar. Her braids were in a perfectly coiffed bun, her suit without a single wrinkle, and even if there had been, it would have smoothed itself at her stern look. She was usually an unflappable model of organization, but her eyes widened when Jack sank down into his chair.

"What's wrong with you?" she asked.

Jack patted himself down from head to ass, stopping only to swipe at his jaw to check for leftover shaving cream. All his clothes were in the right places, and his fly was closed.

"Nothing?"

"You're smiling. It's creepy." She reached across the table and pinched his chin, yanking his head back and forth as if he were a champion horse she wanted to buy.

"Knock it off. I'm fine."

"Hmmm." She leaned back in her chair. "I printed out the resumes for your new backing musicians. I assume you read the files when I sent them over last week?"

Jack peered around the restaurant for a distraction. "Oh, look! Isn't that Kristen Bell over there?"

"Nice try, Jack. Too bad you weren't at the auditions. You'd already be acquainted."

The day they held auditions earlier in the fall, searching for musicians that would work in both a studio and tour setting, Jack had spent the afternoon on his couch sampling a bottle of whiskey and two nameless blondes. Pre-Lucy, of course.

Kim fanned the resumes across the table. "Lainey Mills is your new lead guitarist. She's already played some prolific tours, and before that, she was a concert tech for two years." Jack read over her background but stopped when the waiter appeared.

"Mike," Jack said, checking his name tag. "I'm going to need a mountain of scrambled eggs. Not a spoonful, not a dollop, but a mountain. Is that something you can do for me?"

The waiter flashed a conspiratorial grin and dashed off to the kitchen. Kim stared at him, and her features fell with sheer disappointment.

"Jack..." She covered his hand with hers, patting it gently. "Are you doing coke again?"

He sputtered and dribbled hot coffee onto Lainey's resume. "What? No! Jesus. I'm fine, I swear." He mopped up the coffee drips with a cloth napkin and went on to the next resume.

"That's Maya Rodriguez," Kim said. "She really impressed me. She's young and doesn't have tons of experience, but she'll make a good utility player. Guitar, keyboards, bass, you name it, she knows it. Even trombone, which I'd like to see because she barely clears five feet. And this last one is

Hasan Desai. Percussion. Mostly a session musician, but he has a tour or two under his belt."

"All the contracts are signed?"

"Of course. They'll work well with you. As long as you work well with them." She tipped her head, a subtle warning. Jack tried to ignore her jab, but he really didn't have the best track record in the studio or on tour.

"I'll be good," he said, gratefully diverted as his plate of eggs arrived. As he scooped them into his mouth, Kim examined him like a newly-discovered mythical creature.

"What?" Jack said through a mouthful of eggs. "They're delicious. Try some. You can't subside on whole-wheat toast alone." He held out a forkful to her mouth, tapping her closed, thinned lips. "Here comes the airplane, Kim. Open up." She pushed the fork aside with as much dignity as she could muster while he made buzzing engine noises.

"Is it pills?" she asked. "Speed?"

"No." The airplane fork returned to its hangar for another bite of fluffy, eggy goodness. His phone chimed with a text and a picture from Lucy.

LUCY: The hell is this?

The picture was a crooked crop of a receipt she must have found in his "office"—a room where he threw important paperwork to die—for sixty pounds of exotic bird food. Jack chuckled and texted her back.

JACK: Ask Josh Groban.

When he lifted my eyes, Kim no longer looked disappointed. Instead, her eyes were lit with something like gleeful insanity.

"Holy shit." She let out a maniacal laughing noise that he'd never heard from her or most rational human beings. "It's her."

"Her what?" he asked, slathering a piece of toast with strawberry jam and licking the knife clean while Kim cackled.

"Holy shit." She clapped, her immaculate nails clicking together like crustacean claws. "Holy shit."

"I'm confused." *And worried for your mental health.*

She swung her head like an eager, wet puppy. "I haven't seen you this relaxed in years. It's Lucy, isn't it?"

Jack felt a flush of heat travel over his cheeks. "Don't be ridiculous. She's entertaining. That's all."

Another text pinged through, this time with a photo of a receipt for a crate of instant lemonade powder and a latex scuba suit.

LUCY: *Do I want to know about this?*

JACK: *What Groban wants, Groban gets.*

"Your cheeks are actually pink!" Kim's cackle wound up again, like a flawed science class model of the Doppler effect.

"Stop. It's all pretend." He took another sip of coffee and ignored the flipping sensation in his chest.

"Mmm-hmm." His distinguished, no-nonsense manager was actually bouncing in her chair.

"I don't know what you want me to say."

"I'd normally ask when the wedding is, but as I'm planning it, that won't work here." She tapped her lips thoughtfully. "How many children do you want?"

He cleared his throat. "Kimberly."

"Ooooh, maybe one grumpy, all scowls and shit, and one sunshine. Just like you two."

"If you think Lucy is all sunshine, you clearly don't know her well."

Although, she was her own brand of sunshine, wasn't she? Sometimes soft and beautiful, sometimes hiding behind her own cloud cover. Sometimes too bright just when you think you need to hide in the darkness, but once she draws you out, you realize it might be for the better.

"We're going to be late," he said, changing the subject.

"Do we need to go over how you need to act today?" she asked, flagging Mike, the waiter, for the check.

"I'm sober today, and that's half the battle usually."

"All you need to do is be patient and hold back your temper. No prostitutes, preferably."

"That was one time."

"One very expensive time." She raised an eyebrow.

"Fine. No alcohol, no tantrums, no sex workers." He held his hands out in his best mea culpa gesture. "And everything will go well, right?"

Everything did not go well.

Jack's reputation naturally preceded him, like a town crier in front of a naked emperor. Lainey, Hasan, and Maya were professional, but a cool wariness between the four of them made Jack second guess every one of his words and actions, and then every one of *their* words and actions. His scrambled egg-sponsored good mood dissolved within the first hour.

As they spent the morning fleshing out his songwriting scribbles, the tension ratcheted so tight that they sounded like a squeaky middle school band. The day was woven with missed notes, wrong entrances, and mistaken chords, and by afternoon, the atmosphere was a powder keg just waiting for a welcome spark.

Hasan, a dark-eyed man with muscled arms toned by years at the drums, descended from neutrally impartial to sullen as a schoolkid. For the gazillionth time, he played his drum solo too fast on "Ruby Road," and by the way his jaw jutted forward, Jack knew it was on purpose.

"For fuck's sake." He raised his voice to a hair's breadth below a yell. "I've told you three times to slow it down."

Hasan's eyes flared, and he attacked the drums with the ferocity of a Viking guard warning his village against pillagers.

"Dude, what's your problem?" Jack asked after he banged into the cymbals an absurd amount of times.

"Why do you have to be such a diva?" The drummer stood, squaring his shoulders. "This is our first day. Of course, it's going to suck."

"Maybe you need to spend more time practicing and less time showboating."

"I don't think I'm the one who needs practice." He crossed his arms smugly, having landed a perfect blow.

The voices of a dozen journalists hypothesizing *Has Jack Hunter lost his touch?* wormed their way into Jack's brain, and suddenly, he wasn't sure if he even knew how to hold a guitar correctly anymore.

Jack snarled and kicked a nearby folding chair with a ferocity born of humiliation and a third grader's temper. It startled Maya, who tripped backward and knocked over her amplifier. Banshee-like feedback squealed throughout the room, and she knelt on the floor, frantically resetting it.

A welcome but tense silence followed. Jack whipped his head back to Hasan, unsure if he would yell or apologize, but Hasan's angry expression had been replaced with puzzlement. He peered at the doorway to the room, and Jack whirled around, ready to unleash his frustrations on whoever had disturbed them.

Lucy stood there, her face ashen and her hands cupped over her ears.

"Take five, everyone," Jack said with a deflated tone. He took a careful step toward her, and she flicked her calf's eyes toward him.

"What are you doing here?" he asked.

"That was loud." She leered at the amplifier as if it had threatened her first-born child. Her hand twitched, fingers flexing at hummingbird speed.

"Yes. Maya fixed it. It's okay now."

She tore her gaze from the amplifier to Jack. "You were yelling." Her head tilted to the side, and she frowned.

Three words said so matter-of-factly, and yet Jack was overcome with shame. Anyone else would have tried to butter him up or downplay his behavior, all in the spirit of celebrity coddling. But Lucy, as always, was just stating the facts: Jack had been yelling.

"Yes," he said with an exasperated sigh. "I probably shouldn't have."

"No, you shouldn't have." She reached for her tote bag. "I brought cookies from Batter Up. Adrian says hi."

"You went to the diner?" He attempted a meek smile, hoping to win back a smidgeon of her favor.

"Yes. I brought some for everyone." She rummaged around and extracted a cellophane-wrapped cookie. "He said peanut butter is your favorite."

This was true. Peanut butter cookies were the world's equivalent to the nectar of the gods.

"Thanks," said Jack, already tearing into the cookie. She gave a curt nod, her narrow gaze darting around the room, cataloging and calculating. The others returned from their break and eyed Jack, waiting for his next dictatorial decree.

"They don't look happy," Lucy whispered.

"They aren't," he whispered back.

"Because of you?"

"Most likely, yes."

Jack called the others over. "This is my fiancée, Lucy."

She flashed a bright, hopeful smile.

Lainey whipped her head from Jack to Lucy and back again. "You're marrying *him*?" she blurted out.

Jack pinched the bridge of his nose and squeezed his eyes shut.

"I am." The corner of Lucy's eyes crinkled, and she leaned toward the others with a conspiratorial air. "He made you mad, didn't he? He does that."

Jack couldn't hold back an irritated groan, but Lainey surprised him by bursting into laughter. Hasan and Maya followed suit, and Lucy looked genuinely pleased.

"I brought cookies." She shook the tote bag. "Let's sit."

Jack sputtered in protest—they obviously needed more practice—but Hasan grabbed some folding chairs and set them in a semi-circle. Jack flopped down in a chair while Lucy passed out treats like a mall Easter Bunny. Somehow, she had usurped the entire rehearsal through the power of baked goods.

"I got you an extra one." Her eyes sparkled when she gave Jack his second cookie.

Jesus. This woman. Jack would have married her for her cookie management skills alone.

"How has today been?" Lucy asked the other musicians.

"It's been...good." Maya sent a wary sidelong glance Jack's way.

"I'm so glad to hear," Lucy nibbled at her own cookie, wrapped carefully in a napkin. "I'm sure it's been nerve-racking meeting new bandmates. Like going on a blind date." Her gaze slid to him. "I know Jack was so nervous this morning about meeting you guys."

Jack choked on his cookie. "I was what now?"

"Oh, really?" Hasan smirked. "That's very interesting."

"Oh, yes." Lucy's head bobbed as she retrieved another napkin. "You know how it is with celebrities. Everyone already has an opinion on you just by what's reported in the press, and you don't get a chance to defend yourself. It gets depressing sometimes."

Jack inhaled and counted to ten. And then to twenty, for good measure.

"Lucy, I—" He stopped, unsure of what to even say. *Stop making me sound...human?*

"It's crazy sometimes," she continued, ignoring him. "You should ask Jack about some of the stories that are out there. I'm not saying there aren't some that are true, but there are definitely some creative falsehoods out there." She picked at some crumbs on her lap, utterly indifferent toward the rest of the room.

There was a prolonged, uncomfortable pause. Then Lainey leaned back, her cream and ebony locs falling over the back of her chair. "The concert in Aruba. Is that all true?"

Jack winced and shifted in his chair. "Well, mostly. I've heard a few different versions, but yeah. Not my proudest moment."

"What about the drummer you punched?" Hasan asked, leaning forward, more relaxed than he'd seen him all day.

"True. He was sleeping with the guitarist." His brow wrinkled before Jack added, "And so was I. Also, he couldn't keep time worth shit."

"Oh. Well, fuck that." He looked satisfied as he stuffed the last of his cookie in his mouth.

"Um." Maya coughed, a flush creeping up her heart-shaped face. "The sweet potato?"

"The what?" Jack racked his brain, trying to remember any rumors about vegetables. Lucy leaned over and whispered in his ear.

"Oh, God! Not true, not true!" He barked out a humiliated laugh and covered his face. "I can never look at any of you ever again."

When he dropped his hands, his face still burning about his alleged abuse of root vegetables, the atmosphere had changed entirely. The other musicians started hammering him with questions, and Jack answered them all with humble modesty. There were the true legends—that summer in Japan, the Skype incident, the cruise ship debacle—and the fun but false ones—the rodeo, the harmonica, and the sword fight with the ambassador to Burundi.

Seething looks became snorting laughter, and snapped remarks became inside jokes. When they moved from the past to the present, they threw ideas back and forth on musical arrangements, giving genuine, honest criticism. And when they all packed up to go home, they weren't best friends forever yet, but there was the beginning of a new camaraderie.

As they collected their gear, Hasan sent Jack a questioning glance. "We're good?"

"We're good." Jack held out his hand, a peace offering, and Hasan shook it with a few enthusiastic pumps before calling out, "Nice meeting you, Lucy!"

"Oh, fuck me! Lucy!" Jack had completely forgotten she was there. He turned to where she was perched cross-legged in a chair, a book in her lap.

"Probably not the best use of this room," she said, closing her book with a snap and brushing her unruly hair behind her ears.

"No, I mean—not fuck me, but you know, fuck me!" *Why was he stammering?*

Her rosy lips tipped up in a bewitching grin. "I get it, Jack."

"You could have gone home. Sorry, I should've offered to call a car."

She lifted a shoulder. "I liked listening."

Somewhere between telling her to fuck-him-but-not-fuck-him and that, Jack had made his way in front of her chair. "I don't know if Adrian put something in the cookies, or if you're just magic, but that was the best time I've had in a recording studio in years." He lifted her chin and rubbed his thumb against her velvety cheek. "Thanks, Cottontail."

"Not my name." Her eyes sparkled with amusement, and Jack became dizzy, like a syringe of pride and something entirely unfamiliar had been shot into his veins.

"Do you really not like the nickname?" he asked.

"I didn't at first. I thought it was just you being crazy." The corners of her eyes softened, and her hand slid into his, warm and snug. "But now it's mine."

His voice roughened. "Always."

"Kinda like 'Mad Jack.' To heck with the stupid press. It belongs to you now."

Jack's eyes went wide. He stumbled back, dropping her hand and clapping both of his to his skull with a resounding gasp. "Cottontail, you genius, you!" He lunged forward and pressed an enthusiastic, smacking kiss to her forehead.

She furrowed her brow in bewilderment. "What did I do?"

"Everything," he said, taking her hand again and near-sprinting to the car waiting for them in the street outside. He had to go home and get to work. After all, shenanigans didn't plan themselves.

Chapter 16

Too dark too dark too dark too dark

Lucy thrust her hands out, reaching for some semblance of freedom, even though she knew that she'd only find the damp, tiled walls of the bathroom. She yanked at the doorknob, the cold brass stinging the half-moon cuts on her palms where her nails had bitten into the flesh. The door wiggled enough to give her hope of escape, but despite pulling it with all of her body weight, it held firm.

Blood blood blood blood blood

Her temple had been bleeding, but it was now at the tacky, gluey phase. Blood had congealed in her eyebrow, hardening it so that when she blinked, the skin resisted. She needed to wash it away, to hide it, but it was too dark to find a washcloth, and even if she did, she couldn't get blood on their best towels. He'd find them. He always found them. Fumbling around, she found the faucet and splashed water on her face, rubbing at the split skin.

Footsteps footsteps footsteps footsteps

He shouldn't have returned so soon. Lucy curled into a ball, rocking and rocking, her hands cupped around her ears, blocking all noise, all sounds. Now, she wished the door was stuck firm, but it wouldn't be for long.

He opened the door again, yanking her into the harsh, bitter light with a clawed hand tight around her wrist.

She tried to fight. She kicked and shrieked, but no one heard her. Not there.

Please please please I'll be good so good

She wrenched her wrist free, beating at his chest. Her palms left bloody prints on his best shirt, and each time she pounded and hit his chest, it echoed louder and louder until her ears buzzed like a broken radio.

He caught her fist before she could hit him again, dragging her across the carpet, and she went limp as a rag doll to prevent further injury. His hands were reaching, pulling, tugging, twisting, but then—

A crash. Distant, and yet not.

Stop stop stop stop stop

"Lucy!"

A silhouette hovered over her, and she shrieked. Her arms were mercifully free again, and she launched them forward, slapping, hitting, scratching until someone grabbed her wrists, lifting them above her head. The taste of warm copper stung her mouth, and she twisted against his manacle-like grip.

Still holding her thrashing hands away from his body, he flipped her arms around in a pretzel-like hold as if she were hugging herself, but with his solid chest rising and falling against her back.

"Lucy, wake up. Now." It was a demand, an order, a plea. "You're going to hurt yourself."

Stiffening, Lucy blinked her eyes open, hesitating. It was still so dark, darker than when she had gone to bed.

What happened to the light?

"Stop it." The command was low and soft against her ear, but she couldn't obey. She needed to find the light.

Lucy ripped her left hand free, stretching toward the lamp, but the light didn't turn on. As she clicked the switch back and forth, a keening wail rose in the room, and it took a moment before she recognized it as her own.

The arms around her loosened so hastily that she nearly lost her balance. Rapid footsteps filled the room just before a pane of light shone in from the adjoining bathroom—and then it was over. The light acted as an instant relaxant, a shot of reality, and she fell back onto her tear-dampened pillow.

She was safe.

She was in her bedroom.

And so was Jack.

Their eyes locked, both panting from the dream-induced battle. He wasn't wearing a shirt, and in the dim light, red streaks across his chest from her nails stood out, raw and painful.

"You don't like the dark."

She hung her head, full of shame. He disappeared into the bathroom and returned with a wet washcloth. His steps were deliberate and unhurried, as if he were approaching an unbroken horse, and her humiliation rocketed from shame to self-loathing.

When he wiped at the blood on her lip, where she'd bitten it while struggling, she squeezed her eyes against stubborn tears, and her muscles slumped in surrender.

"There you are." His earlier commanding tone melted away as he brushed sweat-sticky hair from her temple. "There's my Cottontail. There's my Luciana. Your bulb burned out, honey. That's all, just a burned-out bulb. We'll get you a new one tomorrow." There was a weighted, awkward pause. "And a new door."

The last vestiges of sleep vanished as she glanced at her entryway. The door frame was splintered on one side, and the lock hung loosely from its screws.

"Oh," she said. "That door sticks."

"You don't say." His fingers reached for hers in the dark, a brush of warm skin against her shivering hand. "You were screaming."

"Oh?"

"I thought you were in trouble." He tapped her forehead gently. "You were, weren't you."

She nodded, burrowing her cheek into the pillow.

"Well, then." He tugged at his bottom lip, then crawled across the bed, laying down next to her, flat on his back. Only their fingers were touching, yet his body so near to hers felt like an embrace.

"I'm okay now," Lucy said. "There's a light. You don't have to stay."

"We're friends," he said through a leonine yawn. "Call it a slumber party."

She had no time to protest before he hauled her heavy duvet up around both of them and snuggled himself into its flannel folds.

"Fuck, this is fantastic." He buried his face into the duvet like a sleepy kitten. "Pick me up one of these, will ya?"

"I'll add it to the to-do list." He was right—they were friends, they were adults, and this wasn't the first time they'd shared a bed. If he felt like he was helping her by staying, she wouldn't deny him that. And if she took extra comfort because he was the person she wanted most in the world just then, she wouldn't deny herself that either.

She closed her eyes in hopes that her adrenaline-spiked body would stand down from its battle response. Jack slid his thumb over her knuckles, over and over, until the rhythm nearly lulled her back to sleep.

"Lucy?" His voice was weary, and rough as gravel.

"Yeah?"

"What was it?"

She froze, eyes snapping open. "It's late. And we have a busy day tomorrow. We have to catch a flight, and you have to fix a door."

"Well." A pause. "I'll call someone to fix a door. I don't know how to fix a door."

"They didn't cover that in Rock Star 101?"

She could practically feel his dramatic eye roll. He lifted a hand as if to poke her in teasing retaliation, then halted. His fingers hovered above her for a moment, tense with indecision, before he lowered them and curved them around the flat plane of her belly. They lay like that for a moment, spooning with distance, with only the whisper of an occasional car outside as background.

"He hit you," Jack said slowly. The words hung above them like thunderclouds, dark and brooding. Words that had never been spoken aloud.

"Yes," she said, and even now, even though she knew better, she was compelled to add, "Only sometimes."

"Sometimes, all the time, it makes no difference." The hand around her waist tightened.

"Brock liked things a certain way." Her lips curved with dark humor. "I am not that certain way."

"What did he do?" asked Jack, and his breath caught in anticipatory apprehension.

I told you to stop that tapping, but you never fucking listen, do you?
This is all your fault.
You're a freak. No one will ever love you the way I do.

She bit the side of her cheek until pain supplanted the voice in her head. "Does it matter?"

He exhaled. "No," he said, sounding surprised at his own answer. "Only that he won't be doing it anymore." The words were final and substantial and believable, so believable that Lucy felt relief in every bone in her body. The hand splayed across her waist tugged her closer, the curve of her back fitting perfectly against his chest.

"Are you nervous about tomorrow?" she asked, her voice unsteady. A disgruntled hum vibrated near her ear. "You'll be fine, you know. My family isn't a pack of serial killers or anything."

"I've never met a girl's parents before," he mused. "I barely dated in high school, and by eighteen, I was on tour, so it wasn't going to happen then. I'm not sure I know what I'm supposed to do."

"Well, you play guitar, so you can bond with my dad over that." She pinched the skin on his wrist. "My mom will say you're too skinny and try to feed you, but she does that to eighty percent of the people she meets. Dante and I are her beanpole kids—skinny and tall—and it makes her crazy."

"Is she at least a good cook, or am I going to have to fake enjoyment as she force-feeds me?"

Lucy smiled at the thought of the plates and plates of food that would fill the table the following day, the scent of basil and garlic hovering over the room in a savory fog. "She's amazing. It's not a stereotypical Italian mom thing, either. I sometimes wonder if she hadn't had so many of us if she would have gone into the food industry."

He hummed again. "Am I supposed to bring her flowers or chocolates or three goats and a mule or something like that?"

"Well, actually," Lucy bit her lip. "About that. I mean, you could, but it's already going to be a lot. Handing her a bunch of daisies might add fuel to the fire."

"A lot?"

"Yeah, I uh, haven't told them you're coming."

His hand stiffened. "Um—what?"

She sighed and flipped over so that they were face to face, and immediately wished she hadn't. Spooning had been comforting, a cuddle puddle of warmth, a reminder that neither of them was alone. Now, they were chest to chest, nose to nose, Jack's hand now cupping her hip instead of her waist. She could count every one of his sable lashes, follow the slope of the indent above his mouth, study his stubble as it faded into smooth skin and hard cheekbones.

"They don't know you're coming," she said, distracted by the way his nose crooked slightly to the left. She liked it.

"You're telling me that I'm showing up to turkey dinner uninvited?"

"Well, actually, it's spaghetti, not a turkey," she said. Jack's mouth opened as if to protest, and she tucked a finger under his chin, closing it again. "That's a completely different discussion. And, secondly, we're a huge family—unexpected guests show up all the time. Ari's best friend and his husband have crashed every major holiday at least once. We'll just pull up another seat."

"The issue isn't whether there's a place for me to sit," he said. "The issue is that your half-insane rock star fiancé is showing up without warning."

"Well, actually—" she began, but he cupped her chin between his fingers with a firm look.

"I'm beginning to think that 'well, actually' is a dangerous phrase coming from your mouth," he said, brushing his thumb against her bottom lip. "But go on."

"Well—" She paused. "*Incidentally*, they don't really know about you. At all."

He blinked at her. "Luciana."

"I mean, I told you I wanted you to meet them before we went live with everything—"

"—I thought that meant I just had to *meet* them, not that I'd be jumping into their lives cold turkey!"

"Well, actually—" She swallowed a laugh when he groaned. "I believe in this case it would be cold spaghetti, not cold turkey."

"Oh, Jesus," he said with an exasperated huff. "Do they even know you're in New York?"

Her smile drooped a little. "Yes, but they don't know why."

"I'm not sure I know why either."

The words jumbled in her mouth, a traffic jam of panicked verbs and nouns. She dipped her head from his gaze to a scar across his collarbone, intersecting with the red scratches she had inadvertently inflicted. She closed her eyes and traced the raised ridge with her index finger, back and forth.

"Bike accident when I was thirteen," he murmured. "They had to reset the bone."

She exhaled. "I told you Brock didn't like me seeing my family," she said, still running the tip of her finger over his scar. "When Gianna was born, I wanted to go see her, but he was in the middle of a case —he's a lawyer—and he didn't want me to go by myself. But I went, I met my niece for the first time, and I went back home to him. Unsurprisingly, he was not happy."

Jack's head tipped forward, just enough that their foreheads met.

"The next day, I packed a bag and picked the first flight I could get on out of Indy."

Jack's eyes glittered, dark as obsidian in the faint light. "And then?"

She shrugged as best as she could manage in their position. "I stayed in the rental. Let the bruises heal. Made a plan." Her eyes darted to his. "And then I punched a guy in a record store."

Jack lifted his chin up just enough to brush a light kiss on her forehead and mumble something into her skin.

"What was that?" she breathed.

"I said, a *completely* innocent guy in a record store."

"Oh, yes." She smiled drowsily. "So innocent. An angel, really." She rubbed her cheek against the crisp cotton pillowcase. "So my family knows that I broke up with Brock, I'm working on a contract in New York, and I live somewhere with a roommate. It's all technically true."

"Technically," he whispered, but Lucy scarcely heard. Half of her mind wanted to drift away to sleep, feeling steady and safe and secure for the first time in years, and the other half wanted to sit there and analyze exactly why that was. But as Jack drew her closer, tucking her head under his chin, that formerly unattainable sense of shelter took her by the hand and shepherded her into the land of dreams—quiet, quiet dreams.

Chapter 17

Sparrow Hill, Indiana, was a lie. Jack did not see one single hill. He was not greeted by sparrows. Someone might call it a one-horse town, or in modern terms, a one-traffic-light town. Even that wasn't technically correct because it was really just a blinking four-way stop, the unpaid intern of traffic lights.

As they drove through the town in their airport rental car, Lucy rambled out trivia, pointing out her elementary school, the only pizzeria, and a grocery store that could fit inside his house. She glowed with pride when she mentioned that they had not one but two gas stations, as if that elevated the prestige of the entire village. They were in and out of the town in less than five minutes in their whirlwind tribute tour to rurality.

If New York City could be considered all verticals with its skyscrapers, then out in the heartlands, the world was one big horizon. There was nothing but farmland and telephone poles for miles in all directions, with an occasional farmhouse popping up out of the ground like a curious prairie dog. Jack's head spun, dizzy from the sheer openness of it all, as if someone had suddenly switched his internal settings from fullscreen to widescreen.

Lucy turned the car into a gravel driveway, parking in front of a farmhouse straight out of a Grant Wood painting. He recognized bits and pieces from her photos—the sail gray barn, the yard as vast and expansive as the rest of the land, and bare, skeletal fields as far as he could see. Trees across the property were shedding the last of their autumn colors, giving the entire property a sleepy sense of hibernation, paused for the cold season.

"Any last advice?" he asked, lifting their suitcases from the trunk, his palms clammy around the plastic handles.

She paused on the rickety wraparound porch, her head tilted in thought. "Hold onto your butt," she said and ducked inside.

The first thing Jack noticed about Lucy's childhood home was the smell. It smelled like burning firewood, fresh-baked bread, and pasta sauce, but above all, it smelled like *home*. Not like his cold Brooklyn townhouse or the garish Manhattan penthouse he'd grown up in, and certainly not like any of the stock hotel rooms he drifted in and out of on tour, but this ethereal, primitive idea of the sense of home, the sense of belonging.

They shucked their shoes and coats in the mudroom—a feature Jack didn't think even existed in the city—and added them to coat hooks already weighed down with several layers of down jackets. They headed down a hallway lined with braided rugs that opened into a dining room.

As they stepped inside the chaos, the cackling laughter, raucous conversation, and even the clinking of plates and silverware came to an abrupt stop. Nine heads swiveled their way. Jack felt like the villain in a Wild West movie, strutting into a saloon and startling all the patrons from their respective poker games.

There was a moment where Jack wondered who would recognize him first and what the proper way to react might be. Acknowledge and change the subject? Sign autographs and then stuff his face to avoid additional attention?

"Oh my God," one woman said, breaking the silence with sharpened shock. "Lucy brought home a guy."

Lucy's cheeks bloomed with rosy color, and she cleared her throat. "This is Jack," she said. There was no descriptive noun, no *fiancé/boyfriend/friend/roommate*. "He came home with me."

"We can see that," said another woman.

Another silence descended, one built on confusion and curiosity and innate protectiveness. Lucy shifted on her feet.

"Well, come on in," said a middle-aged man from his seat at the head of the table, and the tension shattered into the mayhem of friendly voices and creaking chairs and footsteps on an old wooden floor. Jack was flooded with *hello* and *nice to meet you* and *oh, I like your hair* and was half-panicked trying to remember everyone's names. Halfway through the introductions, he just gave up and started assigning nicknames in his head. Lucy would have to give him a cheat sheet later.

Jack was passed between them, a human baton in a relay race, but as he was handed off to the last person, a hush fell over the room. A woman entered from the kitchen, a wooden spoon clutched in her hand like a nun's disciplinary ruler. Jack felt like he was being cornered by the school principal, or perhaps General Patton.

She crossed her arms and peered at him through half-moon glasses. "Who are you?" she asked. Any sense of bravado melted away, and Jack stared at her, liquid apprehension flitting through his veins.

"I'm Jack," he said, because he was. Just Jack.

"Hmmm," she said, eyeing him from head to toe with an arched eyebrow.

"Jack," Lucy said, coming from behind him. "This is my mother, Rose."

"Jack who?" her mother asked.

"Jack Vincent."

Another unreadable "hmmm," and then, "He looks familiar."

"Well," Lucy paused. "He's a musician."

"Hmm." Her eyes narrowed, and she looked him over once more. Sweat dampened Jack's hairline, but then Rose nodded a curt, satisfied bob. "Ben, set another place at the table."

Lucy's father left the room and returned with a black thigh-high metal bottle, painted with a quaint design. Jack stared at it, not quite sure what he was supposed to do with it.

"It's an old milk can," Lucy whispered. "We have to get creative with seating sometimes." She sat on a wobbly piano bench and laid her napkin in her lap before adding, "The milk can is a seat of honor."

Jack perched on the milk can, his eyes darting around the dining room as plates of food were carried in. He offered help as they were set around the table, but was waved off by one family member or another until, at last, everyone was seated and ready for Thanksgiving dinner. He stared at the food like Tiny Tim at Scrooge's born-again-nice-guy feast, his mouth watering at the scents and sights and sheer massiveness of the meal.

"Am I allowed to ask about the spaghetti thing yet?" he whispered to Lucy, but Twin #1, the overly cheerful one sitting on his right, overheard.

"Ma, Jack needs your spaghetti speech," she said, snagging a still-steaming bread roll.

"The pilgrims came over, committed genocide, and then wanted us to celebrate it," said Rose in a clearly-practiced recital. "I'm not following their xenophobic rules and I'm not serving some dried-out bird. This is my family. My dinner. My rules."

Jack paused, a ladle-full of crisp green beans hovering mid-air. "Oh." While he absolutely agreed with her sentiment, he hadn't expected to discuss genocide within ten minutes of meeting his fiancée's family, and felt woefully incompetent. Lucy flicked his elbow, and he unfroze, dropping the green beans onto his plate.

"So, you're a musician?" Lucy's father—Ben, a name Jack remembered because it was short—asked, passing a plate of chicken parmesan around the table.

"You look a lot like Jack Hunter," another sister said. Her hair was cut into a pert pixie, and dyed with red and orange streaks. He would call her Flamehead until further notice. She peered at him, and then her eyes rounded. "Holy cow, you *are* Jack Hunter, aren't you?"

Lucy stiffened at his side, and he laid his fork down. "That's my stage name, but yes, that's me."

"Damn, Lucy," Flamehead whistled. "You've started bringing home live specimens for your music collection."

"Watch your mouth," chastised Rose.

"Jack Hunter?" Ben tapped the fork to his mouth in thought. "Would I know your songs?"

Jack opened his mouth to answer, but one of the brothers beat him to it. "He did that 'Slow Down' song. You know, the one that goes 'da da duhn da duhn.'"

Ah yes. Da da duhn da duhn was his biggest accomplishment.

"Oh, yes, I know that one," Ben said with a head nod. "So you sing then?"

"Guitar and piano too," Jack answered. "I dabbled a little with the bass guitar, but it wasn't for me." It was strange, discussing his music so casually, as if he were a plumber or a teacher instead of a triple platinum artist, but he liked it.

"Dad plays the guitar too," said Twin #1, drowning her salad in a deluge of dressing. "So does Matteo."

"I had all the kids take at least one year of music lessons," said Rose. "Good for the brain, you know. Only Matteo and Sophia stuck with it."

"I've been focusing on banjo lately, though," said Matteo with a proud grin. Jack said a silent thank you—Matteo was the brother that reminded him of a golden retriever, all bouncy and happy-go-lucky. *One sibling name down, six to go.*

Twin #2 snorted. "Yes, Matteo plays the banjo. Loudly."

"Sophia, be nice to your brother. He's getting better," said Rose, and Jack assigned *Sophia* to *Twin #2* in his brain.

"He's not getting better," whispered Twin #1 from the corner of her mouth.

"The banjo is a difficult instrument," Jack said in a placating tone. Matteo held up his hands in a *Right?* motion.

"And yet a puppet frog plays it better," muttered Sophia, receiving another glare from her mother. She passed a container of cottage cheese to her twin sister, who, to Jack's horror, took a spoonful and plopped it on top of her spaghetti and sauce.

"The fuck?" Jack said.

"Jack, watch your mouth," said Rose, her tone firm. "And Ariana, put the phone away. It's dinnertime. Business can wait." Flamehead—a .k.a. Ariana—scoffed and whispered something that sounded like "goddamnit."

Lucy's lips were pressed thin against imminent laughter. She gathered a scoop of cottage cheese curds in the serving spoon and held it above his spaghetti. He stared at it, wide-eyed, nose flared.

"Cottontail," he whispered.

"Mmhmm?"

"Nowhere in our contract does it say I have to eat your weird spaghetti."

Her nose scrunched in amusement, and she dumped the cottage cheese on top of his pasta.

"I know where you live," he hissed. Lucy burst into laughter, her shoulders shaking with giggles as she pressed a napkin to her mouth to stifle it. Jack loved her laugh. It was like happiness and mischief and pure, uninhibited glee molded into a sparkling sleigh-bell sound. But when he looked up, he found the entire family staring at them as if they were some sort of zoo exhibit.

Jack's cheeks burned. He must have said or done something completely wrong, so he did the only thing he could think of to salvage the moment—he closed his eyes and dove into the cottage cheese-spaghetti concoction. It was surprisingly edible, delicious even, adding a hint of ricotta taste. Lucy grinned at him, oblivious to her gawking family, and ate a forkful of her own.

"So, Jack," said The Tired Sister, which probably wasn't a polite way to remember her, but her eyes were lined with exhaustion. She had a dazed expression as if she'd learned that aliens were real, but she still had to act normal. "How did you meet Lucy?"

"We ran into each other at a record store," Jack said, and half of the people at the table let out a simultaneous "ohhh" as if that were no surprise.

"Did you get any records while in New York?" asked her father, his focus intent on his daughter. Affection mixed with a bit of bewilderment reflected in his countenance.

"A few," said Lucy. "I found a good Sam Cooke live album."

"Oh, yeah?"

"Yeah, the 1963 show at the Harlem Square Club," she said. "Oh, and also, Jack and I are getting married."

Jack gasped, causing a strand of spaghetti to catch in his throat. He sputtered and coughed, eyes tearing as he drew in sharp inhales. Twin #1 clapped him on the back a few times until he waved her off, reaching for a glass of water and downing it in one gulp.

"You good?" asked the oldest brother—the one that reminded Jack of a grizzly bear—as Jack's coughs diminished into watery eyes and the occasional hack. He bobbed his head between coughs, and Grizzly nodded once in acknowledgment before focusing on Lucy. "Now, the hell did you say?"

"Nico, watch your mouth," said Rose, but her earlier conviction had faded.

"Jack and I are getting married," Lucy repeated. Jack scrambled for her hand in a frantic show of solidarity.

"No, you aren't," laughed Matteo, but he stopped when no one else joined him. "Wait. Really?"

Lucy nodded and gave a half-grimace, half-smile. Suddenly, three very large, very angry, very overprotective brothers dropped their forks and were glaring at Jack. Jack tried to match their glare as best he could, but it ended up as more of a neurotic wince.

"How did this happen?" Sophia gestured at the two of them like a scolding schoolteacher, and then she gasped and shoved a finger toward Jack. "Did you knock her up?"

The three brothers kept their eyes tracked on Jack as if they expected him to run for the non-existent hills. The third brother—the one that looked as if he would sneak out of a corner, break someone's neck without a sound, and then go casually drink a glass of Merlot—cracked his knuckles.

"I'm not pregnant," Lucy said in exasperation, fidgeting in her seat.

"Uh-huh. Where's the ring?" asked Rose, pointedly looking down her nose at Lucy's left hand.

"Here." Jack fumbled inside his pocket and slid it on her finger. "We didn't want to shock you right away."

"Yes, because the delayed shock is so much more preferable," muttered Ariana.

"Have you set a date?" asked Rose.

"Errr," Lucy looked at Jack for backup.

"We were going to do it next week, actually," Jack said. "In New York."

The room went silent again except for the ominous drumming of Rose's fingers. "New York," she said as if it were a curse word.

"It's complicated," said Lucy. "We wanted to tell you first before the media found out."

"Media," repeated Ben, a little hoarsely.

"You're actually serious," said Grizzly Nico, throwing his arms in the air.

"Jack, Lucy," said Ben, his forehead creased in confusion, as if he weren't exactly sure how he had found himself in this situation. "You have to understand our concerns."

"Of course," Jack said, because he would be blowing a gasket if any child of his were dating Jack Hunter. "But I can promise you, I'll take good care of Lucy." He wove their fingers together.

Partners. Equals. We've got this.

"And vice versa," said Lucy with a modest smile.

"This is messed up," growled Nico. "Lucy, he's taking advantage of you somehow. You haven't known each other long enough."

"Nico," warned Rose, but Jack was already halfway out of his chair, ready to smack him in his grizzly bear face. Lucy hauled him back down into his seat while Ariana muttered something about the ridiculous constructs of masculinity.

"I'm not taking advantage of her," Jack seethed. "Yeah, it hasn't been long, but anyone who spends a minute with Lucy can figure out how amazing she is. And I'm going to do my best to get as many of those amazing minutes with her as I can, for as long as I can."

His voice wavered, and something behind his sternum stretched and squeezed, something that knew his speech wasn't a lie. Lucy was frozen in place, gazing at her water glass with a blank look.

"Eh, not bad," said Sophia, raising her glass as a salute. "Could've used some work on the delivery."

"Jesus Christ, Sophia," Ariana snorted.

"Ariana, your mouth," groaned Rose before returning to Jack and Lucy with a softened gaze. "You know, Nonno and Nonna only knew each other six weeks before they got married."

Matteo made a disgruntled sound and reached for a roll, shredding it apart with his long fingers.

"But," Rose added, "We're discussing this 'getting married in New York' thing tomorrow."

"Ma—" started Nico, but she held up a hand to silence him.

"Tomorrow." She fixated each and every one of her children with a cool *end-of-discussion-or-else* look.

Jack jumped as the crackle of the baby monitor cut through the air, and a distorted wail echoed through the dining room.

"Now the baby's up," huffed The Tired Sister, rising from her chair. She jabbed her pointer finger in the general vicinity of the table. "Nobody have any other life-changing news until I'm back."

"There's pumpkin pie for dessert," said Rose casually, as if the past half hour hadn't even happened.

"Do we have ice cream?" asked Twin #1.

"I picked up vanilla bean yesterday," said Ben.

"I failed my geology midterm," said Sophia. Everyone's head spun to face her. "What, so Lucy gets to be spontaneous, and I don't?"

Jack clenched his jaw against the sudden urge to laugh. Despite the lingering tension, that sense of acceptance covered him again, like a velvet magician's cloak. He felt calm and hopeful and—and slimy. Definitely slimy.

"Oh God," he inhaled, his body stiffening as a rough, squelchy wetness enveloped his right heel. "What's happening?"

"Oh," Twin #1 said, glancing down at Jack's feet. "Jack, meet Larry. Larry, meet Jack."

Jack lowered his head to regard the pot-bellied pig, nuzzling and glomming his heel. The black and white, jowly, solid tank of a creature blinked and regarded him as well.

Lucy leaned down and whispered into his ear. "Welcome to the family."

Chapter 18

After dinner, Lucy didn't bother showing Jack around the rest of the house, not yet. He had that dazed, slightly winded look of someone uninitiated with the ways of her family. They trudged up the first flight of stairs to the second floor, and then up the creaky wooden stairs to her bedroom in the attic.

When she was six, her parents had realized that she would require a break from time to time from their very loud, very talkative family. Ben partitioned off part of the attic and built her a bedroom of her very own. It was small and drafty, but it was quiet, and it was just for her, a rare thing in a family of ten.

"This is mine," Lucy raised her hands in a "tah-dah" gesture, though anyone who saw the room would know it was hers. One wall was lined with wooden bookshelves, filled with rock memorabilia. A robin's egg blue suitcase record player, her first, was folded up on one of the shelves. Another wall displayed framed concert posters for Janis Joplin, Jimi Hendrix, The Band, and more. The only things absent were her actual vinyls, which Brock had let her bring to their house in Indianapolis, and she had left them behind the day she escaped to New York.

"So this is the rabbit's warren." Jack circled the room, glancing at the wall art and pausing in front of a child's drawing, framed with the same prestige as the albums.

"What's this?" he squinted, turning his head back and forth.

"The Beatles. I drew them for art class in fifth grade. My mom framed it."

"Why is George screaming? Is it because he's holding a snake?"

"He's singing, and that's a guitar," she said. "Elena got the artistic talent in the family."

"Hmmm." He fiddled with a miniature Grammy award replica and looked around the room, clearly stalling.

"That went better than it could have," she offered. "My brothers still might castrate you, but overall, not bad."

"I'm pretty sure everyone in your family could castrate me," he said, cupping his hand in front of his jeans protectively. "Especially your one brother that looks like he knows at least twenty different ways to dispose of a dead body."

"Oh, that's Dante. And yeah, he probably does know."

There was a sharp knock on the door, and Lettie's muffled voice asking if she could come in. She entered, one hand holding a quilt and the other supporting Gianna in a cotton sling. Lucy's heart throbbed when she saw her niece, wrinkly and pink and puffy and *beautiful*. She had only met the child once before, for barely an hour, but every part of her was already completely devoted to her happiness. She reached out a tentative finger, and when Gianna grasped it, nearly cheered despite the minutia of it all.

"An extra quilt," Lettie explained. "It gets pretty cold up here." She sent a pointed glance at Jack, who barely noticed. Unlike Lucy, he was staring at Gianna, nostrils flared as if she were one of the horsemen of the apocalypse. Had he ever even been near a baby in his life?

"Thanks," said Lucy. Jack stopped looking at his future niece like she was Rosemary's baby long enough to catch the not-so-subtle dismissal in Lettie's eyes.

"I'm gonna go take a shower," he said, tipping his head toward the door.

"Down the stairs, past the reading nook," Lucy directed. "Towels in the closet inside the bathroom."

When the door closed behind Jack, Lettie tossed the quilt haphazardly onto the bed and folded her arms. "Explain. Now."

Lucy didn't answer at first, too busy dancing her hand in front of Gianna in hopes of capturing a baby laugh.

"Nope," Lettie tilted her body so that the baby was out of reach. "No baby giggles until I get answers."

"What's there really to explain?" Lucy sighed. "I went to New York. I met a guy—"

"Not a guy. A rock star."

"He's still a guy." She fought back a wave of protective anger. "He's still a person."

"Of course he is," Lettie said with a note of placation.

"It's not like I brought home another stray," Lucy added, looking pointedly at her older sister, who was responsible for the presence of a pot-bellied pig in the house in the first place.

"Isn't it, though?" Lettie rubbed her temple. "Look, I'm just worried. This is very spontaneous."

"Agreed."

"You don't do spontaneous."

"Also agreed." Lucy picked up the quilt, shaking it until it billowed like sailcloth across the bed.

"And you're going to marry him!" Lettie shook her head. Gianna watched her mother's dark auburn hair bounce with fascination. "You're going to marry Jack Hunter!"

"No," said Lucy, meeting Lettie's eyes. "I'm marrying Jack Vincent."

Lettie's expression softened, and she sat down on the bed, patting it. Lucy joined her, sitting hip to hip. Her sister lifted her hand and looked at Lucy, a little questioningly, a little pleadingly, and she nodded. With a small smile, Lettie held Lucy's hand in hers as she had since she was a child. The hand sizes might have changed over the years, but the love never had.

"You didn't question me at all about Gianna's father when everyone else was freaking out," Lettie said. "I'll trust you on this."

Lucy went through that wild, unpredictable brain of hers, searching for the right word to describe Jack, but *wonderful* and *fantastic* and *handsome* and *kind* and every other adjective were just blind platitudes, little pieces that made up his whole being.

"He's good," she finally said. "He's good." And by the way Lettie squeezed her hand, she knew her sister understood.

"He made you laugh," Lettie said. "At dinner."

"Yes?"

"I don't think any of us have heard you laugh in years."

Lucy's stomach knotted. "Really?" Lettie just nodded, and it was she who wouldn't meet Lucy's eyes, not the other way around.

After a moment, Lettie cleared her throat. "You know, if a guy looked at me the way Jack looks at you, I'd marry him too," she adds.

Lucy scoffed. "What do you mean?"

"Like you hung the moon. I mean it. Every time I looked over, he was watching you, and his eyes had sparkles. I swear to God, fucking—" She glanced around the room on instinct as if their mother would pop out of the closet upon utterance of the curse word. "Fucking sparkles," she continued in a lower voice. "And you had some sparkles of your own, Lucy."

Lucy traced her finger along the fine, wispy tendrils of Gianna's scant hair. It was a ruddy blonde, the color of honey. She knew better than to speculate out loud, but she wondered if the color came from Gianna's father, or just some rebellious gene passed down.

Lucy," her sister said, drawing her away from *soft soft soft* and *blonde blonde blonde*. "If you're happy, we'll all be happy, you know that. It might take those knuckleheads some time, but they'll love Jack, too, because he's yours."

Lucy touched her engagement ring, rubbing against the sapphire and diamond petals, petals that reminded her of a certain sunflower left in tribute on tiles in Central Park.

"He's mine," she said. "He's mine, and I'm his."

In the sad case of Jack vs. Farmhouse Bathroom, Jack was clearly the loser.

It began when he reached into the linen closet for a towel, and the towel hissed back. He yelped, stumbling backward as two glowing yellow eyes stared at him from within the crevices of the closet.

"Mr. Lincoln, I presume," he muttered, poking a tentative finger inside the closet. The finger was batted away with a furious yowl and a painful swipe of claws. He shimmied a towel from underneath the cat and undressed, pausing only to close the closet door just enough that Lincoln could escape but that he wouldn't be leering at Jack as he stripped.

After that, Jack reached into the antique farmhouse shower, twisting the faucet toward his favorite temperature between *right there* and *not right there*. Nothing happened. He wrenched it harder, tilting an ear toward the brass pipes, listening for some clanking hint that it was working. It wasn't until he tugged the movable showerhead toward his face that he heard a gunshot-like bang seconds before a frigid stream of water blasted out, soaking him, the floor, and his pile of folded clothes. This led to his third challenge—he was going to have to trudge back to the attic bedroom wrapped only in a towel unless he wanted to squeeze himself back into soggy clothes. It might have been acceptable behavior for some of the hedonistic haunts he'd visited in the past—the ice hotel near Stockholm came to mind—but it felt a bit faux pas in his fiancée's family's farmhouse.

Jack showered quickly, not trusting that the hot water would last in plumbing that had existed since before he was born. The cat sulked in the closet as Jack wrapped the towel around his waist, a disgruntled grumble near the washcloths the only hint of his existence. He calculated that if he dashed out at the speed of a mall walker, he could go from the bathroom and up the attic stairs with a minimal chance of anyone seeing him. His course plotted, he unlocked the door, only to hear—

"Hello, Jack." Dante drawled his name in a voice like a midnight glass of brandy.

Jack peeked out of the door into the reading nook and froze at the sight of Lucy's three brothers: Nico and Matteo relaxing on the brocade sofa, fingers tented in mirror gestures, and Dante sprawled in an easy chair, his legs crossed up on an ottoman, a book in his hands.

"Hello," Jack choked out. He cinched the towel at his waist, trying to cover up all his essential bits.

"We're going to have a little conversation," continued Dante, shutting the book with a snap.

"A conversation?" A trickle of water dribbled between his bare shoulder blades.

"You know," Nico said, contemplating Jack over his fingertips. "The trouble with being a celebrity is that anyone can quickly find out anything about you. Crucial information for brothers to have."

He flicked a hand at Matteo, who began reading from his smartphone.

"It has been reported," he recited with a haughty air, "that Jack Hunter's favorite color is yellow."

Nico smacked his brother on the arm. "The post under that, dummy." Matteo rubbed his bicep with a whimper.

"You're already wrong," muttered Jack. "My favorite color is blue."

"'Jack Hunter may have given the world hits like "Slow Down" and "Midnight in New Orleans,"'" read Matteo, "'but he's just as well known for his diva temper, ridiculous stunts, and an endless line of romantic paramours.'" He swiped downward. "Here's an interesting article."

Jack wanted to rub at his temples, but that would mean releasing the towel, and nudity wouldn't improve the already precarious situation.

Matteo continued to read to himself before staring up at Jack with incredulity. "You did *what* at Disneyland?"

"It wasn't that bad," Jack said. "I'm still allowed back on the premises."

"Ooh, this link takes me to a list of every woman you've been tied to, in alphabetical order. Let's start with A. Angeli—"

"Is there a point to this?" Jack cracked his neck to hide a shiver.

"Look," Nico sighed, pulling off his glasses with one hand and rubbing a wide hand over his face. "Even if you weren't a celebrity, we'd be having this talk."

"Don't these talks usually involve looking down the barrel of a shotgun?" His patience and body temperature were waning.

"Mrao." Lincoln crept out from the bathroom, rubbing his head on Jack's bare ankle, his fur sticking to his clammy skin.

"Not you too," Jack hissed at the cat, who flicked his tail and jumped onto the couch between Nico and Matteo. "Look, I'm going to marry your sister because I care about her. The end." Once again, the lie didn't feel quite so much like a lie. Jack clamped his arms against his side, attempting to look stoic but also to keep warm. "Can I go now?"

"Mrao," said Lincoln.

"It's just that—I mean, so soon after Brock—" Matteo frowned, clearly struggling with whatever he was trying to say. "Fourteen years, that's a long relationship to get over."

And that's when the realization hit Jack. Brock had limited Lucy's interactions with her family—which limited accidental discovery of any evidence of his behavior. Did they even know the whole story?

"Lucy's relationship with Brock is her story to tell," he said. "But I'd think as her brothers, you'd have a little more faith in her judgment."

He had struck a nerve. Matteo blushed, and Nico looked away. Only Dante still gazed at him, dark eyes narrowed.

"You must be cold," proffered Nico after a moment. "You should probably get dressed or something."

Jack huffed in exasperation, suppressing another shiver. "Thanks for the advice." He strode past them, heading for the attic stairs.

"Jack," called Nico, his voice lighter. "If you're absolutely honest about all this—well, it'll be nice to have another brother in the family. God knows we're outnumbered as it is."

Jack stopped short. *Brother?* All of his childhood fantasies of having a sibling had faded by the time he was ten. What even went into having a brother? Lots of manly hugs with enthusiastic back slaps? G.I. Joe battles in the backyard?

"But if not..." Matteo trailed off, drawing a warning finger across his neck and making a dramatic gagging noise.

"Mrao," Lincoln added, somehow adding a feline threat to the sound.

"Understood." Jack nodded and bolted up the stairs, freezing his ass off and somewhat terrified for his life.

Lucy was already in bed reading when Jack padded in, clutching his damp clothes like a security blanket. Her eyes trailed over his half-naked form, and she frowned.

"That was a longer shower than normal," she said.

"Unexpected complications," he answered. *Feral brothers. Feral cat. Feral plumbing.*

She covered her eyes and flicked a hand at him. "You can get dressed."

Jack rifled through his suitcase for lounge pants and a sleep shirt. "You always close your eyes when I'm naked."

"Your lips and your nipples are nearly blue," she said. "Do you really want me to ogle you now?"

Yes, please, he thought. *I'll dance the "Macarena" naked if you would just look at me the way I look at you.*

"No, I guess not," he said, rubbing at his called-out nipples and slinking into his pajamas, thankful for the long sleeves and flannel in the drafty room. "You can open your eyes now." He held his hands over the space heater. "Are you good with sharing the bed or do I need to camp out on the floor?"

"Jack," she said with a sigh. "Get in here. We're well past the 'only one bed' trope in our relationship." He perked up at the word *relationship*, and then immediately panicked that he was perking up about *anything* regarding relationships.

Fake fiancée, fake fiancée, fake fiancée, he chanted in his head, but the past twenty-four hours had whipped every thought regarding Lucy into a mental Jell-O fruit salad—shaky, full of mysterious bits, and terrifying to bite into because it could be wonderful and filled with marshmallows, or it could be dreadful and filled with some experimental hipster concoction like coconut and cubed ham.

"You look awful," Lucy said, putting down her book again. "What are you thinking about?"

I'm falling in love with you. And also, cubed ham.

He stretched and faked a roaring yawn. "Just tired."

She tilted her head, indicating his side of the bed. "Come on."

He slipped into the bed, not in a seductive way, but in a methodical, comfortable manner, as if they'd been doing this for years, and suddenly, he wanted that so badly it ached. He wanted to lean over and say things like, "How was your day, dear?" and "I missed you today, dear" and "Did you see that the Millers got a new rhododendron, dear?" and "Should we get a boat, dear?" And then, when he got tired, he'd fold up his reading spectacles, close whatever Oprah self-help book he was reading, and fall asleep with his arms wrapped around his wife. No, not just his wife—his Luciana.

But instead, he tucked the quilt around his shoulder, turned to face the wall and its poster of a wailing Diana Ross, and simply said, "Good night, Lucy."

Chapter 19

When Jack woke the following morning, he was tangled up in an armful of Lucy. It was still dark out, the November sun having been granted an extra hour of sleep by the U.S. government and their antiquated rules on Daylight Saving Time. In Lucy's bedroom, though, her small bedside lamp glowed, sending scatterings of light into the nooks and crannies of the attic space. Jack gazed at her face, studying how the faint light tripped over her freckles, highlighted the slope of her nose, and added layers of shadows to her dark lashes. He tugged her a little closer, enthralled by the way her body seemed to fit in all the empty spaces of his own—an elbow here, a shoulder there, cold toes intertwined with cold toes in the hollows of their blankets. She felt natural, and complementary, and utterly *necessary*.

But, unfortunately, it wasn't just his heart that believed her necessary. He carefully untangled her arms in a Jenga-like process, making sure there was no chance that Lucy would swipe her hand down to be greeted by the tent in his pajama pants. He crawled out of the bed and tiptoed downstairs in search of coffee.

As Jack neared the dining room, he heard an alternating chorus of baby whimpers and guitar chords. Ben hunkered by the brick fireplace, picking at his guitar. Lucy's niece—soon to be Jack's niece, he realized in horror—fretted and whimpered in a yellow swing by Ben's feet. Jack stepped into the room cautiously, and Ben's face lit up with frenzied relief.

"Thank God," he said, rubbing at glazed-over eyes. He thrust his guitar into Jack's arms. "I'll give you a million dollars if you take over. I can't feel my fingers."

Jack's coffee-deficient mind wasn't quite sure what was occurring as he blinked first at the baby, then at the vintage instrument in his hands. "You want me to play?"

"It normally works," said Ben with a sigh. "Lettie came over about two hours ago. They had a rough night. She's on the couch trying to catch some sleep." He leaned over the baby, who was champing at her fist. "You need to go to sleep, Gigi. It's a big day." The baby narrowed her eyes as if to say, *Old man, I do what I want.*

"What's wrong with her?" asked Jack, taking a seat and fiddling with the tuning pegs on the guitar.

Ben snorted. "You haven't been around babies much, have you?"

"Never." Jack cocked his head at the tiny gremlin. "I'm an only child."

"Well, every baby is different," explained Ben, flexing his fingers. "But you get good sleepers and bad sleepers. Eventually, they work out a sleeping rhythm, but the first few months, even the first year, can be brutal." He cooed down at the fussy baby. "Yes, pumpkin, you're so brutal!"

Jack tore his gaze away from Miss Brutal Pumpkin and inspected the guitar. It had a few spiderwebbed cracks in the lacquer, and "I Love You, Daddy" was written in a shaky, childlike script along the waist, but other than that, it was in excellent shape.

"Elena has always been our artist," Ben said, pointing at the blocky words. "But we hid the permanent markers after that. I couldn't bring myself to clean it off though. Now, start playing."

Jack obeyed his future father-in-law immediately, playing mellow chords and miscellaneous melodies that would disappear from his memory as soon as they hit the air. Ben nodded in approval and peered over his silver reading glasses at the fire. "I'm going to get more firewood. Keep playing like that. She's nearly there. I think."

Jack looked at the baby skeptically. Her bright blue eyes were wide and round. Their definitions of "nearly there" were vastly different.

And then Ben was gone, and Jack was alone with an actual, real live child.

Fuck.

He squinted at the baby. She whined back.

Fuck. Fuck.

Jack struck a few chords, a progression he had percolating in the back of his mind that he hadn't yet tried on an actual instrument.

"Eh? What do you think?" He waggled his eyebrows at the baby. "Should I go with this, or switch to D minor?"

The baby's face went from pale to raspberry-colored, and her eyes squeezed shut as she arched her back, sucking in air for what was projected to be a mighty wail.

Fuck. Fuck. Fuck. Fuck. Fuck!

"Kid, please don't cry, please," Jack pleaded. "I'll play any chords you want, just don't cry." He glanced around the dining room, praying that a more responsible adult would pop up out of nowhere and save him.

"Here, how about this?" He started an easygoing blues riff, knocking the guitar every so often in rhythm, often with a dramatic flourish of his hand to distract Gianna. Her face relaxed and her bleary eyes tracked the movement of his hands with curiosity.

"There we go. I'm not so bad, see? Not a big ol' scary rock star at all."

The baby continued staring at his fingers as he extrapolated on the riff, adding a key change and an improv solo. Then, she cooed—a sweet, snorty noise that could have been amusement or maybe just gas—and Jack stopped playing to pump his fist triumphantly in the air.

Which startled Gianna, who began to cry again.

"Kiiiiiiid," he groaned, picking up the guitar for more chords. She calmed down with a squeaky snuffle, watching his fingers pluck and strum. And then finally, whether the music was working or the planets had aligned just right, she fell asleep.

"You put her to sleep," Lucy whispered behind him, her voice thick and groggy. Her gaze swept from his hands, still strumming, down to his foot, which was balanced on the swing so he could rock it and still play at the same time.

"You forget," Jack said, cooing in a singsong voice toward Gianna, "I'm Jack motherfucking Hunter." He tilted his head back until it rested on the top rail of the chair. Lucy smiled down at him.

"Where's everyone else?" she asked, rubbing at the corners of her eyes.

"Your parents are working on breakfast. Lettie's on the couch."

"We should move the baby," Lucy said. "Before everyone shows up." She knelt down and scooped up Gianna with gentle hands, moving at a snail's pace. Tucking the child against her shoulder, she swayed a little as she tiptoed for the door, humming something that sounded a lot like "Knockin' on Heaven's Door." Jack was taken aback by how relaxed and natural she looked holding a baby, and disturbed by how much it made his chest twinge. He didn't even know if she wanted kids, but by the way she gazed down at the sleeping child, he was pretty sure she did. He wondered if her next husband would also want to have children. He pictured her in a van with a passel of dark-haired boys and girls, husband in the passenger's side as she drove them to Disney World and lectured them on the effect of the Beatles on modern-day entertainment.

"Jack?" murmured Lucy from the doorway, her lips pressed against Gianna's chubby cheek. "You okay?"

"Yeah," he grumbled. "Why?"

"You just growled to yourself."

"Just hungry," he said with a scowl.

Lucy shook her head and disappeared with the baby.

Jack soon learned that the Meyer dining room and adjoining kitchen were the equivalent of Grand Central Station in the old farmhouse. As soon as one person popped in, another popped out. Once Lucy took off with the baby, Sophia came in, still dressed in pajamas and carrying a messy three-ring binder. She eyed Jack warily. He eyed her back.

"I know I'm supposed to treat you like any other guy," she said, sitting across the table from him. "And ignore the whole rock star thing."

"Okay," said Jack, raising an eyebrow.

"But I need help," she said, tossing him an uncapped pen.

"Okay," repeated Jack. "Do you want an autograph or something?"

She stared at him. "Dude, you're marrying my sister. I'm not going to use you for some nefarious eBay scheme." Her face turned thoughtful. "Unless you want to. We could go 50/50 on the profits."

"I think I'm good."

"I need help with my homework." She started flipping through her binder, somehow finding what she needed by way of crumpled sticky notes and fingerprint-smudged tabs.

"Um." Jack twirled the pen in his hand. "I didn't go to college. I won't be much help."

She rolled her eyes and tossed him a few sheets of paper. "I'm a musical theater major. I need help with my composition final."

"You're a musical theater major?" Jack tilted his head at her. She reminded him a little of Lucy, if Lucy were spliced with Wednesday Addams in a genetic experiment gone wrong. Sophia's hair was dark and stick straight, and her eyes were dark brown with flecks of chaos and mayhem.

"Not every theater kid is sunshine and rainbows," she said, crossing her arms.

"Well, you're definitely more *Sweeney Todd* than *Sound of Music*," he said. He perused the composition paper in his hand. "Where do you need help?"

"This is the main character's eleven o'clock number," she said, and when Jack gave her a puzzled look, she clarified, "A big showstopper number in the second act. I can't get the bridge right, no matter what I try." She flipped through the pages full of erasure markings and scribbles until she found the section she needed. "Going from the bridge to the final chorus, right there."

Jack squinted, then plucked out the melody on the guitar. He paused, read the lyrics, and looked up at her. "What the hell is this musical about?"

"The U.S. Senate during the zombie apocalypse," said Sophia matter-of-factly. Jack opened his mouth to speak, then thought better of it. He ran through the bridge a few times, and then, like it so often did in the early days of his writing career, the pieces fell into place.

"There," he pointed at a measure. "Switch those three notes with those two, change that chord to a sixth, and add a half-rest there."

Sophia's eyes darted back and forth as she went over the changes, humming to herself. When she lowered the page to the table to look at Jack, her eyes were filled with shocked appreciation. "Holy shit."

"Sophia," said Rose, coming into the room with a cup of coffee. "Language."

"Ma, Jack just fixed my final for me," Sophia said, holding the song pages in front of her mother's face.

Rose glanced over the song. "Zombies again, Sophia? Can't you ever write anything happy?"

"It's about the implicit failure of elected officials during the country's times of crisis," said Sophia.

"Oh." Rose nodded and took a seat next to Jack. "That's okay, then."

"Thank you so much," said Sophia, sliding the pages back into her unwieldy binder.

"Honestly," Jack said. "The songwriting is the best part of what I do. Performing is fun, but writing is what I really love."

"Did you ever want to write full-time?" Rose asked, sipping at her coffee.

"I've thought about it," he admitted. "I've ghostwritten a few things here and there. But then—" He shrugged, a single movement that encapsulated writer's block and failure and maybe a little alcoholism all in one.

"Hmm," said Rose in that hum that could mean anything. "You're an interesting guy, Jack Vincent."

Jack wasn't sure if *interesting* was a good or bad thing in this instance, but since he was pretty sure Lucy's mother could murder him in his sleep, he simply answered with, "Yes, ma'am."

Decorating for Christmas at the Meyer household was *a thing*. It started the morning after Thanksgiving with an official kick-off meeting—yes, a meeting—in the basement of the old farmhouse. Ben Meyer had grown up in a picturesque town straight out of a Hallmark movie and was determined to keep the holiday spirit alive by way of two bedecked Christmas trees, flickering electric candles in every window, nutcrackers on every surface, and, if he had his way, a partridge in a pear tree somewhere in the house.

Of his children, Lucy was the most enthusiastic about the holiday. Christmas meant warmth, safety, contentment, and above all, tradition. For someone who needed things to be *just so*, it was truly the most wonderful time of year. It was also the only time of the year she put her foot down with Brock, and they would go to the farmhouse, where Brock would hole up in a bedroom writing legal briefs while the rest of the family bustled around decking the proverbial halls.

By the time Lucy came back downstairs dressed for the day, Matteo and Dante had arrived. Nico, who lived outside Indianapolis, had stayed the night, as had Ariana, who lived outside Chicago. Lettie had woken up, and though her eyes were still bleary, she bounced Gianna on her knee with renewed energy.

Jack and Lucy took their spots at the dinner table, Jack, of course, taking the milk can again. A light breakfast spread filled the table, and Lucy handed Jack the coffee pot and sugar bowl without a word. He mixed his sugared sludge and inhaled it with a sigh before snagging a cherry pastry.

"Have as many of those as you want," said Rose, pushing the plate toward him. "You're too skinny, eat up." Lucy sent Jack an *I told you so* smile before Rose continued. "Before we start decorating, we're going to discuss the wedding."

Lucy took a deep breath, bracing herself against her mother's unpredictability.

"We want you to have it here," Rose said. "Dad and Matteo finished remodeling the granary in September, and we could fit enough chairs in there for something small." She flicked her eyes to Lucy. "No crowds, no loud reception. Just us, maybe Nonna and Nonno, and you two."

Lucy loved the idea. "You're sure? Jack's PR guy will have to okay the decor and everything, and he's—"

"A menace," said Jack through a mouthful of pastry. "But good at creating an image."

"You're worried if I can handle your PR guy?" Rose's eyebrow arched, and Jack gulped.

"No, ma'am," he said. "Let's have a good old-fashioned Indiana wedding, then." He raised his coffee in a mock toast. "I can't believe I'm getting married in a barn."

"Granary," corrected half of her family members, and Jack waved them off.

"Now that's taken care of," said Ben, "to the basement!"

As Lucy followed her siblings down the basement stairs to where all of the holiday decor was kept, the front doorbell rang.

"Lucy, can you get that?" called Rose. "I'm supposed to be getting new tree lights from Amazon."

Lucy made an about-face and headed to the front door, stopping only to pat Larry on the head as he snored in front of the dying fire. She opened the front door, finding the lights her mother had been expecting. She brought them into the living room, working the cardboard box open with her index finger and releasing serpents of green wire onto the carpet near the bare tree. Sitting cross-legged next to the fake branches, she untangled the lights and plugged them in, inhaling in delight at the *bright bright bright* and the *red green blue yellow pink*. She began to wind them in and out of the fuller branches at the bottom, twisting and turning and creating a pattern all her own.

She didn't notice the shadow behind her until it was too late, and the heavy hand touched her shoulder.

Chapter 20

Jack clomped up the basement stairs, holding not one, not two, but *three* tree toppers, even though no sane household needed more than one at any given time. "Lucy," he bellowed. "Your mom says it's your turn to pick the tree topper—" He rounded the corner and stopped short, his eyes narrowed.

Nico was kneeling in front of Lucy, his face pale and frantic. Lucy was curled into herself, her ears covered by trembling hands and her eyes squeezed tight. Tremulous inhales of shock tore through the air.

"What did you do?" asked Jack, speaking slowly despite his instinct to yell. Nico's head snapped up, eyes locking on him.

"I just touched her arm. I did it gently. I know she doesn't like to be touched, but she's never done this before," Nico shook his head over and over. The juxtaposition of this tall, self-assured man and his stunned expression was almost laughable. "I don't know what I did. I don't know what I did."

Jack laid the tree toppers on the sofa and knelt next to Lucy. He pushed at Nico's arm, and her brother jumped up, stepping away and tugging at his hair nervously.

"Hey, Cottontail," said Jack. Lucy flinched and shied away from his voice. "It's just me. It's just Jack."

"I didn't hurt her," Nico repeated as if trying to convince himself.

"I know you didn't," said Jack in a calm, singsong lilt. "Nobody did anything wrong. Right, Lucy? You didn't do anything wrong. No one is in trouble. No one is getting punished."

Her eyes blinked open, and she tilted her head. Her eyes darted from Nico to Jack and back again, her brow furrowed in confusion.

"It's just us," Jack said. "Just your brother and me. No one else. He isn't here."

"He?" asked Nico, but Jack shook his head. Now was not the time. He reached out a hand, and let it hang in the air, patient and hopeful. After a few seconds, Lucy touched her fingers to his, the tips bumping against one another, and then slipped her own fingers in between his, braided together in a semblance of comfort.

"Hey," he whispered. "Why do bees have sticky hair? Because they use a honeycomb."

Lucy let out a half-laugh, half-gasp, as if surfacing from an icy ocean, and crumpled against him. He adjusted until he was cross-legged and she was sitting in his lap, face curled against his neck. There were no tears, only tremors that shook her body and transferred to his own. Jack's hand traced her cheek and brushed her skin in a simple rhythm. *Back and forth, up and down.*

"Why is Peter Pan always flying?" she whispered in between jagged breaths. "Because he never lands."

Jack rocked a little and nuzzled her hair, maintaining that same stroking pattern on her cheek. "How do you row a canoe full of puppies? You use a doggy paddle."

"Where did you learn these?" she murmured against his shirt. "They're awful."

"Google is a powerful tool." He risked a glance at Nico, who looked stricken, his back pressed against the wall. "I'm going to take her upstairs for a bit, okay?"

"Okay," her brother rasped. "I'll—I'll finish the lights." Nico ducked his head low as Jack helped Lucy stand, keeping his gaze from his sister as he untangled endless strands of bulbs with quaking hands.

Meyer family tradition involved watching *It's a Wonderful Life* after a day of holiday decorating as a way to either kick off the merriment of the Christmas season or to insinuate the evils of small-town monopolies by men in ornate wheelchairs. After a long rest, Lucy and Jack had rejoined the family in time to hang the ornaments, and no one mentioned their absence, though Nico refused to make eye contact with either of them.

Ten minutes into the film, Nico stood up, his stance jittery and tense. "We need more firewood. Jack, come help."

"I can help you," offered Matteo, starting to rise, but Nico held out a hand to halt him.

"No, Jack's been here for a few days; it's about time he helps with the goddamn firewood."

"Watch your mouth," everyone in the room echoed.

"Nico, *It's a Wonderful Life* is on," Rose chastised.

"Jack doesn't care; he's seen it."

"Have you seen it?" Rose asked with a wary squint.

"Which answer gets me in the least trouble?" Jack asked.

Nico threw his hands up and stormed out of the room. Jack followed, grabbing his coat and heading outside to the firewood pile, and possibly a reckoning of sorts.

Lucy's brother stood alone in the moonlight, an ax gripped in his hand. A pane of cold, blue light from the motion-sensor lamp illuminated him, casting a gauzy, stretched shadow across the brown grass. Jack began gathering logs from the nearby firewood pile, the bark scratching at his ungloved hands.

"Drop them. They need split first." The edge of the ax glinted like a tiger's fang. Jack swallowed a lump of trepidation and obeyed.

"How long?" Nico finally asked with an eerie stillness.

Jack cocked his head. "How long what?"

"How long was he—" Nico swallowed as if the words were foreign and unfamiliar. "How long was he hitting her?"

Jack ducked his head. "Long enough."

Nico exhaled, long and slow. "She doesn't like being touched, but she doesn't mind us. But that—that was different. That was *something else*."

"It was," Jack agreed, his voice low and rough as sandpaper.

"I hated the guy," Nico said, biting the words out behind clenched teeth. "I always hated him. And still, I never figured it out. I never saw. We never got along, but I thought it was just him and me. He was arrogant, and I'm a hothead, I admit, but Lucy seemed fine. I never thought there was an issue between them." He relaxed his arms with an exhausted sigh, dropping the tool, the ax head sinking into the snow. "One month," he said. "One month with her, and you know her better than any of us." His eyes met Jack's, and they weren't angry or accusing. They were the eyes of a brother desperate to save his sister from her demons. "Here." Nico handed Jack the ax. "Ever split wood before?"

"Nope. Not a lot of reasons to use an ax in New York." The tool was top-heavy and clumsy in his hand, and Jack couldn't get a comfortable grip.

Nico grunted, his eyes gleaming. "That's not an ax; that's a maul." He steadied a thick log on the homemade chopping block. "Look here, you want to hit right where it wants to naturally split."

Jack lifted the maul into the air and swung downward with all his might—and missed by seven inches.

To his credit, Nico didn't laugh. "Try it again."

Jack gritted his teeth and swung again. This time, the air echoed with the snap of the log as it split into neat pieces that tumbled to the ground. Jack grinned at Nico, and miraculously, he smiled back.

"Ma sent us out to make sure you haven't killed him yet," Matteo announced as he joined them at the chopping block, Dante lumbering behind him.

"Step back; he's busy," said Nico, putting another log on the block. Matteo and Dante halted at a safe distance. As Jack's breath puffed out in frosty clouds, there was a new sense of determination flowing through his muscles.

"Put your feet further apart." Dante spanned his hands out to demonstrate. Jack adjusted his stance and swung again, missing twice but splitting the wood cleanly on the third time.

"Wiggle your ass a bit," said Matteo. "You're too tense. Stretch out."

"Matty, you can't tell people to wiggle their ass," Nico said. "Let alone a famous rock star."

"No." Jack held up a hand. "I'm Jack. Just Jack. Tell me to wiggle my ass if you want." He paused. "Well, maybe not. Now, more wood. Please."

Nico balanced another log on the block and stepped back just before Jack slammed into it, funneling every frustration, every fear into his arms.

Thwack. Derelict Records and their stupid contracts.

Thwack. The suffocating pressure of the album, the fans, a tour that may not happen.

Thwack. The fear that he'd become his father—or worse, his mother, distorted by the allure of fame.

And the fact that he was falling hard for his fake wife. *Thwack. Thwack. Thwack.*

Jack swung and split and chopped until his hands were as raw and pink as an uncooked shrimp.

"You're good." Nico clapped him on the back, and Jack wondered if he was referring to more than his firewood skills.

His chest stung from gulping in the cold night air, and his arms were already burning with overuse. And yes, he should have wiggled his ass a bit because his lower back was stiff and sore. "So," Jack panted, wiping sweat-damp hair from his forehead. "What are you guys doing tomorrow?"

"Dunno," said Matteo, "But that look on your face tells me you've got something fun planned out."

"Depends," Jack said. "Any of you know how to throw a punch?"

Nico and Matteo both grinned wildly and glanced at Dante, who simply raised the evilest eyebrow imaginable.

"Well then, boys," Jack said, attempting to throw his arms around Nico and Dante's shoulders, but as he was several inches shorter than them, it felt like he was trying to reach for a dish on the highest shelf. "Have you ever taken part in a good shenanigan?"

Jack explained his idea and then the four men tromped back to the house in silence, like soldiers coming home from battle. When they returned to the living room, Ben raised a single eyebrow that Nico answered with a curt nod.

After everyone replenished their plates of snacks and cookies, Rose shushed everyone because "It's sacrilegious to talk during Jimmy Stewart!" Jack and Lucy traded their spot on the couch with the twins, opting to sit on the floor in their place. Jack claimed it as an act of fairness, but really, he just wanted to pet Larry, who couldn't jump up on the couch with his awkward piggy legs.

When everyone's attention was glued to the screen, Jack took a moment to gaze around the room, amazed by the sheer improbability of the situation.

He was curled up on an old carpeted farmhouse floor in the middle of nowhere, Indiana, watching Jimmy Stewart stammer about flower petals and angels.

He had spent the night chopping wood with his future in-laws.

His fake-ish wife was nestled in one arm, red and violet and yellow speckled light from the Christmas tree dancing over her skin like tiny holiday fairies.

And, of course, his other hand was resting on top of a snoring pig.

Jack had never been happier.

Chapter 21

The whine of the suitcase zipper woke Lucy the next day. Jack was pulling his clothes on in that awkward, tiptoeing fashion people did when they were trying to be quiet and ended up being louder than if they just got dressed normally. His back was to her, and he was still shirtless, and though she should probably cough or say hello to alert her wakefulness, she kept silent, burrowed in her pillows.

It was funny how attraction worked. Millions of fans swooned over Jack's face, the product of the perfect genetics of the film and music worlds, and yet Lucy's heartbeat was ramping up over his back. The symmetry of the reversed L's of his shoulder blades. The smattering of birthmarks just to the right of his lower spine, a miniature constellation of melanin. The trail of his backbone, leading to—

"I can hear you thinking," whispered Jack. He turned and winked at her, and her face burned. She nestled her face into the pillow. "What's going on inside that head? No editing."

"I like your shoulder blades," she mumbled against the flannel pillowcase.

The bed dipped as he sat next to her, his hand outlining her own shoulders. "Huh. I like yours too."

"You're up early again," she said, moving on before she blurted out more of his body parts that she admired. "This is two days in a row. It's a miracle."

Jack's laugh was barely above a breath. "It's so quiet here that it's almost too loud. Keeps me awake." He patted her shoulders once more and stood again. "I'm going into Indianapolis with your brothers to pick some stuff up. We'll be back this afternoon."

"You're going with them?" Lucy lifted her head, eyebrows raised.

"This is my chance to ride in a pickup truck. *A pickup truck.*"

"My God," she whispered, pursing her lips against a smile. "You're a real Hoosier now."

He waggled his eyebrows, and then his expression softened, little lines creasing perpendicular to his dense lashes. "Hey."

"Hey?"

He smoothed his thumb over her cheekbone. "You know I'm gonna take care of you, right?" His tone was suspiciously neutral.

"Yes," she said, because she did know that. She wasn't sure why he was bringing it up while wearing that peculiar expression though. "Because we're friends, or something."

"Or something," he repeated, and then he kissed her on the forehead. It was a display of affection he did more and more, because that's what friends did.

Or something.

It wasn't until darkness had blanketed the farm, the barren fields fading from existence into the velvet night, that the front door opened and Jack came in, stomping off powdery snow onto the rug. Lucy's heart clenched as he flashed her a smile full of sunshine, his face more relaxed than she had ever seen. She searched his eyes and flushed at the sheer joy reflected back at her. She wanted to question him, to ask him what had happened to give his eyes that extra glitter of happiness, but instead, her awkward mouth stuttered out, "What are you wearing?"

"Huh? Oh, this." He tapped at the threadbare navy and gold Notre Dame ball cap. "It's Matteo's. Just so I didn't get recognized."

"You look very Indianan."

He crinkled his nose, and she pecked a kiss to his cheek—and then squawked like a peacock in his ear as Matteo strode into the room, sporting a very nasty black eye.

"What did you do?" she hissed as Jack scrambled back, rubbing at his ear. Nico came in, cradling his right hand like a newborn kitten. Her eyes nearly popped from her head as she saw his bruised, bloody knuckles.

"What did you do?" she repeated, enunciating each word.

"So, uh, well," said Matteo, scratching behind his ear. "So don't get mad."

"*Matty.*" She turned to Jack with a pointed look. "What happened?"

Jack opened his mouth, closed it, and then the three men exploded into a typhoon of explanations.

"They wouldn't let me do anything," complained Jack, throwing his hands into the air. "I had to sit back and watch with a hat and sunglasses on!"

"You're getting married in a week!" protested Matteo. "And you can't fuck up your guitar hand!"

"Matteo Michael!" snapped Rose. Her son held up a culpable hand and ducked from her anti-profanity glare.

"Yeah, but all I got to do was trip him," Jack grumbled, kicking at the carpet. "You guys got to have all the fun."

"Fun?" Matteo pointed to his swollen eye, looking like a knock-off Popeye. "Does this look like fun?"

"What—"

"I mean, it was pretty fun," grinned Nico, sucking on the distended knuckle of his index finger.

"Did—"

"Yeah, watching Dante was probably the best part," admitted Jack. "Has he always known how to kick that high?" He attempted his own karate kick and nearly fell backward, saved only by Nico's grip on his shoulder.

"You—"

"Who knows with that dude. I know he spent some time with the Rockettes before he—"

"Do?" Lucy finally finished, but as she did, the room fell into a hush. Dante entered the room with the solemnity of a warrior priest, bereft of a single scratch. He smiled down at his sister, and without a word, handed her the square object in his hands.

Her throat tightened as she drew her fingers over the fine edge of the record sleeve, finding the tiny tear in the corner she had accidentally made when she was nine. Her heart filled with bursts of *safe* and *secure* and *home* and *love* as she traced the solitary figure howling his heart out in front of dozens of brilliant red lights, each one contributing to a letter in his name.

E-L-V-I-S.

"Ah-ah-ahhhhhhhhhhhhhhhhh-AH!"

Lucy snuggled into a layer of comforters on Matteo's futon and watched as four of the most precious men in her life shriek-sang Led Zeppelin's "Immigrant Song" from the carpeted floor of her brother's living room.

She had ridden in the truck with her three brothers, Jack, and her recovered records and record player to Matteo's house, where he was going to store her belongings until they arranged for shipping. As they unloaded the albums into the safety of Matteo's house, she managed to squeeze the story from the others.

The men had ridden to her former house in the city, and when Brock answered the door, they walked right in and started packing up her albums. Brock had gotten angry, and then he hit Matteo, which started a chain of events: Nico punched Brock. Brock went for Nico, and Jack tripped him. Then Dante took Brock into another room and did, well, elusive Dante things while the others packed up the rest of the albums.

"Suffice it to say, he will not be bothering you anymore," Dante had said.

"Did you—did you *kill* him?" Lucy had almost been afraid to ask.

Dante only raised a dark eyebrow in response, until Matteo shoved him and told him to stop being creepy.

"He's fine," Nico had corrected. "A little bruised, but he knows what's up now."

Before Lucy could get any further clarification, Matteo pulled a joint out from his shirt pocket, and the rest of the story was lost in a haze of smoke and giggles and Robert Plant's voice.

Now she perched on the futon, a sober mama eagle observing her four extremely high eaglets with both amusement and tenderness as they lay haphazardly across the floor. Having her albums back had realigned her crooked world a little bit, and she owed that extra sense of rightness to her brothers and Jack.

"You know, Jack, for being a big ol' celebrity, you are pretty down-to-earth," said Matteo, rubbing at his red-rimmed eyes. "A real man of the people."

"Me?" sputtered Jack, a Cheshire Cat grin stretching across his face. "Dude. *Dude.* You are so wrong. My piano cost a half-million dollars. I once flew to Greenland just to pet a prize-winning sheep. I have an *actual* skeleton in my closet." He puffed on the end of the joint and delivered it to Dante.

"I'm sorry, what?" asked Lucy, her brows skirting her hairline.

"Don't worry, Cottontail." He patted her calf, and then left his hand there, curled around her ankle. "It's just a monkey skeleton."

"Why do you have a monkey skeleton?" snorted Nico, tucking a couch cushion under his head.

"I could tell he had a good soul," Jack said with soft-spoken reverence. Lucy made a mental note to have the monkey's remains taken care of once they returned to New York.

"See, you say all this, but we know you, Jack. We *know* you. You're one of us." Matteo ruffled Jack's hair. "You have a good soul. Like your monkey, man. You have a goddamned monkey's soul. And really good cheekbones."

"Shit, Matty, you think so?" Jack's gaze was filled with awe.

"I know so." Matteo waved a hand at Lucy. "Lu, tell your man that he has beautiful cheekbones."

She couldn't help her budding smile. "You have beautiful cheekbones."

"See?" Matteo swatted at Jack's shoulder. "Beautiful cheekbones, and a beautiful soul."

"You know," Nico mused, tapping his index finger against the side of his nose, "Plato once said that thinking is the talking of the soul within itself."

"Whoa. Whoa. *Whoa.*" Jack's eyes grew wide. "For a cartoon, Mickey's dog sure was wise."

Lucy shut her eyes for a moment, attempting to quell her imminent laughter. "Oh, sweetheart." The epithet rolled off her tongue before she could prevent it. "That was *Pluto*. He's talking about *Plato*."

Jack's carefree laugh in return was worth a hundred accidental "sweethearts." He gasped and turned to Matteo, shaking her brother. "I need your guitar." He dashed off at roadrunner speed in the direction Matteo pointed.

Nico glanced up at her from his makeshift pallet on the floor. "You all right?"

"Yeah. Just—" She blinked back a sudden sting of tears, surprised at their belated appearance. "I love you guys. And I'm sorry I haven't been around. But now you know why."

All three brothers smiled up at her, and she didn't have to struggle for any more words. They already knew anything she could have said.

"Love you too, Lu," murmured Nico. Then they all jumped as the room exploded into mariachi-style guitar chords.

"Cheekbooooones," crooned Jack, strumming the guitar and sashaying toward Matteo, who had the expression of a teenage girl at a Backstreet Boys concert.

"Oh my God," Matteo exhaled. "Jack Hunter is singing to me." Jack knelt down next to him, somehow balancing the guitar as he rested on his heels.

"Matteo's cheekbones have never been better," Jack sang. "Matteo's cheekbones are sharper than cheddar..." He placed a hand on Matteo's forehead as if he were a revivalist preacher, and her brother squealed.

"Okay, Jack." Lucy tugged on his shirt, putting an end to the madness. "Time to come up here." Jack sent her a fool's grin and laid the guitar down, crawling next to her on the futon.

"You okay?" he whispered. "I want you always to be okay, you know."

"I'm okay. Thank you for today." She hesitated. "You know this won't change everything, right? The nightmares, the flashbacks, they won't magically go away. And even with that, I'm still me. I'm still a weirdo."

"Shhhhhhhhhhhhhhhh," hushed Jack, stretching the sound out for far longer than necessary as he snuggled against her shoulder. "But you're my weirdo."

"Yes," she said. "Your weirdo."

Jack reached for her hand, plopping it down on top of his head, nodding in approval when she started working her fingers through his hair. "And I'm your asshole," he declared. They both paused for a moment, and he shot her a puzzled look as he thought through his words. Then he wrapped his arms around her waist like an octopus, planted his face on her chest, and placed her hand back on top of his head.

Okay, then. High Jack was apparently very into physical affection.

"You know," said Nico, crinkling his nose at them. "It has also been said that love is a serious mental disease."

"Who said that?" slurred Jack, nuzzling further into her like a baby koala. "Goofy?"

"No, that was Plato too."

"Man." Jack sighed, a sound saturated with utter contentment. "I bet he had a beautiful monkey's soul too."

"Cheekbooooones," sang Dante at last, and for once, all was right in the world.

Chapter 22

Eight days before their wedding, Jack and Lucy informed Jack's manager and PR team that they were moving the wedding to Sparrow Hill, Indiana. Kim groaned. Trent laughed. Martin yelled something about *#destinationweddings* and *#farmhousechic*, and it was game on.

Five days before their wedding, Jack—back in New York while Lucy held down the fort in Sparrow Hill—spent the day in the recording studio, stitching together random chords and lyrics scribbled on crinkled paper. He had yet to find his magnum opus, but he felt it coalescing just out of sight, if he could just push away enough of the clutter in his brain to find it.

Four days before their wedding, Matteo, Nico, and Dante video-called Jack in a secretive attempt to throw him a virtual bachelor party, which ended up being a two-minute video of Larry dressed in a bikini while "Pour Some Sugar On Me" played and Lettie walked by in the background muttering about toxic heteronormative rituals.

Three days before their wedding, Jack burned his microwave popcorn. It was a pretty boring day.

Two days before their wedding, Jack realized that the weird atmosphere of the house wasn't because of a faulty HVAC system or the foundation shifting or even a rogue ghost, but because a very vital person wasn't there. He cut his grilled cheese into squares and slept in the guest room tucked in the world's greatest duvet.

One day before their wedding, Jack was on the way to Sparrow Hill from the Indianapolis airport. They had chartered a private plane from New York to fly him, Kim, Martin, Emery the photographer, and Parker, as well as lighting equipment and wedding decor. It wasn't Jack's preferred method of travel, since he was a rock star, and rock stars and private planes often led to tragedy. Kim had taken one look at a map of the area, declared that she was only driving out to "the sticks" once, and booked a hotel in Indianapolis for the night.

Meanwhile, Jack was scrunched in the back of Dante's sedan with his future...well, Nonna-in-law might have been the right term. His future Nonno-in-law was in the front seat, lecturing Dante on everything from the benefits of celery salt to the mating rituals of animals.

"And when the male giraffe prepares to mate," boomed the ruddy-faced former professor, his coarse voice peppered with a faded Italian accent, "he drinks the female giraffe's urine to make sure she's fertile."

"He does what?" The sides of Dante's lips twitched as he wrestled back a smile.

"He drinks her urine!" said the white-haired man, clearly irritated.

"He drinks her what?" asked Dante loudly, white teeth on full display.

"Her urine!" Nonno repeated. "Goddamnit, kid, I know you can hear me!"

"Watch your mouth," warbled Nonna, smacking her husband on the arm as Dante cackled in the driver's seat. She turned to Jack with a secretive expression. "If they get to be too much, I usually grab a bottle of champagne and go sit with the pig. Come find me if you need it." She winked at Jack, and he was saved from responding by an incoming text.

LUCY: Almost here?

JACK: Your grandma winked at me and I think your grandpa suggested that I drink your urine. Save me?

LUCY: I will.

And though it was meant in jest, Jack wondered if she knew that she already had.

Three hours before their wedding, Jack burst into Lucy's bedroom, clad only in his trousers and half-buttoned shirt, slamming the door behind him as he clutched a wrapped box to his chest.

"We've got five minutes," he panted. "Thank God you're still undressed."

Lucy cocked her head at him, tapping her fingers on the wooden vanity.

"That's not what I meant," he said as red blooms snaked across his cheeks. "I've been trying to sneak up here all day, but your mother and Nonna won't let me near you."

"They're superstitious," she said. "It's bad luck to see the bride before the wedding. So now, we're cursed."

"Well, maybe this will counteract the curse." He thrust the gift at her without ceremony, wiping his palms on his trousers. "Open it."

"Thank you," she said, her fingers tracing the loop-de-loop of the taffeta ribbon, the raised ridges of the embossed wrapping paper. She unwrapped it, and her smile fell as she opened the box. "Oh, Jack," she breathed, blinking back tears because if she cried and ruined her makeup, Martin would probably banish her from her own wedding.

"I thought you could use them as your 'something blue.'" Jack scratched at his pressed collar, shifting on his feet.

She lifted one of the high heel shoes out of the box as if it were a family heirloom. Her thumb caressed the material, tracing and brushing all that *blue soft blue soft blue.* "Blue suede shoes," she whispered, holding both shoes up to the light.

"I'm sure the King would approve." Jack gave her a shy smile, and Lucy threw her arms around him. He staggered back a step before he caught his balance, and she held him tighter, throwing away thoughts of contracts and social media quotas and two-year deadlines, just for one day.

"Thank you, Jack," she murmured, her voice cracking just a little. "I'm glad it's you."

I wish it could always be you.

"Me too, Cottontail." He trailed his hand up and down her back, his fingertips catching on her hair. "Me too."

A loud rapping shook the bedroom door, and they jumped back like teenagers caught with toilet paper. "Jack? Are you in there?" Nonna's voice was somehow both cheery and menacing.

"Oh God," whispered Jack, tugging Lucy a little tighter. "The call is coming from inside the house."

"Lucy? Is that man in there?"

"It's no use," she whispered. "You'll have to face her." Jack's shoulders slumped and he opened the door to be greeted with a Hitchcockian gasp of horror. Lucy shook her head to herself as Jack disappeared down the stairs, followed by an angry Nonna berating him in full Italian.

Two hours before their wedding, Jack took Larry on a panicked speed walk around the farm, because he might as well get physical cold feet in addition to his mental cold feet. After his second lap of the yard, he slowed as Ben fell into step next to him.

"Nerves?" asked Ben, his hands shoved into his coat pockets.

"Uh-huh," said Jack, his lips too cold and numb to articulate more than that.

"It's normal, you know," his future father-in-law said.

It's not normal, Jack wanted to say. *Nothing about this is normal. Two years from today, your daughter is going to leave me, and I'll be all alone again.*

"Do you get stage fright before your concerts?" Ben asked.

"Nuh-huh," said Jack, wondering if his eyeballs were going to freeze and if that would be enough to call off the wedding.

"Maybe visualize it as a concert, then," said Ben. "That might help. I was lucky; I wasn't nervous at our wedding. I knew I was doing the right thing."

I'm doing the exact opposite of the right thing, Jack thought.

"Uh-huh?" he sounded out instead.

"Of course," Ben paused, gazing at the distant, bare soybean fields, "I was high as a kite. It was the seventies, everyone at the wedding was."

He thumped Jack on the shoulder. "You haven't lived until you've gone through a Catholic mass completely high, son."

Jack turned his head very slowly and gaped at the man, because *what even was this family?*

"By the way," Ben said nonchalantly, his eyes twinkling, "why did the two melons have a wedding? Because they cantaloupe!" And with that, he patted Jack's arm, patted Larry's head, and went back to the house, whistling the entire way.

Thirty minutes before their wedding, Larry the pig ate his custom-made boutonniere and yakked all over the kitchen floor.

Two minutes before their wedding, Lucy entered the granary to find the antique building transformed into a winter wonderland. Fairy lights and glittering snowflakes hung from the rafters, and a shimmering blue carpet ran down the center of the floor to a mounted platform filled with white holly berries and pine boughs. Kim was still adjusting white tulle bunting down the aisle, even though everyone else was already seated. She winked at Lucy, gave an *it's just what I do* shrug, and sat in her chair next to Martin.

To Lucy's left, Emery, the photographer, beamed up at her, holding the camera and clicking occasionally, the sound as soft as snowy footsteps. To her right, her father looped his arms through hers.

"Ready?" he asked. She nodded, and they began the paced walk, lace and silk swirling around her. She gazed at each and every member of her family, her heart growing fuller with every step, every smile, every tear on their faces. They were hers and she was theirs and she *belonged*.

And then she lifted her head and locked eyes with the man she was going to marry. He was pale and shaky, but his eyes were *sparkles fucking sparkles*, and she knew that for this one moment, he belonged to her too.

One minute into their wedding, Lucy kissed her father on the cheek and joined Jack at the homemade altar, taking his shaking hands in hers.

And then she frowned, dropped his trembling fingers, and placed her hands firmly on his cheeks. She tugged him closer until their foreheads met.

"Elton John once let Stevie Wonder drive his snowmobile," she said in her calm, clear, no-nonsense voice. "If he can survive that, we can survive this."

Jack burst into laughter, and family and photographers and insane PR agents melted away into fuzziness just outside of Jack's awareness. "I once got drunk and broke into a 'swimming with dolphins' event," he whispered. "I got caught when one of them humped me, and I yelled for help."

"What are they saying?" Nonno barked out to no one in particular.

"I think it's the Lord's Prayer," Nonna yelled back.

Lucy's lips quirked. "Keith Moon drove a Rolls Royce into a swimming pool at a Holiday Inn."

Jack grinned. "I rode a golf cart into a dinosaur museum in Madrid, petted a triceratops thigh bone, and rode out."

She tapped a finger against his cheekbone. "Rock stars are unusual creatures."

"You have no idea," Jack said, taking her hands in his now-steady fingers. Somewhere behind them, Martin hissed out a "finally!"

Jack cleared his throat once, then once more, before realizing that the golf ball-sized tightness in his throat was there to stay. The minister said a few words in his calming drone before turning to Jack, asking him to repeat after him like a pet parrot.

"I, Jack, take you, Lucy, to be my—" his voice cracked like a middle schooler, "—my wife, to have and to hold from this day forward, for better or for worse, for richer or for poorer, in sickness and in health, I promise to love and cherish you."

Lucy repeated the vows, her voice clear as a bell. The words were more earnest, more honest coming from her lips. Jack imagined her saying them in her real wedding, at least two years from now. The thought of her starry eyes gazing lovingly at some other lucky son of a bitch made his stomach twist like an over-wrung washcloth.

The officiant cleared his throat, and Jack snapped to attention.

"The rings?" he prodded. Jack held out his hand to Trent, who dropped the banded diamond and sapphire wedding ring into his palm. He slid it onto Lucy's finger, and her eyes rounded.

"It's lovely," she blurted out before covering her mouth with an "eep!" and whispering an apology to the officiant. Lucy's smile grew as she placed Jack's ring on his finger. He held it up to examine it, watching the twinkle of the fairy lights strike the silver and bounce off like a comet. Through the center, a strange, ribbed metal line was threaded through the metal.

"It's a guitar string," she whispered. "The one you broke. I took it out of the trash when you weren't looking."

Jack bit back a groan at the sheer unfairness of it all. The ring was perfect. Lucy was perfect. And none of it was real.

Five weeks, one day, twenty hours, and sixteen minutes after a singular moment in a Brooklyn record store, Jack Vincent kissed the hell out of his new bride and realized he was absolutely and undeniably in love with her.

Chapter 23

It was Lucy's wedding night, and she couldn't find her husband.

After a quick dinner with her family—a thankful trade-off to a noisy and crowded wedding reception—the New York travelers had boarded their chartered plane and headed back home. Jack had opted to stare out the window for the two-hour flight, not even engaging as Martin posted their wedding picture to Twitter and Instagram. Lucy and Jack had gotten home around nine, at which time Jack set his suitcase in his room, grabbed his wallet and house keys, launched a half-hearted "I'm going out" at Lucy, and left.

It was nearly midnight when her phone chirped, Jack's name blinking across the screen. She answered so quickly that she almost dropped the phone. "Jack, where are you?"

"Hey, Lucy." Jack drawled. "Guess what?"

"What?"

He sighed like a teenager with a new issue of *Tiger Beat*. "I got married today."

Lucy rubbed her temple. "I know. I was there."

He lowered his voice. "You should have been there. My wife was so beautiful. Sometimes I just look at her, and I want to—I want to—" He paused and shouted something away from the phone speaker that sounded suspiciously like Latin. "You should come here. I'm at the Blue Monster."

Lucy was frozen in shock at his almost confession of—well, *something*. *You want to what?* "Jack, it's almost midnight."

"Well, get over here before your Uber turns into a pumpkin then."

She sighed, looking down at her flannel pajamas. "I'll be right there."

When Lucy entered the bar, she was immediately pelted with a tsunami of cheers and applause. She scrunched her shoulders, ready to back out through the door into the street, but a grinning man ran up to her and shouted in a brash but friendly voice, "We got another one!"

The man dunked a beat-up Yankees cap on her head. As she recoiled, he asked, "Which house are you?"

"House?" she stammered, unable to see past the low brim.

"Yeah. Gryffindor, Slytherin…"

"Oh." She twisted and looked back at the door sign to make sure she was in the correct bar. "Ravenclaw, I guess?"

He raised the cap from her head and declared in a haughty tone, "Ravenclaw!" From one corner of the seating area, a group of people whooped and banged glasses against their table. The rest of the bar patrons were separated into the other three corners, each group filled with a handful of very drunk, delighted people.

"Lucy?" A familiar voice shouted from the back of the bar. Jack's head popped up from his usual booth, which was definitely not the Ravenclaw table. He sprinted to the front of the bar—knocking over a bar stool in the process—and seized her hips with his long hands, lifting her into the air and then drawing her close into his arms. He was very inebriated, but unlike their last visit to this establishment, his eyes were shining with humor and happiness.

"You were Ravenclaw, weren't you?" he murmured into her ear, nuzzling at her neck, his lips warm against her chilled skin.

"Naturally." She closed her eyes, attempting to tune out the rowdy laughter and general noise of the bar. "What's going on here?"

He clutched her hand and tugged her toward the middle of the barroom. "Everyone!" he announced. "I'd like you to meet my new wife, Lucy! We got married today!"

He boosted her fist into the air as if she were the victor of a boxing match, and everyone cheered. She immediately covered her ears, and Jack waved his arms in the universal "lower your volume" gesture.

"Now, as a wedding present, if you could all keep your voices down, that'd be awesome," he said, winking. "We've had a long day."

"Why should we do something for a Slytherin?" someone hollered from another corner, their entire table booing.

"Ten points from Gryffindor!" shouted a female bartender, scaling a step ladder and erasing some numbers from a dusty chalkboard on the wall.

"Because it's the Hogwarts way," Jack said solemnly, but then he turned to Lucy with a faint smile. "Dumbledore, could we have a little music, please?"

"For the last time, my name is Dave," mumbled an older bartender, but he fiddled around with some electronic equipment mounted on the wall. The classic rock switched to some guitar chords, pure and sweet, that Lucy knew all too well.

"Mrs. Vincent, our wedding dance?" Jack bowed at the waist and held out his hand, humming along to Elvis's "Love Me Tender" in his low rasp. Lucy took it with a sheepish laugh and looped her arms around his neck, fingering the thick, dark tendrils at his nape.

"You are so very, very..." she trailed off, grimacing in place of the missing adjective.

"Oh, I am absolutely *very*," he said, dipping his head closer to her ear. His breath was warm and ticklish against the surface of her neck, sending shivers sweeping down her spine.

"You organized the whole bar into Harry Potter houses?"

"At least you missed the wizard duels earlier." He bit his bottom lip in a hangdog expression before continuing. "On a related note, we have to buy the bar a new table."

"Of course we do." She paused. "You do realize Slytherin's symbol is the snake."

He glowered. "And all the snakes are evil, which just supports my point."

"I didn't realize you were such a Harry Potter fan."

His eyes glinted, and he looked away. "Something about dead parents and a shitty childhood resonated with me, I guess." He gave an apologetic smile. "Sorry I ran off earlier."

"You're fine," she said, even though she wasn't. "It was a strange day." *The best day of my life.*

Jack gazed at her, his eyes trying to impart something that his intoxicated tongue could not. "I just—I don't know what's real anymore. All of it? None of it? Half of it? Three-eighths of it?" He closed his eyes with a long-suffering sigh. "I'm not good at fractions."

"Wingardium Leviosa!" bellowed a man across the room, tossing his whiskey glass into the air. His face fell in bewildered despair as it plummeted to the ground and shattered.

Jack clicked his tongue and shook his head. "Those are the Hufflepuffs."

"Clearly." Lucy bit her lip and looked at Jack again, unsure of how to draw out whatever he was trying to say through his drunken mumbles. She wasn't sure if it was good or bad, but it felt *important*.

He wiggled his fingers into the belt loops of her jeans and pulled her closer. "You know, we're in public," he said, his eyes darkening and darting to her lips. "And I don't want the other Slytherins to think I'm not capable of seducing my wife."

"There's a lot of competition, but that may be the weirdest thing you've ever said to me," Lucy whispered.

He brought one of his hands to her face, cupping her cheek and stroking his thumb against her skin before he pressed his lips to hers. The kiss was light and wistful, a wedding dance of its own. He moaned, and deepened the kiss, sliding needy hands into her hair and winding a tendril around his fingers as if it were his soul's only tether to his earthly existence.

But then he drew back, his eyes glossy and delirious, and she snapped back to reality. They couldn't do this. He was drunk and not in his right head. Anything he was trying to say was null and void. He wouldn't even remember this the following day.

But she would.

For the next two years, every feigned embrace and deceptive kiss would be etched into her memory, unforgiving and unforgettable. For Jack, they were memories drawn in the sand, just waiting for the tide of alcohol to wash them away in its never-ending ebb and flow.

This kiss was just another drunken shenanigan, and she had signed up to suffer through them all. When Elvis's last chord played, Lucy's heart broke.

"Fellow students, I must take this beautiful Ravenclaw home," yelled Jack, swinging another arm around Lucy and buzzing her cheek with his lips, not noticing her consequent flinch.

Another round of cheers and one woman shouted, "Show her your wand, Jack!"

"Now, now." Jack winked and flashed his half-grin, in total Jack Hunter, flirter of fans mode. "Thank you for tonight, and until next time, don't let the muggles get you down." He stumbled forward, and Lucy caught him, wrapping his arm around her body to steady him.

In an all-too-familiar process, she escorted Jack out of the bar and they rode back to the townhouse without speaking. Then she walked him up the stairs to his bedroom, placed a rolled-up blanket behind his back, and waited until he fell asleep before she began to cry.

The following morning, Martin was saying words. Loud, loud words. Words that wriggled their way into Jack's hungover brain and spun around like a ballerina in a carwash.

"I want to talk to Lucy. Put me on speakerphone," demanded Martin. Jack waved Lucy over with an exasperated gesture before tossing the phone on the table next to his breakfast.

"Lucy, what the hell," said Martin. "Couldn't you keep your husband under control for five minutes?"

Lucy didn't even wince at his harshness. "I'm his spouse," she said flatly. "Not his nanny."

"It's the same thing when you're married to Jack Hunter." Martin muttered a few curses before continuing. "Let's just walk through this, shall we? Yesterday afternoon, we posted an amazing, very romantic wedding picture. The buzz starts." He pitched his voice higher and quoted, "'OMG, Jack Hunter is married!' You were trending; you had a gazillion likes on your Twitter post; Mark Hamill wished you well, and then you know what happened next?"

"No, but I'm sure you're going to tell me," said Jack, adding an additional spoonful of sugar to his coffee.

"Five hours later, there's a picture of you in a dive bar, without your wife, on your wedding night, holding a pool cue like a sword—"

"Technically, like a wand," Lucy corrected.

"And then the Internet thinks you abandoned your wife. Next thing we know, *#wheresmrsjack* is trending. Not even who you are, *where* you are. Like Jack left you on the doorstep of an orphanage or some shit like that."

"I was at the bar later," she offered.

"Oh, I know you were." Martin's snarl smacked of sarcasm. "Because there are pictures of you helping your husband's drunken ass out the door and into a car."

Jack squeezed his eyes shut and rubbed the center of his forehead. "So, let me get this straight," he mumbled, his tongue tripping over itself. "I sorted an entire bar into Harry Potter houses, then the world thought I misplaced my wife, and now they think I'm a drunk?"

"Pretty much!" snapped Martin.

Jack glanced over at Lucy, but she averted her eyes, her fingers smoothing out the edges of a placemat.

"But...isn't that just...the status quo?" Jack asked.

Martin made a strangled noise, hung up, and then called back ten seconds later. "We need to fix this now," said Martin in a false, methodical tone. "Get out there and do some romantic shit." After he hung up again, Jack squinted at Lucy.

"Was I at least a Gryffindor?" he asked.

Lucy threw him a pitying look before retrieving her own phone. "Okay, something romantic," she said, tapping at the screen. "Let's check and see what people are posting on Instagram. It's the holidays, so there's bound to be some basic themes out there." Her voice was peculiar, a little shaky, almost as if she were winded.

"You're not getting sick, are you?" asked Jack, searching her face for signs of distress.

She hummed tightly, and Jack's heartbeat flopped like a fish out of water, gasping for precious air.

Something was wrong.

"I'm fine," she said, scrolling through her phone without glancing up. "We could get a tree and take selfies in front of it while we decorate."

"I don't have a tree," he admitted. He'd never really wanted one before, but now that Lucy had requested it, its absence felt like a vacuum.

She shrugged. "We can get one."

"I also don't have lights."

"We can pick some of those up."

"I'm also fresh out of ornaments." He sent her an apologetic grimace.

"Okay, that might take more time than we're ready for," she said with a resigned sigh. "I'll order some ornaments and we can decorate next weekend. What about Christmas cookies?"

"That sounds simpler," he said absent-mindedly, still studying her pinched expression.

"I have an errand to run; I can pick up some supplies on the way back," she said, rising and pushing her chair in.

Jack stood as well, his knee knocking into the table and splashing coffee onto Lucy's placemat.

"No." She held up a hand with a smile, and Jack's chest throbbed. He knew each and every one of her smiles, and *goddamnit*, that was not a genuine smile. She touched him on the shoulder, her thumb rubbing against the seam of his shirt. "You stay and rest." He followed her to the hall, watching dully as she slipped into her coat and picked up her purse.

"Are you sure you don't want me to come?" Jack asked. He ran his finger over the crest of the guitar string in his wedding band. "It won't take me long to get dressed."

Lucy halted, her hand curled around the doorknob. She turned to him slowly, locking her cocoa-brown eyes on his. There was a flash of something like fear and pleading and guilt all at once, and then it was gone, replaced by a carefully crafted expression. "I'll be fine," she said, and then she bolted out the door, quick as a jackrabbit.

Jack stared at the door before trodding back to the table, where Lucy's breakfast plate lay untouched. He sat down, unsure what had just happened, unsure if anything *had* happened. His face felt swollen and strange, and he wondered if he'd gotten into a fight last night that he couldn't remember. But his nose looked fine with no bruises—so why were his eyes stinging?

Jack got dressed in what he thought was an appropriate outfit for Instagram cookies, which, of course, was his standard T-shirt and jeans. He went to his studio and picked up his guitar and continued to work on his new song, "THE SONG" as he called it in his head, all caps included. He hadn't played any of it for Lucy yet, but Hasan, Lainey, and Maya were extremely enthusiastic about what he had so far.

It wasn't a Jack Hunter song, to be sure. It was...different. It was fun and had its share of *br-ahws* and *hwah-chas* and even a little bit of Diamond-esque musical foreplay. But the chord progression wasn't right and had evolved into a musical Rubik's Cube, something Jack had to twist and turn until he found the right sequence. It was difficult when his mind was consumed by thoughts of anxious brown eyes above lightly freckled cheeks.

His phone rang after an hour, breaking his concentration further. A glance at the caller ID showed it was Parker, most likely calling to have Jack confirm the album art proofs. Jack hadn't even opened the file yet, so he ignored the call and tried to get back into the writing zone.

He hummed and tapped out an accompanying drumbeat on the guitar's waist. The phone rang again, and once again, it was Parker.

"Hold your damn horses," Jack said, flicking the phone across the sofa with a feigned drum roll. The phone dropped between the cushions and the ringing ceased. Jack struck a victory chord on the guitar, but seconds later, Elvis Presley's sultry tones began to play from the phone, muffled through fabric and cushions.

Jack froze. That was Lucy's ringtone. Suddenly, Parker's previous calls seemed a lot more ominous. He dove across the seat and scrambled for the phone.

"Lucy?"

"You're screening me," said Parker.

"Why do you have Lucy's phone?" Jack asked, ignoring the pointed accusation. Parker's lengthy pause caused the hair on Jack's arms to stand stiff as icicles.

"You have to promise not to freak out," Parker said. "Or I'll hang up."

"I won't freak out," lied Jack. "I never freak out."

"You're freaking out now," Parker said.

"Parker," Jack said, over-pronouncing his name. "Why do you have Lucy's phone? Where are you?"

"So," Parker sighed. "We're at the hospital."

Jack, as predicted, freaked out. "What? You're where? Why? Which hospital?"

"Brooklyn City ER. She'll be fine, but—"

"I'll be right there." Jack hung up, tossed his guitar onto a chair, threw on mismatched shoes without socks, and ran out the door to get his wife.

Chapter 24

Jack dashed through the automatic doors at the Brooklyn City emergency room, flailing his arms as if he could make the doors open faster with some sort of Jedi power move.

"Where is she?" he growled at the check-in attendant, skidding to a halt in front of her window. "Lucy. Luciana. Meyer. Vincent. Whichever goddamn name she gave. My wife. Where is my wife?"

The attendant blinked at him, unaffected. "Sir, you need to slow down—"

"Slow down?" he yelled, slamming his palms down on the counter. "Slow down? Oh, ha fucking *ha*, let's make fun of the freaked-out rock star with terrible puns about his career!"

She closed her eyes and inhaled with the shared exasperation of customer service workers everywhere. "No. You need to slow down because I can't understand what you're saying."

"Oh." Jack flushed, took a breath, and tried again. "I need to find my wife."

Elvis's crooning belted from Jack's phone. He snagged it from his pocket with such force that it slipped from his grasp like a cake of soap, spiraling in the air and smacking the attendant on her upper arm. She glared at the phone, unbroken and taunting on her immaculate counter before fixing her executioner's gaze on Jack.

"Sir," she said, the singular word heavy with warning as she cracked her neck.

"Please," said Jack. "Please." A nineties' television character popped into his head, courtesy of life with Lucy, so he went for it. "Have mercy."

Elvis began to sing again. The attendant and Jack stared at the phone before he snatched it away and answered.

"Jack, we can hear you all the way back here," said Parker.

"'Back here'? Where is 'back here'? Where are you?"

"Well, now I'm staring at you." Jack turned to where Parker was frowning through an internal pair of glass sliding doors, putting Lucy's phone away in his pocket.

"Oh, thank God," Jack groaned. "Assist me." He motioned at the attendant, and Parker approached her. After a few animated words, she waved them off with a dissatisfied grunt. Jack bolted through the automatic doors, sprinting until Parker's hands clamped onto his shoulders.

"Wrong way," he said, spinning Jack's body until he faced the opposite way. When he let go, Jack started running again, like a wind-up toy that only knows to go forward as fast as possible. "She's in here."

Jack plowed through the door into a small, hygienically pristine room. The harsh fluorescent lights were dimmed, but not darkened. Lucy was perched cross-legged on the bed, a thin white blanket draped over her shoulders. Her skin was a little pale, with shadows under her eyes, but she glanced up at the door with a cheerful grin—until she saw Jack. She snapped her head toward Parker.

"I told you not to call him," she said.

The assistant merely shrugged at her.

"What happened?" Jack asked, struggling to keep his voice steady.

"I'm fine," she said with an exasperated sigh. "I just fell and hit my head. Not even a concussion." Another glare at Parker. "I don't need to be here."

"You fell?" Jack tried to force oxygen into his lungs before he passed out and they both needed a hospital bed. "How did you fall?"

"Well, I fell after the bike messenger knocked me over."

"The bike messenger." He rubbed a shaky hand over his face and took another deep breath. "I'm getting this story in the wrong order. Start from the beginning."

"I was dropping off a package at UPS," she said in her recitative tone. "I wasn't paying attention. I stepped in front of a bike messenger. He crashed into me."

Jack spun to Parker with a fierce frown. "I want his name. And badge number."

"They're bike messengers, not cops," said Lucy. Her eyes widened with sudden worry. "Do you think he still got his package delivered on time?"

"Lucy."

"Fine, I fell and hit my head. I was only knocked out maybe thirty seconds." She picked at the flimsy threads of the hospital-issued blanket. "The biker made me call someone to get me. I called Parker, and then Parker—" she shot daggers at their assistant, "—made me come here."

"Head injuries are no joke," he protested. "Eighty percent of concussions are—"

"Not now, Parker," Lucy and Jack said in tandem.

He clamped his mouth shut before muttering something about brain trauma and impossible employers.

"You called *him*?" Jack asked, loathing the bitter, itchy feeling running down his spine—confusion, worry, relief, and hurt all fused together and infiltrating his bones. "You called *Parker*?"

Lucy dropped her gaze. Her hand tapped and twitched against the blanket. "Yes."

"But not your husband."

She sighed and met his eyes. "I mean, you're not my *real* husband."

A rattling noise reverberated as Parker stumbled backward, clambering for the door handle. "I'm just—I'm going—you know—Christmas shopping," he mumbled, escaping through the door and shutting it fast behind him.

"Not your real husband?" repeated Jack, cocking his head.

Lucy winced but kept her eyes fastened on his.

"If I remember correctly," he said, tapping his finger to his lips, "I was in a wedding yesterday."

"Jack."

"And if I recall, you were there." He stepped forward until his thighs bumped the safety rail of her bed.

"Jack."

"And I'm pretty sure you gave me a ring." He looked at his left hand and mock-gasped. "Oh, look! There it is!" He wriggled it in the faint light. "Look, it's so shiny!"

"You know that's not what I meant," she protested. "Not real as in—"

"I *am* real," he gritted out. "I *am* your real husband."

Lucy started to turn away, her jaw clenched, but then she paused, giving his expression a double take. Her brows unknitted, and her face relaxed. "I hurt your feelings. I'm sorry." She exhaled, a sound of surrender. "I should have called. We're friends and—"

"Honey," he said, reaching out to cup her chin, tipping her face toward him. "We are not friends. We haven't been friends in a long time."

A kaleidoscope of emotion spun across her face—shock blending into sadness, and sadness blending into puzzlement.

He dropped his hand and twisted away from her. "If you need help," Jack said, "you call me. I don't care when. I don't care why. I don't care if you're lost in the city, or you need bailed out of prison. I don't care if your entire arm fell off, or you just have a paper cut. You call me, and I'll bring a

Band-Aid, and I will bandage up that fucking paper cut. *Just call me.*" He swung open the heavy door.

"Where are you going?" asked Lucy, her voice bewildered.

He turned to her with a much braver smile than was truthful. "I'm going to send Parker home," he said. "Then I'm going to find a doctor and get you out of here. And then, I'm going to murder myself a bike messenger."

After being released several hours later, Lucy barely stayed awake on the ride back to the townhouse. Jack helped her to her room, undressing her clumsily as he tried to pull her shirt over her head without hitting the swollen knot on the side of her skull.

"I can get undressed on my own," she murmured just before snuggling herself into her pillow, clad only in her bra and jeans. Any other time, he would have probably gone mad with lust at the sight, but right now, it would be a bit like seducing a sleepwalker. He tapped a finger between her shoulder blades.

"I finally get to see your tattoo," he said. "Tell me about it. It'll keep you awake 'til you're dressed."

"It's a guitar," she mumbled. "The end."

"Come on, Lucy. You're not falling asleep in your street clothes."

She groaned and rolled over, unzipping her jeans so Jack could shimmy them off her legs. "We all have tattoos. All the siblings. Ariana has the most. We all like to go together and get them. Family bonding and all that."

Jack worked a pair of plaid flannel pants up her calves and thighs, handing the waist off to her so she could wiggle it over her behind. "And you got a guitar?"

"Yeah," she said, rubbing her eyes. "I like music."

He huffed a low laugh. "I know, baby, I know."

"It has the lyrics to 'I Dig Rock and Roll Music' around it." She curved her back so he could see it properly.

"Very appropriate," he said, tossing a sleep shirt over her head and yanking downward. She reappeared through the neck hole with an addled scowl, like a kitten enduring her first bath.

"All right, Cottontail," he said. "I'm done bothering you. Lay down." She burrowed back under her duvet as he tucked it around her. He retreated toward the door as her breathing steadied.

"You don't bother me," she said. "I should have called you."

"Just go to sleep." He hovered in the doorway, watching her—for what, he wasn't sure. He just needed reassurance that she was okay. That *they* were okay.

She raised her head again, her rumpled hair slipping over her face like black lace curtains. "Good Lord," she muttered. "Stop your mother hen impression and get in the bed."

Jack bit back a chuckle, more relieved at her catty response than any previous apology. "Good Lord. Let me get undressed."

She arched an eyebrow and burrowed herself further into the blankets. He stripped down to his boxers as quietly as he could and, since it was too early to join her in sleep, grabbed a book about Motown from her bookshelf, and slipped under the world's most magnificent duvet.

Jack was long gone by the time Lucy finally awoke, the only remnant of his presence a scribbled note on her bedside table that read "EAT. SLEEP. TAKE TYLENOL." and was accompanied by something that was either a sketch of a rabbit or a vacuum cleaner.

A flicker of movement caught her eye through the cracks of the curtain. She peeked out and was greeted by cotton ball clouds and a slate-gray sky.

Snow was coming, and Lucy loved snow.

She stretched with caution, testing for any sharp pains. The lump above her ear was swollen and tender to the touch, but no headache persisted beyond that. A few bruises and stiff joints were the only other effects of the previous day's ordeal.

Well, and also total, utter, absolute, completely bonkers confusion about Jack.

Trying to get a read on his feelings was like trying to get a straight answer from a magic eight-ball. She wanted to shake him and get an "it is decidedly so" or even a "my sources say no" just so she could escape this awful, indeterminate limbo. Instead, she was bombarded with "reply hazy, ask again" every step of the way.

She didn't know what Jack wanted. She didn't even know exactly what *she* wanted. But, what she did know was how to make cookies. Lots and lots of cookies.

Since she hadn't made it to the grocery store yesterday, and she wasn't sure what the forecast for dangerous bike messengers was for today, she ordered groceries for delivery. Within a few hours, she had enough sugar, flour, eggs, and sprinkles to put the Keebler elves out of business.

Lucy loved the way cookies could be both uniform and unique, and she could create the same shape over and over in a flawless, sweet pattern. Back in Indiana, she had a whole box of metal cookie cutters that had been passed down from her paternal grandmother, found in every shape from angels to zebras. Miles away and on short notice, though, she had to work with a cheap cellophane-wrapped four-pack consisting of a star, a stocking, and a gingerbread man and woman.

As she worked up a batch of gingerbread cookies, she bobbed her head and danced around the kitchen to holiday music from Chuck Berry, John Lennon, and Queen. Most of the gingerbread troops were the typical sort, rusty cinnamon brown with polished frosted details. Two, however, she kept aside for customization as *I'm sorry* cookies. Or maybe *Thank you* cookies. Or even, *Are we cool?* cookies.

She first cut out a standard gingerbread man, but then added a silhouette of a guitar, shaped carefully with a butter knife. An adjacent gingerbread woman had a tiny circle placed in her hand, scaled to the cookie size of a vinyl record.

Several hours later, the gingerbread cookies were iced, the sugar cookies were cooling, and her hands had been washed often. Lucy mixed a mass batch of frosting, separating it into smaller bowls and adding food coloring. She lost herself in absolute tranquility as the color rippled out from the drops in precise, orbicular *red green yellow blue*.

A shadow descended over the bowls of rainbow frosting. Lucy jumped and glanced up at the source. Jack stood in the doorway of the kitchen with a peculiar, disoriented expression.

"You scared me," she said, clasping at her heart and planting the wooden spoon in one of the bowls. Jack said nothing, his gaze tracing over her, examining her, that odd, pinched look never fading.

"It's snowing," she said. "So I made Christmas cookies." She peered out the window where the snow shimmered as it caught the city lights' reflections.

Jack's dark eyes shot to the window, then back to Lucy. He raked his hands through his hair, leaving a few rebellious strands saluting upward.

"Fuck." He dropped his head back, staring at the ceiling with his hands on his hips.

Lucy frowned. Maybe he didn't like snow.

"I know we were going to do cookie pictures," she said. "But I wanted to make you a surprise." He tilted his head forward again, his mouth set in a pained grimace. She picked up the plate with her *I'm sorry/thank you/are we cool?/please don't hate me/my sources say I might be in love with you* cookies.

She pointed to the girl first, twirling her hand like Vanna White. "Look, she's holding a little record." She glanced at Jack, who was chewing his bottom lip. This wasn't going well.

"And look at this guy." She held the plate closer to Jack. He looked at the gingerbread man, his finger outlining the edge, sending a few crumbs bouncing across the plate.

"He's got a guitar," she said. Jack's brow knitted together. He ran his fingers through his hair again, and the muscle in his jaw ticked.

"You play guitar," she added, her voice a little wobbly. He lifted his gaze from the cookie very, very slowly until their eyes locked.

Then, in one fluid, startling motion, he snatched the plate from Lucy, tossed it on the counter, cupped her face with his long, lean fingers, and kissed her.

Chapter 25

Lucy tasted like vanilla and frosting, sweet and sugary and addicting, and it was ruining all of Jack's plans.

He pressed his mouth to hers, hard and intent, dancing and exploring, his teeth grazing her bottom lip. She made a small noise—one might call it a *yummy noise*—and slipped her hands around his neck. When she entangled her fingers in his curls, lightning shot down his spine, and he groaned and broke away.

"This isn't—" he began, and then took her mouth again, because *why the hell not?* He walked her backward until her back grazed the counter, and she let out a little "Oh!" at the contact, a squeak of surprise that somehow made him crazier.

"This isn't—" he tried again, speaking between kisses because that was more efficient. "This isn't—" a kiss just below the ridge of her lip "—how this—" another to the slant of her cheekbones "—was supposed to—Christ, I love your nose—" a nuzzle of the feverish skin below her ear "—supposed to go."

Her eyes flew open. "What are you talking about?" And Jack was going to answer, he *really* was, but instead, he kissed her again. Her elbows shook against the counter in a feeble attempt at support, so he scooped his hands under her glorious ass and lifted her onto the surface.

"Okay, knock it off for a second." She slid back onto her feet and ducked under his arm, grabbing the wooden spoon from the table and aiming it at him.

"Are you holding me at spoon point?" he asked. She nodded, jutting the spoon out like a javelin. He took a careful step forward, and green frosting splattered onto his black T-shirt. He looked down at his shirt, swiping at the icing and tasting it in thoughtful appraisal.

"Vanilla?" he asked. She dipped her chin, and he hummed in approval. She poked him with the spoon again and he raised his hands in surrender, taking a seat at the table. Lucy sat on the opposite side, her cheeks flushed and her mouth post-kiss pink.

"What do you mean, 'this isn't how it was supposed to go'?" she prodded.

Jack rubbed at his jaw, surveyed the bowls of colored frosting, and dipped his finger into the purple batch.

Lucy smacked his hand with the spoon. "It took me twenty minutes to get that color."

He sucked the violet icing from his finger. "I was going to tell you tonight that I'm done with all this. I can't do it anymore. This pretending shit. Public pretending is bad enough, but this pretending we're doing in private, it's killing me." He flicked his eyes to hers. "I was going to tell you that I'm done with contracts and planned public poses and separate bedrooms and just *all of it*."

Lucy's eyes had a faint, sorrowful look and he held up a finger. "But then I get home, to this house that I've always hated, and there you are. *There you are.*" The corner of his mouth tipped up just slightly. "Making cookies and dancing around my kitchen—*our* kitchen—getting frosting everywhere and wearing the ugliest apron I've ever seen—"

She squawked. "Hey now!"

Jack raised a finger again. "I was going to do this one thing right. I was going to come home and woo you. Woo the hell out of you. And now that I'm here, I can tell you that that is absolutely not going to happen."

"Why not?" she whispered.

"Because I am about ten seconds away from throwing you back up on the counter and fucking you until neither of us ever thinks about pretending again."

Lucy blinked. And blinked again. Jack used the opportunity to steal more purple frosting. He raised an arrogant, challenging eyebrow at her, but his stomach contorted with nerves.

Lucy stood, and walked to his chair on newborn foal legs. Every step sent electric spikes into Jack's chest, piercing and exhilarating at the same time. He held out a trembling hand to her and—

"Prince played the Super Bowl once."

Jack paused mid-reach, inhaled sharply, and then straightened, letting his arm fall. "All right. Let's see where this one goes."

A smile played around her lips. "It was Prince, so you knew it was going to be amazing. But then the show starts, and it's raining. Pouring. It had never rained during halftime at the Super Bowl, not once, and for Prince, the entire heavens opened up, and he didn't even flinch."

Jack was a little confused, which was normal. But he was also mesmerized, shocks of awareness stirring and boiling his blood into a frenzy, and they weren't even touching yet.

"And at the end, fireworks shoot into the sky, and he breaks into 'Purple Rain,' right there in the rain, and my God. You could feel the electricity from your head to your toes, and you just knew you were witnessing something you were so goddamned lucky to see. Everything good or bad, right and wrong, aligned in one perfect performance. One perfect moment."

She gazed at Jack, her eyes flickering across his face, searching. "We may not have picked each other the conventional way, but we did pick each other, and every time I look at you...it's Prince at the Super Bowl. Everything aligning in one perfect moment."

She reached out to sweep a curl off his brow, and his hand caught hers, tugging her into his lap. This time, the kiss was tender, each brush of his lips questioning her, pleading with her, promising her.

When he broke away again, he pressed his forehead to hers, his hands cupping her jaw and his thumbs caressing her cheeks. "I can't tell you how all this will play out. I can't make it easy and organized and predictable, the way you like it. But I can promise you that if I have to go through one more day and you're not actually mine, not actually *real*, I'll lose my damn mind."

Lucy nodded, just once, but it was everything he needed. He shuddered with relief and held her close, smoothing her hair with his hand. She kissed his forehead, then moved down his cheekbones and across his jaw. Jack let her explore, staying perfectly still, his eyes closed, his head tilted back, his lips parted and breathless. He shivered when she finally nipped at his bottom lip, and Lucy smiled against his mouth. Then she kissed him, deep and hard, her tongue flitting and thrusting inside, and Jack was done with being still.

With a savage growl, he angled his head, driving the kiss deeper, plundering her mouth. His hips rolled upwards, eliciting tandem needy moans. He gripped her ass and lifted her, pinning her against him as he stood. She wrapped her legs around his waist, and he gasped against her lips.

The distance from the kitchen to her bedroom was the longest of Jack's life. There was a brief moment where he thought about giving up halfway and just rutting her right there on the stairs like a buck in heat. Twice, he crushed her against the wall long enough to free his hands for cupping and caressing, squeezing, and savoring. Finally, after kiss-fueled stumbles and gasp-filled gropes and one severely stubbed toe that would hurt like a bitch in the morning, they made it.

Jack laid her down on the bed, her dark hair falling across the blankets like a spilled bolt of silk. Her crimson cheeks, swollen lips, and glazed, expectant eyes were so much better than any lonely cold shower or late-night fantasy, though there had been many of those lately.

He settled on top of her, his hands shaking. "Anything special I gotta do?" he asked.

She tipped her head, studying him, and then ran her thumb against his stubbled jaw. "Whale songs," she whispered with a mischievous twinkle in her eye. Jack dropped his forehead to her collarbone, muffling his laughter against the fabric of her— *wait, why was there still fabric anywhere in the vicinity?*

An awkward, frenzied tussle followed, with clothing flying across the room like flags of surrender. Two pairs of pants. A cheap snowman-print apron. One standard black T-shirt stained with green frosting, and one band T-shirt that was most definitely not a Jack Hunter shirt. Boxers, a bra, one inexplicable sock, and a pair of panties, and then they were exposed to each other at last.

And Jack simply *touched*.

He touched the sparse freckles on her nose and followed them with his finger down her neck like a treasure map. He trailed a hand over the small curve of her breast, admiring the way his faintly food-dyed green and purple fingers danced over her smooth flesh like broken crayons on creamy parchment. He strummed the gentle bend of her waist and brushed the sloping arc of her pelvic bone. And then his finger dipped lower, into welcome wetness that led to writhing legs and arched hips and an inherent need to repeat the journey all over again with lips instead of hands.

There was the clack of a side drawer and the ripping of foil, one more kiss against the pulsing point at Lucy's neck, and he settled into the welcome cradle of her thighs.

And then, despite a sordid history filled with debauched forays into bedrooms and exotic hotels and that one memorable shed in Iowa, Jack Vincent freaked the fuck out.

Every muscle froze, panic racing through his limbs like a spooked stallion. Lucy's eyes widened immediately, and she reached a hand to brush his damp hair back, smoothing it behind his ear in a soothing rhythm.

"This doesn't change anything," he stammered out, his voice hoarse. Her brow wrinkled, but she continued running her fingers through his hair, gentle and calming. "I mean—it changes everything, but it changes nothing, right?" His voice lowered. "Right?"

Lucy wriggled a little until she could thread their hands together, and then she craned her neck upwards and brushed her lips against the tip of his nose. It was silly and spontaneous and somehow exactly the reassurance he needed.

Jack thrust inside, gasping as his mind disintegrated into simple one-word thoughts like *tight* and *wet* and *necessary*. Lucy's eyes fluttered and she rocked upward, wrapping her legs around his back until their hips were flush.

"You feel..." Jack shook his head, at a loss for coherent words.

"I know." Lucy nodded, and her eyes glistened. "You too."

And then Jack moved again, and Lucy moaned, and it was *everything*. It was Prince at the Super Bowl and it was Neil Diamond's teasing synth chords. It was Bowie howling and Elvis crooning and Diana wailing. It was wilted flowers on black and white tiles, and whispered assurances in the dark of the night, and a gentle hand on a warm forehead. It was cocoa and lavender, and it was a single stuttered sentence in the middle of a record store. And above all, it was something a whole lot like love.

And afterward, when legs gave out and heartbeats slowed and breathing evolved from jagged pants to satisfied exhales, Jack tucked her to his side, tracing her back with a lazy finger.

"Still real?" he whispered into her ear, brushing aside her bed-tangled tendrils.

"Still real," she said, sliding her hand into his, her lost butterfly fingers dancing against his palm.

Pinky, ring, middle, index. Repeat.

Chapter 26

Jack awoke to a hand trailing down his backbone. A rustle of rumpled sheets. A chill as blanket-warmed flesh was exposed to room air. And then—

"Holy moly, it's a unicorn," said Lucy.

Jack refused to open his eyes, groping first for the covers to tighten them back around his bare buttocks, and then for Lucy, hooking an elbow around her and hauling her back into his arms.

"I told you," he said, buzzing her temple. "First rule of ass tattoos. Don't talk about ass tattoos."

"But—but—how? Why?"

"Cough syrup," he muttered, kissing the side of her neck, "and John Goodman."

"I see," she said in a tone that suggested she did not see at all. But then Jack kissed lower, and her breath hitched in a way that he hoped meant she had forgotten about unicorns and tattoos and poor John Goodman.

"Your phone is ringing," Lucy breathed out, grasping his wrist. Jack paused his ministrations long enough to acknowledge the dull buzz of the phone vibrating against his nightstand.

"It's fine," he said. "Ignore it." The noise ceased and then restarted.

Lucy grabbed his wrist again, halting his progress. "But what if it's an emergency?" she asked.

"It's not—" Jack remembered the last time he had that particular thought process and checked the phone. "Eh, it's just the Anti-Christ."

"The Anti-Christ?"

"My mother. Ignore her."

The phone stopped vibrating and then began again, because what was more indicative of demonic behavior than calling non-stop while he was trying to gain carnal knowledge of his wife?

Lucy pinned his wrist again, and he groaned. He slid a hand out from the sheets and dipped it into his glass of water on his bedside table, flicking the droplets at the phone. "Stop calling. The power of Christ compels you!"

Lucy sighed and snagged the phone from the nightstand, accepting the call.

"Wait, she usually does—" Too late, Jack's mother's face materialized on the screen. "Video calls," he finished hoarsely, yanking the sheet up and over their nude bodies.

Lucy sat up, her back against the headboard, holding the phone in front of her face and regarding Jack's mother with a clinical expression.

"Who are you?" Rita Rae asked, peering down her expertly sculpted nose.

"I'm Lucy," she said.

"Where's Jack?"

"He's right here." She panned the phone toward Jack for less than a second before bringing it back to her own face.

"You must be the wife," Rita said in a dry tone.

"I must be," said Lucy, just as dryly.

Jack's eyes widened at Lucy's passive sass, unsure if he was worried or aroused by it.

"Charming." The older woman rolled her eyes. "Give the phone to Jack."

Jack took the phone from Lucy, who seemed disinclined to give it up. "What do you want?"

"Darling." His mother's voice turned to velvet. "What is this nonsense? Is this a cry for help?"

"No, I got married." He paused. "Pretty sure you're familiar with that concept."

"Jack," she purred, though her eyes had thinned to slits. "There's someone I want you to meet. She's a runner-up from that reality show, the one with the roses. I've taken her under my wing as a bit of a mentor. You would love her."

"Mother." Once again, he wondered why he didn't just call her by name, or even some sort of variation of *hellspawn*.

Lucy squinted an eye in disbelief. "Is she setting you up on a date?"

"You're not famous enough," Jack mouthed at her.

"Jack, pay attention," Rita snapped. She smoothed her ombre hair, flipping the tendrils behind her shoulder. "I'm on *Angie in the Afternoon* on Friday. Maureen might be there."

"Who's Maureen?" Lucy piped up.

"I think she's the reality star," Jack said out of the corner of his mouth. "Mother, I think we've already established that I'm married."

"Fine. Have it your way." Her eyes flicked to Lucy with distaste. "Angie suggested that you appear on the show with me, and we could do a duet. A Christmas one."

And there it was. There was always a self-promoting reason for Rita's calls. "No. Also," Jack stroked his jaw with a dramatic pondering pout, "no."

"Oh, but Jack, dear." Rita's mouth widened in a devious grin. "I'm sure Kim would think it's a great idea."

Jack's grim smile stayed in place, but his heart sank. If Rita went to Kim, Kim would ask Jack, and though she'd respect his decision, she'd know as well as he did that it was a good idea, even if it was painful. Who wouldn't want to see a mother-son Christmas duet? It was as holly jolly as overdosing on dollar store candy canes.

And then there was Lucy. Now that she was his, he had the sickening desire to make sound business decisions, like strengthen his public image or carry a leather briefcase.

"Fine," he said in resignation. "But only to promote the new album. I'm not doing this as some sort of vanity project for you."

His mother paused, coiled like a combat-ready rattlesnake. "I'm just trying to look out for you, darling. If you hadn't wasted the past few years being such a drunken idiot, you'd be the headliner, not me."

Jack tried not to flinch at her venomous strike, but it was inevitable. He'd been hearing *if you hadn't* statements his whole life, but they never ceased to cut into his chest like an arrowhead.

"And you wouldn't be resorting to marrying groupies," Rita added.

Now she'd done it.

"Groupie?" Lucy snatched the phone from Jack with such force that she nearly took his fingers along with it. "Groupie?! I am many things, but I am *not* a groupie." Jack strained to take the phone back, but she squirmed away and continued. "And how dare you talk like that to your son!"

Rita didn't even blink, and if Jack weren't so familiar with her habits, he wouldn't have noticed the threatening set to her jaw. "Do you even know who I am?" Rita drawled.

Oh, Mother. Jack pinched the bridge of his nose and waited.

Lucy made a choked scoffing noise. "Rita Rae. Genre, pop. Instrument, vocals only. First album, *Girl Downstairs*. 1979. Second album, *Corner Dance*. 1982. One Grammy." Her nostrils flared. "Your last album, *A Rita Rae Christmas*, only sold—"

And that shattered his mother's calm demeanor. "I won't be talked to like this by some star fu—"

"Uh, yeah, no." Jack ended the call and tossed the phone on the nightstand. It skidded across the varnish and fell to the carpet below.

Lucy let out a long, exasperated sigh. "So, that's my mother-in-law?"

Jack rolled over until Lucy was pinned underneath him. "Holy shit," he breathed.

Lucy frowned. "Yes?"

"You're like an Avenging Angel." He kissed the tip of her nose. "A Harbinger of Havoc. A Bad-Ass of...Bad-Assery."

She blinked. "Jack."

"I mean, you took on my *mom*!" he said. "She's a celebrity!"

Lucy tilted her head and gave him an expectant look.

"Oh yeah." he scrunched his nose. "But she's the scary kind of celebrity. I'm just the drunken idiot kind."

Lucy's body went rigid beneath him. "You're not an idiot."

"Yeah?"

"And except for your visit to Hogwarts, you haven't been drinking as much."

Jack thought back to the past week. Except for that night in the bar, he hadn't had a drink since before they went to Indiana. That siren's call to drink was always there, but it hadn't been that loud in many days. The change both elated and terrified him, and suddenly, all he wanted was something to ground him.

Or someone.

"Need you," he said hoarsely, rolling his hips against hers and kissing her in the hollow of her collarbone. Her eyes flitted shut and her neck tilted back in a sensual arch. He traced the sunlit slope with his fingers, committing every tender inch of skin to memory and claiming it all as *mine, mine, mine.*

Lucy gasped when he slid into her tight warmth, and the sound was a breath mark, the hush before the conductor raises his baton. Then they moved together, legs tangled and lips meeting. Every moan was a melody, every sigh a symphony. And when at last they tipped over into oblivion together, it was a perfect, sweet, duet.

The soundstage of *Angie in the Afternoon* was the exact opposite of Lucy's concert experience. Yes, there were people, and yes, there were lights and noises, but it was much calmer, more of a gentle rain than a roaring typhoon. Parker had gotten her an aisle seat, just in case, and he would sit next to her during the taping.

Jack had struggled that week, though he would have never admitted it to her. He'd spent his days at the studio and his nights—and sometimes afternoons—and, oh hell, mornings too—in bed with her, but there were moments outside of that when his honeymoon eyes had lost their luster, the grim line of his mouth tightened, and his hand grasped and flexed around a phantom glass. As the day of the interview neared, the episodes grew more frequent. Lucy had refrained from mentioning his mother, and he never brought her up, not even as they arrived at the television studio before recording.

Parker took his seat next to her a few minutes before the scheduled start time.

"How was he backstage?" Lucy asked.

"We holed up in the dressing room until I had to go," Parker said. "He seemed resigned to his fate, for the most part. There may have been some punched pillows and a flying water bottle, but yeah, resigned to his fate."

Lucy rubbed at her forehead. "And everything is set up for afterward?"

Parker cracked a grin. "Of course. The food should be —"

He was interrupted by a round of applause as the show began taping. Angie, a bubbly middle-aged woman who somehow made her viewers feel like her best friend, sibling, child, and student all at once, came out to a roar of clapping over a saxophone solo of "Rudolph, the Red-Nosed Reindeer." Between covering her ears and Parker's single, soothing hand on her back, Lucy managed to stay grounded. As the interviews began, she was able to appreciate the intricacies of daytime television talk shows. They laughed through an interview with an amiable Broadway composer and clapped for a children's a cappella act. During breaks, Parker pointed out different electrical equipment, cameras, and recording devices he had mastered in school.

And then the lights dimmed to blues and whites and twinkling fairy lights, and Rita and Jack descended onto the second stage, hand in hand, until they sat in two high-backed wooden chairs in front of a microphone and Jack's guitar perched on a stand. Jack flashed his mother a tender smile, and it was clear he had inherited some of his late father's acting talent.

After one of Jack's saucy winks at the audience, they began a simplistic cover of Bing Crosby and David Bowie's arrangement of "Peace on Earth" and "Little Drummer Boy," accompanied by Jack's acoustic guitar.

Though she kept her eyes on her husband, who "pa rum pum pum pum"-ed like a champ, Lucy admitted to herself that Rita Rae did have a lovely voice. It was just one of those cases where the metaphorical bubble was inherently better than the bubble blower herself.

"He deserves an Oscar," grumbled Parker as the song ended and Jack leaned over and kissed his mother on the cheek as they acknowledged the audience's applause. He grabbed Rita's hand in one hand, and his guitar in the other, and they made their way to the main stage, hugging and kissing Angie like a long-lost relative.

"Riiiiiiiita, always a favorite guest!" cooed Angie in her usual singsong voice, stretching her vowels like taffy as she hugged the slender pop star. "And Jack, it's been a while, but it's always an adventure when you're here."

Jack gave her round cheek a smacking kiss and flopped down onto the guest sofa, guitar in his lap like a purring pussycat.

Jack usually brought his guitar to interviews, a gimmick that had started when he was a nervous teenager on Conan O'Brien's show and simply forgot to put it down after his performance. It spurned several unforgettable moments over the years, including an impromptu duet with Aretha Franklin and a flirtatious serenade of Dolly Parton on her birthday. Usually, though, it was just there to hold and occasionally pluck, like an oversized fidget spinner.

"So, first off, congratulations on getting maaaaarrrr-ieeeeed," squealed Angie, grasping Jack's left wrist and displaying his ring for the audience to see. Jack grinned and wiggled two bunny-like fingers in Lucy's direction. Lucy wasn't sure if he could see her, but she curled two fingers in response just in case.

"Rita, what was it like seeing your baby boy go down the aisle at last?" asked Angie, unknowingly igniting the end of a pop star-shaped firecracker. Parker's forearm tensed on the armrest between them. Lucy wasn't sure if she needed to preemptively call the police or make the sign of the cross.

"Well, he's forty years old," said Rita with a sickly smile, "It's about time he settled down." She laughed without humor and patted Jack on the shoulder. "But I actually wasn't at the wedding. Lucy and Jack wanted to keep it private and—I suppose *rural* is the right word."

Jack's hand went to his guitar, softly plucking at the E string. Lucy tapped her palm in sympathetic anxiety.

"Yes, we got married in a small ceremony in Indiana." He winked at the audience again. "Go, Hoosiers!" A few attendees whooped in response.

"Yes, I wish I could have been there, but it makes me so happy to see how happy Jack is." Rita gripped her son's bicep as if he were still a naughty child she was yanking into the corner to punish.

"It's hard to miss a family member's wedding," Jack said. "I haven't been able to make your last—" he counted off on his fingers, "—four weddings?" He beamed puppy dog eyes at Angie. "Tour schedules, you know?"

"Hmm, yes," agreed the television host. Her top lip was curved in a smile, but her bottom lip was well on its way to a grimace. Angie turned her attention to Rita, prompting her about the upcoming season of her singing contest show. Lucy tuned out her mother-in-law and tried to concentrate on Jack's fingers, which were traveling all across the guitar. It sounded a little like "Slow Down," but when she repeated the notes in her head—

Lucy groaned and buried her face in her hands as her husband plucked out the tune to "You're So Vain" on national television while his mother discussed her career.

The interview went downhill from there.

Jack talked about the upcoming album, which Rita turned into a discussion about her own extensive catalog. Jack countered by picking out Darth Vader's theme, "The Imperial March" on the guitar while Rita extolled her partnership with a new makeup company. By the time the interview was well past done, Rita's face was the color of a turnip, Angie was stammering and flustered, members of the audience were smirking with apparent schadenfreude, and Jack was playing "Ding-Dong! The Witch is Dead" on his guitar with a deluded grin.

"Well, as alwaaaaaaaays," Angie swallowed with the expression of a robot who had just learned to smile, "thanks for coming on the show, and we'll have you back soon!" She winked at the camera. "Maaaaaaaybe not on the same day though." The cameras cut away, and two stagehands came out to lead Jack and Rita back to their dressing rooms.

"I'm going back there," sighed Lucy, rummaging for her pass. "You go get things ready back home."

Parker shook his head. "I feel like I just watched a boxing match. I think I need a nap." He flashed Lucy a nervous glance. "See you tonight?"

"If Jack is still alive, yes," she muttered, heading backstage. Before she made it down the hallway, though, her phone buzzed in her purse with an incoming text.

MARTIN: Your husband's an idiot. But Twitter is in love with him right now. Good work.

Lucy's nose flared, and she leaned against the wall, inhaling to keep her temper in check. Even so, her response was texted with fierce, thunking taps against the glass screen.

LUCY: He's not an idiot.

Martin's response was sluggish and simple, and she knew he was probably gritting his teeth just as much as she was as he texted it. Still, the single word was a revelation coming from the prickly man.

MARTIN: Sorry.

Unsurprisingly, Jack was alone in his dressing room when Lucy found him. There was a sound like a parrot going through a wind turbine a few doors down, which Lucy assumed was Rita in the midst of a tantrum. Jack laid on his back on the sofa, legs sprawled over the cushions he bounced a tennis ball off the ceiling and caught it.

"Well," said Lucy. Jack startled and hurled the tennis ball careening into a fluorescent ceiling light, which shattered and dimmed the room. He gawked at the broken glass, then flipped his head upside down over the armrest to look at Lucy.

"Well," he said.

She knelt by the sofa and ran her hands through the askew strands of Jack's curls, hanging mid-air over the upholstery. "Tell me," she said with a smile. "Tell me what's going on in that head. No editing."

He tilted his chin until their lips met in a sweet but bizarre-feeling upside-down kiss. "My mom's a dick," he murmured against her cheek.

"Yeah?"

"Yeah." He frowned, though it looked like a smile from this angle. "Your mom fed me pasta."

"Yeah?"

"Yeah." Something like defeat, even grief, flitted across his face. This went beyond pasta, and they both knew it.

"Come on," Lucy said, kissing his forehead. "Your face is turning purple in that position, and I promised Sully I'd pick some stuff up at the music store later."

Jack groaned. "Can't we just go home? Home has cookies." Lucy shook her head and pushed on his shoulders until he sat up. "I'm in distress. The only cure is gingerbread. Lots and lots of gingerbread."

The drive to the music store was quiet except for the plink of light sleet against the glass. Once there, Jack followed Lucy out of the car and into the store with no small amount of grumbling. By the time they reached the door, Lucy laid a finger across his pouting lips, which he promptly nipped.

"Hush for five minutes," she said. "Please?"

He nodded, she opened the door, and—

"Surprise!" a chorus of voices surrounded them like a woolen blanket. Jack's nostrils flared, and he tugged Lucy to his side, shielding her with his arm.

"I thought you didn't like surprises," he said, his jaw clenched and his dark brows wrinkled.

She shook her head and smiled. "It's not a surprise for me," she said. He blinked again at the people gathered in front of him. Parker, finishing up the last bits of decor on a Christmas tree. Sully and Maya, laying out a tray of cookies. Trent and Kim arguing as they set up a Bluetooth speaker of holiday music. Lainey and Hasan waving like loons as Lucy and Jack approached. Even Martin was there, scowling at everyone whenever he looked up from his phone. They were all there, in his building, in his safe place. There for *him*.

"I don't understand," Jack said, his voice quiet as he brushed over the tree's tinsel with a cautious finger. "It's not my birthday."

"Read the sign," Hasan suggested, pointing to the crooked banner hanging off a pair of bookshelves. In spindly script, it read, "Happy Holidays & Congrats On Your Wedding & You Survived Today Even Though It Sucked."

"Oh," said Jack in that strange, withdrawn voice. Lucy tugged him around to each guest, and he exchanged hugs and thanked them in a daze.

"One more surprise," she said, checking her watch, and he followed her upstairs to his studio. She unplugged her tablet from its charger and beckoned him to the couch, snuggling in next to him as she started a video call. One by one, his in-laws popped up on the screen like a virtual game of whack-a-mole. Ben and Rose sitting on the couch in the old living room. Sophia and Elena in a cramped off-campus apartment. Nico and Ariana calling from their respective offices, and Dante and Matteo from one or the other's house.

"Hi Jack!" they all intoned, not at all in sync or rhythm. Then an explosion of questions and conversations came at him, asking him *How are you?* and *How was the show?* and *We can't wait to see you and Lucy* and *Are you getting enough sun because you look a little pale* and *Don't forget to call Nonna next week because it's her birthday* and *Did Lucy make you her gingerbread because it's really good but she should use more molasses because it's a good source of iron*. It was pure, unfiltered chaos wrapped in a long-distance hug.

Afterwards, he shut down the tablet and handed it to his wife with shaking hands. Then Jack Vincent, award-winning and platinum-selling artist, former teen idol, and worldwide rock star, who not so long ago had millions of fans but no one to take care of him when he was sick, put his face in his hands and began to cry.

Chapter 27

"I have something for you," Jack said a month later as they ran through the back door of the Stewart Theater in Albany, dodging January winds and unyielding snow. The theater wasn't Madison Square Garden, but it was the best venue Kim could get on short notice, booked when public interest in Jack had begun to grow again.

"You do?" Lucy frowned, stamping the snow off her boots. "I don't like surprises."

"I know." He gave her an odd look. "It's not a real surprise. More like an unexpected action that I have taken."

She squinted an eye. "That's literally the definition of a surprise."

"Oh. Well, then." His confident, cocky half-smile was nowhere to be found, replaced with anxious, tight lips. He folded her hand in the crook of his arm like a tense prom date.

"You look nervous," she said. "Is it Uncle Jesse? Has he come to steal me away?"

"No." He scowled at her. "And the poor man has a real name, you know." They stopped by a dinged metal door, a crinkled sheet with his name attached by peeling masking tape. His throat bobbed, and he gestured for her to enter.

Lucy pushed the ajar door open with her index finger, half-expecting someone to jump out from inside. Instead of the stark, fluorescent-lit dressing rooms of other venues, the room was filled with soft, warm light, emitted by a cozy standing lamp that looked plucked from an antique store or a grandmother's living room. Jack's acoustic guitar was already leaning against the wall, and some helpful concert tech had loaded a folding card table with bottled water and snacks. And on the other side of the room...*oh*.

"Jack?" she asked. Her voice trembled and wavered like newsprint in a summer breeze. "Is this...for me?"

She took a shaking step forward. The other half of the dressing room had been converted into the epitome of cozy comfort. A plush plaid blanket laid folded over the arm of an oversized, squishy easy chair in a scene right out of an L.L.Bean catalog. In front of the gray chair was a television, and on the screen was a clear view of the empty stage.

"Look here," Jack said. The tips of his ears were piglet pink as he guided Lucy to a coffee table next to the chair. "You can use this remote to zoom in however you like, or move the camera from side to side." He clicked the buttons to demonstrate, zeroing in on an unsuspecting stagehand.

"I can watch your concert. I can really watch it." How could her heart hurt be this full?

He expelled a long breath. "Is it okay?"

Lucy couldn't speak. She was stricken silent with awe and amazement and absolute, absolute love.

She loved him. She loved Jack.

Lucy clapped a hand over her mouth, preventing the declaration from rushing out of her lips like a careening river.

"You're editing. I can see it in your face." His smile fell.

She dropped her hand and clamped her mouth shut. Her fingers were twisting and twitching, little flickers of movement that were the only barrier keeping the words from spurting out. She shook her head and stumbled toward him, throwing her arms around his waist and squeezing a startled "Oof!" from him. An attempted inhale mutated into a hiccupped sob.

"Are you crying?" His tone was bewildered as he ran his fingers through the tangles of her hair. "Please don't cry."

Lucy buried her face against his chest, her fingers trailing back and forth against his collarbone. Thankfully, his shirt was black, and it hid the tear stains.

"Is it a sad kind of cry?"

She managed a weak head shake.

"So you're happy." He tipped her chin up, wiping away her tears with his rough thumb. Their eyes locked, and it was over; the dam was broken.

"Oh God, I'm so in love with you," she breathed out. His body froze in place, his eyes flared, and Lucy's mind shut down.

Wrong wrong wrong wrong wrong

He dropped his hand from her chin and stumbled backward.

Wrong wrong wrong wrong wrong

Both of his hands covered his face, and he scrubbed at his scruffy jawline. "What did you say?"

"Nothing." Lucy's eyes snapped to the floor, studying the lines of the faux-wood flooring and trying to lose herself in the patterned swirls.

"No, Lucy," he commanded, stepping back toward her, cupping her face in his broad hands. "You don't get to do that. You don't get to spring that on me and disappear into your head." He tilted her head again until their eyes met. "What. Did. You. Say?"

Lucy was trembling, her heart racing, but still his gaze seared into hers, fury and lust and something wholly more complex twisting together into a flame that burned away at the last of her defenses. "I'm in love with you."

He made a pained, guttural sound and touched his forehead to hers. "No one—*no one* has ever said that to me."

"I'm sorry. I just—it came out. But we can pretend I didn't and just have everything go on as normal. It's okay, I—"

"Hush." He dipped his head to meet her eyes. "Are you going to let me say it back, or do you need to keep talking?"

She blinked. "Wait—what?"

He leaned in, brushing her lips with his before smiling. "I love you, Luciana. Good God, how I love you."

Lucy pressed a hand to her sternum, her chest prickling with a beautiful, wondrous ache that made her want to laugh and cry and run and fall, fall, fall, deeper and deeper.

"Really?"

"Really. You're it for me, Cottontail. Contract or no contract." He flopped back into the easy chair, drawing her onto his lap. "I'm not sure where we go from here. You've already moved in, and I've already proposed." He nuzzled her nose. "Are we at the matching pajamas phase yet?"

"Let's start with matching slippers and work our way up." She leaned forward, kissing him with tiny, affectionate pecks. He drew her closer and deepened the kiss, grinning against her mouth as he rolled his hips upward, the friction and pressure causing a tug deep in her belly.

"Guess what," he whispered, nipping at her lip. "I love you."

"Guess what," she said, dipping her fingers into his waistband, the metal button of his jeans cold against her skin. "I love you too."

A knock at the door interrupted them. "Ten minutes to soundcheck, Mr. Hunter."

Jack dropped his head on her shoulder with an agonized moan. "Can we just postpone the concert?"

"Nope." Lucy pressed a chaste kiss to his hairline, where silver and espresso alternated in a monochrome symphony. "The show much go on."

"And what a show it will be." His impish mouth cocked to the side. "But first, Cottontail, you need to help me with my eyeliner."

Lucy had always wondered what it would have been like to be in the audience during Elvis's comeback special. To see the legend of all legends brought back to life more potent than ever, like a rock and roll phoenix rising from the ashes of frivolous movies, nonsense songs, and the pressures of fame and fortune.

As Jack descended on the stage, flanked by Hasan, Lainey, and Maya, Lucy's heart stuttered. This was something different. Something new. Something *legendary*.

Lainey broke into a wailing intro to "Slow Down," and as her fingers danced over the strings like an electric ballerina, Jack pointed to where Lucy's camera was hanging from the catwalk. With a Cheshire Cat smile, he wriggled two fingers in his rabbit symbol, just for her, before breaking into the performance of a lifetime.

Guitars screamed. Fans roared. Lights flared. And despite the *crowds* and the *lights* and the *noise*, Lucy was safe and calm, curled up in an armchair that felt more like a hug than a piece of furniture.

At the end of the show, Jack approached the microphone with a flirty but sheepish smile. "So, uh, we're gonna try something new," he said, crinkling his nose teasingly at the consequent cheers. "We're gonna finish up with our new single from the upcoming album. Hope you like it."

Lucy crossed her fingers on both hands, wishing she could cross her toes as well. This was Jack's first single in nearly five years, and she didn't know anything about it. Was it going to be a love ballad? Something wistful? Something darker? All she had to go on was the occasional roguish smirk and a "You'll see, Cottontail" whenever she had asked about it.

And then the lights went out. A single spotlight, pale as a moonbeam, shone down on Jack where he stood, center stage, strumming in a minor chord as he began to sing.

"*Listen, my children, and you shall hear of a demon king from hell,*
A dark-eyed knave from New York town, whom you all know so well."

Lucy clapped a hand over her mouth, her eyes wide as tea saucers.

"His name is known throughout the world as a genius or a hack,
But oh, the many stories,
The rumors and the stories,
The legends and the stories of the bastard called Mad Jack."

Lucy slapped her second hand over the first, because *holy shit, it was a sea shanty.*

The stage lights exploded into an array of swirling colors, unveiling the rest of the band as Lainey burst into a wild guitar intro, turning it into—a punk rock sea shanty? But on stage left, Maya had brought out a fiddle—an *actual goddamned fiddle*—transforming the song into what could maybe be called a Celtic-influenced folk punk rock sea shanty. All the while, Hasan was in the back, thumping away at his drums, and Jack was front and center, grinning and laughing like the veritable madman he was as he leaned in for the chorus.

"With a hey—" and Maya, Lainey, and Hasan all yelled "hey!" in response.

"And a ho—" (Again, a shout of "ho!")

"And to hell with them all,
Mad Jack is somewhere out there following the devil's call
Watch your gin, watch your gold, and above all, watch your back,
'Cause no one here on earth is safe from that bastard old Mad Jack."

The audience absolutely lost their minds. Whoops and hollers and cheers echoed like fireworks through the theater as Jack went on to croon about "a bed fire down in Rio," a "holy man and a monkey," a "sword fight with an ambassador," and countless other tales—no, not *tales*, but *shenanigans*.

When the bridge came, the drums, guitar, and fiddle dropped out, leaving Jack alone with a guitar and a smirk, waving his hands at the audience.

"You gotta be quiet so I can finish," he said, ducking at the barrage of cheers that came at him before singing.

"He nearly was thrown in jail because of one ticked-off prince,
And went back to the big city and hid there ever since
But before he hung up his guitar and let life fade to black—"

Jack moseyed closer to the microphone, speaking the following lines in a libidinous purr that demonstrated just why so many fans launched their bras on stage at his concerts.

"A rock and roller rabbit,
A jumpy sort of rabbit,

"An elusive little rabbit—" and he paused and sneered in the most Elvis-y fashion imaginable,

"—Tamed that bastard, poor Mad Jack."

Lainey struck a power chord. Lucy fanned herself. The song finished with a raucous repeat of the chorus, with fans yelling the "hey!" and "ho!" and Maya's hand flying as she fiddled, and in the midst of it all, Jack singing and laughing and possessing the stage like a maniacal trickster god of rock and roll.

The stage went dark, and the house lights went up. Lucy turned off her television as running footsteps thundered in the hallway outside, and Jack sprinted into the room like a kid on Christmas morning. His hair and shirt were slick with sweat, and his chest was pumping like a locomotive engine.

Lucy met his gaze, then tipped her head toward the doorknob. Jack's grin unfolded across his face, and he flicked the lock with a sultry, teasing pout—and then staggered back as she flung herself at him, lips meeting lips in rough, gasping cadences.

"What was that?" she demanded between kisses. "I mean—seriously, what *was* that?"

"That, my darling," Jack growled, biting below her jawline, "was a motherfucking *shenanigan*."

She yanked his shirt over his head, ignoring the rent sound of a torn seam, and reciprocated with her own shirt.

Jack stared down at her, pupils blown, his face lit with lust and adrenaline. "Have mercy," he breathed, grinning wickedly as she shivered from head to toe.

Then Lucy seized his hand, dragged him to the easy chair, and proceeded to show him exactly what she thought of that bastard poor Mad Jack.

Chapter 28

One month, and everything changed.

Derelict Records released "The Ballad of Mad Jack" as Jack's first single from his new album. Despite its unusual composition, the song climbed the charts faster than a spider monkey up a tree, and requests for bookings and television appearances filled Kim's inbox until she could barely keep up.

Frank and Keith reached out directly to have a discussion about renewing Jack's contract. With no lack of smugness, he told them he was swamped and had Parker handle their correspondence instead.

He continued to polish the album, readying it for release into the world. Lainey, Hasan, Maya, and Jack worked together like clockwork, each one supplementing the other in ideas and trust and laughter. And at the end of every session, Jack went home.

Home to his Lucy.

They made love in every room of the townhouse until they were gasping and giggling and sore. They watched old reruns and classic concerts tangled in each other's arms, snacking on homemade cookies. They took stupidly adorable selfies and posted them on social media, documenting how their life together had become so happy.

Until one day, it wasn't.

There was a ringing phone in the evening. A stuttered greeting. A gasp, a whimper. A promise to be there soon.

And when Jack folded his arms around Lucy and wiped the tears from her cheeks, all she could say was, "We have to go."

Hours after, Dante retrieved them from the Indianapolis airport, his eyes red-rimmed, crescent shadows curved under his eyes. He hugged Lucy first, then embraced Jack, his chest shuddering. Bittersweet warmth filled Jack's chest. This was what family meant too. Not just loud dinners and late-night laughter, but sweet, sharp grief, clutching each other in search of love and comfort.

"Tell us everything," Jack said as they got into Dante's car. He sat in the back with Lucy, each needing the assurance of the other's hands, but Dante didn't seem to mind.

"You know how Nico is with cars," he said, his voice hoarse. "It was icy. He took a turn too fast, and that was it. The way he ended up, his leg was crushed. And his internal injuries..." He swallowed. "He was still in surgery when I left."

"Is everyone at the hospital?" Lucy asked, and he nodded.

"Ariana got there about an hour ago." He shrugged, the movement dissolute and hopeless. "And now we wait."

The drive was much shorter since they didn't have to go all the way to Sparrow Hill, their destination being one of the city's hospitals. They rode in silence, their abilities to speak or even cry lost to the strange purgatory of unknowing.

There was a parking garage, a lobby, an elevator, but Jack barely processed them. He held Lucy's hand, his eyes darting to her every so often for an assessment. She was pale, but hadn't cried since New York. He half-wished she would, to let out some sort of tension, but she held herself in a cocoon of static suffering instead.

The waiting room was graveyard quiet, filled only with the Meyer family in their vigilant watch. Lucy went to her mother, tucking herself in the older woman's arms.

"Anything new?" he asked as Lettie approached him, curling an arm awkwardly around his shoulder in a half-hug as she tried not to squish Gianna in the crook of her elbow.

"Should be soon," she sniffled. "The last update was about two hours ago. They're still trying to relieve the swelling in his brain." She shook her head, and fury rolled off her in waves. "He's so stupid. So fucking—" she glanced over to where her mother sat, and lowered her voice, "—so fucking stupid. If he dies, I'm going to kill him."

Jack was saved from responding to that logic by a wail from Gianna, who was not having any of this nonsense. Lettie stared down at her daughter, eyes brimming with frustrated tears, and Jack said the one thing he'd never thought he'd say.

"I'll take her," he offered. "Go rest."

Lettie blinked at him. "Are you sure?"

"Yeah," he said with feigned, foolish confidence. "Give her here."

Lettie stared at him as if he'd just revealed that he was part dinosaur. Then she pressed a kiss to the baby's head and handed her over.

For the first time in his life, Jack Vincent was holding a baby. He tucked her into his elbow, hiding his shaking fingers from her mother as he shooed her away. Gianna was heavier than he imagined and didn't feel at all like the bag of flour he'd had to take care of in high school home economics classes. He grimaced, remembering that his bag of flour had ended up in a dusty explosion on the floor of the Lexington Avenue subway, and he held the baby a little more securely.

Gianna looked at him with an unimpressed scowl, and Jack relaxed a little. Scowls he could handle. He was a scowler. His wife was a scowler. And apparently, his niece was a scowler. He strolled around the waiting room with the baby, using his footsteps to walk away his worry. He received an appreciative nod from Ben, and a small smirk from Sophia, but the love and awe reflected in Lucy's eyes erased the last traces of baby-holding nerves. For the first time in nearly forty-one years, Jack had a real family, and if that meant carrying around a small human that had nothing in common with a bag of flour, he was ready to do it.

"Hey, Gigi," he murmured, readjusting her until her head was resting on his shoulder. "How can you tell a tree is a dogwood tree? By its bark."

The baby didn't laugh, of course, but neither did he. He worked his way through his scanty joke repertoire, then moved on to a lullaby-soft version of "The Ballad of Mad Jack." By the time Lucy joined him, he was pretty sure Gianna was asleep, if the drool on his shoulder seam was any sign.

Lucy took the baby from him and motioned toward the doors to the restricted area. A doctor had entered, and her family approached him like apostles to a prophet.

"Hi, I'm Dr. Avery," he said, rubbing at fatigued eyes. "I've been in surgery with Nico." There was a hush, a collective holding of breath. "We reduced the swelling, but he's in a coma. His body is basically shutting down to heal. He could wake up in thirty minutes, or thirty days." The unspoken *or never* sent a shudder through the room, but it was still better than a spoken *he didn't make it*.

"I recommend you go home and rest," he said. "We'll call if anything changes."

The rest of her family picked up coats and bags and tired feet and headed out, one by one, but Lucy stayed, frozen on a stiff, upholstered chair.

"Come on," Jack said, kneeling in front of her, wide hands on her knees. "It's late. Parker booked a whole block of hotel rooms for your family. Let's head over and get some sleep."

Lucy shook her head. "No." Her lips thinned, and her fingers tapped furiously at her palm.

"Honey," he said. "We don't know if —"

"I can't," she bit out. Her eyes darted around the room, bouncing off every object and person except Jack. "I have to stay."

Jack stood, reaching out a hand to swipe a tendril of hair from her cheek. She jumped, her shoulders tensing as if electrocuted. "All right, Cottontail," he said. "Then we stay."

Her eyes finally met his. "You can go sleep," she whispered. "It's fine. I'll stay."

He sat next to her, shaking out his coat and draping it over their legs. "Nope. We stay."

Morning came and went, and Nico did not wake up. Lettie went home to her own farm to care for the animals and wait for news. Lucy held her brother's bruised hand and recited stories and facts about her favorite musicians, hoping he would hear her voice.

Two days came and went, and Nico did not wake up. Sophia and Elena went back to school to attend classes and wait for news. Lucy held her brother's hand and played "Space Oddity" over and over until she fell asleep on the armrest of her chair.

Four days came and went, and Nico did not wake up. Dante and Ariana each went back to reopen their respective businesses and wait for news. Lucy sat in the hallway, rocking herself back and forth to prevent a meltdown, while inside, the nurses moved her brother back and forth to prevent bedsores.

One week came and went, and Nico did not wake up. Matteo went home to finish a job contract and wait for news. Lucy held her brother's hand and read to him from one of his textbooks until her voice was cracking, and then past that point until she felt Jack's hand running through her hair, gentle and soothing.

"Luciana," he said, clearing his throat. "We—"

"No," she said, not even glancing up at him. She brushed her hand over Nico's knuckles, over and over, her fingers tapping at his sallow skin.

"We can be back here in a few hours if something changes," he said quietly. "Your mom and dad are here. He won't be alone."

"No." She shook her head. Her place was with her family, and her family was here, in this room, in this bed.

Jack expelled a long breath. "I've got two interviews in two days. And my meeting to negotiate the contract is three days after that, and another interview after —"

"You can't miss them," said Lucy. She didn't look up at Jack's silent, assenting nod, but his fingers slowed as they trailed through her hair. "You should go."

His hand froze in place. "Without you?"

"I can fly back if you need me to make an appearance somewhere," she said.

"If I need you to—" he stopped, stepping back from her chair, pacing across the room, his back to Lucy. His voice was forced and strange when he spoke again. "What if I just need you?"

Lucy faltered for a moment but said nothing. Her place was with her family, and she had gone too long without them to give them up now.

"This is what you want?" he whispered, his voice sounding so much younger. She nodded. "Alright then. I'll have Parker get me a flight. And I'll come back as soon as I can."

Again, another nod. She was tired of nodding, nodding, nodding, but her voice was long gone and the lump in her throat prevented even the simplest of whispers.

Jack tapped off a text on his phone, then pulled a chair up next to Lucy, taking her hand. They sat like that for several hours, Nico connected to Lucy and Lucy to Jack. Then there was a whispered goodbye, a last kiss on the forehead, and Jack was gone.

Three more days came and went, and then, there was no need to wait for news. Jack felt his phone vibrate in his pocket as he returned from a radio interview to the empty townhouse. He scrolled past a text chain under the header *Cottontail*, past three days of unanswered texts on Lucy's part, to a single sentence text from his mother-in-law.

ROSE: He's awake.

Chapter 29

Upon waking from his coma, Nico blinked. A lot. He was a veritable blue-ribbon champion of blinking.

Lucy, Ben, and Rose took turns holding his hand, answering the mass of texts in their family chat, and retrieving coffee for each other. He wasn't awake for more than a few minutes at time, but he was awake, and that was something.

Several hours later, he progressed to humming. Matteo had driven up from Sparrow Hill by that point, and he hummed back at his brother as if they were holding a conversation.

"Maybe he thinks he's talking," said Matteo, shrugging at Lucy. "Hmmm?"

"Hmmm," agreed Nico, his voice hoarse and crackly.

"It's okay," Lucy said, stroking his forearm. "We're here."

"You gotta say it in his language," said Matteo. "Hmmm, hmmm."

"Hmmm," said Nico, his eyes blinking slowly, as if they were weighted with sandbags.

"He says you need to go back to the hotel and nap," Matteo said as he ran his gaze up and down her. "And maybe shower."

"He didn't say that." Lucy glared at him. "I'm fine."

Matteo clucked, and then in a softer voice, "Seriously, Lu. You look like shit."

"Watch your mouth," she said, her jaw clenched. "Nico needs me."

"You're no good to Nico like this," her brother continued. Lucy's throat worked, her lip quivering as she balled her hands into defiant fists.

"Hmmm," said Nico, soft and low.

"Promise me you'll go shower," Matteo said. "Please?"

Lucy bit her lip, unable to find the words amongst the jumble of fluorescent lights and machine beeps and the constant buzz of nurses, doctors, and patients outside the room.

And suddenly, she didn't have to. Nico turned his head, ever so slowly, and blinked at her once more.

"Lucy?" he said, his lips cracked and pale. Her eyes filled with exhausted tears at the sound of her name. Another of his prolific blinks, and then, with brows furrowed as if he were trying to explain the meaning of life, he asked, "Where the fuck is Jack?"

Jack walked into the main conference room at Derelict Records for his nine o'clock meeting with Frank and Keith Taylor. His head ached, and his eyes were bleary from lack of sleep. Trent, Kim, and Parker were already inside, but the Taylors had not yet arrived. He slumped into an office chair and gratefully accepted a cup of coffee—two creams, five sugars—from Parker, who stood at attention, eager to take notes.

"You ready for this?" Trent asked, his eyes glinting. Trent approached contract negotiation with the same hunger of a lion hunting down a gazelle. Jack had actually once seen him bare his teeth in a snarl at another lawyer.

Jack shrugged at his lawyer. "Might as well get it over with."

Trent sobered and lowered his voice. "How's the brother?"

"Awake," Jack said. "Not talking yet, the last I heard. But awake."

"These things take time," said Trent, wincing a little at the words. It was a generic *hope things get better* saying, and they both knew it, but Jack appreciated it all the same.

Frank and Keith Taylor entered the room, trailed by Ted, their gangly yet terrifying lawyer. Hands were shaken, greetings were given, and then they got down to business.

"Well, Jack," said Frank, his white teeth spread in a proud grin. "I can't believe it, but you've really turned yourself around in a few short months. I really didn't think you'd be able to after the Prince Harry incident, but look at you."

"Your single is climbing the charts," added Keith. "Your social media following continues to grow, and your interviews are getting great ratings."

"And I haven't been called in to clean up after you," said Ted in a dry voice. Jack narrowed his eyes, but the lawyer shrugged nonchalantly and handed over a copy of the new contract as well as a tour agreement.

"Derelict is really happy to have you," said Frank in a softer, fatherly tone. "And I look forward to our future together."

The room was silent as Jack, Kim, and Trent flipped through the contracts, broken only by the occasional question or statement. The further Jack got into the paperwork, the more the words swam on the page. At one point, he had to stand up and refill his coffee, as an escape from the legal jargon that was causing his chest to compress and his hands to twitch. All he could think of was the last contract he'd signed, a few sheets of paper locking him to one enigmatic woman for two whole years. A contract that signed away a small fortune and all freedom to be a drunken buffoon, just to obtain this contract.

Jack had been much happier signing that contract.

When he sat down again after a few tremulous breaths, he leafed through the tour agreement. "I want this changed."

"What do you want to be changed exactly?" asked Ted, narrowing his eyes.

"Hasan Desai, Lainey Mills, Maya Rodriguez, I want their tour agreements to match mine."

No one spoke for a moment, then Frank snorted in disbelief. "That's a lot of money, Jack. We don't have that in the budget."

"Take it from mine, then," Jack said. "Split everything evenly amongst the four of us. Same for any profits from shows."

Trent's eyebrows were furrowed in confusion. "What are you doing?" he hissed in Jack's ear. Jack swatted him away gently.

"Alright," said Frank. He gaped at Jack as if he were a crazy person, which of course, he was. "We can do that. They haven't signed their agreements yet; the changes can still be made."

Jack contemplated the other contract, which would tie him to Derelict for at least two more years. He fiddled with the plastic lid of his coffee cup until the tab broke off and drops of coffee splattered onto the table, inches from the pristine legal document.

He took a deep breath, and for a moment, he missed the scent of cocoa and lavender.

"I'm not signing that one," Jack said.

Trent perked up, ready to counter, and Kim flashed him a questioning glance.

"All right, Jack, what do you want?" asked Keith, tenting his fingers. "I'm sure you'll agree this is a lucrative offer."

"I'm sure I do agree," Jack said. "I'm just not signing it."

Trent tilted his head at Jack, staring as if he had grown antlers. Jack almost felt sorry for his lawyer. He got off on negotiations, and Jack was about to yank that away from him.

"I don't understand," Keith said, baffled. "What do you want to be changed?"

"Nothing." Jack stood, pushing his chair back in. Trent rose next to him, but his brows were still wrinkled. "I'm just not signing with you."

Frank turned bedsheet white, and Keith jumped to his feet. "What the hell are you talking about? Did you already sign with someone else?"

"You could say that." Jack pictured Lucy's long, lacy handwriting on their contract, written with a gimmicky Elvis pen. "Just not another label."

Keith made a strangled, huffing noise, and Jack offered an apologetic smile. "Send Trent the new tour agreement when it's updated. It'll be a successful tour. People love a farewell tour."

"A farewell tour? What the hell is going on?" Keith's jaw dropped. Frank, however, was studying him with speculation, his earlier anger replaced with thoughtfulness. Across the table, Kim, his wonderful, unflappable Kim, had her hand to her heart and a smile dancing around her lips.

"I'm done, Keith," Jack said, and as he did, he felt the tension in his shoulders dissipate into nothingness. "I'm retiring."

"You can't retire!" the man stammered. "We can make so much money together, Jack! Come on, now!"

Jack shook Frank's hand, then Ted's. When he held his hand out to Keith, he stared at it, the color draining from his face.

"Keith," Jack said. "Did you know Elton John once let Stevie Wonder drive his snowmobile?" He patted the executive's shoulder. "If he can survive that, you can survive this."

And with that, Jack picked up his coat, winked at his former team, and walked out the door.

———◆———

Lucy gave in and went back to the hotel and took a shower. Afterward, she laid down for a one-hour nap. She dreamed of a surly rock star under the world's most magnificent duvet, and a one-hour nap somehow turned into fourteen hours of the deepest sleep she'd had in weeks.

By the time she rushed back to Nico's side, Matteo was already there, sipping his morning coffee and reading to their oldest brother. Nico wasn't quite sitting, but he was at a slightly higher incline than the previous day.

"Hey, Sleeping Beauty," said Matteo. She gave a quick head jerk in greeting and then did a double take at the book in his hands.

"Are you reading him *The Baby-Sitters Club*?" she asked, tilting her head for a better look at the title.

"He's a literature professor who can't fight back." Matteo grinned with the evil that only little brothers could manage. "Besides, he's learning a lot."

"Are you?" she asked Nico.

He twisted his mouth in a half-grimace, most likely a less painful version of a shrug. "Mary Anne loves Logan. I think." His patter was slow, and every expression and movement had a bewildered sluggishness to it, but her brother was there, alive and on the way to wellness.

"Do you remember anything?" she asked, taking a seat next to her brother's bedside.

He started to shake his head, winced at the movement, and went for a muttered, "No" instead. "I was in an accident," he said with halting, jerking words. "But I don't remember. And my leg is hurt." The latter was an understatement, and by the way his face clouded, he was quite aware.

"But we'll get you fixed up in no time," said Matteo with blustering cheer. "You'll be helping me repair Mom and Dad's fence this summer for sure."

Nico's lips twitched but his eyes dulled. Fence-building was a long way away for him. His gaze crawled to his little sister.

"Lucy," he said. "You should go home."

She shook her head. "I slept all night. I'm feeling much better. I can stay with you all day."

"I meant New York." Nico swallowed and closed his eyes with a weary sigh. "Jack's probably a mess without you."

"I can confirm that," Matteo said. "I love your husband, but he's making us all crazy." He handed Lucy his phone, the screen showing a chat between Matteo, Dante, and Jack that was probably ninety percent texts from Jack. "Dante gave up and just started replying in Jack Hunter reaction gifs."

Lucy smiled at a looped animation of her husband performing an exaggerated eye roll during a stint as an awards show presenter. "I'm sure he's thrilled with that."

Nico's eyes fluttered open again. "I'm not a timeshare."

Both Matteo and Lucy stared at him. "He's been saying weird stuff," Matteo sighed. "It's the brain-scrambling he's had."

Nico did his best insouciant glare without moving his head too much. "My brain isn't scrambled. Mostly." He flicked his eyes back to Lucy. "I know you, Lu. You hold guilt tighter than anyone I know."

"I don't understand."

"I'm trying to explain," he said. The corner of his mouth tipped up in a close approximation of a smile. "Just because you were kept away from us for so long, doesn't mean you need to bank up time with us now."

Lucy inhaled sharply, her eyes stinging. "But you're hurt."

"I'm not going anywhere," Nico said. "Trust me. Everyone else had to go back to their lives. Even this loser here."

"Hey, now!" protested Matteo. "Remind me to shove you later when you're not a giant bruise."

"I'm gonna be fine," repeated Nico. "Don't put your life on pause for me. It was on pause for too long as it was."

Lucy looked away, focusing on the heart rate monitor attached to her brother, trying to catch her breath.

"Okay, bring in the big guns," Nico said, and she whirled back to him. He wiggled an index finger at Matteo, and despite her imminent tears,

Lucy never thought she'd be so happy to see something as minor as a finger wiggle.

Matteo pulled out his phone and dialed someone via video call. Lucy wiped at her eyes, preparing to see Jack again. God, how she missed him. Instead of Jack, though, Parker's face filled the screen.

"Parker?" She glanced at Matteo. "How'd you get his number?"

Matteo snorted. "Are you kidding? Jack sent all of us a phone tree of everyone they should call if you so much as sneezed. I might have Celine Dion's number at this point."

"Lucy," Parker said, scratching at his neck. "Jack, uh, did something yesterday."

"Oh no," she said, hands going to her temples. "How much bail do we need?"

"No, no, no." Parker waved his fingers in a "calm down" motion. "Nothing illegal. I mean, the day's still young, of course. But he's making an announcement tonight on *The Late Show with Jerry Manning* and I think you should be there."

"What announcement? What's happening?" Her head reeled, possible scenarios spinning through her brain like a tilt-o-whirl of anxiety. She glanced over at Nico, biting her lip.

"Literally," he said dryly, wiggling his finger toward his mangled leg, "not going anywhere."

"I've got a comp ticket to the show," added Parker. "And a one-way ticket from Indy to New York, if you know anybody who needs to get here in a hurry."

"I'll be right there," piped up Matteo. "Lucy, you take care of Nico."

Lucy laughed and jumped to her feet, planting a kiss on Matteo's forehead, and then Nico's. And then a kiss to Parker on the phone screen, just for good measure.

"Go on," grumbled her older brother, closing his eyes with an exhausted sigh. "Trust me—I'll be here when you get back."

Chapter 30

Lucy realized how out of it Jack really was when the snakes came out.

The first guest on Jerry Manning's nighttime talk show was a zoologist with the Bronx Zoo. He brought several animals for the audience to fawn over and for Jerry to use as a comedic foil. Jack was on stage to interact with the animals, adding that celebrity color that viewers loved. He smiled and followed the zoologist's cues—patting a toucan on his hollow-sounding beak, scratching an adorable baby ocelot behind the ear—but when the ball python was brought on stage by its handler, the only sign of Jack's discomfort was the slight shifting of his hips in his chair. He petted the snake with eyes as dull as the reptile's own.

When the zoologist's section was over, the show cut to a commercial break while Jack, Lainey, Hasan, and Maya situated themselves on stage. Jerry introduced them, and they broke into "The Ballad of Mad Jack."

And, of course, it sounded fantastic, and of course, the audience loved it. Jack flirted with the camera while strumming the guitar, and the atmosphere was charged with the ionic pleasure only found around a stellar performance. The stage was his domain, his kingdom, and he ruled it with an iron fist clutched around the neck of an electric guitar.

Afterward, he rambled toward the main stage, waving and aiming finger guns at the crowd. Parker had found a single seat for Lucy in the very last row, so she doubted Jack saw her, especially with the harsh lighting pointed at the stage.

After charming the audience, Jack settled into a stiff-looking armchair next to Jerry Manning's desk, his long legs sprawled out as if he were just lounging on the sofa in their living room instead of in front of a studio of captivated viewers. His guitar was laid across his lap, and he plucked at it absentmindedly.

"So, Jack, glad to have you back on the show after all these years." The bespectacled host gave him an exaggerated look of disapproval. "You're not planning on running off mid-interview like last time, are you?"

"No," said Jack with an amiable chuckle. "My running days are over. I'm not even wearing the right footwear." He kicked up a leg like a Rockette to show off his scuffed leather boots, and the audience laughed.

"So it seems. You've had quite the past few months. A new wife, a new album, and a new single that's defying convention."

"Yeah, the new song, it's sort of a—" Jack tipped his head, "—a sea shanty, I guess? But kinda glam rock. Let's go with a *glanty*. I like that."

"Well, whatever it is, it's very popular. And you've got some more news, don't you?"

"I do." He took the smallest of breaths, and his false confidence faltered for a millisecond. "At the end of the month, tickets will go on sale for the tour. My farewell tour."

Low gasps punctuated the studio as audience members reacted to this news. Lucy's inhale was so sudden that she started coughing. Jack's head perked up, and he squinted at the audience, but by the time she got her hacking under control, he had lost interest again.

What the hell was he doing?

"So you're really retiring from music? You're so young." Jerry rested his head on his fist, studying Jack with a perfectly sculpted, thoughtful expression.

"Jerry, look at this hair." He leaned over and hung his curls over the host's desk. "I've got more salt and pepper than a potato chip factory." He sat back up, shaking his hair back into place. "Besides, I've always enjoyed the songwriting aspect much more, so I'd like to put more of my focus on that." He switched keys on his guitar, strumming a few chords that sounded vaguely familiar.

"And what about your new wife? How does she feel about all of this?"

His new wife is not amused, thought Lucy, her hand clasped over her mouth as she shook her head over and over.

"She's very supportive of me, no matter what I do," said Jack. "As long as I stay away from the Royal Family and woodland creatures."

"Your engagement and marriage was a bit of a whirlwind, wasn't it?" asked Jerry after the audience's laughter died down.

"Yes, well, when you know, you know. I met Lucy, and I just had to, you know—" he stopped and looked straight in the camera as if imparting some secret message. "I had to woo her."

Lucy's mouth went dry as the Sahara in summer.

"Woo her, huh? Well, she definitely has charmed your fans on social media. Your Instagram account is extremely entertaining." They displayed a photo on the screen, one that Parker had taken of them posing by the Christmas tree at Jack's party, holding an ornament that said, "Just Married." He had snapped the photo before they were ready, and instead of the cheesy grins they had prepared, they gazed at each other with something that looked a whole lot like love.

His fingers repeated the same chords, and suddenly, Lucy recognized it, a simple picked melody that was clean and fresh and sounded like summer.

"Neil fucking Diamond," she whispered.

Jerry continued, gesturing at the photo. "So, how did you two meet?"

"Well, Jerry, what you've first got to understand is that Lucy is an expert at rock history. It's awesome, like she's got the whole Rock and Roll Hall of Fame up there in her head."

"So she knows which of your albums to listen to and which ones not to?" Jerry winked at the camera. The audience tittered and Jack laughed right along with them, a sheepish grin spreading across his lips.

"That and more. You can name a line from a Marvin Gaye song, and she'll tell you the song, the album, the year it was recorded. She can recite the Billboard hits of Gloria Gaynor and the dates of every Beatles television appearance. It's her special gift, her passion. So, of course, we met at a record store. I was going through the albums, minding my own business, and I picked up one, and I hear—"

"You don't want that one." Lucy's voice shook, and before she could stop herself, she rose to her feet. Jack turned his head, one mischievous curl tumbling down his forehead. Her heart leaped as he craned his neck, and through the *lights* and the *noise* and the *crowd*, their eyes locked. His throat bobbed, and then he stood, taking a few jolting steps forward.

"Oh no, he's running again," Jerry said, but his voice sounded distant, far away from that beautiful snow globe world that belonged to just Jack and Lucy.

He dashed off the stage, nearly tripping on a camera's power cords before vaulting over them with a clumsy leap. He strode up the stairs two at a time, through the bewildered audience, and then he was right in front of her, launching himself at her before a single word fell from her trembling lips.

"There you are." He clutched Lucy to his chest, holding her in his shaking arms, his face buried in the crook of her neck. His rapid breath warmed the drumming pulse point at her throat.

"Here I am." She tangled her fingers through his dark curls as he nuzzled her shoulder, rocking her back and forth. She pressed a kiss to his hair, and he tilted his head upward, bringing their foreheads together.

"You came back."

"I came back." She gazed at his brown eyes and dark lashes and everything was beautiful *brown black brown black brown*. She leaned forward to whisper in his ear. "You're still on television, you know."

"I don't care." His lovestruck eyes shone as he bellowed to the stage. "Hey, Jerry, how much time do we have?"

The host sighed with a browbeaten expression, but he played along. "You're on for another forty-five seconds, Jack."

"Got it!"

A portly cameraman pointed a handheld camera into their faces, and Jack gestured into it. "World, this is my wife, Lucy. Say hi to the world, Lucy."

"Hi, world." Her face heated and she suppressed a nervous hiccup. Instinct told her to hide her face in Jack's shoulder, but she stood strong and waved at the millions of people that would watch this when it aired later.

Jack's rough hands cupped her cheeks, and his eyes glowed with such utter adoration that her throat tightened, and she had to press her lips together because she couldn't really cry on national television, could she?

"She's my best friend and the absolute love of my life."

Apparently, Lucy *could* cry on national television. The first of several tears slid down her cheeks as Jack swept a tendril of her hair away, his gaze intent and full of so many promises. He didn't even look at the stage when he called out again.

"How much time do we have, Jerry?"

"Ten seconds."

Jack raised an eyebrow and said the two words that caused every producer in the room to thank the heavens for delayed recordings. "Fuck it."

He kissed Lucy, slanting his mouth over hers, soft and pure and possessive. His hands shuddered against her cheek, and really, she agreed with him because *fuck it*. She threw her arms around his neck and kissed him back, her heart revving like a race car as the audience broke into applause and cheers. Jack drew away with a crooked grin, fiddled with his collar, and tossed his wireless mic to the floor. He reached under her legs and hoisted her into his arms like a newlywed, heading for the exit as Jerry attempted to bring sanity back to the broadcast.

"Well…that was Jack Hunter and his wife Lucy, and we'll be right back with our special guest, John Stamos."

"Don't even think about it, Cottontail," he said when Lucy looked hopefully back at the soundstage. He plowed through the double doors and didn't put her down until he found a private nook at the end of an empty hallway. He ran his hands up and down her face and arms and sides, over and over, as if he expected her to vanish without his touch.

"You're here, you're here." Lips replaced wandering hands, and Jack trailed kisses up and down her temple, her cheekbones, her jawline, edging her backward until she bumped against the wall. His hands cupped around the swell of her hips.

She felt safe. She felt loved.

"Matteo and Parker staged a convincing intervention," Lucy said.

His thumb brushed her arm, circling and tracing her wrist bones. "I know you needed to be there. And I would have waited for you as long as it took. But good God, I missed you."

"What are you doing, Jack?" she said. "You can't retire. Everything is going according to plan now. Everyone loves you again."

"For now they do," he said, his mouth a firm, pale line. "For now, I've got a hit song and a happy marriage and a good reputation. For now, I'm the most goddamned perfect Oreo in the world."

Lucy studied his face, saw the utter exhaustion there, and at last, she understood. She leaned forward and kissed the worry lines at the edge of his eyes.

"No more watching where you step," she whispered. "No more looking behind your back. No more pretending to be someone you're not. No more Jack Hunter."

He didn't hug her. He didn't kiss her. He simply exhaled, and yet in that one single, stuttered breath, Lucy felt the weight of everything that she was to him and everything that she would be.

"I'm still going on tour, Cottontail," he said, dropping his forehead to her shoulder. "One last tour and then it's all over. I won't ask you to come with me. We both know you'll be miserable. And it's going to be a long time before we're together every day. But if you wait for me, I promise, I'll spend every day making you so happy. We'll listen to music, and go to the diner for cookies, and I'll take you to Central Park and laugh at your incredibly awful jokes, and I'll annoy you while we watch television, and I'll take you to bed and possibly annoy you there, too, and—"

"Shh." She placed a soothing finger on his lips. "I'll wait. I'm not going anywhere."

He took a deep, shuddering breath. "I love you. I love you so much that I thought I was going to die when you weren't here. I love you so much that I might just die anyway because there's no way one person can hold all this love in without exploding, and then pieces of love shrapnel will fly everywhere."

"Love shrapnel?"

"Hush, woman, I'm working on the fly here." He tipped her head up, his gaze burning with intent. "I need you in my life, in my bed, in my house, because if you're not there, it's not home. Please be my home."

Lucy took his hand in hers, tracing the guitar string in his ring, the half-moon scar across his knuckle. "I love you too. I think I've loved you since the first time you proposed to me. You're mine, and I'm yours."

"Wait for me?"

"I will." Her fingers fluttered against his palm—*pinky, ring, middle, index. Repeat.* "But for now, let's go home."

Epilogue

18 Months Later

August in Indiana always started out blistering hot, but by the end of the month, a slight chill underlined the suffocating heat, as if autumn was chipping away at the wall of sweaty misery until it could break through at last. That barely perceptible chill was the promise of a new school year, of football and apple cider, of hayrides and harvest. It was the bittersweet feeling that accompanied all endings, though new beginnings were never too far away.

It was the end of another beautiful summer, which Lucy spent in Sparrow Hill with her family on the farm. She read in the rope hammock under the catalpa trees, listened to music in her childhood bedroom, and took long walks along the fields outside the property, alone except for the stars above, the waving cornstalks at her side, and the snorting pig at her feet.

Other days, she spent with Matteo working on the fixer-upper farmhouse that she and Jack had bought that spring. The property next to Lettie's farm had gone up for sale, and they snatched it up, despite the many repairs it would need.

The end of summer also brought about the transition from babyhood to toddlerhood for Gianna. The entire family felt that twinge of sadness, however brief, as her baby face melted away into the visage of a two-year-old toddler—a very rambunctious one.

For her birthday, they threw a simple family-only party in the backyard of the Meyer farmhouse, complete with Elmo-themed decorations, toddler-sized party games, and a huge table filled with an over-abundance of homemade food. Most of the family was there, and Lucy never stopped being amazed at what a blessing each and every person was. The moments that Brock had stolen from her had been replenished tenfold. More family members had been woven in since the day Lucy placed a guitar-string ring on Jack's finger, each bringing their own personalities and memories and *love, love, love.*

Of course, it meant they still had to get creative with their seating arrangements. Ariana's fiancé roosted on top of a pink Power Wheels car, and the extended family was spread out across camping chairs and lawn recliners. Dante had given up entirely and just lounged in the grass, long legs sprawled out like a late-summer spider.

And yet, they all felt the absence of one crucial member of their wild and wonderful family.

After nearly a year and a half of grueling travel, stolen moments in hotels around the world, and hundreds of lonely text messages and phone calls, Jack's farewell tour ended that week. It hadn't been easy for either Jack or Lucy, but they had made it work. Her unique concert set-up was moved around with the tour equipment, and when she could fly out to one of his shows, the concert techs set it up in his dressing room. Other times, when he had a few days off, he flew to Sparrow Hill or back to New York, wherever Lucy was, and they spent every waking moment together.

His last show had been in Paris two days prior. They had celebrated with a virtual dinner and video call with the whole family, where they dined on fondue and baguettes and spoke in exaggerated French accents while Larry pranced around at their feet, wearing a navy beret.

Jack had business at Derelict's UK office that week, and then next week, he would be coming home to Sparrow Hill for good, and their new normal—whatever that would be—could begin at last.

The birthday party was in full swing, or as much as it could be with the honorary guest sprinting naked through the sprinkler, shrieking as Lettie's new husband chased after Gianna with her discarded swim diaper.

"All right, people, time to sing," barked Rose as she inserted two tiny candles into the top of a lopsided red and yellow cake. Gianna—now half-dressed and bouncing in her seat of honor—swiped a glob of frosting from the side with a gleeful cackle.

"One, two, three..." counted off Ben, and they began an off-key, warbling "Happy Birthday." Before they could continue onto the second line, Nico paused, craning his neck to look beyond Lucy to the driveway.

"You're late!" he called out with a sly grin.

The rusty hinge on the picket fence gate squealed in protest. Lucy turned in her seat, shielding her eyes from the sun with her hand—and jolted up from the chair, nearly tripping over her own feet.

Jack strolled through the picket fence gate, his guitar slung over his back. He looked tired, and his clothes had the limp, wrinkled look caused by hours on a plane, but his cocky half-grin was lit up as bright as August sunshine.

Lucy didn't even realize she was running until she was already in his embrace, her arms slung around his neck. Tears streamed from her eyes onto his mussed collar as he lifted her off the ground by her waist, burying his head in her neck and peppering it with ardent kisses.

"I thought you weren't coming 'til next week," she said between sniffles.

"Kim's idea. I know you don't like surprises. Is this one okay?"

"This one is amazing." And then there was no more talking, just kisses upon kisses, soft and caressing as a dragonfly's wing, and—

"Are we singing here or what?" bellowed Rose. "The candles are melting all over the cake. Someone's going to end up with wax poisoning."

"Shit, oops," he said, waving off his mother-in-law's obligatory, "Watch your mouth!" He swung the guitar from his shoulder, retrieved a pick from his jeans pocket, and played a fanfare of chords to kick them off. Backed by her Uncle Jack's strumming, everyone serenaded Gianna as her eyes shone with the endless, simple wonder that could only belong to a toddler. After multiple tries, she managed to blow out the candles, and everyone cheered.

Lettie started serving everyone, handing out paper plates that wilted under the weight of the cake. Jack took a plate for Lucy and himself, crooking his neck to indicate that she should follow him for a bit of privacy. She glanced back at her family, but Rose shooed her off with an impatient wave.

They sat under the maple tree, legs tangled and backs resting against the rough bark.

"I've got something for you," he said, pulling a wrinkled envelope from his back pocket. He handed it to her with a stern look. She would have been worried, but his lips twitched as they fought back an impending smile.

"What's this?"

"Letter from Trent," he shrugged, stuffing a frosting-laden bite into his mouth. Lucy opened the letter and read it.

And then reread it.

"What is this?" she repeated.

"Exactly what you read," he said. "A ninety-day notice. Our marriage contract expires in November."

"Uh-huh."

"Look, Trent signed it and everything. That makes it official." He pointed at the lofty signature, smearing yellow frosting on the high-end paper.

Lucy handed him a napkin from the stack she had brought from the table. "So...you don't want to stay married after November?"

"Nah." He wiped his hands and retrieved another envelope from his other pocket. "I had Trent work up another contract."

"Another one?" She read the letter and burst into laughter.

Dear Lucy,

This is an invoice. The son of a bitch is actually paying me fifty bucks to write this out. Please pay attention to him, and may God have mercy on both your souls.

Yours, Trent L. Roberts, Esq.

When she looked up, Jack's face was flushed with timid tenderness, despite the streak of yellow frosting across his cheekbone. She wiped it with her napkin, and he caught her hand in his. He wriggled the wedding ring off her hand, but before she could protest, he wriggled it right back on.

"I, Jack, take you—"

"What are you doing?" Lucy interrupted.

"Saying the vows for real," he said. "Hush a minute." He cleared his throat. "I, Jack, take you, Lucy, to be my wife, to have and to hold from this day forward, for better or for worse, for richer or for poorer, in sickness and in health, I promise to love and cherish you."

His face was so earnest, so vulnerable, and her cheeks ached from smiling. She took his hand and removed—then replaced—his guitar-string ring, repeating the vows back to him. They kissed, and though that nervous kiss in front of a handmade wedding podium in a granary full of people nearly two years ago had been as crisp and real as could be, this one brought with it a renewed sense of promise and partnership and absolute love.

"Well," he said as they broke apart. "What happens now?"

"That's the best part," Lucy said, weaving their fingers together, soft skin meeting roughened fingertips. The canvas of their future stretched out, blank with possibilities. Kids or no kids. Cats or dogs or maybe pigs. A home in Sparrow Hill or New York or both at once. It all lay before them, unscheduled, unplanned, untamed. "I have no idea."

Acknowledgments

Once upon a time, a girl tried to write an epic fantasy series and it just wasn't working. In a fit of exasperation, she fell back on the old "write what you know" saying, turned up her Elvis music, and wrote what became Jack and Lucy's story.

This book couldn't have been completed without the support of a lot of amazing people:

My editor, Jessica McKelden.

My beta readers, J.N. Smith and Celia Shadrach, whose comments not only made me braver but also kept me laughing throughout the process. (A rhododendron is not a Pokemon)

My fellow Squanchchat Slackers, who put up with my random requests of "what's that thing with the thing and the thing?" called again.

Dan, for creating my beautiful cover.

Stella, Vita, and Tresa, for all the summers of writing Hanson fan fiction and Barbie musicals in the basement that laid a very...unique...foundation for my adult writing habits.

Mandy, for your Laverne-and-Shirley level of support, and for that one night on the bus back from COSI when you played Billy Joel for me through shared headphones, and my music world was forever changed.

Cordelia, Leonidas, and Esmeralda, for being the bestest of dogs and laying with me while I write.

My daughters, for providing cuddles and giggles, and listening when Mommy says, "Let me go write so we can go to Disney World."

And my husband, for listening to my endless monologues, reading random scenes, and recognizing that the little pieces of us in this book are little pieces of love.

About the Author

Belle Chapin lives in the Midwest with her husband, two children, and a plethora of animals. She spends her time writing, reading mushy books, obsessing over Broadway musicals, playing the piano loudly, and leaving unfinished knitting projects around the house.

Printed in Dunstable, United Kingdom

74170149R00180